ONE BAD THING

Also by M. K. Hill

Sasha Dawson series
The Bad Place
The Woman in the Wood

ONE BAD THING

M.K. HILL

HEAD
of ZEUS

An Aries Book

First published in the UK in 2022 by Head of Zeus Ltd,
part of Bloomsbury Publishing Plc.

975312468

A catalogue record for this book is available from
the British Library.

ISBN (HB): 9781788548342
ISBN (XTPB): 9781788548359
ISBN (E): 9781788548373

Typeset by Siliconchips Services Ltd UK

Printed and bound in Great Britain by
CPI Group (UK) Ltd, Croydon CRO 4YY

Head of Zeus
First Floor East
5 -8 Hardwick Street
London EC1R 4RG

www.headofzeus.com

For Eileen

Everybody, sooner or later, sits down to a banquet of consequences.

ROBERT LOUIS STEVENSON

1

What you have to understand is, it was a very bad time for me.

That's not to excuse what I did, which was indefensible, and I will never forgive myself. I fully accept responsibility for my actions. But I wasn't in the right headspace. I was immature, full of anger, grief-stricken. And besides, what we did – what *I* did – was intended, in a clumsy and callous way, to redress a wrong; to balance the universe.

I'm truly sorry for what happened, and all I can say is, lesson learned.

In the months that followed, when my mental health hit rock bottom and I finally dragged myself out of depression, I often thought about apologizing to our victim. But I was never able to find him. I tried the bar where we picked him up, and even went to his flat, but he had left a few weeks before, leaving no forwarding address. So, no, that didn't happen.

At first, I thought the guilt would poison my life, that I'd never get over it; but it didn't, and I did. And in the years and decades that followed, a lot of what happened has drifted from my memory. I suppose if I was really sorry for what I did, and truly contrite, I would think about it more often

– every day, every week, once a month. But I don't, and it all seems such a long time ago now. A lot of things have happened in the years since, and it's almost like it never took place at all.

Almost.

It's true to say that in the intervening years I've tried to be a force for change, and to help people where I can – and I think on the whole I've succeeded in that. I'm not saying I'm a completely good and perfect person, but I'm not a bad one either, I'm really not. After all, no one is all good or all bad. We all just muddle along the best we can, trying not to hurt people, don't we? Sometimes we let ourselves down, but if we're determined to do the right thing, if we make a conscious effort to treat people well, I don't see why we have to let the guilt of our previous bad behaviour, those silly mistakes we all make from time to time, tear us apart.

However, I've learned to my cost that you can never totally leave behind that one bad thing you did. You may try to forget it, and to drown out its nagging echo by living the best life possible, but it will catch up with you. And if you're unlucky, it will turn your life upside down.

But here's the thing. I've also learned that when the past comes back to haunt you, and you face the prospect of losing everything you love, there's only one way to escape that one bad thing.

And that's by doing something worse.

2

'Our Queen of Hearts is here for you, caller, go ahead!'
It's my last time behind the mic on Craig's radio show, which is broadcast every Saturday afternoon across London. I've been appearing as the show's resident psychologist, its agony aunt, for two years now, but all good things come to an end, as Craig explains at the top of the show.

'Our Queen of Hearts is going up in the world, she's got a gig on television, some little daily morning magazine show with, oh, just a few million viewers. But the saintly Hannah is all ours for one last time, and she'll be here for the next hour to sort out your problems. If you're feeling down about something – and the world is an anxious and scary place right now, so who can blame you? – call us and she'll give you good advice on how to cope.'

'There's always a first time,' I say into my mic.

He laughs, says, 'Ring us now on the usual number!' and punches in a jingle with the telephone number on it.

Phone lines on the console in the production gallery next door light up as people begin to ring in. The calls are always a mixed bag. It could be people who are struggling to cope financially, or whose relationships are crumbling; sometimes, if someone says they're feeling suicidal, I may speak to them after the show to make sure they seek help from the Samaritans or their local GP. The truth is, all I can ever really do is provide a sympathetic ear. But it's been proved that sharing a problem, taking it out to examine it in the cold light of day, is the best way to begin to tackle it. It's when you bottle up those negative emotions, toxic feelings and secrets that the situation can spiral from bad to worse.

And on this, my last show, the calls come thick and fast. One of our regular callers, Simon from Dollis Hill, bless him, phones to say he's feeling sad because I'm leaving. Melissa from Crystal Palace cries on-air because she's fallen out with her daughter. Family problems like hers are common, and I try to encourage the pair of them to keep communicating. Finally, Nicholas from Acton, who is agoraphobic, speaks very movingly about the debilitating anxiety he experiences whenever he leaves his house.

'Thanks, Nicholas,' says Craig. 'You stay safe.'

'And thank *you*, Hannah. I think I speak for all us listeners when I say we're going to miss you,' Nick says, and in an echo of the words that have become something of a catchphrase for me, adds, 'Always be kind.'

I feel quite choked up. 'Aw, thank you, I'll try.'

Glancing at the studio clock, I see I've been on-air for nearly an hour. As usual, the time has flown by. There's another half hour to go, and then I can go home to my husband and my baby.

But then *she* calls, and everything is changed forever.

Her name flashes up on the screen in the studio and Craig fades her up. 'Hi Diane, how can Hannah help you today?'

Craig can't believe his luck when the woman on the line

4

begins to tell listeners the story of what happened to her brother, Martin. How he met two people who bullied and traumatized him. He grins at me across the studio, and I try to mirror his enthusiasm, but beneath the table my hands, damp with sweat, are clamped between my knees. Every bitter word she utters is crystal clear in my headphones.

'And then those people, people he trusted, and believed were his *friends*,' she says in a menacing throaty rasp, 'this Cameron and—'

'Just a reminder, Diane,' Craig says quickly into his microphone, 'for legal reasons, we're not allowed to use names.'

'The man and the woman, they treated him no better than a dog and left him confused, shocked, humiliated.'

'That's terrible.' Craig eagerly catches my eye. 'I don't think I've heard of anything so cruel.'

He tries to sound sincere, but hunched close to the mic, his eyes flashing with excitement, he struggles to hide his glee. There's no question this call will go straight into the end-of-year compilation of the best moments on the show. Diane's story about the humiliation of her brother at the hands of two strangers is broadcasting gold.

'And your poor brother, how is he now? How is Martin?'

'He's dead.' The caller sucks down a deep, shuddering breath. 'He killed himself years ago.'

'Oh, Diane, I'm sorry to hear that.' Craig's voice is full of compassion, but his eyes sparkle. 'Do you think... could he have done it because...'

'Martin was a sensitive man, and I believe he never got over what happened to him. It ate away at his confidence and self-respect. And my life is a mess too, Craig. I can't stop thinking about what was done to him, it keeps me awake at night. Martin didn't deserve being treated like that, nobody does.' You can hear a pin drop in the dismal silence between her words. 'I miss him so, so *much*.'

'I understand,' says Craig softly.

'I want to know what Hannah thinks.' Diane's deep voice is a growl in my headphones. 'I'd like to hear what she says about it.'

'Hannah Godley, our Queen of Hearts, is here for you, Diane.' Craig's voice oozes concern. 'And I personally want to thank you for sharing your story with our listeners. I understand how difficult it must be for you.'

It's my turn to speak, to dish out advice. We're live on-air, hundreds of thousands of people are listening across the city, so I try to gather my thoughts. But my hands tremble beneath the table, my mouth is parched.

Craig raises his eyebrows, *go ahead*, because there's nothing worse for a radio show than dead air.

'Diane.' When I'm finally able to speak, I try to sound my usual bright and positive self, but my voice is a croak, and I have to take a sip of water. 'Thank you for your… thanks for calling in. What happened to… Martin, is it?… is clearly bringing up a lot of feelings for you right now, and I'm not sure talking about it here is really going to help.'

Across the desk, Craig stares at me as if I've gone mad. As far as he's concerned, Diane's raw emotion and macabre story are dynamite, and he wants to keep her on-air for as long as possible.

'I'd like to help you,' I say, ignoring him. 'But your story is very personal and I don't think speaking about it in such a public way is the correct thing to do.'

'No,' she says quietly, 'I bet you don't.'

'So I'm going to suggest that I talk to you after the show,' I continue quickly. 'We've got your number, and I promise that as soon as we're off-air, I'll ring you back and we can talk. I'm going to help, I *want* to help.'

'I didn't call for sympathy, or for help.' Diane's angry voice fills my head. 'I called to tell you that I'm going to make the people responsible for Martin's death suffer for what they did. I'm going to make them *pay*.'

Craig sits bolt upright, eager to get involved in the conversation now it's taken an unexpected twist. 'Diane, thoughts of revenge are perfectly normal, but it's not something that...' He frowns. 'Diane, are you still there?'

There's a deafening silence in my headphones; all I can hear is my own panting breath, the blood thrumming in my ears. Craig glances quickly at the producer in the gallery, who slices a hand across his neck. *She's hung up.*

'That's a shame,' Craig tells the listeners. 'We've lost Diane, but we'll take more calls right after this news bulletin. Join us then, and remember...'

He looks across the desk at me and I say unsteadily, 'Always be kind.'

The news jingle plays and an announcer begins to read the bulletin from another studio. Craig pulls down the faders to shut off the mics, drags his headphones down his neck.

'Is she gone?' he says, pressing a button to talk to the gallery. 'Can we get her back?'

'She's not answering her phone,' the producer says over the internal speaker.

'Bloody typical.' Craig is annoyed. 'She was just getting

warmed up, we could have had some more good stuff if she'd hung around.'

'She was in pain,' I tell him.

Craig remembers to sound concerned. 'Sure, she was in a bad way.' He frowns at me. 'You all right? You're as white as a sheet.'

'Am I?' I smile weakly. 'I didn't eat much at lunch.'

After the show, Craig and the team pop a bottle of bubbly to celebrate my new job in TV, and we drink it out of polystyrene cups. It's a nice gesture, but I barely taste the bubbles, and when I get a chance, I take the producer of the show aside.

'Diane, the woman who hung up,' I say to him quietly. 'I'd really like to help her. Can I have her number?'

'Ah.' He makes a face. 'Unless she gives us permission, I can't give it to you. Sorry, data protection laws. But I can give her a ring to see if she's happy for you to call.'

'Do you mind?'

'Not at all.'

'Thank you,' I tell him, and I pick up my bag.

The show has been a big part of my life for two years and I've a lot to thank it for. I've been podcasting and writing advice columns for magazines, but this regular Saturday slot has got me noticed by the people in television – the *Morning Brew* show, no less, which is the Holy Grail of daytime TV. When the champagne is finished, Craig and his team want to take me to the pub to continue the celebration, but I'm not in the mood.

We're in Soho, in central London, and the streets are busy with shoppers and tourists. The world is finally coming back to life after a weary couple of years going in and out of lockdown, and people are pouring into town this Saturday afternoon, many of them still wearing masks.

I wouldn't recognize Diane, with or without a mask. I've never met her – up until a few minutes ago, I didn't even know of her existence, how could I? But I can't help but scan the pavement as I come out of the building. I'm nervous, on the lookout for someone following me, someone who wants to make me pay.

Because of one bad thing I did many years ago… something stupid, something bad, something hateful.

3

The lights in the compartment blink on and off as the Tube train rattles up the Northern Line, throwing the passengers into intermittent shadow. Sitting in the seats, standing in the aisle, or peering into the carriage from the platform as we slide into each Underground station, their faces are mostly obscured behind masks or phones.

As the train clatters along the tunnel, shunting left and right, a woman at the end of the carriage looks over in my direction. Every muscle in my body clenches as she moves towards me, eyes staring over her black mask. But then she steps over my feet in the aisle – I draw them in quickly – and drops into an empty seat further along the row.

It's stifling and uncomfortable in the enclosed space, I can barely breathe, and when the doors finally open at Kentish Town station, I hurry up the escalators to street level. It's early evening, approaching six, as I scurry along the pavement carrying a glittery bottle–shaped bag containing Prosecco, a leaving gift from Craig and his team. Despite the dipping sun, it's still as hot as hell – we're a couple of weeks into another summer drought and even the breeze seems to scorch my skin – but I've never been so grateful to suck down the foetid, polluted air of the inner city in summer.

Listeners of the show will have written off Diane as a crank, one of the many attention-seeking souls who regularly call radio phone-ins, and have probably already forgotten her bizarre and unlikely story.

But I know better. Because the threat she made was aimed at me.

That cruel thing Cameron and I did all those years ago is still the biggest shame of my life. And now it turns out that the man we did it to, our victim – I'll never forget his name: Martin – later committed suicide. Diane's story could be a bizarre coincidence, she may not even know she was talking about me. But I wouldn't feel so shaken, so full of a nameless dread, if I hadn't had at the back of my mind all these years the lurking feeling that sooner or later that incident would come back to haunt me.

All I want to do is get home and shut out the world. I'll play with Amber, make something to eat, relax in front of the telly. Maybe tomorrow Diane's call will seem like a bad dream.

I've had problem callers before on the show, people who are overly persistent, even borderline intrusive, in their attempts to get me to help them. But they're often just desperate for someone to listen to their problems. Sometimes their close attention, bombarding me with emails and letters, trying to get my home address, can be scary, but they always drift away eventually. The important thing in dealing with them is to remain helpful and patient, but also to put in place clear boundaries.

But when I turn into the tangle of roads off the high street and onto my narrow curved street with its stately rows of ornamental apple and Judas trees, and let myself into our house, I discover Sean standing at the kitchen island, peering at his phone with a gin and tonic in his hand.

'You've started early,' I tell him.

He slugs down the last of the drink, crunching on the ice. 'Just getting warmed up for tonight.'

'What are you talking about?'

Sean flings his arms wide to reveal boxes of beer and wine stacked on the counter. 'Ta-da!'

My heart sinks. 'Oh no.'

'Oh *yes.*'

He comes over, doing a little dance as he moves, and beneath the overpowering smell of all the lotions, balms, hair products and the cologne he wears, I detect the tang of alcohol; he's had more than one already, that's for sure.

He's dressed smartly, too. Sean is always careful about his appearance – honestly, it's just as well we have a bathroom and an en suite, because he can hog the mirror for hours – but this afternoon he's catalogue-ready in a tight pale-blue cotton short-sleeved shirt that emphasizes his hard torso, ankle-length casual trousers and slip-on canvas shoes. His bouncing dark hair is carefully oiled, and his neat beard immaculately groomed.

'The party starts at eight o'clock sharp. Be there...' He strikes a Usain Bolt thunderbolt pose, forefingers pointed at the ceiling, imagining it's somehow charming. 'Or be square.'

'No, not tonight, please.' I dump my bag on the counter, already exhausted by the idea. 'I'm not in the mood.'

'Don't be a spoilsport.' Sean takes my hands, determined to talk me around. 'It's to celebrate your new job!'

The patio doors are flung open, revealing chairs placed all over the decking and lawn. Fairy lights hang from the trees, and a candle flickers on the garden table. 'I figure most people will want to be outside in this weather,' he explains.

'Honestly, Sean, it's a lovely thought,' I say, choosing my words carefully. 'But I'm shattered, and I need an early night.'

He grimaces, *no can do*. 'I've invited people.'

'How many people?'

Tipping his head side to side like a metronome, as if trying to add them all up, he finally settles on an infinitesimal figure; places a thumb and forefinger together. 'This many people,' he says, grinning. 'Less than a few, really.'

'A few,' I repeat, because Sean's definition of a *few people* is not the same as yours or mine, it's not even in the same universe. 'How many?'

'I don't know, a dozen.' He winces, because *he* knows that *I* know he's not telling the truth, and he's probably invited every single person we know. 'Maybe a few more.' As a distraction, he reaches for the bottle bag and reads the gift tag. 'Hey, it was nice of Craig to get you this.'

'Seriously, Sean, call it off.'

'We've got to celebrate,' he insists. 'Because you're going to be a TV star.'

'A star! That's pushing it a bit, don't you think? Besides, someone's got to get up in the morning with Amber.'

Which could be any time from five o'clock, the way our daughter has been sleeping recently, and there's no chance Sean is going to get up if he's sleeping off a stonking hangover. Plus, that phone call on the show has really spooked me, and I don't think I can face people tonight.

It's my own fault, really. We'd spoken in a vague way about organizing a small get-together to celebrate my new gig on *Morning Brew*, but then I forgot all about it. I should have known that Sean, who can't bear a quiet night in, despite the fact that he's a father with responsibilities, would use it as an excuse to throw a massive party for our friends – and probably all his other mates – on the pretext of a celebration.

'I promise I'll get up with her.' He shovels ice into a bucket of water, then places bottles of beer in it to chill. 'And make sure everyone's gone by midnight.'

I've heard it all before. Once Sean is surrounded by his boozy mates, playing the perfect host, being the life and soul, he won't want the party to stop. But there's no point in forcing him to call it off, not this late in the day, not unless I want him to go into a massive sulk.

It's tiring being the sensible one, the one who always has to say, *let's call it a night.* I don't want always to have to be that person, but someone must.

Sean and I tried so hard for a baby – we went through the slog of IVF, it was the most emotionally draining thing I've ever done – and thought it would never happen for us. But it did, thank God, even if we're both in our late thirties now. We're a family, it's the three of us, and Sean loves Amber dearly, but he still finds it a struggle to let go of his social life. The dinner parties and restaurants and bars, the drinks in town, the mini-breaks with childless friends. The pandemic didn't dampen his enthusiasm for staying out till all hours getting wasted, and nor has being a father. It's not like I don't want to have fun any more, of course I do. But every now and then, not all the time. These days I'm much happier staying home with our beautiful girl. She always comes first.

'Everyone will be gone by midnight, they've got to be, because I've got a footie match tomorrow morning. And Izzy and Ollie are coming, of course.' So at least my best friend will be here, which makes me feel better. Just in case I'm still not convinced, he places his hands together, as if in prayer. 'Remember, always be kind.'

'Get lost,' I tell him, because he always throws that phrase back in my face when he wants his own way, and he laughs.

Sean starts making himself another gin and tonic. 'Do you want one?'

'You're going to be drunk before anyone turns up.' I look around for our little girl, but she's not in the room, and I glance at the baby monitor. 'Is Amber asleep?'

But Sean's attention is once again on his phone. He dabs at the screen, messaging someone. 'Sean, where is she?'

Just at that moment, our nanny, Siobhan, comes into the room with my baby girl in her arms. It's a bit of a shock, because Siobhan isn't meant to work weekends. I give Sean a look, like, *what the hell*, and he grins.

'Here she is, here's Mummy,' Siobhan tells Amber quietly, and hands my eighteen-month-old to me.

'Mama!' squeals my daughter, as I take her gratefully in my arms.

'Hello, baby!' Positioning her comfortably on my hip, I press my nose to Amber's scalp to drink in the lovely warm fragrance of her light, springy hair and skin. Her small hands reach for my face to pull me closer as she talks nineteen to the dozen. Just holding her makes me feel a hundred times better already. About today, about tonight; about everything.

'She's been as good as gold, as always,' says Siobhan, picking up her bag.

'Thank you, Siobhan, but why are you here?'

'Mr Godley phoned to ask if I would come in for a couple of hours,' she says. 'And I'm always happy to do that if I can.'

'Had to go to the supermarket.' Sean gestures at all the boxes of beer and wine, although I'm not sure why he couldn't have taken Amber with him. 'It was good of you to come in on your day off, Shiv.'

'No problem.' Siobhan gives him a thin smile.

'You staying for the party, Shiv?' Sean drains his G&T. 'You're very welcome.'

I tense, because I've always been careful to keep a professional distance from Siobhan. Also, if I'm honest with myself, there's something about her that I don't like, and I know exactly what it is. It's a horrible thing to admit, and I obviously wouldn't tell her in a million years, but the way she looks, with her unruly red hair and her pale, porcelain skin and hoop earrings, the cheap jeans cinched tight with a massive buccaneer-style belt, the black plimsolls she wears… she reminds me too much of Natalie.

When she walks into a room, all I see is my dead sister.

'I'm sure Siobhan has better things to do than hang around with old farts like us,' I tell him.

'Seriously?' Sean flings his arms out, as if to say, *look at how young and fit I am!* He's being *lovable funny employer guy* for the benefit of our young nanny. 'Speak for yourself!'

But thankfully Siobhan shakes her head.

'That's very kind of you both, but I can't tonight.'

'What a shame,' I say as she hovers at the door. 'Have a lovely evening, Siobhan.'

'Cheers, Shiv,' says Sean, moving furniture around.

On her way out, Siobhan closes the front door carefully. The lock is sticky and if you bang it too hard, it opens again.

I jog Amber in my arms, talking to her, making her giggle and chatter, as I wait for Sean to finish sending another message and toss the phone down, and then I ask him, 'Did you listen to the show?'

I'm anxious to know whether he heard anything in my voice during Diane's call that made him suspect there was something wrong.

'Sorry, Han.' He's distracted by looking for a corkscrew. 'I was at the supermarket getting the booze, so I didn't catch the show. Go all right, did it?'

It doesn't matter, really, it's not like I expected him to listen, and part of me is relieved he missed it. I've never told him what we did to Martin, I've never admitted it to a soul. Only one person in the world knows about that night, or so I thought until today, and that's Cameron, and I don't think he'd tell anyone either. Sean doesn't even know about Cam, who I haven't seen since university.

For one fleeting moment I think I should tell him what Diane said. *I'm going to make the people responsible for Martin's death suffer.*

But I don't, I can't, because all these years later I'm a respected psychologist, a middle-class mother, and how do I explain why I did such a thing? Sean probably wouldn't believe me anyway, or he'd laugh about it, which would just make me feel worse.

'Yes,' I tell him. 'It was a lot of fun.'

Putting down a box of wine, Sean comes over to wrap his arms around me and Amber. For a few moments, maybe for the last time, everything's the way it should be, and the way I have always believed it would remain. The three of us stand holding each other on the cool tiles, swaying with a gentle rhythm; Sean and I, our arms entwined, Amber snug between us. He kisses us both on the forehead.

The party is probably a good idea, I have to admit – it'll be good to see friends, and it'll keep my mind off that low, malicious threat.

I'm going to make them pay.

Sean takes Amber from me, lifting her to his chest. 'Why don't you relax in the bath before everyone gets here?'

4

And, yeah, I enjoy the party for a while.

Sean's right, it's good to get dolled up in something nice and welcome people to our home, even if a lot of them are his mates rather than our mutual friends. Everyone is genuinely happy for me, and many kind visitors arrive with gifts. Not just bottles of wine, but soaps and smellies and stationery, lovely knick-knacks. It's an unexpected opportunity to catch up with people I haven't seen for absolutely ages, and for a brief time I forget all about the radio show and Diane's threat.

We've got a roomy double-fronted house you enter through one of those colourful stained-glass front doors I used to dream of having. There's a spacious living room to the left of the long, wide hallway, but it's the big kitchen on the right where everyone gathers, to drink and chat. People drift into the garden, where it's still hot and bright, and I have to keep reminding everybody to keep the noise down, because Amber is asleep upstairs.

'Don't you worry, love,' says Kath, enveloped in a cloud of vape smoke, before immediately screaming with laughter at someone's joke.

Holly, who is Sean's PA at his marketing company, comes

tottering across the white floorboards on ridiculous heels, screeching so loudly that I worry she's going to wake up Amber; Isaac and Steve arrive with a big bouquet of flowers; Kath came straight from the pub. Claire hugs me tight, won't let me go, and tells me again and again how proud she is of me, and that her mum wants my autograph, which she pesters me into signing on a piece of kitchen towel.

I'm careful not to drink too much, and never stray far from the baby monitor on the kitchen island. Sean keeps turning the music up on the Wi-Fi speaker, and whenever he wanders away, I turn it back down. Minutes later, he turns up the volume so his football mates can sing along to a Queen anthem, and I have to tell him to stop. He's very drunk by now, and flaps a hand dismissively, as if I'm being a bore.

The doorbell rings again and again over the din of conversation in the crowded kitchen – just how many people have been invited, exactly? – and Sean welcomes the newcomers inside. The front door bumps against the stopper at the skirting, and I watch until I'm satisfied he's closed it properly. I know it seems like I'm paranoid about the door, but we live in an inner-city area where there are a lot of burglaries, and you really don't want to leave it wide open on a Saturday night.

At half ten, Ollie turns up – but without Izzy.

'Hey, man,' Sean calls from outside. He's coming down the lawn – God knows what he's been doing at the top of the garden – and opens his arms wide to accept Ollie's hug. There's a lot of loud and elaborate backslapping. 'Good to see you! Where's the wife?'

'Izzy's not coming,' Ollie says with a wince. 'She didn't

want to miss it, but she's got a bug, so she's snuggled under the duvet on the sofa.'

'Bloody hell!' Sean seems even more disappointed my best friend is not here than I am. 'We should get together soon, yeah?'

'We're meant to be meeting in town next week,' I remind them.

'Let's get you a drink, fella.' Sean throws an arm over Ollie's shoulder – he gets very tactile when he's drunk – and they march into the kitchen. 'What you having?'

My enthusiasm has faded now I know Izzy's not coming, and I want to escape to bed. But the kitchen is still full, and there are a lot of people smoking and drinking in the garden; many of them I recognize from Sean's company. Maya's one of the account managers there, and Irene is from accounts; Julius is one of his designers. Sean's also invited practically everyone from his Sunday morning football team. They're meant to be playing a match tomorrow morning, so I'm amazed they're all drinking so heavily. Sean looks absolutely wrecked, he's been mixing drinks all night, and his eyes slop about in his head. Whenever the doorbell goes, he rushes over to drape himself all over the new arrivals, and it's embarrassing. Standing in the kitchen, Ollie smiles at me in sympathy.

Half an hour later, I've had enough, and tell Sean I'm off to bed. Most of our mutual friends have left; it's mostly his who are left, and they're all drunk and loud.

'Hey, babes.' Sean tries to look disappointed, but he's so pissed that he's leering. 'Stay up for a little while.'

'Someone's got to get up with Amber in the morning,' I tell him.

He gives a heigh-ho shrug, like I'm being a spoilsport. I tense when I think I hear Amber's voice on the monitor, but I must be mistaken.

'I'll just be a little while longer, yeah?' Sean presses his hands together, as if his word is holy, but nobody looks like they're planning on leaving soon. He seems jittery, the pupils of his eyes seem unnaturally wide, and when he pinches his nostrils, I wonder if he's taken anything. Sean used to do a bit of coke when he went out of a night – at one stage it was becoming a problem – but when Amber was born he solemnly promised that he wouldn't touch it any more.

'Please keep the music down.' My eyes flick to the hallway. 'And make sure the front door is shut.'

'You got it.'

As I trudge tensely upstairs, the thump of music vibrates the floorboards beneath my feet. But halfway up, the volume drops, it's been turned down at least, and by the time I reach the landing all I can hear is mostly the low thrum of chatter.

When I go into Amber's bedroom, she's blissfully asleep. It's a sanctuary of calm in her small room. Soft light from a rotating lamp scatters warm colour across her body. She lies on her back, her arms flung wide, tiny fingers curled. Her chest rises and falls slowly in her sleepsuit.

Stroking her soft hair, my heart pounds in my chest, because I love her so much. Eighteen months ago, against all the odds, this amazing little person came into our lives, this miracle of life, to transform my whole world.

When Amber was born, I discovered what it means to love someone utterly and completely. My love for her is sacred, pure, absolute. She's the greatest thing that's ever happened to me, or will ever happen.

It's tempting to climb into bed and snuggle up beside her till morning, but we'll no doubt be getting up with the larks, so I turn off the lamp, close the window to a crack, and leave the room.

Our bedroom is at the front of the house, and I hear another knock on the front door below. Someone has just arrived – even now, at nearly midnight – and my heart sinks when Sean bellows a greeting. Closing the shutters, I change into my pyjamas, then pad across the landing to the bathroom.

But when the light goes on, I get a terrible shock.

The mirror above the sink is an angry mess of thick red lines, scribbled and scrawled every which way. The entire surface is smeared with it, so that as I come closer, my own stunned reflection is almost obliterated.

The red is a rich, dark colour – like blood. And the sight of it triggers a memory – one I've not had for many years. I see bed sheets and pillows, my own hands, my face and body, smeared crimson; spurts and splashes along my arms and legs, sodden red and sticky.

Staggering back, I make out something written beneath the chaotic smears and scribbles. It's nearly hidden, as if someone wrote it and then tried to obliterate it. I can only make out some of the letters. The looping curves of a *B*... A jagged *A*... The manic curl of an *S*...

But I know instinctively what the word is.

When I touch the mess, a glittery sheen comes away on the end of my finger – it's lipstick. A messy stub, which must have broken off the tube, has been dumped in the sink.

Staring in horror at the mirror, steadying myself against the sink, I feel sick.

Who would do this, and why?

A door creaks, and when I rush onto the landing, a woman I don't recognize is coming out of the spare bedroom.

'Oh, hi!' She's young, with peroxide blonde hair, a minidress and oversized trainers.

'What are you doing?' I ask her sharply.

'I'm sorry.' She looks embarrassed. 'I was looking for the toilet?'

'Did you just do that on the mirror?' I point into the bathroom.

She's flustered. 'Uh, sorry?'

But I don't stop to listen, because there's a draught on my legs. From the top of the stairs, I see the front door is flung wide open, revealing the dark, empty street beyond the gate of our front garden, the houses opposite. Anybody could just walk in. The party is in full swing in the kitchen, everyone's laughing and chatting, so I slam the door shut, shoving the heel of my hand hard against the wood to make sure the lock clicks home, and rush into the kitchen.

'Where's Sean?' I ask, because I can't see him. 'Where is he?'

His football mates shrug, and maybe one of them smirks.

'In the garden, I think,' someone says.

When I get outside, Sean is standing up by the shed, almost hidden in the shadow of the wall at the end of the garden. He's talking to a young woman from his work; they're standing close to each other, their faces just inches apart. Laughing at something she says, he reaches out and lightly touches the underside of her arm.

'I need to speak to my husband,' I tell her with a tight smile. Seeing my pyjamas and tense expression, she steps back. 'Who did that upstairs?' I ask him.

'Wait.' He sniffs. 'What are you talking about?'

We walk back towards the house. 'Someone's smeared lipstick on the bathroom mirror.'

He looks confused. 'Why would anyone do that?'

'I don't know, Sean, but someone has been upstairs. They could have gone in Amber's room.'

He stares at me, bewildered, as I walk back inside and turn off the music, raising my voice above the conversation in the room.

'Who's been upstairs?' Everyone turns to listen. 'Who scrawled red lipstick over our bathroom mirror?'

'Come on, Han,' Sean says, slurring slightly, and Ollie comes up behind him. 'Nobody would do anything like that.'

'Somebody did.' My heart thumps in my chest. 'And I want to know who.'

'Accidents happen, though, right?'

But it's not an accident, no way. Whoever did it smeared the lipstick so hard onto the surface that it broke in two. And the front door was wide open – for how long I have no idea – *anyone* could have walked in and done it.

'Yeah, love, I did it,' shouts one of Sean's soccer mates. 'That colour never suited me.'

He laughs, until someone elbows him in the ribs.

'You're spoiling the party,' Sean tells me in a low voice. 'Come and look.'

Upstairs, he frowns at the mirror, smeared with the angry red scribble. 'Someone's just being a bit of a prat.'

'But why would anyone do such a thing?'

But of course, all I can think of is the caller to the radio show today. Diane, or whoever she is, could have walked in off the street and done it. After all, she knows all too well the significance of that obliterated word.

The thought that Amber was up here, sleeping just a few feet away, makes me nauseous.

But I can't tell Sean about Diane now, not after midnight, with him drunk, and a party in full swing downstairs, and I wonder if I'll have the courage to tell him tomorrow.

He cocks his head sideways, peering at it, following the messy curves of the letters. 'It says something. B... a... there's an e.'

'Banshee,' I tell him quietly. 'It says Banshee.'

He screws up his face. 'What is that, a boy band or something? I'm so out of touch these days. Christ, I feel old.'

I know exactly what the word means. And so does Diane.

'Don't worry about it.' He waves a hand at the mirror. 'I'll clean it up in the morning.'

'I don't want to see it,' I tell him.

'I'll do it first thing,' he promises. 'I'm gonna get rid of everyone downstairs. Give me ten minutes and I'll come to bed.'

He kisses me on the forehead and heads downstairs. But I know he won't come up. He'll get pulled into the orbit of a conversation, or someone will pour him a drink, and he'll forget about me. Not long after I get into bed I hear him roar with laughter, and the volume of the music goes up.

I don't know how long I lie there before I finally drift off to sleep, and the laughter and music transforms into the echo of another party I didn't enjoy, in another time, another place.

5

Twenty Years Ago

Looking back, I have no idea what on earth Cameron saw in me. Right from the beginning of our relationship, if that's what you want to call it, he was having to manage my bad behaviour. That time of my life was turbulent, and my head was all over the place. A lot of people regard their university days as the best of their lives, but it's not a period I have any fondness or nostalgia for.

Living in London and separated from my family for the first time, I was dealing with a lot of complicated teenage emotions and feelings, even though I couldn't wait to get away from my parents and sister. I had a lot of resentful feelings about Natalie's illness. My sister – she was a couple of years older than me – suffered from severe depression and mood disorders, so she always received a lot of attention from Mum and Dad. It wasn't their fault, they did the best they could in difficult circumstances, but growing up I felt like I was always treading on eggshells, that Natalie's emotional needs always took precedence over mine, so there was always a lot of tension at home. Natalie couldn't help it, of course, she was battling her own demons, but I'd get angry and lash out when Mum and Dad already had enough on their plate. So I couldn't wait to leave home, and thought that going away to university would improve the situation for everyone. But hundreds of miles from home, I felt isolated and still carried a lot of unprocessed anger. The truth is, well – I was a mess, and probably not the easiest person to be around.

The very first time I met Cameron was at a house party in Dalston, when I was drunk and behaving badly. I didn't even want to be there, because that afternoon I'd rowed with Mum on the phone about all the usual stuff. She had started talking about how Natalie had taken a turn for the worse, or how well Natalie was doing on her new meds – I can't remember which, but it was always one or the other – and as usual she hardly asked anything about my new life in London. It was a big and scary time for me, I was alone in a strange city; but preoccupied as usual with Natalie, she just took it for granted that I could cope, and I inevitably got upset.

Anyway, some people I knew were going to the party, I wouldn't even call them friends, they were just people I knew from uni, but they invited me, and I was so desperate to get out of my grotty digs that I thought, what the hell.

But as soon as I got there, I regretted it. It was a three-storey student house and there must have been nearly a hundred people crammed inside. I immediately got separated from the people I went with, and ended up standing on my own in the kitchen. I'd found a six-pack of beer and was drinking them all – not a good idea on an empty stomach – when this guy came over and started making conversation.

'You don't want to talk to me,' I told him.

He was thin, with an earnest baby face that made him look

a lot younger than his eighteen years, and he was wearing an enormous parka, which was probably meant to be trendy but looked bulky and ridiculous on his slight frame. He seemed nice enough, but I wasn't in the mood to chat.

'But I do,' he told me. It was his smile, which was gentle and honest, and not at all predatory, that stopped me telling him point-blank to go away. I'd already had a lot of guys try to chat me up in the short time I'd been standing there, and I'd told them all to get lost. 'That's why I came over.'

'Why are you wearing that massive coat?' He looked hot in the packed, smoky room.

'I'm worried if I put it down somewhere, it'll be stolen.'

'You're going to get heat stroke wearing that.'

He blew his damp fringe off his forehead. 'I think you might be right.'

'No offence, Mr Anorak, but I just want to be left alone to think about stuff.'

'You know what they say,' he said with a shrug. 'A problem shared is a problem halved.'

'How do you know I've got a problem?'

'You look like you need a friend.'

'You really don't want to be my *friend*,' I told him with a scowl.

He looked around the crowded room. 'I won't know unless you talk to me.'

'Look, you seem like a nice bloke, but I'm not just going to spill all my secrets to some random who comes up to me at a party.'

He finally got the message and shrugged. 'Sure, no problem. You have a good evening.'

'Yeah, you too.' To take the edge off my rudeness, I said, 'Wait, what's your name?'

'Cameron,' he said with a smile, and disappeared into the crowd.

I should have gone home then, but the alcohol had hit my system and I went in search of more. This time, I found a bottle of cheap red wine, and poured as much of it as I could into a plastic beer cup. Wandering from room to room, mostly avoiding everyone and wallowing in self-pity, I picked up a few more drinks, unwisely mixing beer and wine and spirits. I even spoke to a few people, I think, but I'm sure by that time I was so drunk and annoying they weren't keen to speak to me.

Everything became a blur. The noise of the party, the thumping bass, the throb of chatter and laughter crashed around in my head; a procession of lurid faces passed in front of me as I walked around. Maybe I danced a bit, swinging my arms too widely, spinning too fast, stumbling into people. I vaguely remember being sick somewhere.

And then I don't remember anything until someone woke me up.

'Hey,' said a guy who was gently shaking my shoulder.

It took me a few moments to work out who I was, and where I was. Feet lifted past my head. I was slumped on the stairs, so that all the people coming up and down had to step over and around me, and everyone was getting annoyed. There was a plastic cup in my hand, but it was empty; red wine had tipped all over the carpet, and the thigh of my jeans.

'You probably need to go home.' The guy's face was haloed by the fur of a big parka.

I could barely stand, I was so drunk, but knew I had to get out of there.

'Yeah,' I murmured.

'Hey fella,' someone said. 'Get your girlfriend out the way, nobody can get past.'

'I'm not her boyfriend,' he said.

'Come on.' I pulled at his arm. I felt sick and giddy, and needed to get outside. 'Let's go.'

Outside, I felt immediately better when the cold winter air hit my hot face.

'I'll call you a cab,' he said.

'No.' I didn't trust myself not to throw up in the back of a car. 'I'm going to walk.'

'Where do you live?'

'Camden,' I said.

He frowned. 'You can't walk to Camden from here. You'll freeze to death, or get mugged or worse.' He looked back at the house. 'Do you have friends still inside? I'll try and find them.'

I didn't know if the people I'd arrived with were still there or if they'd gone home, I hadn't seen them for hours. I'm not sure I'd even have recognized them. 'You can walk with me.'

'You don't know me,' he said. 'I could be anyone.'

'You seem okay, and I want you to take me home.'

'If you want.' I was wearing a tee-shirt; in the chill of the night, I hugged my bare arms across my chest. 'You're going to freeze, where's your coat?'

'I put it down somewhere inside.' I didn't want to go back inside because I wouldn't even know where to start looking for it, I just wanted to get home. 'I'll come back for it tomorrow.'

The guy shimmered and swayed in my vision, and I squinted at him. 'What's your name again?'

'Cameron,' he said. 'Call me Cam.'

'I'm Hannah.'

'Come on, put this on.' He took off his parka and placed it over my shoulders as he led me down the road. It felt warm and snug. 'Or you'll catch your death.'

6

When I wake up, it's gone eight o'clock. I must have been completely exhausted last night, because it's the longest I've slept in since Amber was born.

Panicking that she's been crying for hours, that she's starving and needs changing, I scramble out of bed. But her room is empty, and I hear Sean's voice downstairs. He's talking to her above the comfortable Sunday morning burble of the radio, and I relax. Until I remember the bathroom.

But the mirror is spotless; gleaming. Sean has been as good as his word and cleaned it.

When I go downstairs, Amber has already eaten, and is sitting quietly in her high chair playing with a couple of bendy figures. I pick her up and hug her, pressing my nose against the top of her head.

'Hey.' Sean moves around the kitchen, furiously cleaning. Most of the mess from last night has been cleared up; everything smells of surface cleaner. Two bulging recycling bags sit on the floor.

'Did you even come to bed?' I ask him.

He grins wearily over a glass of fizzing Berocca. 'Yeah, I got a few hours.'

Sean looks wretched. Bleary eyes peer out between pale,

puffy lids; his face is drawn and grey, and he stinks of booze. It's obvious he's in the grip of a powerful hangover. God knows I've tried to talk to him about his drinking many times, but he just dismisses my concerns, as if I'm exaggerating the problem or being a killjoy.

A memory from last night comes back to me, of Sean pinching his nose and sniffing, and I want to ask him whether he's doing coke again. But I don't want a row this morning, so I say nothing, and gently bounce Amber in my arms, watching him rinse a cloth in the sink. His phone dings, he's got a message. His thumbs dab across the screen.

'Who's that?' I ask. 'The girl from last night?'

He looks up at me. 'What girl from last night?'

'The one you were talking to outside the shed.'

'Uh.' He gives me a stern look, as if I'm overreacting. 'Zeta? She's just someone from work who was having a cigarette and didn't want to bother anybody with the smoke, which is why we stood by the shed. I didn't inhale, if that's what you're worried about.'

'She seemed very young.'

There's an edge to his voice, as if I'm being unreasonable asking questions. 'She's on the undergrad scheme, I think.'

I'm just being paranoid. Sean is a terrible flirt, he admits it himself, but no more than that. I've let my own anxiety about the events of yesterday cloud my judgement.

Holding up the phone, he says, 'And *this* is just someone thanking us for the party.' He makes a sweeping gesture around the room. 'Look, you'd hardly know it happened.'

Everything is very tidy, I have to admit. 'It's very impressive, and thanks for cleaning up the mirror.'

'No problem.' He finishes tying a sack. 'Nobody owned up

to it, but it was probably one of my idiot mates thinking they were being hilarious.'

'It's not funny,' I say. 'How is it even funny?'

'Couldn't agree more.' He grimaces. 'Can we talk about this another time, Han, I've got a bit of a headache.'

But I can't help myself and say, 'The front door was left open.'

'No, it wasn't.' He opens a cupboard and takes out a bottle of painkillers. 'I made sure it was closed all night.'

'It was open when I came down. Anybody could have walked in off the street, Sean. We need to get that door fixed.'

Sean palms a couple of pills into his mouth and gulps them down with the last of his vitamin drink.

'Nothing's been taken,' he says. 'The telly, the laptop, the phone, your beloved silver teapot, they're all still here. Nobody is going to come in off the street just to deface our bathroom mirror, and then...' He flutters his fingers. 'Disappear into the night.'

Now is the moment to talk to him about Diane, and her threat. But that would mean having to tell him about Martin and Cameron, and a turbulent part of my life that he knows nothing about, and I'm not sure I want to open that can of worms. Sean wouldn't believe at first that I could be so cruel. It's a running joke between us that I'm always so prim and correct, a fine upstanding citizen, and he's the uncouth tearaway.

Maybe he'd laugh off what Cameron and I did as a nasty joke. A vicious, spiteful thing to do, but a prank nonetheless. But I've always been deeply ashamed of what we did. And if what Diane said is true, and her brother Martin later took his own life as a consequence, that makes me feel even more wretched.

So it's no wonder I try to convince myself that Sean is right, and it was one of his loser friends who vandalized the mirror – there were certainly enough of them here – and that I conjured up the word I saw, *Banshee*, out of the chaotic loops and whirls of the blood-red scrawl. Because it was on my mind, because *she* was on my mind. Diane surely can't know my address, unless she followed me home yesterday...

No, I'm just being paranoid.

As Sean takes the sacks outside, my mobile rings. Continuing to jog Amber gently in the other arm, I put it to my ear. It's the producer from yesterday's show.

'Sorry to bother you on a Sunday morning, Hannah,' he says. 'But I've got that number you asked for.'

It takes a moment to realize what he's talking about, but then my heart begins to pound. 'Let me get a pen.'

'I'll be honest,' he says. 'I didn't manage to ring the lady to check it would be okay for you to contact her, but I don't suppose she'll mind – she did ring to speak to you, after all. Just don't tell anyone I gave it.'

My hand trembles as I write it down. I've got her number now – this mysterious Diane – and I'll make contact with her during the week to get this situation sorted out and put my mind at rest. Until then, I'll not let it spoil what remains of our weekend.

'How about we grab breakfast somewhere?' I suggest to Sean when he comes back in. 'My treat.'

Because I've worked on the radio show nearly every Saturday, and Sean usually plays football on Sunday mornings, it's not like we get to spend a lot of time together at weekends. We can grab something to eat and then take Amber to a museum or gallery, wander around a farmers' market, or walk on the Heath; we've got the whole day.

'But I've got a match,' he tells me, and I realize he's wearing trackie bottoms and a hoodie.

'You look terrible, Sean, you're not going to be able to play football in your state, surely?'

'I feel freaking awful, yeah, but I can't let the lads down.' He leans in to kiss me, and his stinky breath makes me rear back. 'What, that bad?'

'Please.' I bat him away, making a joke of it, but also kind of disgusted, because he really has no idea. 'Go and gargle with some mouthwash.'

'I have already,' he says and pretends to sob, hanging on to Amber and me and making us both laugh. Then he pulls us in for a hug. 'Oh God, I'm so disgusting.'

'You really are!'

I push him off and he picks up a rucksack. 'I'll probably go for a quick drink afterwards with the lads – you know, hair of the dog – and then maybe we can do something after lunch?'

He kisses me again, and gently cups Amber's face in his big hands, pressing his lips to the top of her head.

At the door, he stops. 'By the way, it's a spirit whose wailing foretells death.'

'Excuse me?'

'A banshee. I looked it up.' Then he slams out of the door.

A chill drops down my spine, I don't know why, maybe it's just the mention of the word. But I try to force down my unease, because there's so much I should be doing; the washing needs to be done and Amber's lunch has to be made. I need to book a restaurant. My parents are coming to London this week, it's been an age since I've seen them, and I've been anxious about where to take them.

The sad truth is, I see my parents only very rarely because they live up north, but also because things haven't been good between my father and I for many years. A trip down south is a rarity for them, and I don't kid myself it's because Dad has a burning desire to see his daughter, or even his granddaughter, it's because they have a funeral to attend. However, they did agree to meet for lunch.

But when I phone the restaurant I've chosen, it's closed – hardly surprising on a Sunday morning – and I leave a message saying that I want to book a table for Wednesday lunchtime.

Amber and I play together on the floor for an hour. We have a fine time banging multicoloured bricks into holes of different shapes, and building towers and populating them with animal figures. She does all the hard work and I make myself useful by handing her the bricks.

'Look how clever you are!' I say, when she's built one precarious construction, and she celebrates by shoving it over. When I offer Amber a yellow brick to start again, she takes it with an exquisite gentleness that makes my heart swell. They say that the universe gives you exactly what you need at any given moment, and this time alone with my daughter is exactly what I need right now.

But the universe has also placed a more sinister and worrying possibility in my path, and I struggle to get Diane out of my head. If I'm honest, I don't want a cloud of uncertainty hanging over me, and I feel anxious about waiting several days before making contact with her.

Amber begins to get grouchy, so I fill a sippy cup with juice, which she grabs in her fists and pulls to her mouth, and I pick up my phone to tap in the number I wrote on a slip of paper.

The next thing I know, I'm pressing the green button to connect the call. Amber's still grumbling, so I pick her up and together we pace the kitchen.

The phone must ring seven or eight times, and I don't think anyone's going to pick up, but then the call connects, and I recognize instantly Diane's gruff voice. 'Yes?'

'Is that Diane?' I ask lightly.

'This is she,' she says carefully.

'Hi.' I try to sound as casual and pleasant as possible. 'It's Hannah, Diane – Hannah Godley from Craig's radio show. You phoned yesterday?'

There's several seconds of silence, and then Diane says, 'What do you want?'

'I hope you don't mind me calling, but I think there must have been a problem with the line yesterday because you were cut off, so we never got to speak properly.' We both know she hung up on purpose. 'Your story really…. well, it really resonated with me, Diane, and I wanted to… reach out.'

Her breath rasps. I rang a mobile number, so I've no idea if she's in her house or somewhere else. There's no background or ambient noise, comfortable burble of a radio, whistling kettle, or birdsong. All I can hear is her voice; once again, it's almost as if she exists only in my head.

'Reach out,' she repeats.

'I'd like to help you.'

'And why would you want to do that?'

Because I'm afraid you're going to tell the world about the terrible thing I did, just as my career is about to take off. I want to find out just what you know, and to persuade you to leave me alone.

'I… just want to help, Diane, if you'll let me.'

She sniffs, and says, 'So what are you saying?'

'Let's meet up,' I say chirpily, as if we're old friends who have left it far too long to get together. 'I think it would help you to chat about things. Why don't I come to your—'

'I don't want you here,' Diane says quickly.

'That's okay,' I say. 'There's a café, it's very central, just off Warren Street. Maybe that would be a good place to—'

'I can't meet right now,' she says. 'But maybe in a couple of hours.'

That catches me off guard, because I was expecting we'd arrange a date for later this week. But I'm also afraid that I'll antagonize her if I try to delay, and frankly, I want to put my anxieties to bed as soon as possible. So I say, 'That's perfect!'

'Is it?' she asks, surprised.

After I tell her the name of the café, and the address, I add, 'I'm looking forward to meeting you, Diane. As I said, your story really… it touched me.'

Diane's response is flat and guarded. 'Did it?'

When the call ends, my heart thumps in my chest. Amber is exploring my face with her damp fingers. She's laughing now, and normally I'd laugh too, but I'm too shaken up.

'I'm sorry, baby,' I tell her, because I'm going to have to make another difficult call.

We've only been in this house for a few months, it cost us an arm and a leg and the mortgage is way too high, but Sean and I fell in love with it. We're in a vibrant part of North

London, and reasonably central. Sure, there are problems with living here, but you name me a part of the city that doesn't have any. One issue, though, is that it's difficult to get childcare at such short notice. We don't have friends close, or family in the area. My parents are in Lancashire and Sean's family live south of the river.

So I have to call Siobhan again. It's her day off, like yesterday was her day off, but I really have no choice. There's no chance I'm going to take Amber with me to meet Diane.

When Siobhan answers, I hear footsteps and people talking in the background, a church bell in the distance.

'I'm so sorry to ask you this…' I tell her I've got to go out unexpectedly, it's an emergency and can't be helped, and can she look after Amber?

'Um,' she says, hesitating. 'I mean, if you really think—'

'I'd be very grateful,' I tell her quickly. It's a good thing we're not on Zoom, because she can't see my anxious grimace. I'm desperate for her to say yes, and terrified she won't.

'Sure,' Siobhan says, after what seems like an age. 'What time?'

'Can you get here within the hour? I'll make sure to feed Amber, and then scoot.'

'Okay,' she says after a long pause. 'I'll come over.'

7

A n hour later, I'm back on the Tube, travelling into the centre of town.

Usually, I'd put in my AirPods and listen to music, but I'm nervous about meeting Diane and need to think carefully about what I'll say to her. She'll likely be aggressive and accusatory, so it's important that I remain calm and patient and sympathetic. But I'm not going to make any kind of admission until I know what her motives are. There's still a chance that I've gotten the wrong end of the stick, and that she wasn't threatening me directly. That's the hope I cling to as the train trundles along the black Victorian tunnels beneath the city.

When I step off the Tube, the platform at Warren Street is half empty, but I look around, just in case someone's watching me – which is ridiculous, because Diane can't possibly know how I'm going to arrive, or when.

It's another sweltering day. We've had weeks of intense heat – the records keep tumbling one after the other – and today it's also very humid. The air feels like a heavy weight on my shoulders, everything feels soporific and sticky. There are lightning storms up north, apparently; the heavens have opened and dumped a month's worth of rain onto the earth in a day, causing flash floods. But not here in London, where the grass in the parks is brown, the mud hard and cracked, the pavements bone dry, and all the bins give off a foul stench, because the storms aren't heading in this direction. So it's a relief when I finally get to the café. It's one of those small independent places, with half a dozen tables and matching chairs and a big glass-fronted counter with too many shelves and too few cakes.

Walking inside, I spot Diane immediately, because there's only one person here.

A woman glares at me from a table near the window. She knows who I am, because she's probably seen me on TV, or my photo beneath a magazine byline. It's obvious how tall and broad she is, even sitting down, and when she stands as I approach, I see she's over six foot. She wears garish zigzag leggings in rhubarb and yellow, which gather beneath the gladiator sandals clenching her shins. Her body, with her wide shoulders and large breasts, is smothered by a shapeless grey hoodie, and I can only imagine how hot and uncomfortable she must be in this unbearable heat.

About my age, in her late thirties, Diane looks like someone who was a Goth when younger, and has never completely shaken the look. Her make-up is dark and thickly applied; her jet-black hair is worn away from her ears in a stiff, bulbous helmet; there are puckers of ghost piercings climbing the edge of her large ears, and on the side of her nose. But her wide and watchful blue eyes, obscured by the thick clumps of messy mascara that cling to the long lashes, are beautiful and expressive.

'Diane?' I plonk my bag on the table and offer a hand, as

if we're here for a business meeting. The shake she finally gives me is limp.

She glares, she looks angry, but I have to take control of the situation. The most important thing is to show I'm not afraid – I came here to offer help, after all – and I absolutely will not admit to anything that will compromise me. If she's in any way aggressive or threatening, I'll leave.

'Did you have any problems getting here?' I ask, making small talk as I take a chair. Most of the tables are in the shade, but Diane is seated in the window, with the blinding midday sun directly overhead; she really couldn't have chosen a worse place. 'I hope not.'

'No,' she says, sitting down again.

Diane's posture is stiff. Her arms are pressed tightly to her side but her big hands, the short, blunt fingernails painted brown, flutter in her lap. Cheap gold rings sit on nearly every finger, and her wrists jangle with a variety of bracelets and bangles.

She's already got a glass of Coke in front of her, the ice cubes almost melted. I'm not thirsty, I don't want to be here any longer than I have to be, but it'll look rude not to order anything, so I ask the waitress for a peppermint tea.

'My goodness, it's hot.' It's like a furnace where we're sitting, and I eye the empty tables in the shaded part of the room. 'Shall we move?'

When she finally meets my gaze with a scowl, I remind myself to be wary. This is a person who could very well have crept into my house last night. 'I'm fine.'

'Okay, then. The first thing to say, Diane, is thank you for meeting me.' I place a hand on my chest. 'Your story really touched me.'

There's an urgent question in her intense gaze. 'Do you usually meet people who call the show?'

'I'll talk to callers after the show sometimes, but your call made me especially upset.' Diane's mouth twitches, and her dark-red lips once again make me think of my vandalized mirror. 'And I knew I wanted to speak to you again, because I want to help.'

'What do you mean, help?' she asks in that deep voice I heard in my headphones yesterday.

'Well, sometimes I find it's just good to talk things through with someone, isn't it?'

The thumb of her right hand tensely spins a ring on her middle finger. 'I still miss him.'

'Our grief for the loved ones we have lost never really leaves us, so that's only natural.'

The waitress comes over and places tea in front of me. I don't bother stirring the pot, just pour it straight into my cup; it's not like I'm going to drink it anyway.

'Why don't you tell me about Martin?'

'He was a nice man, kind and gentle,' she says, scowling again. 'He wouldn't hurt a fly.'

My mouth opens because I remember just what kind of a man Martin was, but think better of contradicting her. 'Go on.'

'He killed himself a few years back.' She talks to the top of the table. 'Hung himself from a banister.'

'So he didn't... it wasn't straight after what happened to him?'

'No, but that was the beginning of the end. Martin was happy and confident before it happened, and he was never the same after. He became frightened and withdrawn, and prone to black moods.'

'I'm so sorry, Diane.'

'Are you sorry?' Those pale eyes snap to mine. 'Are you really?'

The midday sun pounds at the back of my neck and makes my shirt cling wetly to my shoulders and spine. I shouldn't have come here – what on earth was I thinking?

'Of course I am.'

She nods. 'You're not who I thought you'd be.'

'Really? In what way?'

'I thought you'd be stuck up and very grand, but you're not, you're… nice.'

'That's very kind of you,' I tell her, and for the first time Diane's face softens. Now seems like the right time to address why we're both really here. 'Was there a reason you phoned the show, Diane? Maybe you wanted to speak to me in particular?'

Diane's hands squirm in her lap. Despite her threats on the phone, and her tense demeanor, I realize that she finds meeting me an intimidating experience.

'I didn't…' She mumbles something but I don't catch it.

'I'm sorry, Diane.' I lean forward. 'What did you say?'

Her gaze drifts over my shoulder to the street, as if she's looking for someone. 'It was important that I tell you… about him.'

'About Martin. I understand.' Now is the time: I can continue to maintain the lie that I'm an impartial observer, a benevolent professional who wants to help, or I can admit the truth. But I'm not ready to take that plunge, not until I'm sure it's the right thing to do. 'But I think you wanted to speak to me, Diane. Why was that?'

'You know why.'

When her gaze lifts sharply to mine, I glimpse the fury behind her scowl, and it makes my blood chill. It's gone in a split second, and Diane's face again becomes a mask. But I saw anger there, *rage* even, and it makes me wary of admitting anything.

'You blame me, don't you, Diane?' I say softly.

My question makes her flustered. Maybe if I hadn't been in such a hurry to contact her, the whole thing would have blown over. She phoned the show on an impulse, just to let off steam, and it was never her intention to take her grievance any further.

'It was you,' she says finally. 'You were with him that night.'

'What makes you say that?'

'He said one of the people he met was called Hannah, and you look like her.'

Did I use my real name that evening? I can't remember how much Cameron and I spoke about ourselves, but I can't imagine we admitted more than a fragment of truth. And Martin was heavily drunk. He surely couldn't have described me so accurately that all these years later Diane has been able to identify me. Yet somehow, incredibly, she's added two and two together – my name and description – and come up with the right answer. It doesn't make sense how she could have found me.

And now I have to find the moral courage to admit responsibility for the bad thing I did to her brother. If I can do that, who knows, maybe I can finally let go of that memory, and also the guilt that has ached at the back of my mind for so many years. We all have these moments in our life when we're invited by fate to do the right thing, to make amends; when we're given the opportunity to repair the hurt and pain we've caused, and can finally release that burden and begin to heal.

That moment has arrived for me. I should tell her how Cameron and I humiliated her brother.

My direct memories of Martin have evaporated over time; all his physical features have eroded, become less precise and focused; the details of his face, his complexion, the colour of his hair, the clothes he wore, become a blur. One by one, they disappeared, until finally I even forgot his name. In my mind, Martin has become less of a human being than a symbol of my own weakness and capriciousness.

However, it's not too late to admit my shame, to finally do the right thing, and part of me is eager to confess. But I can't shake the feeling that I've made a terrible mistake by coming here, and that I'll give Diane the ammunition to demolish my reputation. If I admit what I did, I'd be encouraging her in the delusion that I'm somehow responsible for her brother's death. And for all I know, she could be taping this conversation.

I feel a sudden burning resentment at being put on the spot. Being made to feel somehow responsible for the death of a man who I met for a matter of hours many years ago.

'Do you mind if I use the toilet?' I say. 'I won't be long.'

Diane looks surprised when I hurry to the cubicle at the back of the café. I don't need to go to the loo, I just need to cool down in the small space; give myself a couple of minutes to take a few deep breaths in front of the mirror. Then I wash my hands, dab my perspiring face with paper towels, and head back outside, determined not to give her any ammunition to use against me.

'Sorry about that,' I say, sitting back down. 'Diane, I think you're under the impression that I was one of the people who met Martin that night, and who... made fun of him.' My intention is to close this situation down quickly. I'll say what I need to say, then go home to Amber and forget any of this ever happened. 'But I'm afraid you're mistaken.'

When Diane finally replies, her voice is quiet. 'But you did.'

'It wasn't me,' I tell her firmly. 'And as far as I'm concerned, that's the end of the matter.'

She frowns at the table, her dark lips pressed tightly together in a terse line.

'I notice you're wearing lipstick,' I say.

She blinks. 'Yes.'

'Were you...' My own voice sounds hard and accusatory. 'Did you come to my house last night?'

She blushes – from shame or anger, it's difficult to tell – and the sides of her mouth curl up in a sour smile, as if a hard truth has been confirmed to her. 'I thought you were nice,' she tells me.

'Someone came into my house last night, Diane, and made a mess in my bathroom, was it you?'

I want to accuse her of writing Banshee on the mirror, and say that she's the only one who could have known the significance of the word, but then I'd have to admit that I know it too. I'd be admitting my guilt.

She eyes me steadily, her expression pained and resentful, and it takes all my effort not to look away. But I don't wait for her answer; part of me doesn't even want to know if she was creeping around my house. Coming here has been a mistake.

'I see now there's been some misunderstanding. You think I'm someone else. You've probably seen me on telly and I sort of fit the description of the person you had in your head. I'm sorry about what happened to your brother, but the fact is, Diane, I never met him.' I know I sound brittle and make an effort to soften my tone. 'I'm not going to take the matter any further, because I can see how badly his death has affected you. But, believe me, all this toxic talk of revenge isn't going to help anyone, least of all yourself. My suggestion is that you get yourself counselling, talk to someone about your emotions, and work through your grief. I'm happy to provide the numbers of some helplines if you think that will be useful.'

'So it wasn't you.'

'No, Diane, it wasn't me,' I say in exasperation, and I begin to take things out of my bag, looking for a pen and paper. 'As I say, I can give you numbers to help you begin your journey of acceptance.'

Diane picks up her own bag. I watch, fascinated, but also with a sick feeling in my stomach, as she takes something out and places it on the table between us.

It's a photograph of three people, taken at a table in a basement bar nearly two decades ago. A bar called Banshee. I'm sitting on the left of the image and on the right is Cameron, and between us is another man. Memories of that night rush back.

I remember now Martin's braying laugh, his wet bottom

lip, the soft patch of hair below his ear that he hadn't shaved his disgusting hands all over me.

Like poison racing into my veins, I remember his sobs and screams of self-pity...

Please. Just leave me alone.

A hot shame rushes up my chest, neck and shoulders. My face burns. I'm dumbfounded, because I've no recollection of this photo ever being taken at the Banshee Bar. Cameron and I couldn't have been so careless and arrogant as to allow it to have been taken, could we? But we were young then, and thought we were invincible, so maybe it's possible. Instinctively, I reach for it with trembling fingers, but stop, because I don't want to touch it.

'Pick it up if you need a closer look,' Diane says.

I feel light-headed, giddy, in the impossible heat, and desperately want to leave. I'm furious that Diane, with her scowl and hoodie and garish leggings that twist around her big thighs, her badly applied mascara, has put me in this intolerable situation. What was she even thinking, sitting in the window where the sun pounds down on the top of our heads? Or maybe she knew exactly what she was doing, sitting here. I pick up the bits and pieces I pulled out of my bag, my diary and purse, keys and receipts, and throw them back in.

'What do you say now?' Diane asks me.

'I've got to go.' I stand. 'I have to get back.'

'I see.' She nods at the photo. 'Take it.'

And stupidly, because I'm hot and angry and ashamed, and I just want to get out of there, I snatch it up. And then slam out of the door into the blazing midday sun.

8

Grimacing as I replay our encounter in my head, I must look a loon sitting on the Tube train home.

By storming off like that, I've made myself look foolish and guilty, and I can't stop thinking about the look of disappointment on Diane's face as I fled the café. But it doesn't matter, I tell myself, because the fact is, I'm never going to contact her again.

I reached out, I listened, I did nearly everything expected of me... except maybe take responsibility for my actions. My hope now is that she'll just go away.

Another hot flush of shame races up my chest at my own cowardice. I should have just come clean. *Yes, I played a cruel trick on your brother, please forgive me.*

All Diane wanted from me, I think, was an admission and an apology, and that most likely would have been the end of it.

But I failed her, and let myself down.

As the train grinds to a halt in a tunnel, waiting at a light, I take out the photo of Cameron, Martin and me. The image is cramped and grainy, and the camera flash in the low light of the basement bar makes the faces of the people pop like ghosts. I've changed so much since then, but that's undeniably me on the left – no wonder Diane was able to find me.

This photo was apparently taken on the day of my sister's funeral, which was taking place hundreds of miles away. While I was sitting in the Banshee Bar, my sister was being laid in the ground. My expression is blank, and the white flash in the dark surround makes me look gaunt. My face is cheekbone sharp and my long, cinched-back hair dyed a fiery red. These days, I'm a content and healthy North London mum; a caring professional, no less. My face is curved and heart-shaped, with a dimpled smile, and my naturally brown hair falls around my jaw in a gently waved bob. Everything about my appearance is soft and approachable, as befitting an agony aunt.

I want to take the angry girl in this picture in my arms and give her a big hug and urge her to be kind to herself. Everything's going to be okay. The edges of those big, negative emotions will get worn away by time and she'll find happiness.

On the right of the image, Cameron's long hair falls to the shoulders of the scruffy corduroy jacket he always wore. His hazel eyes sparkle, and his nice smile into the camera belies our dark intentions of that evening,

And in the middle is Martin – I guess that's him, it's been so long since I've seen him now – his heavy-lidded eyes staring unfocused into the camera lens, his unshaven jaw slackly open, as if he's been taken by surprise by whoever took the photo.

It's inconceivable that this image exists, I don't know how Cam and I could have been so stupid as to have posed for it, and my stomach churns just looking at it.

I need to try to switch my brain off, so I drop the photo back in my bag and reach for the smooth white case containing my AirPods, intending to listen to music.

But I can't find my phone anywhere. I check the pockets and compartments of the bag, and in a panic pour everything onto the empty seat beside me. But it's not there – my phone is gone.

My mind whirls as I desperately try to recall the last time I had it. Did I take it out at the café? Did I even take it with me when I met Diane, or leave it at home? That's ridiculous, I wouldn't go anywhere without it.

And then I remember that I left my bag on the table when I went to the toilet.

Did Diane take my phone?

When I get back home, Siobhan is in the living room, playing with Amber. Usually, I'd rush straight to my daughter, but instead I shout 'Hi' and race into the kitchen to look for my mobile, because sometimes I leave it charging there.

Siobhan carries Amber in to see me. 'Here's Mummy!'

'Have you seen my phone?' I'm looking all over for it: in the dish on a shelf where we dump random stuff, beneath a pile of papers on the counter, even among a heap of Amber's toys. But I know in my gut that it's not here.

'I tried to call you,' Siobhan says. 'But a woman answered it.'

My heart leaps. 'Diane?'

'Yeah, that was her.' She bounces Amber gently in her arms. 'She says you left it behind, and she's going to bring it here.'

'Bring it here?'

'She offered to return it,' Siobhan says hesitantly. 'She sounds like a nice lady.'

'Did you give her my address?'

She looks confused. 'She would need the address.'

'But did you offer her the address, did you just tell her it, or did she ask for it?'

'I...' She shakes her head. 'I don't remember, I think I just gave it.'

'I don't want her here.' Siobhan looks at me as if I've lost my mind. 'I mean, she doesn't have to come. I'll call her back and tell her to leave it at the café, and I'll pick it up later.'

But when I try to call my mobile number, the phone is switched off – or maybe Diane is already on the Tube coming here. I don't want her coming to my house – if she hasn't been here already – and I certainly don't want her near my daughter.

'I'm going to take Amber upstairs,' I tell Siobhan and pull Amber from her. 'So do you mind answering the door and getting my phone from Diane? Just, whatever you do, don't let her in.' I know I must sound barking mad. 'It's complicated.'

'I was hoping to get away.' Siobhan looks embarrassed. 'I was meant to meet some people for lunch, and if I go now I can probably still make it.'

'Oh.' I'd completely forgotten that she's come here on her day off, the second in a row. It's unfair of me to ask her to stay any longer, particularly if she's got somewhere else to be. 'Of course.'

'I'm really sorry.' Siobhan looks genuinely worried that I'm annoyed. The truth is, I'd like her here, it would make me feel better, because I really don't want to see Diane again, but I can't force her to stay.

'Of course you should go,' I say reluctantly, and she looks relieved. When she's gone, I place Amber in her playpen in the living room, pour myself a glass of water, and wait for the inevitable knock on the door.

An hour later she's still not arrived, but the front door opens and Sean comes in.

'Hey.' He chucks his keys on the kitchen island and kisses me. 'How has your day been?'

Sean thinks I've been here the whole time. I haven't a clue what to tell him, and change the subject. 'How was football?'

He rubs his head to show how hungover he still is. 'We lost 4-0.'

But then the bell rings, and I tense. Sean is closer to the door and is already reaching for the handle.

'Sean,' I say quickly. 'Wait—'

But he opens it to reveal Diane standing there in her hoodie, leggings and sandals.

'Hi,' he says, intrigued by the stranger. 'Can I help you?'

'I've got Hannah's phone,' she tells him, trying to look inside. 'She left it in the café.'

Sean turns to me, making sure Diane can't see his face, and his wide-eyed expression is pure, *what the hell?* 'There's someone here for you, Han, she says she has your phone.'

'Oh, Diane. Thanks so much for bringing it, it's very kind of you.' Stepping between them, I turn to Sean. 'I thought I'd lost it.'

What I want to know is how Diane came to be in possession of my phone, but I can't accuse her of taking it from my bag. Sean smiles at the strange woman on our doorstep; Diane really doesn't look like someone I'd have as a friend. I hold out my hand for it. If she thinks she's coming in, she's got another think coming.

'You're welcome.' Diane reaches into her bag, a cheap

beige thing in the shape of a clamshell, with a fake gold chain for a strap, and hands it to me.

'Thank you.'

I'm just about to close the door when Sean steps forward.

'Wait, we can't just send this good Samaritan away after she's travelled all the way from wherever. Come in, mysterious lady, have a cup of tea, or a cold drink.'

I wince. 'I think Diane's got things to do.'

'Have you, mysterious Diane? Do you have important things to do this Sunday lunchtime? I bet you don't or you wouldn't have been so kind as to come here.'

Diane looks like a rabbit caught in headlights as he ushers her inside. 'Not really.'

'No, of course you don't, nobody does, so come in and make yourself at home.'

Stepping inside, Diane glares tensely at me; she looks almost as mortified as I feel. Sean is smiling, and I know he's being mischievous. He wants to know who Diane is, and my connection to her.

Closing the door, Sean folds his arm and thrusts his elbow forward in this new way of greeting we all have, and she knocks hers against it.

'There you go. Houston, we have contact!' he says, and clapping his hands together goes into full gracious-host mode. 'What would you like, Diane, a cup of tea, or a cold drink? Maybe something a bit stronger, a glass of wine?'

Diane looks at him as if he's just offered her heroin.

'Just a tea, please.' She gives me a pained look, to show that she didn't ask to be invited in, and doesn't want to be here any more than I want her here.

Sean eyes Diane with undisguised interest as he makes the

tea, taking in her zigzag leggings and sandals, her helmet of hair, and the make-up congealing on her damp cheeks.

I've got my phone back now, thank God, but there's a smudge of fingerprints on the screen. Are they mine? Has this smear of prints always been there, revealed by the bright light shining in from the garden, or has Diane been tapping at the screen, trying to access my diary, numbers, photos, messages and emails? My whole life is on that phone.

I don't know much about phone security, other than that it's protected by a password. If Siobhan phoned her, and Diane answered it, was that enough to enable her to get to the information inside it? Also, it took her over an hour to arrive. Is that enough time to get it unlocked at one of those high-street phone shops?

'So you found Hannah's phone in a café?' Sean asks, fishing for information. 'It's good of you to bring it back.'

Diane is about to speak, but I interrupt. 'I met Diane for a coffee today, actually.'

Sean does a double take. 'Really?'

'She's the sister of someone I used to know from university.' I hope she's not going to contradict me, and to my relief she nods shyly.

'Someone from uni?' he asks.

'My brother Martin,' Diane tells him.

'And because you weren't here, I thought it would be nice to catch up with Diane over a coffee, for old time's sake.'

'I bet Amber enjoyed the cake.'

'Siobhan looked after Amber,' I tell him and he raises an eyebrow, because he knows how much I disapproved of him asking her to work yesterday.

'Gotcha,' he says, bringing the tea over. 'Anyway, it's always good to meet new people, Diane.'

'Yes,' she says, looking uncomfortable.

Sean is losing interest, I know the signs. Diane's not engaging with him, and hasn't even asked his name. Sean needs constant affirmation from people, he needs to be loved and admired, and Diane's lack of enthusiasm is frustrating him. A moment later, he stares at the screen of his phone, pretending he's just received an important message, which is his usual way of disengaging from conversations. It's classic Sean; he's invited her in and now he's leaving her with me.

'Oh,' he says, walking to the door. 'I'm going to have to reply to this. I'll be next door with Amber.'

When I'm sure he isn't listening in the hallway, I turn to Diane.

'Thank you for not saying anything about... well, you know...' The kitchen door is ajar, I can hear Sean laughing with Amber in the living room, so I close it softly. 'First of all, I shouldn't have run off, and for that I apologize. It was very rude. I'm afraid I... panicked. The photo, it was... a shock seeing it. I suppose what I'm trying to say is, yes, that's me with Martin.'

Diane attempts a smile. 'Thank you for telling me.'

'I'm not proud of... what happened that night. It was a difficult time for me, you see. My sister had—'

The kitchen door opens suddenly and Sean looks in, surprised. 'The door is shut.'

'Yeah,' I say, blushing. 'What do you want?'

'Just popping to the local shop. Anybody want anything? Diane?'

Diane shakes her head.

'Amber's playing happily,' he says. 'But keep the door open so you can keep an eye on her.'

When the front door slams and Sean's footsteps head down the path, I try to pick up where I left off. 'The point is, Diane, you're right, it was me and Cameron who...'

But Amber is visible from where we're standing, and the way Diane keeps stealing glances at my daughter makes me uncomfortable.

'Amber is a lovely name,' she says.

I don't want Diane to keep looking at Amber, and to get her attention back I touch her hand, which makes her shudder in surprise and pull away quickly.

'And thank you for not saying anything to my husband, because he doesn't know anything about it.'

She nods. 'It's a relief to finally know for sure.'

'Where did you find the phone?'

She eyes me carefully. 'You left it on the table.'

'Did I?'

I'm pretty sure I didn't, but I can't just accuse her of stealing it.

And then she says an unexpected thing. 'I don't want to fight. Can we be friends?'

'I'd love that, Diane.' I'd rather she wasn't here in my kitchen, or near my daughter, but this has to be a better outcome than her making threats.

Despite her tense exterior, Diane seems perfectly harmless – passive and withdrawn, even – but I have to remind myself that I know nothing about her, and once again I think of the smeared mirror in my bathroom. I don't want to make things worse by making accusations, not now that we've reached an understanding.

She presses the palms of her hands down her hips, maybe trying to rid herself of perspiration.

'I'm so happy,' she says, exhaling. 'It's such a relief to meet you, Hannah, and to find out that you're actually nice.'

'I'm not sure about that.' I certainly don't feel like I've shown my best nature this afternoon, but I can try to repair some of the damage. 'I let you down and let myself down, and I would have completely understood if you chose to leave my phone in the café where you found it. But you didn't, you brought it to me, and I'm grateful for that. I feel I've learned an important lesson.'

I can't tell if she's smiling or grimacing when she says, 'You're welcome.'

'And I'm glad we're friends now.' We're both riding on a wave of good feeling, but I'm afraid she's going to stay all afternoon, that I'm going to have to entertain her, when really I just want her to go.

And then Sean comes back and I could kiss him, because he looks at his watch and says, 'Remember we're due at my parents in an hour, Han.'

'Oh God, I completely forgot!' I exclaim. 'I'm so sorry, Diane, but we're going to have to go soon.'

Diane frowns. 'It's fine. I've taken up too much of your time.'

'Of course you haven't! Thank you again for bringing my phone.' I roll my eyes as I walk her to the door. 'I'd be totally lost without it.'

'See you again, then,' she says hopefully.

'Of course.' My reply suggests I'd like nothing better. 'Let's stay in touch.'

When she finally leaves, I watch her walking down the pathway through the stained glass of the door.

'Okay.' Sean holds up his arms. 'What the actual fuck?'

'She got in touch and we went for a coffee, that's all there is to it,' I say, trying to dismiss the whole thing.

'She's an odd woman,' he says. 'Why would you want to do that?'

'She's lonely, I think, and it just seemed like the right thing to do. You weren't here, and I was bored. And then I stupidly left my phone in the café.'

'You're just too good for this world, Hannah Godley, you truly are my Queen of Hearts.' He comes towards me, holding out his arms for a hug. 'I'm shattered, so I'm going to go lie down for a bit.'

'No you're not,' I tell him. 'We're not going to waste the rest of the day because of your hangover, we're going to take Amber out.'

We have to go out now, for a walk or a drive, because I told Diane we were leaving, and I can't shake the feeling that maybe she's watching the house.

Maybe she's waiting to catch me out on the lie.

It wouldn't be the first time she's done it.

9

My working day is spent mostly in my home office, writing commissioned articles for magazines and online sites. This Tuesday afternoon I'm finishing one for an airline in-flight mag, about how people have rediscovered their love for travel after the pandemic, and the mental health benefits of a holiday. It's only eight hundred words long, but it's taking forever because I'm distracted by the sound of Siobhan singing to Amber downstairs.

It's always tough to hear them together. It's undeniable that Siobhan is good with my baby. She's always talking to her, encouraging her in activities, keeping her stimulated, and Amber loves her to bits. But it can be hard to concentrate if they're downstairs, and not at the park or lido, or any of the other places Siobhan takes her to every day. I want to be the person playing with her, or taking her to the pool.

So it's a relief when Siobhan knocks on the door to tell me they're going to the local playgroup.

'Okay, have fun.'

Soon after they've gone, I'm sitting at my desk, stuck on a sentence, when my mobile rings. Mum's name appears on the screen, and I take a long breath. She and Dad are coming to London tomorrow for that funeral. I suggested they could stay in our spare room for a couple of nights so they can get to know Amber a bit more, they've hardly met their granddaughter, but of course Dad doesn't want to.

Which is probably just as well, considering my difficult relationship with him; having them here would most likely be a massive disaster. Ever the peacemaker, Mum suggested lunch instead the last time we spoke, and I promised to book a restaurant for tomorrow lunchtime. But I was surprised and disappointed when she gently hinted that I don't bring Amber.

'Oh, darling, it'll be lovely to see you, but maybe leave her at home this time, it's just a flying visit.' I let her fill the tense silence. 'We'd love to have stayed with you, but you know how your father doesn't like to be away from home for long. He doesn't travel well.'

She'd forgotten she'd told me already that they'd booked themselves a hotel on the South Bank for a couple of nights, and it took all her powers of persuasion to get him to even see me.

'It'll be lovely to meet,' Mum tells me now when I answer the phone, 'but please let's not reopen old wounds.'

We both know it's not me who's going to do that. Dad is old now, and the chances of he and I repairing our fractured relationship are slim. I've bent over backwards to make things better between us, but he's made it clear that he can't – he won't – forgive me for what happened when my sister died.

'That's the last thing I want to do,' I tell her.

'I know that.'

'I can bring Amber,' I suggest again.

'That's sweet of you, but we don't want to make a fuss. We'll see her at Christmas, I'm sure.'

Dad has probably put his foot down about me bringing Amber. It's another way for him to punish me.

It takes an hour more to finish the article and send it to the magazine editor. There's some internet research about climate anxiety I've got to do, but then I'm going to treat myself to an afternoon off. I'll be able to spend a few hours with Amber before I go out. I'm meeting Izzy and Ollie tonight in a bar in town, and don't want to ask Siobhan to work yet another evening, so Sean's reluctantly agreed to stay home.

But when I try to phone Siobhan to tell her to come home earlier, her phone is off, which irritates me. I've had to speak to her before about leaving it on. She'll be at the playgroup, so I ring there instead.

'Who did you say again?' asks the woman who answers.

'Siobhan Linden,' I tell her. 'She's there with my daughter, Amber.'

'Hold on a minute,' she says. 'I'll go and check.'

There's the chatter of voices in the background, of mums and childminders and children; it sounds lively and friendly, and I feel a pang of regret that I'm not there.

A moment later, the woman picks up again. 'There's no one of that name here, I'm afraid.'

'Oh.' I'm surprised because that's where Siobhan said she was going. 'You must know her, she's always there with my daughter, Amber.'

'Is she? I thought I knew most of our regulars, but I've only worked here a few weeks. Does she come here very often?'

Only three days a week, I want to say. But Siobhan is

unprepossessing, she's not someone who stands out from the crowd. So she's not there and she's not answering her phone, and that makes me anxious, because if she's not been going to playgroup as she says she has – 'she really loves it, Mrs Godley!' – then where has she been going?

It's another thing that annoys me about Siobhan. She's so good with Amber, they really have a connection – sometimes, when Amber's upset, Siobhan can quieten her in seconds – so I don't have any problems on that score. But she can be quiet and a bit distant where adults are concerned; she really needs to learn to communicate with us more.

It's a bit of a sore point for me that we even employ a nanny in the first place, but the whole thing happened so fast. We'd talked vaguely about getting one because I was getting weighed down with work, and then Sean literally bumped into Siobhan in the park. There was little in the way of a formal employment process – she gave me the name of a couple she had worked for, who I emailed for a reference – and Sean offered her the job before I even had a chance to interview other candidates.

Her resemblance to my sister Natalie spooks me, to be honest. That's not her fault, of course, and it's certainly not something I'd feel comfortable bringing up with Sean.

Siobhan has been with us for nine months, but my new job on *Morning Brew* may give me the opportunity to ease up on other freelance work going forward; we may not even need a nanny. I remind myself to talk to Sean about it. He's hopeless about delivering bad news, he just wants everyone to like him, so if anyone is going to fire her, it's going to have to be me.

I'm reaching for my phone to try to call Siobhan again to

find out where she is when it *dings* with a new message. My heart skips, because I know immediately what it is.

It's not a threat, but I knew it wouldn't be. It's a positive message – big red letters in front of a background of glittering stars.

YOU'RE NEVER ALONE IN THE UNIVERSE
WHILE ONE PERSON LOVES YOU

It's the kind of inspirational epigram people post on social media all the time, and which is intended to make the reader feel good about themselves and the world. This is the eighth I've received since Sunday. Each one is written over an image of a galaxy, or a scene from nature: an epic waterfall, meadow of wild flowers, or beautiful sunrise. They're all on my phone in one long, mawkish thread:

THE KINDEST SOULS FIND THE GREATEST LOVE

IF YOU LOSE BALANCE, LEAN ON ME

THE SUN SHINES BRIGHTEST ON A CLOUDY DAY

SOMETIMES UGLY ROADS LEAD TO
BEAUTIFUL DESTINATIONS

YOUR LOVE IS A LIGHT THAT ILLUMINATES
THE DARKEST PLACES

YOU BURN BRIGHTLY BECAUSE
YOU ARE STARDUST...

WE ALL TAKE DIFFERENT PATHS, BUT WE ARRIVE
AT THE SAME DESTINATION, SO BE KIND

It's her, it's got to be.

Diane doesn't write anything else, these inspirational messages are all she ever sends, and she never identifies herself, but they all come from the phone number I rang at the weekend. The first arrived four days ago, the day after we met.

I don't understand how she got my number in the first place, because I withheld it when I called her on Sunday. When she had my phone, and answered Siobhan's call, did she somehow manage to find out what it was? My diary was in my bag, all my personal details are written on the first page; did she look in there while I was in the toilet at the café? Is that how she got the number?

As silly and banal as these messages are, at least they aren't threatening.

The question is, should I respond?

My hope was that if I didn't reply she'd get bored and stop sending them, but Diane knows where I live, and if she feels slighted or ignored, she could turn up again. Against my better judgement, I decide to reply.

I've never agonized so much about what to write. I want to be polite, but I don't want to encourage her to send more. So I sit with the phone in my hands for a long time, formulating a response. In the end, I decide to keep it short and terse.

Too true!

I hit the send button, and off it *whooshes*.

A few moments later, and to my relief, the front door

opens downstairs and I hear the wheels of the stroller bang on the hardwood floor, as Siobhan angles it over the step and into the hallway.

'Home again, home again,' Siobhan sings to Amber, as I come downstairs.

'Hello, baby!' Amber's face lights up as soon as she sees me and already I forget about Diane. Siobhan collapses the buggy as I lift my daughter into my arms. 'How was the playgroup, did Amber enjoy seeing all her friends?'

'Oh, we didn't go today.' Siobhan grimaces, in case I'm annoyed.

'Really?' I say, as if it's a surprise. 'Why not?'

'It's such a lovely day, and it can get so stifling in that community centre, that I thought it'd be nicer to go to the playground.' She looks worried. 'I hope you don't mind.'

'No,' I have to admit. 'That's probably a good call. But please keep your phone on, Siobhan, so I can contact you at all times.'

'Will do.' She must catch something in my tone, because she asks, 'Is something wrong?'

'Not at all.' I smile, but add, 'You haven't seen anyone hanging around?'

Her eyes go wide. 'Hanging around? What do you mean?'

I wish I hadn't mentioned anything. All Diane has done is send silly inspirational messages telling me I'm stardust, it's not like she's nailed a dead rat to our door.

'Forget it. But please make sure to tell me where you're both going, and keep your phone on.'

Siobhan nods quickly. 'I'm really sorry, it won't happen again.'

'The good news is, I'm going out tonight, so I'll take the rest of the afternoon off and you can leave early.'

'Great.' Siobhan smiles. 'Thank you.'

When she walks into the kitchen, I sneak a look at my phone, and am relieved there's been no response to my reply.

10

'You look fucking amazing.' Izzy's voice carries across the bar as she comes hurtling towards me with her arms wide. 'Come here.'

When we hug, she already smells of booze, and there's a glass of cold white wine on the table. She's come straight from work, and is already a couple of glasses ahead. As usual, she looks tanned and healthy in a summer dress with a plunging neckline that shows off her slim figure and long, sharp shoulder blades; D&G sunglasses are embedded in the crown of her thick blonde hair, which tumbles to her shoulders. Before we've even let go of each other, she's talking nineteen to the dozen, gesticulating wildly, firing questions that I don't get a chance to answer, and trying to catch the eye of one of the bar staff to order a bottle of wine.

She's telling me something when she suddenly interrupts herself, which is typical Izzy. 'Oh God, I'm so sorry I didn't come to your party, but I was feeling a bit shit. You don't hate me, do you?'

'Of course not, you didn't miss much.'

'Ollie said some tosser vandalized your mirror.' She looks disgusted; Izzy is one of those people whose every emotion is revealed instantaneously on their face. 'What kind of animal guzzles all your drink and then does something like that?'

I'm so tired of thinking about it that I don't have the energy to explain. Fingers crossed, it's all in the past, and anyway Izzy's already started telling a story about a mutual friend.

We may not see each other as much as we'd like now that I'm a mum, and Izzy works long hours in an administrative role at a hospital and is totally loved-up with her new husband, but we're still best friends after all these years, and always will be.

'Ollie can't make it till later.' She smirks over the top of her glass. 'I think he's only coming to make sure I get home at a reasonable time.'

'The days of staying out to all hours are long gone.'

'Bloody hell.' She laughs. 'We really could cane it back in the day, couldn't we?'

When we order food, Izzy picks at a Ceasar salad, which doesn't look anywhere near substantial enough to soak up all the wine she's drinking, and I opt for a prawn and chorizo pasta dish. The conversation never stops, we both have a lot to catch up on, and it shoots off at unexpected tangents, the way chat with your bestie always does. Part of me wants to tell her about Diane and my eventful weekend – Izzy is probably the only person in the world I can discuss it with, but she's already a bit pissed, and I know she'll get aggressive about it. She'll force me to block Diane on my phone and contact the police, when all I want to do is let the whole situation fade away.

Izzy's eyes bulge with indignation as she tells me about another of the endless feuds she's got into at work, and she's filling our glasses again when I become aware of somebody standing beside the table.

And when I look up, it's Diane.

'Oh my goodness, it *is* you,' Diane says under her pale-blue disposable mask. 'Hannah!'

'Diane.' I gawp up at her. For a moment, I think I'm hallucinating. I've been thinking about her so much that I've made her manifest in front of me. 'What are you doing here?'

'Would you believe it?' she says.

Izzy doesn't look amused at being interrupted. 'I'm sorry, darling, I can't understand a word you're saying, do you mind taking that thing off?' Diane pulls the mask off her face. '*Now* we can meet properly.'

'Izzy, this is, uh, Diane.' My compulsion to be polite and welcoming takes over, when what I really want to do is scream. Izzy nods coldly at the newcomer; she clearly doesn't know what on earth to make of her. 'What are you doing here?'

'I was just passing.' Diane points over her shoulder. She's wearing a purple velvet skirt that sweeps down to her ankles, the kind of thing people wore in the seventies, and a matching waistcoat over a white shirt worn to grey.

'*Love* your outfit, by the way,' says Izzy with barely concealed derision.

If Diane hears her, she doesn't show it, and tells me, 'I couldn't believe my eyes when I saw you as I was walking past.'

I don't believe it for a second. We're sitting at the back of a long bar, the lighting is low, and the chances of her seeing us from the street are small, unless she cupped her hands at the window to peer in, and what would make her do that?

She smiles shyly at Izzy. 'I'm Hannah's friend.'

'In that case, why don't you sit down?' Izzy says with a distinct lack of enthusiasm. 'Unless, of course, you have somewhere more important to be.'

'No.' Diane pulls a chair out from under the table. 'I can stay for a bit.'

She's the last person I want here, and I feel a hot flush of discomfort. Izzy is already giving me sly, smirking glances, as if to say, *who is this creature?*

Diane places a theatre programme on the table in front of her, and Izzy snatches it up.

'*Cats*, bless!'

'It's my favourite musical,' Diane says.

'You went to see this today?' Izzy flicks through the programme as if it's an alien communiqué from another dimension. When she bends the pages slightly, Diane visibly stiffens. 'Grizabella and all that shit?'

Diane tells me, 'I've seen it over a hundred times.'

'Stop it!' Izzy closes a fist under her chin to lean across the table towards Diane in mock fascination. 'I mean, *why?*'

She's making fun of her. Izzy doesn't mean any harm but she can be sarcastic and tactless when she's had a drink, and Diane, with her velvet waistcoat and passion for musical theatre, is easy game.

'I like it, the story and the songs make me feel... joyous.' She starts talking about the story and the songs, and it's the first time I've heard Diane speak at length about anything. Izzy tries to look interested but her eyes begin glazing over, and after a couple of minutes she interrupts by pointing to our empty glasses.

'You need a drink, Diane. I think we all do. My God,

Cats.' She rolls her eyes at me and whispers, 'I'd rather kill myself.'

A lot of people can take Izzy's jokey digs, they'll even play her at her own game. But Diane is unconfident and vulnerable. Feeling protective of her, I make a face at my friend: *please stop*.

'I think it's nice that you can enjoy something so many times,' I tell Diane. 'And it continues to give you such comfort and pleasure.'

'Yes.' Diane nods, thinking about it. 'That's exactly what it does.'

'I've never seen *Cats*,' says Izzy, draining her glass. 'And if I ever get the urge to book tickets, you have my permission to shoot me. All that singing and dancing and people licking themselves.'

'I've seen it,' I tell her. 'And it's a lot of fun.'

'I bet your lovely Sean doesn't think so, I bet he's on *my* side on this.' Izzy frowns. 'Where is your beautiful man, by the way, why isn't he here?'

'He's looking after Amber,' I say.

'He should be here!' She looks around for the waiter. 'I'm going to get us another bottle, ladies.'

I want to go now. 'I'm not sure...'

'We haven't even celebrated your TV gig,' Izzy tells me.

When she scrapes back her chair and walks off, I'm left with Diane. 'I'm sorry about Izzy, she's had a lot to drink.'

Diane nods as she watches Izzy flirting with the guy behind the bar. You really couldn't find two more ill-fitted people to spend an evening with.

'That was lucky, you seeing us in here,' I say, fishing for more detail on just how she came to be here.

'I couldn't believe my eyes when I was walking past,' she says with a big smile. 'I thought to myself, that's Hannah.'

'Thank you for my messages,' I say reluctantly.

Her fists clench in her lap. 'I'm glad you like them. I find them helpful and nourishing. Maybe they'll help you find peace.'

'Here we are.' Izzy returns to the table with a bottle of wine, and tops up my drink and hers. Diane's eyes widen when Izzy pours her a large glass. 'Don't worry, Diana, it won't kill you.'

'It's Diane,' I correct her, because I know Diane won't.

Izzy raises her glass in a toast to me. 'Here's to our talented telly superstar.' She elbows Diane beside her. 'You know she's going to be on *Morning Brew* soon? She's going to be their new agony aunt.'

Diane nods. 'It's very exciting. I'm sure she'll be very good.'

'She's going to absolutely fucking smash it, is what she's going to do,' Izzy says loudly, and grabs my hand. 'This one here is one of the nicest people you'll meet. She just has to make sure she doesn't belch loudly on live television.'

She laughs. It's a running gag between me and Izzy. Years ago we'd both dressed up to go to a posh hotel in the West End and at the crowded bar I'd coughed, which somehow turned into a loud belch. It was foul and childish, and absolutely hilarious at the time – you had to be there, I guess – and now when we go anywhere, into a shop or a bar, Izzy will whisper, 'Do try to keep it in, dear.'

I can't help but giggle. 'Can you just imagine – on national television.'

'In front of millions of people!' Izzy snorts with laughter. 'I dare you to let rip in front of Simon and Maria!'

Diane smiles politely, but the tone of the conversation

clearly makes her uncomfortable. Izzy dabs a finger at the corner of each eye, and I try to hold in my own laughter, because I'm conscious of Diane's embarrassed reaction.

'Hannah wouldn't do that,' she tells Izzy. 'That's not the kind of thing she'd do.'

'Au fucking contraire, my love,' Izzy tells her dismissively. 'I've seen her in action. Trust me, the whole studio will have to be fumigated.'

She laughs hard at her own joke, she's gone past the point of no return, and Diane's tense gaze drops to the table.

'Honestly, though. I love you, Han.' Izzy lunges across the table to give me a drunken hug, almost toppling the wine bottle and forcing Diane to lean back. 'You're going to be a big success, and I am so proud of you. Just don't take any shit from those television people, because you're the Queen of fucking Hearts. Always be kind, and all that, yeah?'

And that's when Ollie walks over, kissing Izzy on the top of her head and slipping into the remaining chair at the table.

'What have I missed?' He holds out his hand to Diane, who shifts uncomfortably in her seat. 'Hi, I'm Ollie.'

'Yes.' She looks embarrassed, and I get a sick feeling that she knows who he is because she saw him at the party on Saturday night.

'And you are?'

Izzy narrows her eyes. *That's a good question*, they seem to say, as if I'm withholding information from her. She puts minimum effort into the introduction. 'Diana, Ollie. Ollie, Diana.'

Her husband nods, none the wiser, but taking it all in his stride. Ollie is far more laid-back and understated than his wife, or Sean. He doesn't feel the need to hog all the attention in a room, which is just as well when you're married to Izzy. She offers to get him a drink, but he shakes his head.

'I'm shattered.' He scratches his head. 'And if it wasn't for you two I'd be at home in bed right now.'

'Ollie can be so boring sometimes. He's not like Sean, who's got the stamina to keep going all night.' Wine slops over the side of her glass when she lifts it clumsily to her mouth. 'Let's swap husbands, Han, while it's not too late.'

'I've met Sean,' says Diane out of nowhere. 'And he seems nice.'

'He is, isn't he?' says Izzy, mocking Diane's politeness. 'He's a very nice *chap*. Sean's one of the best, he's a diamond. Honestly, you couldn't meet a nicer couple than Sean and Hannah.' She pretends to gag. 'It's *sickening*, really.'

'Thank you for the vote of confidence,' says Ollie wryly.

'Oh, I'm sorry, baby.' Izzy grabs his hand. 'I love you, too, honest I do. Just not as much as I love Sean.'

Ollie grins, used to Izzy's joking outbursts. He's a quiet, steadying presence when Izzy goes over the top. Beside me, I sense Diane watching them both carefully.

'Oh my God,' Izzy says suddenly. 'I've just realized, you're seeing your parents soon, right?'

I take a deep breath. 'Yeah, tomorrow, actually. At a restaurant called Xerxes.'

'Oh, that place in Marylebone. You'll love the food.' She grimaces. 'It's just a shame you have to take your old man.'

Izzy knows everything there is to know about my relationship with Dad, she's followed all the ups and downs of it over the years.

'Don't you get on with him?' asks Diane, and I remember with a jolt that she's listening.

'It's complicated,' I say, not wanting to elaborate.

Draining her glass, Izzy says, 'Hannah's dad has been a complete prick to her.'

I shake my head tensely. 'He's not that bad.'

'He has, and you know it. They fell out years ago when Han's sister died and she didn't go to the funeral. She's tried to make amends, like, millions of times, but he's a stubborn old git.' When I glare at her, Izzy frowns. She thinks I'm annoyed that she's slagging him off, but it's more that she can be indiscreet about stuff – I wish she wasn't talking about it to Diane – and she lifts a hand in apology. 'Sorry, Han, but I've known you long enough to know how much it hurts, and it makes my blood boil. You have the patience of a saint, the way you keep waiting for him to see sense. I would have washed my hands of him years ago.'

I can't let that go. 'It's not fair on Mum.'

'You'd think he'd make the most of the time he's got left with you. You don't deserve this.'

When I don't reply, Izzy finally gets the message that I'm not comfortable talking about it, and shrugs. 'Anyway, give your Mum my best.'

There's a tense silence. Ollie isn't really engaging, he's reading something on his phone, and Diane sits beside me looking down at her hands folded in her lap. I can't help but feel that she's absorbing everything, watching everyone. I want to call it a night, and I'm about to suggest we all go home when Izzy gives me a long look.

'What I still can't get my head around is, how do *you*...' She lifts one shiny-nailed forefinger at Diane and then moves it slowly in my direction. 'Know *you*?'

I'm trying to think of an answer that will satisfy Izzy's curiosity when Diane leans forward.

'Hannah knew my brother a long time ago, and now we're friends.' She glances at me, as if to make sure she hasn't spoken out of turn.

Izzy cocks her head. I know what she's thinking, me and Diane together, it just doesn't make sense. And, of course, she's right about that.

'Her brother? Anybody I know?'

'*Way* before your time,' I say, which is true, because, like Sean, I didn't meet Izzy until after I left uni.

Izzy knows there's something I'm not telling her, because she knows me as well as anyone, and I've never mentioned Diane before, not once, let alone her mysterious brother. She craves more information, but I just smile.

'I'd better use the toilet.' Diane stands. 'I don't want to be bursting on the way home.'

'Too much information, my lovely,' Izzy says sarcastically. When Diane's gone, she practically launches herself over the table at me. 'Please, *please*, explain who that person is, and how you know her.'

I'm certainly not going into it right now, I'll do it when we have more time to speak properly – and when she's sober. 'Diane is… not doing well at the moment, she's not got many friends.'

'No fucking kidding,' says Izzy.

'And I felt sorry for her.'

She gives me one of her sidelong looks to show how deadly serious she is. 'She's weird and gives me the creeps.'

'Don't hold back, Iz.' Ollie glances up from his phone. 'Tell us what you really think.'

'Okay, FYI, you can't just adopt every waif and stray who writes you a sad letter.' She leans her elbows on the table to lever herself nearer me. 'Get *rid*.'

Ollie drops his phone in his jacket pocket and smiles at me. 'What she says.'

Izzy sits back suddenly, because Diane is coming back. Ollie slaps the table and says, 'Right, time to go.'

'I've got to go too,' I say when Izzy appeals for us to stay for one more drink.

'Bah.' Izzy necks the rest of her glass and tries to pull her big bag through the small gap between her knees beneath the table, but it doesn't go well. As patient as ever, Ollie lifts it free, while she flails around trying to find the sleeves of her jacket and place her arms in them.

'Give that big, sexy husband of yours a hug from me, and tell him I'll see him soon. He should have been here tonight, it's not been the same without him. Wait, we can't go yet!' She rummages in her bag for her Android. 'It wouldn't be a night out without a selfie.'

There's no point in arguing with Izzy, because she always insists on a photo, which she'll hashtag to death on Instagram. She swipes the screen and brings up the camera.

'Right.' She pulls Ollie towards her on one side, and me on the other, and hands the phone to Diane, says, 'Do you mind?'

She's being mean, so I say, 'Diane has to be in the photo too.'

'Of course she does, but first, let's just do us three, for old time's sake.'

Diane holds up the phone, her finger hovering over the screen, and Izzy exclaims, 'Friends Forever!'

Then we shuffle closer to one another and I encourage Diane to join us. Izzy holds the phone at arm's length to take the photo quickly.

'I think I had my eyes closed,' Diane says.

'I'm sure you didn't.' Izzy slips the phone back in her bag without even looking at the image – it's obvious which of those photos will find its way onto social media – and she and I split the bill for the evening.

'Bye, then,' Diane says to Izzy and Ollie. 'It was lovely to meet you.'

'Likewise,' replies Izzy with an insincere smile, and Ollie is already heading for the door. I feel an overpowering embarrassment for Diane, and for myself. I don't want my friend's rude behaviour to sour things with her, or for her to hold it against me, so I ask where she lives.

'Bounds Green,' she says.

It's a bit out of my way – a lot actually – but we're both heading north, so I suggest we share a cab.

She grimaces, because she's thinking about the cost. 'I don't think so, I'll just get the—'

'Don't worry,' I tell her quickly. 'I'll pay.'

11

'She doesn't like me, does she?'

It doesn't take long for Diane to bring up what's on her mind as the cab moves smoothly through the dark streets of central London.

The indicators click softly as we turn right and then left, and the car accelerates towards King's Cross. My house is closer than hers, a lot closer, and the cab should really drop me off first, but I don't want her coming to my house again, in case she somehow manages to invite herself in, even at this late hour.

Sitting beside me in the back, fingers tensely rubbing at the glossy cover of the theatre programme in her lap, she rests her forehead against the side window, watching buildings speed past. 'Your friend doesn't like me at all.'

'Oh, don't take it personally.' It's not the first time I've had to excuse Izzy's rudeness and it won't be the last. 'She's not good with new people, she can be a bit... intimidating. But she's actually lovely when you get to know her.'

Diane doesn't turn to me; all I can see is that helmet of shiny black hair. 'She's very fond of Sean.'

'Yes.' It's an odd thing to say. 'She is.'

'She's always talking about him.'

I wrack my brain, trying to remember how many times Izzy mentioned Sean; it surely can't have been more than once or twice.

'I shouldn't have come into the bar, really. It wasn't my place.'

'Honestly,' I lie, 'it was good to see you.'

But we both know she didn't bump into us by accident. I don't know how – she saw it in my diary, or on my phone – but Diane knew I was going to be there.

'I'm sorry about your sister,' she says.

I don't want Diane talking about her. Natalie died a long time ago and her death, and all the confusing emotions it caused in me, was in many ways the catalyst for what Cameron and I did to her brother.

'We've got a lot in common, haven't we?' When Diane finally turns to look at me, her features are hidden in the dark of the car. 'We've both lost siblings. Me my brother, and you your sister. I suppose that's one of the reasons we get on so well, why we're kindred spirits. It's taken me so long to find someone I can talk to. To truly talk to.'

Her tone makes alarm bells go off in my head, and I stiffen. I've been very patient with her, I think, but if Diane thinks we're friends, *kindred spirits*, then she's living on a different planet. We're very different people, practically strangers, and I want to tell her that we haven't got anything in common. But then I think of the smeared mirror in my bathroom, and her turning up out of the blue this evening, and something tells me it's best not to antagonize her.

'I really wanted you to suffer, you know, when I called in to the radio show.' Her eyes glint in the gloom. 'I wanted Martin to know that I hadn't forgotten him, and that there was still someone who loved him and was fighting for him, even all these years later. But when I met you, you were nice to me, and genuine, and I felt ashamed for putting you on the spot like that. I was so confused about what I had been told about you.' She shakes her head. 'I don't know what he was thinking, saying you could do such a thing. None of what he told me makes sense.'

I know I've a chance to spin what Martin must have told her. Diane seems... malleable, overly empathetic. She's believed the truth of what he said for so long, but already the seeds of doubt have been sown in her mind about what happened. Maybe that's something I can turn to my advantage, to put this whole issue to bed once and for all. God, I hope so.

'It was all such a long time ago now,' I say, 'and my memory of that night is fuzzy, but I'll be honest, Diane, I don't remember Martin's version of things. We were drunk, and yes, I was probably unkind, but... what he said, I'm afraid it's just not something that I would do.'

'Yes.' She nods gravely. 'He must have gotten some of the details wrong. Or more likely I got them all mixed up in my stupid head. That's so typical of me, I get things wrong all the time.' She knocks a clenched fist hard against her forehead. 'I'm such an idiot!'

'Of course you aren't,' I say, alarmed at her sudden violence. 'But sometimes when we're upset, our own minds can play tricks, it's easy to get things muddled, and we come to believe things that just aren't true.'

'I've been living a lie, you mean?' Her face is hidden in shadow, but her eyes shine steadily. 'We all live a lie, don't we? There are things right in front of our noses that we don't want to look at too closely, in case we see they're rotten, and we have to admit we've been fooling ourselves. You must know that more than anyone, the way things are at home.'

I stare at her. I don't understand what she's trying to tell me. What on earth is she talking about?

'Anyway, all I know is, you're not the person I thought you would be, and I feel bad for accusing you.'

'You're a nice person,' I tell her, trying to gather my thoughts. 'Sincere and forgiving.'

'I'm not though, am I?' Street lights flicker down her face, illuminating it for the first time, giving her skin a sickly, lurid pallor. 'I'm not the person you think I am.'

Before I get a chance to ask her what she means about things at home, she leans forward to get the driver's attention. 'You can pull up anywhere around here.'

The dark street of scruffy terraced houses is obscured behind the long chains of cars parked at each kerb. Numerous bins are lined up outside each house, which suggests most of the properties have been divided into flats or bedsits. Depthless blank windows stare across the street at each other.

'It still feels weird living here,' says Diane sadly. 'I had to move out of my last home. It wasn't my choice, but I'm not a very lucky person.' When the cab pulls up in the middle of the road, she pops open the door.

'Diane, what did you mean about my living a lie?'

'Thank you for a lovely evening.' Ignoring my question, her arm shoots out and she grabs my hand – she physically shivers as she makes contact, as if she's just dived into a freezing river, or grabbed a live cable – and the look she gives me is full of compassion... and *pity*. 'Bless you, Hannah.'

'Diane—'

Then she slams the door shut and walks between the parked cars and onto the pavement, the theatre programme shoved in her clamshell bag. The car begins to pick up speed, but something makes me want to know which house she lives in, and I ask the driver to stop at the top of the road.

A moment later, Diane walks up the path of a scruffy house near the end of the row – the front garden is littered with junk, an abandoned mattress, an old fridge, a chest of drawers; the woodwork around the windows is crumbling, the paintwork flaking – and goes to the door, lets herself inside.

'Okay,' I tell the driver. 'Let's go.'

12

'Isn't this nice, Bob? Yes, very... plush.' Mum looks around the expensive basement restaurant doubtfully, intimidated by the sombre décor and the waiting staff walking around with their noses in the air, and I know it was a mistake to bring them here. 'Is this the kind of place where you always eat, Hannah?'

'Not really, I wanted to bring you somewhere nice.' Dad is doing his best to look unimpressed and I wish now I'd booked somewhere cheaper. But it doesn't matter where I'd chosen, it could be fancy and cosmopolitan or cheap and cheerful, Dad will be determined to hate it. 'I've heard the food is really good.'

Dad picks up the menu as if it's about to burst into flames. His lips twitch as he appraises the dishes, and of course the prices. It doesn't matter that I said I'll pay, he'll complain anyway.

'I've never heard of half the ingredients,' he says in his flat northern vowels.

'Tell us about your new job,' says Mum, trying hard to lighten the mood. 'Everyone at my club can't wait to see you on TV. Everyone I know watches that show. You'll be on *Loose Women* next!'

Dad snorts. 'It's very tabloid, that morning show, isn't it? You'll be dishing out morsels of comfort to sad people who watch TV all day and think nothing of airing their dirty laundry to the world.' He shrugs. 'It's a living, I suppose.'

'A problem aired is a problem shared, Bob,' says Mum with a tight smile.

'I just can't get used to how people share their innermost feelings in public, these days. When my mother…' He turns a glass of water slowly in his fingers. 'When she died, God rest her soul, nobody outside our family even knew she was ill. I was just a nipper then, and even I didn't know. One day she went upstairs to bed and never came down. And when my father grieved, well, let's just say he didn't feel the need to ring up a TV show to sob his heart out.'

I know Dad is trying to get under my skin, but I can't help biting. 'As I remember, Grandad was always depressed.'

'Don't be ridiculous,' he snaps, making Mum tense. 'People of his era were made of stronger stuff than your snowflake generation.'

Mum sips from her small glass of white wine. 'But he did cry, didn't he, Bob? I remember him in tears when that dog of his died.'

Dad is annoyed at being contradicted. 'I don't remember that *at all*.'

'And you cried many times after our Natalie died.' Mum winces at her own unexpected mention of my sister. In our phone conversation this week, Mum and I agreed not to talk about Natalie. It's treacherous territory, and Dad always ends up getting angry with me for not going to the funeral.

We didn't speak for a long time because of it. Mum and I would speak on the phone when he was at work, or walking the dog, and she'd tell me everything that was happening at home.

'Will you speak to him?' I'd ask her regularly. 'See if he'll come round?'

She'd sigh. 'You know what he's like, Hannah. He's a stubborn old fool.'

'I made a mistake, Mum, but I wasn't in my right mind.'

'Oh, you don't have to tell me, I've explained all that to him. But he won't listen.'

We did speak eventually, Dad and I, even if it took several years. But our relationship is fragile, and the subject a scab that we both can't help but pick at when we're together.

'Anyway,' I say quickly, hoping to move on the conversation. 'Let's order some food.'

But it's too late, because Dad folds his arms tightly across his chest. 'I don't know why you're trying to embarrass me.'

'Nobody is trying to embarrass you, Bob,' says Mum with quiet reproach. 'Because crying is nothing to be ashamed of.'

'It's a good thing, a normal thing,' I agree. 'That's what I'm trying to say.'

'Look at us,' says Mum with a shrill, unconvincing laugh. 'It's gone all deep, and we haven't even ordered the starter.'

Catching the eye of a waiter, we order food. I go for the sea bass and Mum for a seafood risotto, but Dad takes ages to decide, asking the waiter innumerable questions about each dish, where the ingredients are from, and how they're cooked, and he finally settles on a curry. And when the food arrives, Mum and I actually manage to talk about something else for a few minutes – I tell her all about Amber and how well she's doing, and about Sean's work – but Dad is quiet, still stewing over our earlier conversation.

Finally, he folds his napkin and says, 'Is that why you didn't come to the funeral?' Mum and I throw each other a weary glance. 'Because you were too busy sat in your student bedsit, or wherever, crying and feeling sorry for yourself?'

'Oh, Bob,' says Mum. 'Can't we all just have a nice time?'

I place my knife and fork on the plate. 'Dad, I've admitted many times that I didn't handle things very well, I've apologized again and again for not coming to the funeral, but I'll do it again if it makes you feel better.'

His face goes crimson. 'You couldn't put aside your differences with Natalie, you disliked her so much that you couldn't bear to even say farewell.'

'It was a confusing time for me,' I tell him quietly, while Mum stares at the table.

'If you couldn't cope then, what makes you think you're a fit and proper person to give other people advice on how to handle their emotions?'

'Maybe that's just why I'm qualified to do it.'

'You let your sister down,' Dad tells me; he's said the same thing a thousand times. 'You let us all down.'

'Yes, I did,' I say sadly. Even if he doesn't want to be here, I don't get to see Mum very often, and he's spoiled our lunch – again. I decide I may as well be hanged for a sheep as a lamb. Mum sees something in my expression and silently pleads with me not to inflame the situation, but I ignore her. 'Precious, fragile Natalie wasn't an easy person either, though, was she?'

'How can you say that about your poor, dead sister?' Dad hisses.

I've lost my appetite and push my half-eaten food away.

'Even if you never forgive me, your constantly acting like this isn't fair on Mum.'

'Your mother agrees with me,' says Dad, lifting his nose in the air. 'That what you did was a terrible thing.'

Mum smiles weakly at me. We both know that's not true, but she's not willing to bicker any further. He's a frail old man now – I was shocked to see him leaning on a stick when he arrived – but resentment still pulses off him like a shimmering heat, and I finally have to admit that he will probably never forgive me till the day he dies.

A waiter comes over to top up the wine, but Dad shoos him away. 'No more.'

I take a large gulp of mine. There's been something I've wanted to say for a long time, and maybe I'll never get another chance. 'Maybe it's not about me at all.'

'Hannah,' Mum says quietly. 'Don't.'

'What?' Dad scowls. 'What are you talking about?'

'I'm saying that maybe all these years you've been emotionally transferring all the anger you feel at her to me.'

He glares. 'What claptrap are you saying now?'

'Keep your voice down, Bob,' Mum says, looking around the room.

'You're angry with Natalie for ending it all, for walking onto that train track.'

'How dare you!' Dad slaps a liver-spotted hand on the table, making the plates and cutlery jump. 'It was an accident.'

'Was it, though? Natalie never went there, she never, ever walked along that track. Why did she go there that day, and what are the chances that she just fell and was hit by a train? Maybe she couldn't face her demons any longer, maybe she wanted to end it all.'

Mum and Dad stare at me in incomprehension. The brief feeling of triumph I felt at getting one over on Dad is replaced by self-disgust. I've gone too far, and I don't want to argue any more, I just want to pay so we can all leave.

But then Dad snatches up his stick and stands, and I'm afraid he's going to walk out the door and I'll never see him again. 'Where are you going?'

'To the toilet,' he says sarcastically. 'If that's all right with you?'

'The toilets are upstairs.' He's frail. What the hell was I thinking, choosing this basement restaurant? 'Do you want me to show you where they are?'

'I can manage,' he says over his shoulder. Then he limps towards the archway that leads to the stairs.

Mum finishes her wine. She's not much of a drinker, but she grips the glass tightly. She lost one daughter, and for so many years all she's ever wanted is to reconcile Dad and me, but she looks so very tired. I reach over to squeeze her hand.

'I'm sorry, I haven't helped things very much.'

'The older he gets, the more prickly he is.'

It can't be easy for Mum, she must live on her nerves. My parents live hundreds of miles away, in the same village in Lancashire they grew up in. Neither of them would ever agree to move, and certainly not down south. It's not an ideal situation, but my life is in London. My work is here, so it's not like I can move back up there at the drop of a hat, even if I wanted to. Also, Sean would laugh his socks off if I suggested moving out of London.

'I'm worried about you both being so far away.'

'We've lots of friends, and our neighbours are very helpful, you don't have to worry about us.' Mum gives me a long look. 'Your father is proud of you, you know, despite all his silly bluster.'

'Will he ever forgive me?' I ask her.

Mum dabs a crumb off the tablecloth and drops it to the floor. It would be nice to hear her say, *of course he will*, but she just shrugs. 'I'm sure deep down he knows he's wrong. And despite what you think, he's always loved you just as much as he did Natalie. It's just that we spent so much time looking after her, we were both so focused for so long on trying to get her well, and we feel like we... failed. We know it wasn't fair on you, and we should have paid you more attention. It's easy to say that now, of course.' She smiles sadly. 'He'll come round.'

'I hope so,' I say.

'I always look forward to seeing you, Hannah.' She tightens her hand around mine. 'And maybe next time you can bring that little girl of yours.'

How many more times I'll get to see my parents, I don't know. It'd be good to take Sean and Amber up north to see them soon, but Dad always makes it so incredibly difficult.

He's never going to change, he'll never forgive me for not going to the funeral. I could have gone, I should have. But I was in a bad place at that time, full of pain and anger. And just because she was sick doesn't mean Natalie was an angel, she could be shrill and demanding, and I was full of resentment at the way she soaked up all my parents' attention for so many years. I was angry and—

Someone cries out and there's a noise on the stairs – bang, bang, *bang*. Mum and I look at each other and then I'm out of my chair and running towards the archway. Just beyond, Dad lies in a heap at the bottom of the stairs, his stick beneath him.

When he tries to move, his face twists in pain.

'Dad!' I crouch down beside him, as Mum comes up behind us. 'What happened?'

'She pushed me.' Crying out in pain, he points to the top of the stairs. 'That bloody woman pushed me!'

And of course I feel sick, because my first thought is that *she* did it.

But Diane wouldn't do a thing like that, surely; she wouldn't push an elderly man down a flight of stairs?

She could have injured him; killed him.

That kind of thing, it's not normal.

13

As soon as I'm sure he's unharmed, I go upstairs to see if there's anybody there. But the narrow entrance and hallway leading to the toilets is empty. If somebody did push him, they've long disappeared.

'Who pushed you?' I ask him, trying not to show the panic and upset I feel, when the restaurant staff have got him comfortable on a chair.

'I don't know, they were behind me,' he snaps. 'Who would put a restaurant in a basement, anyway?'

'Then how did you know it was a woman?' I say, but someone has called a paramedic, and when he arrives, my question goes unanswered.

Dad is subdued when my parents announce they're going back to their hotel. He's still clearly shaken by what happened, but insists he doesn't want to make a statement to the police about the mystery woman on the stairs. I think even he's convinced he imagined it.

But I'm not so sure.

All these years, I've told people that secrets are bad, they're toxic, and wherever possible you should try to talk about them with a friend or relative, or someone you trust; get them all out in the open where you can examine them. It's the bedrock of all the advice I give people, because speaking about a secret out loud may not solve the problem, but it will lose some of its poisonous power over you. Sharing a problem is good for your mental and physical health. I tell people this all the time, so it seems crazy that I'm not doing it myself.

What Diane has just done has taken the situation to a shocking new level and I desperately need to talk with someone about it. Trouble is, Sean would probably find the whole thing hilarious, and that's not going to help; and I can't tell Izzy, because she'd command me to take action against Diane: go to the police, or threaten her with an injunction, which could just send her running to the papers.

But there is someone who will understand my dilemma, because he was there with Martin and me on that night, and knows more than anyone about the shame and guilt I felt in the aftermath. So on the way home from the restaurant, I can't stop myself looking up Cameron West on my phone. Everything that's happened has made me think about him again; seeing that photo of him has made me curious about what has become of him. It's not hard to find information about him because the truth is, I've done it before. I mean, we've all googled our exes, haven't we?

The last time I looked, which was admittedly a few years ago, Cameron wasn't on Facebook or Twitter, or any other social media sites, and that's still the case. But it only takes me a couple of minutes to find where he's working as a GP, at a clinic in West Hampstead. Which is a different surgery to the one he worked at the last time I cyberstalked him; that one was in Ealing.

On the 'Meet Our Team' page there's a photograph of the medical staff who work at the surgery. It's an informal image, taken in the reception area.

Cam is leaning against the desk, his forearms resting behind him on the counter, a wall of box files in the background. His legs are crossed at the ankles; he looks casual and confident and professional. In his thirties, nearly two decades on from when I knew him, he looks so different from the Cam I used to know, and yet so familiar. Middle-age suits him, actually. His hair is much shorter than he used to have it, with flecks of grey above the ears, and his lean face and slim body have filled out; he's even got a bit of a stomach. But those hazel eyes and that amiable smile, the one that so often enraged me, are just the same. In his nondescript grey jacket and dark trousers, ironed shirt and dark knitted tie, he looks every inch the friendly neighbourhood doctor.

Because his hands are obscured, I can't tell if there's a ring: if he's married or single. And other than that he's a GP and where he works, I don't know a single thing about his life.

But right now he feels like the only person I can speak to about Diane, and to my shame – because it's not fair to drag him into this situation – I desperately want to get in touch with him. But I can't, because years ago I dumped him in the cruellest way possible. If I made contact after all this time, he'd probably tell me to sling my hook, or just put the phone down – and I couldn't blame him if he did. Poor Cameron, I treated him so badly.

'What number are you?' asks the driver, and I look up

from my phone – I've obviously been gazing at that photo for a long time – to see we're already in my street.

'Just along here,' I say.

Pointing at my house, my heart leaps.

Because Diane is standing outside.

14

'What are you doing here?'

My heart hammering, I slam the cab door and rush up the path, fumbling in my bag for my keys, intending to get inside quickly. The cab roars off, and I wish I'd asked the driver to stay until I got indoors. What if Diane attacks me too? What if she screams and shouts? It's difficult to imagine her becoming aggressive in the middle of the street, but Dad's mysterious accident has made me realize that I don't know what she's capable of.

She's got a plastic bag in her hand, there's something wide and flat and heavy in it, making the thin handles dig into the fleshy joints of her fingers.

'How was your lunch?' she asks, standing close behind me at the door as I chase the keys around the bottom of my bag. 'I've been dying to ask you.'

It could just be the bright afternoon, there's not a cloud in the sky, but she seems less pale, and sunnier in spirit. Her top lip curls in a grim smile, revealing a dark red gum beneath her pink lipstick. Even her clothes – a paisley shirt over a pair of stonewashed jeans, those ever-present sandals – seem brighter. Gold jewellery flashes at her neck and wrists as she hovers at my side.

'I've got a confession to make,' she says. 'I was so full of nerves for you, and, well – I went to the restaurant.'

'You admit you were there?' My hands shake as I fumble for my keys. 'That was you?'

'I didn't stay for long or anything.' She looks embarrassed. 'You all looked like you were having a good time.'

'You watched us,' I say incredulously.

'The food looked delicious. I bet it was expensive though. Not my kind of thing.' Diane hesitates. 'I hope you don't mind, but I spoke to your father.'

Astonished by her admission, I turn to face her. 'Did you push him?'

She looks at me, uncomfortable. 'I don't—'

'Did you *push* him down the stairs, Diane?'

She frowns. 'He asked the way to the toilets. I hope things are better between you now.'

I can't tell if she's tormenting me. All I know is that I want to get inside, I have to get away from her.

Reaching into the bag again, I manage to find the door key; it taps against the metal surround of the lock, my hand is trembling too much to slot it home.

'I was worried all night, it's all I've been able to think about, so I've been so excited to hear about it,' she tells me.

The way she's talking, you'd think butter wouldn't melt. But that's Diane, I realize. Just as with the smeared mirror and the phone, she won't accept responsibility for her actions.

It's obvious now that she isn't just going to fade from my life. So far, out of fear for my reputation, I've remained polite and measured, and stupidly encouraged her to think we're friends. But that's only reinforced her delusions. Diane's attention has tipped over into something more dangerous and insidious. Her supposed affection has become toxic and aggressive, if it wasn't already to begin with.

Crucially, I ignored the threat she made when I first encountered her on the radio show. *I'm going to make them pay.*

'You can't just come here.' I press my back to the door in case she tries to force her way in; Amber could be inside with Siobhan. 'I have things to do.'

Diane blinks. 'You're upset.'

'You can't follow me everywhere, Diane.' I'm doing my best to sound calm, but tears of fear and frustration well behind my eyes. 'Please stay away.'

'I'm sorry, I didn't mean to...' She lifts the plastic bag. 'I came to give you this.'

Opening it wide, she shows me what's inside. Beneath cling film bubbled with condensation is the dark brown skin of something clammy in a casserole dish.

'It's a lasagne. I'm not much of a cook, really, and my kitchen isn't—'

'I don't want it.' I chop my hand in the air for emphasis. 'I'm sorry, but you have to go now.'

'I won't come in if you're busy. But it's my only dish, so I'd like it back, if you don't mind,' she says. 'I can come back for it another time.'

'I don't want it.' I hold my hands up and away from the bag, because I want nothing to do with Diane or her lasagne. 'Take it with you, please.'

Turning back to the door, I get the key in the lock and open it. If Siobhan and Amber were here, I'd hear music and chat, but to my relief the house is silent.

Diane places the bag on the step. 'I'll leave it here.'

'I don't want it,' I tell her, closing the door.

'Say hello to Sean for me.' She smiles grotesquely as I slam it in her face.

Standing against the door, I take a deep breath and sneak a look through the stained glass – the bright world outside is the colour of a bruised plum – and quickly rear back because Diane is still on the doorstep. Her shadow looms for several seconds as she puts her nose to the glass to peer inside, but then it recedes. When I look again, she's walking off.

As soon as she's gone, I pull out my phone with shaking fingers, because I don't want Siobhan to come along the street with Amber, not while Diane's nearby. But of course her phone is switched off, when I've specifically asked her to keep it on.

Five minutes later, I'm still looking down on the street from behind the shutters in my bedroom, but can't see her anywhere.

I'm going to make them pay.

I should go to the police, and damn the consequences to my reputation, but Dad said he didn't see properly who pushed him; and I have no proof that she came into my house on Saturday night.

But there is something I can do.

When Diane made that threat, it was against me *and* Cameron. If that's not a good reason to phone him, I don't know what is.

15

Sliding open the patio door, letting fresh air into the hot, stuffy kitchen, I walk into the garden. After several weeks of no rain, the lawn is brown and scratchy under my bare feet, the cracked ground hard.

I can't believe I'm about to make this call. To a former boyfriend I dismissed from my life years ago.

These days, they call it ghosting, but back then there wasn't a cool word to describe my bad behaviour; how I didn't take his calls or reply to his frantic messages; how I hid behind the door when he begged me to explain why I wouldn't speak to him; how I just removed him from my life without any explanation.

Cameron was devoted to me, and for a while he was the only person who kept me from falling apart completely. But I treated him pretty badly, I think. A memory crashes into my brain of the night when I goaded him at the restaurant. My only excuse is that emotionally I had hit rock bottom and needed to start from scratch; but the way I broke up with him was callous.

So I've no idea how he's going to react to my making contact nearly twenty years after I froze him out of my life. He'll probably tell me to get lost, and I'm not sure

I could blame him, but I've at least got to try to talk to him.

Finding the 'Contact Us' page of his GP surgery, I call the number and wait anxiously for it to connect. Then a woman says, 'Priory Medical Centre, will you hold, please?'

A moment later I'm listening to muzak, and pacing restlessly across the lawn. The door to the garden shed is ajar, which is unusual. It's Sean's domain, not mine, I hardly ever go in there, and he always keeps it locked. There have been a number of thefts from sheds around here, and gardening equipment stolen. But moving closer, I see the padlock and key have been left on the sill. Sean would have taken garden furniture from the shed so people could sit outside at Saturday's party, and he's forgotten to lock up afterwards. But then I remember seeing him walking down the garden more than once that night; he was coming from the shed when Ollie arrived...

'Sorry about the wait,' says the receptionist, coming on the line again. 'Can I help you?'

'Can I speak to Dr West, please?'

'Do you have an appointment?'

'It's... a personal call. Tell him it's Hannah... from uni.'

The thought hits me that Cameron may not even remember who I am. He may have had five – ten – twenty girlfriends in the two decades since, and completely forgotten about me. But, no, that's ridiculous.

'Hold on, please,' says the receptionist.

It's cramped in the tiny shed, and smells of cut grass and paint thinner, but it's cool out of the sun. The garden chairs are folded against one wall, secateurs hang from a nail above them, and the lawnmower is stored with its flex rolled neatly around the folded handle; there's a stack of old paint tins dumped here, even a roll of wallpaper; the metal frame of the barbecue, with a packet of waxy firelighters resting on its bulbous lid, stands in the corner; Sean loves wheeling out the barbecue of a weekend.

There's just enough space to get to the shelf where Sean keeps empty flower pots and packets of lawn and plant feed. It's odd being in this unfamiliar space, I can't have been in here more than twice since we moved in.

After a few seconds, the line reconnects and I hear Cameron's voice for the first time in two decades.

'Hello, stranger!' To my relief, he sounds genuinely pleased to hear from me. 'This isn't a call I expected to receive.'

'Hi, Cameron, how are you?'

'I'm great, Hannah.' He says it slowly, elongating the words, as if he's still trying to get his head around my unexpected call. And then, in that way people do when they don't know what else to say, he repeats it. 'I'm great, but kind of... gobsmacked.'

'I can imagine.' Part of me is pleased to hear his voice again all these years later, and part of me wants to curl up and die. 'I'm embarrassed to be calling.'

'Don't be embarrassed. It's good to hear from you. Better late than never, as they say!' He laughs. 'And to what do I owe this great honour?'

'It's difficult to explain over the phone, really, so—'

'Hang on a moment, Hannah,' he says, and I hear him talking to someone in the background; they're discussing a prescription or something. A door closes, and then Cameron comes back on the line. 'Sorry about that. You were saying?'

'It's... complicated.' I'm trying not to wince. 'The thing is, it'll be easier to tell you in person.'

There's a thick silence on the line and I grit my teeth. It's one thing to accept my call for old times' sake, it's another thing entirely to agree to meet. But then he says, 'When?'

There's a stack of empty plant pots, and a single pot beside it that's turned upside down, and I pick it up, intending to place it on the top of the stack.

Underneath is a small sealed bag containing white powder, and a packet of condoms.

'Hannah, are you there?' Cameron asks.

'Yes...' I stare at them. 'I'm still here.'

'So, when do you want to meet?' he asks.

I pick up the bag of coke or speed, or whatever it is, and place it back down. The packet of condoms is open; there's only one left inside. The paint thinner smells acrid in my nostrils, making me nauseous in that confined space.

We all live a lie, don't we? Diane said in the cab.

A noise comes from inside the house. Through the single scuffed window of the shed, I see Siobhan pushing Amber in her buggy into the kitchen.

Numb with shock, I replace the pot over the coke and condoms.

There are things right in front of our noses that we don't want to look at too closely, in case we see they're rotten, and we have to admit we've been fooling ourselves.

'Hannah, are you there?' asks Cameron.

'How about tonight?' My voice is barely a croak.

You must know that more than anyone, the way things are at home.

'Sure,' Cameron says, and then he laughs ruefully. 'But let's not go all Bonnie and Clyde this time.'

16

Twenty Years Ago

It was his smile that caused all the trouble that night; the fact that he sat there looking like the cat who got the cream. But if it hadn't been that, I'm sure I would have found something else to get annoyed about. Poor Cam couldn't win. I wanted him around all the time, because it was easy and he always came running when I called, but I couldn't work out what it was he saw in me, and resented that he wanted to spend so much time together, despite the fact I treated him so badly.

It wasn't as if we had made a decision to see each other, but we kind of fell into a relationship. It turned out that we were both studying at Royal Holloway – Cam was doing medicine and me psychology – and we had some people in common, and somehow over the weeks and months we became a *thing*; a couple, I suppose.

Cam was good for me, that's undeniable. He was a solid and steadying presence in my life, and always quietly attentive, which I both liked and hated. He wasn't the most exciting person – there were times I yearned for him to do something unpredictable or dangerous – but he was a faithful friend, a shoulder to cry on, and someone who talked me down to earth whenever unhappy emotions threatened to consume me. I was often in conflict with my parents and Natalie, and he listened to my endless rants about my sister. Poor Cam was the right person at the wrong time.

But that particular night, as I sat toying with my food in the restaurant, I was in a mood, and looking to pick a fight. It had just opened on a street near the Southbank, and neither of us could really afford it, but Cam suggested that we go there; his treat, he said.

'You're thinking about her again. What's happened?'

Nothing had happened, not really. I'd argued with Mum on the phone when she asked if I wanted to speak to Natalie and I said I didn't. She got upset and accused me of not caring about Natalie's illness, and I told her she was being ridiculous, and it invariably developed into a full-blown row.

'She does my head in,' I said. 'I don't know why Natalie doesn't just get on with it and die.'

Cam frowned. 'You don't mean that.'

He was right, of course, I was being ridiculous, and the fact that I'd said it made me feel ashamed.

'Anyway, I'm not thinking about her,' I insisted, even though I obviously was; the row was grinding away in my head. 'So please let's not talk about her *again*.'

Cam nodded, because he already knew better than to challenge me when I was in a mood, and changed the subject. It was one of the things that was really beginning to annoy me about him. We'd been 'going out' for several months, and a lot of things about him were beginning to irk me.

'They've changed the timetable of my tutorials,' he said brightly. 'It's a real pain.'

'Do we *have* to talk about uni?' I asked, exasperated.

'No problem.' He cleanly sliced the greasy chicken on his plate with a knife. 'What do you want to talk about?'

'I'll tell you what I want to talk about,' I told him, gulping from a bottle of beer. 'Do you ever stop bloody smiling?'

He knew I was picking a fight, but the smile stayed fixed in place, and then he made things worse by saying, 'I've got a lot to smile about, being with you.'

'I'm being rude to you, Cam,' I snapped. 'Why don't you say something back to me, like a normal person. Tell me I'm being a bitch, or that I'm out of order.'

He pushed his plate away. 'If you're in a mood with me, I can't do anything about that, all I can do is try to cheer you up.'

Part of the problem with our relationship was that it was too comfortable. All I had to do was snap my fingers and he'd come running, day or night. He'd drop everything for me, even if he was meant to be revising for an exam. If I asked him to jump off Westminster Bridge, I'm sure he would have done it. He was just so loyal, so passive; he was like a little lapdog. I should have been flattered by his devotion, but instead I found it suffocating. It must have been obvious to him that he was more into our relationship than I was.

'I don't mind if you're angry with me, because I love you,' he said.

'Don't say that.' In the back of my mind, I kind of knew that we weren't going to last and I didn't want him using words like that. And I had to go and make things worse by goading him. 'If that's true, prove it. If you love me, do something for me.'

He blinked over his glass of Coke. 'Like what?'

'Anything, Cam,' I said in frustration. 'Just do *something* to prove that you're an exciting person, and that we might even be able to have more fun than sitting in this boring place.'

'Fun?' Cam frowned at the table, and I knew that I'd made him feel dull, which made me both triumphant and ashamed. There were a lot of cool, exciting guys at university, I saw them all the time in the student bar, and I didn't understand how I had managed to get lumbered with him. I felt like life was racing away from me; as if I was missing out, living at the edge of things. It was like being back at home all over again.

Cam looked around, as if trying to find inspiration for craziness and fun, something that would impress me.

'Why don't we go to a nightclub after this?' he said finally. 'It's on me.'

I didn't know what I was expecting him to suggest, but it wasn't that, and my frustration boiled over. It was stupid of me to expect him to be someone he wasn't. Cam was always going to be sensible and dull, and it was unfair to expect him to be anything else.

'You know what?' It was a mistake to come to this stupid, expensive place. 'Let's go home.'

'Why don't we get another—'

'I just want to go *home*.'

Cam blushed. 'I'd better go and pay.'

There was a till beside the bar on the other side of the room. I sullenly watched him walk towards it, wondering whether I should just put him out of his misery tonight, and end it.

Sorry, Cam, we're just not made for each other...

Sitting waiting for him to pay, I saw him get his phone out.

A moment later, my own phone buzzed in my pocket, and when I looked at the screen, a message said,

Run!!!

As soon as the barman walked in the opposite direction, Cam launched himself over the bar to open the till – and snatch money from it.

Dumbstruck, I saw Cam slide back over and run towards the exit, just as the bartender shouted at him to stop. In a panic, I jumped up and scrambled out of the door behind him.

'Keep running!' he shouted, as we flew down the street. I dared not look back, but heard the door bang open and footsteps pound on the pavement behind us.

I'd never run as fast in my life. Heart pounding, I could hardly breathe as I followed Cam off the pavement and into heavy traffic. Car horns beeped and tyres screeched as we weaved dangerously between the moving cars; it was only by sheer luck I didn't get mown down, but if I hesitated even a moment the barman would surely catch me. Then we were racing through the tangle of streets, putting distance between us and the guy chasing. After another couple of blocks, when we were sure that he'd given up, we finally came to a stop; which is just as well, because I don't think I had any energy left.

'I can't believe you did that,' I scolded him between panting breaths. 'How much did you get?'

Cam opened his clenched fist to reveal a bunch of notes. 'I just grabbed what I could,' he said, grinning.

When we counted it, there was £140.

'You're a maniac! We could go to prison!'

Neither of us could believe what he'd just done. It was totally out of character for Cam, and I could see in his eyes his own surprise and exhilaration.

'What are you going to do with it?' I asked.

He held out the money. 'Have it, it's yours.'

I pushed him in the chest and he staggered back, but we were both laughing hard. 'I said do something exciting, not rob the place!'

'Do me a favour, H…' Grinning, he wagged a finger. 'Don't *ever* call me boring again.'

17

The handles of Diane's plastic bag are still wrapped around one of Siobhan's wrists as she unstraps Amber with her other hand.

'Is everything okay, Mrs Godley?' she asks, when I stumble into the kitchen. 'You look... upset.'

'I'm just hot,' I tell her, but my mind is still whirling from my discovery in the shed of cocaine and condoms. It confirms my suspicion that Sean took drugs at the party. But we haven't used contraception for years, because we were trying for a baby for so long and neither of us would be upset if I fell pregnant again.

So why is Sean hiding condoms?

We met in the most old-fashioned way possible: he chatted me up in a nightclub. He was charming and funny, and full of an unpredictable energy, and I fell for him hard. Once, when we were drunk, he laughed that when he turned on the charm, women found him irresistible. It was meant as a joke, but there's an arrogance about Sean where women are concerned. I've tried to laugh it off, but there's always a question lurking at the back of my mind: if he can chat me up in a nightclub, what's to stop him still doing it?

He goes out with his friends all the time, to pubs and bars

and clubs, and often gets home in the early hours. I've no idea what he's getting up to when he's out so late. We've been married for five years, and dated for two before that. Is Diane right, have I been fooling myself the whole time about Sean?

I think of that girl he was standing with by the shed on Saturday night, how close they were to each other, the way he touched her arm, and it makes me feel sick.

Something else Diane said pops into my mind, about how Izzy was fond of Sean. They've always been flirtatious together. I remember a few months back when we left Amber with Sean's parents and all went away to an Airbnb, Sean, Ollie, Izzy and I – it was this luxury place in the country – and Sean spent the entire two days trying to throw Izzy in the pool while she was sunbathing. On both evenings, Ollie and I went to our respective rooms and left Sean and Izzy drinking into the early hours. I could hear their roars of laughter until I finally fell asleep. I didn't think anything of it at the time, but did I miss the signals? Did something happen that weekend? Was it the start of an affair between them, or was something already going on?

Diane has put these thoughts in my head. She's made me doubt my husband and my marriage, when, with a baby daughter we both love fiercely, we should be at our happiest. It seems crazy that a stranger somehow knows more about what my husband is getting up to with my best friend than I do.

But I refuse to jump to conclusions; if I'm going to accuse Sean, I want to be absolutely sure of my facts.

'Do you want to sit down?' asks Siobhan, who looks concerned.

'Honestly,' I tell her, 'I'm fine.'

Never mind the coke, there must be a reason he's hiding condoms in our shed – but if there is, I haven't the faintest clue what it could be. I try to force it from my mind, because there are more immediate things to worry about.

'Where did you get that?' I ask, afraid that Diane has intercepted Siobhan on the street and forced the lasagne on her.

'It was on the step outside,' she says.

She hands it to me. Flies crawl over the surface of the foggy cling film, which sucks at the dark, cratered surface of the cheese.

'It's nothing.' Annoyed that Diane has left it behind, I put it on the counter. Amber talks happily to me, showing me the Baby Yoda toy she holds in one hand, and a bunch of wilted daisies in the other.

'Fowers!' Every day she says something new that resembles an actual word. 'Fowers!'

'Are these for me?' I make a big show of sniffing the daisies. 'Thank you, my darling!'

As I smother my daughter with kisses, Siobhan folds the colourful sun umbrella attached to the buggy.

'We went for a walk along the canal. Amber loved seeing all the ducks and swans, and we fed them.'

'I asked you to keep the phone on.' I don't want to alarm her by telling her about Diane, but in the circumstances, it's important that she does as I say. 'I can't stress enough, Siobhan, I need to know where Amber is at all times.'

When she takes out her phone, the screen is blank, and she frowns. 'I turn it off at night, and sometimes I just forget to turn it on in the morning.'

It seems incredible to me that in this day and age someone can keep their phone turned off all day, particularly someone as young as Siobhan. Mine is probably the first thing I look at in the morning and the last thing I check at night. Once again, it makes me consider how Siobhan's priorities are so at odds with mine, and whether she's really the person I want to look after my child.

'I'm sorry, it won't happen again.' I smile, as if to say don't worry about it, but the truth is, I've probably already made up my mind to let Siobhan go.

As she disappears upstairs to get Amber ready for her afternoon nap, I take out my own phone. I'm not the kind of person who sits examining our joint bank account of an evening, but I open the app and scroll down the deposits and withdrawals, trying to find anything out of the ordinary.

Sean's bought plenty of drinks at plenty of bars over the last month, and he's made a lot of cash withdrawals, but there are no unexplained payments that raise alarm bells; no odd hotel bills, unusual travel payments or extravagant gifts.

But there's another app I've got on my phone. When we bought our new car a year back, an Audi, it came with a GPS tracker in it. Sean uses the car every day for work, and I use our old Fiat. Opening the app, I can locate Sean's car. And right now, it's exactly where it should be, parked on a street near his office on the Finchley Road.

I can't believe I'm spying on him like this, but finding coke and condoms hidden in the shed is a shock.

When he gets home from work at half six, the first thing he does is pick Amber up and twirl her around, up and down and over his head, making *whoosh* noises and making her scream and giggle.

His love for our daughter isn't a matter of doubt. At times like this, when they're together, it's hard to believe anything can be so wrong in our household. But the discovery I made in the shed gnaws at me.

Amber is still shrieking with pleasure when my phone buzzes. It's another inspirational message from Diane, and this one says:

WHEN YOU *TRUST* A PERSON COMPLETELY, YOU KNOW TRUE LOVE

The background image is of two blurred figures, a naked man and woman embracing. It's not what I need to see right now; it's like Diane is reading my mind.

Maybe I drop the phone too hard on the counter, but Sean glances over as he spins Amber around like a toy aeroplane. 'Everything all right?'

It's on the tip of my tongue to tell him, 'No, actually, we need to talk.'

I'll tell him what I found. Better still, I'll take him to the shed and show him myself. But Sean can be very persuasive when he wants to be, and he'll come up with some plausible reason they're there. I'm determined not to say anything until I know for certain that he's guilty of something, or that I'm being paranoid and ridiculous.

'Yeah, sorry,' I tell him. 'I've got to go out again tonight.'

He looks surprised. 'Where?'

Sean's not the only one who can lie when he needs to, and I tell him I'm meeting one of the producers from *Morning Brew* to discuss the show.

'Bit late, isn't it?' he complains.

'Mowe, Daddy,' says Amber, wriggling in his arms because she wants to take flight again. 'Mowe!'

I've lost count of the number of times he's phoned from work to tell me he's going out for a quick drink after work, or a business client wants to meet in the pub, and then he's not come home for hours. But all I say is, 'It won't take long.'

'Cool,' he says, losing interest. 'I'll take this little girl up for a bath, shall I, and get her ready for bed?' He stops at the counter. 'What the hell is that?'

He prods at the rubbery skin of the lasagne.

'It's a lasagne,' I tell him. 'I didn't make it.'

'Who did?'

Tipping the soggy mess into the food bin, it makes a sucking noise as it slides reluctantly from the dish. 'Long story.'

He doesn't ask anything else, and instead lifts Amber above his head to blow a raspberry against her stomach, making her screech.

'There's one more thing,' I say. 'I'm going to let Siobhan go.'

He lowers Amber in his arms. 'You're what? Why?'

'I honestly don't think we need her any more.'

'Of course we do.' Sean makes a face. 'We both work.'

'I'm here most of the time anyway. The job on *Morning Brew* will probably lead to more lucrative opportunities, so I'll be able to ease back on the journalism. It's hard sitting upstairs listening to Siobhan and Amber while I'm making podcasts and writing articles about the importance of spending time with your family. Also, it's a ridiculous expense to have a full-time nanny. We can get in a childminder when we need one. It'll be a much more flexible arrangement.'

It's also disconcerting how much Siobhan looks like my dead sister, and it freaks me out every time I see her, but I'm not going to tell him that.

'And another thing, Siobhan spends a lot of time with Amber, but she's not taking her to enough playdates with other kids. It's important Amber socializes with children of her own age. Siobhan's great with her and everything, I just think she could be more... friendly with other people.'

'If that's the way you feel about it. But you enjoy your work, and you'll likely end up looking after her all day.' Sean gives me a meaningful look. 'Are you ready to juggle work *and* be a full-time mum?'

'I'm ready,' I tell him. 'And if it doesn't work out, we'll get someone else in.'

He frowns, and I can see the cogs turning in his head. He's thinking that he'll have to take more responsibility, too, and that he'll not be able to go out as much, it'll cramp his style. He *should* take more responsibility.

'Just for the record, I think you're being mean. Shiv may not be the smiliest person in the world, but Amber will miss her deeply.'

It annoys me that he's making me out to be the villain, but for the moment it's best to bite my lip.

'It's not like I'm going to sack her straight away,' I tell him. 'We'll give her a month's notice and I'll make sure she gets a good reference.'

'I'm uncomfortable about it,' Sean says. 'What will she say about us if we sack her?'

I don't understand. 'What on earth could she say?'

'You let people go like that, without a good reason, and they can spread rumours.'

'What rumours?'

'I don't know, just untrue stuff. She could make up anything.' He sounds anxious, but cuddles Amber close. 'So when are you going to do the dirty deed?'

'I'll speak to her tomorrow morning.' Picking up my bag, I walk into the hallway, ready to head to the pub where I'm meeting Cameron. 'I've got to go.'

'Bye, then,' he says, and walks upstairs without looking back. He's clearly annoyed, but I can't tell if it's because I'm going out or sacking Siobhan, or both. 'Have a good meeting.'

18

It's a measure of how paranoid Diane has made me that I spend the journey into town looking over my shoulder, making sure I'm not being followed; peering anxiously along the platform when the Tube train stops at stations; looking for zigzag leggings and gold sandals in the rush-hour crowd.

Cameron and I agreed to meet centrally, in a pub off Regent Street, because it's easy for him to drop down the Jubilee Line after work. But when I walk into the crowded room and don't see him, I'm worried he's already changed his mind about coming. Maybe he's decided to give me a taste of my own medicine, stringing me along on the phone and then leaving me in the lurch, just like I did to him all those years ago.

Part of me would be relieved if he doesn't turn up, because it doesn't seem fair to drag him into this situation – Diane has likely recognized me from the TV, but there's no way she could identify Cameron. However, I force myself to wait, in case he's late.

I'm getting out my purse to buy a drink at the bar when a voice beside me complains, 'Do I really look that different?'

I've been standing right next to him.

'I'm so sorry,' I say, embarrassed. 'I was in a world of my own.'

'It is kind of weird, isn't it?'

There's an excruciating moment when neither of us know what to do next. Cameron breaks the tension by holding out a hand.

'How do you do.' He grins. 'Cameron West.'

'Hannah Godley.'

'Wait.' He clicks his fingers, pretending to recognize me from somewhere. 'You're... the Queen of Hearts.'

When he turns to get the attention of the barman, I get a chance to look at him. He's no longer the wiry young man I knew. He's still got the thick, dark hair, but it's worn in a scruffy short mop, and those flecks of grey I saw in the photo on his work website now reach around his ears.

With his sensible off-the-peg jacket, knitted tie and jeans, the scuffed brown shoes, he looks exactly the same as in that image. He's even got one of those battered leather satchels that doctors always seem to have hanging from their shoulders. Cameron was never the most trendy of people, even when he was a student, that was part of his charm, and the world-weary look suits him as he approaches middle age; he looks distinguished, even handsome, and he's still got that self-effacing smile.

'I asked you to come here,' I tell him. 'The least I can do is buy you a drink.'

'I wouldn't hear of it,' he says with a firm shake of his head. He asks what I want, and I tell him I'll have a gin and tonic.

'Good choice,' he says. 'Go and find us a table.'

A minute later, when I've found a spot in one of the corners, he comes over with my G&T and a glass of sparkling water.

When he sits down, he makes small adjustments to the position of his glass on the table, maybe playing for time while he thinks of something to say.

'I completely forgot you don't drink,' I say, nodding at the water. Even when we were students, he never really touched alcohol. We were all so drunk back then that nobody even noticed that he was always sober.

'Never really acquired the taste. It's saved me an absolute fortune down the years, I can tell you.' He lifts his glass in a toast. 'You look really good, Hannah.'

It feels weirdly formal for him to call me that. When we were together, I was always just 'H' to Cameron. Here we are, many years later, back to square one.

'I've seen you on the television. You were speaking on a documentary series, on Channel 5 or something. It was one of those shows where they list stuff.'

'*My Favourite Phobia*.' It makes me cringe that he saw it, because that documentary, featuring people with strange fears, wasn't exactly quality TV.

'I don't tend to watch television.' He makes a face, as if he's made a social blunder admitting it. 'My working days can be draining, and I don't have a lot of concentration left in the evening, but I have patients who suffer from phobias, so I thought I'd give it a watch. When I saw you were on it as one of the experts, I couldn't believe my eyes.'

'I get asked to do a lot of shows like that. They interview you in front of a bookcase to make you look clever, and then edit what you have to say down to two minutes, so you end up sounding like a fool.'

'Same old Hannah, still putting yourself down.' He smiles sadly. 'You're a psychologist, an expert.'

'I'm an agony aunt really.' I roll my eyes. 'I write articles on how to stay happy on social media.'

He points a finger. 'You can never remind people enough to do that.'

'It's not like I have my own practice or patients, or anything. It's all a bit ridiculous.'

'It seems to me that your advice reaches thousands... no, millions of people. If you make even half a dozen unhappy souls feel better about themselves, then you're doing a brilliant job.'

I nod, grateful. 'Thank you.'

As unexpected as it is, it's good to see Cameron again, but it's also a bit uncomfortable considering the circumstances in which I dumped him. 'So, look, I owe you an apology.'

He holds up a hand, *stop*, as he shrugs off his jacket and lets it fall onto the chair behind him. 'You did what you—'

'No, I handled things badly.'

'You don't have to apologize to me. You were in a bad way, Hannah. In fact, looking back with my clinical hat on, I'd probably say you had PTSD after Natalie's death.' Cameron folds his arms across his chest, frowning at the table as he considers his next words. 'Having said that, I'll be honest with you, at the time it really fucking hurt. I thought I could make things better for you, but I couldn't, and then you just... vanished from my life.' He looks pained for a moment, then smothers it with a smile. 'But after a year or two... or three, the pain went away.'

'I had to, I'm sorry.' I squirm. 'I felt trapped, after what we did to that man, I just needed to leave everything behind, *everyone* behind.'

'Martin.' Cameron nods, and I'm surprised he remembers the name. 'I shouldn't have dragged you into it.'

'No.' I shake my head, vehement. 'I made *you* do it.'

'All right, I'm not sure that's true, but let's just say that we did it *together*.' There's an awkward silence and then he says, 'It's an unexpected pleasure to see you after all these years, Hannah, but I'm intensely curious to know why you want to see me.'

I take a deep breath. 'It's about that night, and what we did.' Cameron must sense how difficult it is for me to say this, because he rests his elbows on the table to lean closer. 'I was on a radio phone-in the other week...'

He nods. 'I've heard it, you're very good.'

I wonder how he must feel when he hears my voice, or sees me on television; when he sees the woman who ghosted him, who scraped him from her life as if he was dirt on her shoe, giving advice to people on how to be happy and kind.

'A woman phoned in to talk about what happened to her brother Martin. Diane spoke at length about what we did, Cameron, she knew all about it. It was obvious that she knew I was involved. She made a threat on-air, she said she's going to make me – make *us* – pay.'

His eyes narrow as he tries to take in everything I've said. 'Wait,' he says. 'Tell me that again.'

So I tell him about the show and about Diane, and what's happened since. My meeting with Diane in the café, my lost phone, and her admission that she was at the restaurant.

'Okay.' When I've finished, he claws his fingers through his hair, something he always used to do. 'And you think this woman Diane... she's a threat?'

'Yes, no... she could be,' I say, thinking of Dad's fall. 'When I met her, she seemed sweet and gentle, nothing like the person who rang the show, and I may have given her the impression that we could be... friends.'

He waits for me to continue. The palms of my hands are clammy because I've been sitting on them.

'But too many things have happened.' I tell him about my suspicion that she crept into my house on the night of the party, and the mess on my bathroom mirror. The idea of Diane touching all my things, maybe even going into Amber's room, makes me feel sick all over again.

'She knows where you live?' he asks.

The way she spoke about Sean and Izzy in the cab comes back to me. 'I think she knows a lot of things about me.'

'It's good that you've come to see me,' he says. 'But maybe you should be talking to the police instead.'

When my gaze drops to the table, he nods thoughtfully, and I know he understands that what we did to Martin could have repercussions for me. These days, even the hint of bullying behaviour is enough to kill a career, particularly when you're the Queen of Hearts. The fact that it happened so long ago is irrelevant. 'Has she proved her connection to Martin?'

I take out the photo – of me, Cameron and Martin in the bar all those years ago – and place it on the table in front of him.

Cameron says softly, 'Holy shit.'

'I don't remember having our photo taken that night, do you?'

'Is it even real?' he asks, flipping it over to check the blank reverse side.

'It must be,' I tell him. 'That's me and you, and I *think* that's Martin.'

'It's him,' he says quietly, and drops the image on the table. 'What do you want from me, Hannah?'

His voice sounds terse, almost cold, and I'm afraid that now he knows why I'm here he's going to run a mile. None of this is Cameron's responsibility, and it's unfair of me to drag him into this situation – in the circumstances, he owes me nothing – but I've been hoping that he would somehow provide me with a solution to the thorny problem of Diane.

'I suppose I just wanted to find out whether you'd had any contact with her, if the same thing was happening to you.'

'No.' He shakes his head. 'Martin didn't know anything about us, other than our first names, and he was steaming drunk that night. Even if she knows what I look like, and I've unfortunately changed a lot since then anyway...' He pats his paunch. 'I don't see how she could find me.'

Part of me is relieved that Diane hasn't got her claws into Cameron too, but it also makes me feel more isolated and vulnerable. I smile, but there's a hard lump in my throat. 'That's good, then.'

He gives me a sad look. 'I'm sorry that this has happened to you.'

'The truth is, I'm terrified she's going to ruin everything.' Tears spring into my eyes. 'I've never told anyone about that night, not my husband or my friends.'

'Me neither. It's not something I'd feel comfortable telling people.'

'And I just... needed to speak to someone who knows about... about...'

'That bad thing we did.' He sips his water and places it back down. 'But if I remember rightly, he deserved it.'

'Did he, though?'

'I wouldn't lose too much sleep over what we did to that guy. Martin was a weirdo with an unhealthy attitude to women. Men like that don't change, he's probably still the same. And if he was so damaged by what we did, why hasn't he contacted you himself?'

'He's dead,' I tell him. 'He killed himself several years later, according to Diane.'

The idea that we're somehow responsible for his death has burrowed into my mind like a tick. A sick feeling washes over me.

'Did we kill him?' I ask in a panic. 'Are we responsible?' I've an overwhelming urge to leave, and I sling my bag over my shoulder and stand. 'I'm sorry, I had no right to contact you out of the blue like this.'

'Now look.' Glancing around the pub, he smiles and says, 'Everyone thinks I've made you cry. Please sit down, Hannah, and let's see if we can work something out together.'

Reluctantly, I drop back into the chair and sip my gin and tonic. It tastes cheap and acidic.

'First of all, rid yourself of the idea that we're responsible for his death. He could have had long-term mental health problems or a life-threatening illness; he could have been standing trial for sexual offences and couldn't live with the shame. Knowing our friend Martin, that's not beyond the realms of possibility. From what you've told me, this sister of his sounds a confused and depressed woman, who's determined to lay all her unhappiness at the door of someone else. Frankly, she sounds like she needs help.' His assurance that I'm not personally responsible for Martin's death makes me feel better. 'My advice is to stay the hell away from her.'

'I've tried to tell her to go away, but she's not getting the message.'

'I'll speak to her, if you want,' he says, and I feel ridiculously relieved and grateful. Deep down, I think that's all I've wanted to hear him say. I just needed for someone to tell me that I don't have to handle this alone.

But I shake my head, *no*. Because Diane doesn't know Cameron's whereabouts, and it feels unfair to pull him into her unpredictable orbit. 'She'll just start hounding you.'

'I'm a grown-up, and a GP, which means I meet a lot of lonely and miserable people who are clingy and dependent, and I'm sure I can handle Diane.' He taps the table absently with a couple of fingers. 'At the end of the day, it's her word against ours.'

'But she's right about what we did to Martin.'

'Sure she is. What we did was at the very least unkind, and at worst abusive. But, come on, saying we're responsible for his death... that's a bit strong.' He leans back, shaking his head. 'You shouldn't have to go through this alone.'

'What worries me is that she seems very unstable. One moment she's desperately trying to be my friend, sending me inspirational messages and offering lasagne, and the next she's pushing my dad down the stairs.'

Cameron blinks. 'She pushed your father down stairs?'

'He didn't see her, but she admitted she was there. And also, she claims to know a lot about me and about... my husband...'

I stop myself saying any more. I can't bear to tell him

about the insinuations she's been making about Sean, and about Izzy.

But Cameron folds his arms, the way people do when they're really interested in something. 'Such as?'

'It's...' I don't feel comfortable telling a former boyfriend I haven't seen for years about my suspicions. 'I'd rather not say.'

'Fair enough, and I won't ask again.' He nods at my wedding ring. 'So you're married, then. Nice guy?'

'Yes... he is.' I eye the ring on his own finger. 'And you?'

'How are your folks?' he says, ignoring the question.

'They're good.'

'How's things with your father?'

Cameron was my boyfriend back when Natalie died, when she killed herself by walking in front of a train; he was there as my relationship with Dad deteriorated. He's well aware of the unhappiness I felt at the time, the burning anger I had towards Natalie that she could be so selfish and turn her back on us all. And he knows how it led to what happened with... what we did to Martin.

My sister's illness dominated my childhood. Everything revolved around her. It felt to me back then that she hogged all Mum and Dad's love, all their time and attention, so that in the end there was precious little left for their other daughter. She did exactly the same in death – whether it was a freak accident or suicide, we'll never know – and left me reeling in the aftermath.

'Oh, you know.' I wince. 'Same old, same old.'

'Funny, isn't it. Here you are now, helping people cope with their own feelings.'

I shrug. 'Funny ironic, yeah.'

'I don't think it's ironic, or a coincidence, I think that her life and death, and the feelings you struggled with back then, made you what you are. Someone who is empathetic and understanding. As awful as her death was, some good came of it.'

It's been a long time since I've discussed Natalie with anyone outside of my mum and dad, and I feel my chest clog with emotion. 'Thank you, but I'd rather she was alive, so I could tell her how much I loved her really.'

'Of course,' he says gently.

'But what about you?' I'm actually sick of talking about myself and my problems.

'There's not much to tell. I'm a GP now, as you know. And I live a very boring life. Up until tonight, anyway.' A phone rings in his satchel and he digs it out and frowns at the screen. 'I'm going to have to take this.'

'Of course.'

'Hey,' he says into the phone. 'Yeah, she's great, we've been catching up… No, she's not changed at all, she's still the same headstrong Hannah.' He winks at me. 'I'm coming home very soon. Have you taken your medication?… Good, I'm glad. Bye, then.'

'Your wife?' I can't help but ask.

'Yes, Penny. She…' He hesitates as he drops his phone in his bag, and I get the sense that he's choosing his words carefully. 'She's… not well, so she worries if I'm late home.'

'Would you like another drink?' I ask, but he looks tense, and I know what he's going to say.

'I'd better not, I have to get going.'

It would be nice to have another drink, and steer the

conversation into happier waters, but I can't force him to stay.

'The more I think about it, the more I'm not sure you should get involved, not if Diane identifies you.'

Shrugging his shoulders back into his jacket, Cameron shoots me a wry look. 'We're both responsible for what happened, and it's not fair to let you face this alone.'

'Thank you, Cameron,' I tell him.

'I preferred the old days when you called me Cam, and I called you H.'

'Thank you, Cam.'

'You're welcome, H.'

He lifts the glass to his lips, about to drain it, but contemplates me instead, and I have to ask, 'What?'

'Once upon a time, we got up to some stuff, you and me, because we were too young and stupid to know better. And now here we are, a doctor and a celebrated psychologist, sitting here talking politely, virtual strangers. Funny how life goes, isn't it?'

'We did a bad thing,' I say.

'Sure, we did a bad thing, but I'll say it again.' He drains his glass and places it on the table. 'You were under terrible strain and full of conflicted emotions about what happened to Natalie, so you have to be kind to yourself.'

And he's right, because I was in a bad way.

19

Twenty Years Ago

'Can you come round?'

'I'm not in London.'

'Where are you?'

'I'm still at my parents. Why, what's happened?'

'She's dead, Cam. Natalie's dead.'

'What, how?'

'It was an accident... or suicide, nobody knows... she fell in front of a train. She left the house yesterday afternoon to go to the shops and didn't come back. Nobody can work out what happened, it just doesn't make sense.'

'And how do you feel about it?'

'How the hell do you think I feel about it?'

'It's just, I know you have conflicted feelings about her.'

'She was my sister, Cam, and now she's gone, and it's my fault.'

'Hey, wait, how?'

'Because of how I treated her, because she desperately needed my support, but I turned my back on her, I couldn't wait to get away.'

'That's ridiculous and you know it, H. Are you going to see your parents? They'll want you there.'

'I don't… I'm too upset right now.'

'They'll want to see you.'

'But how can I possibly face them after everything that's happened? I didn't help her, Cam, when she needed me. I wasn't there.'

'They're going to need you now.'

'Please come here as soon as you can, I can't be on my own right now.'

'I'll get the first train, and I'll call you as soon as I get into London.'

'Please hurry.'

'And listen to me, H. Whatever happened to Natalie isn't your fault. These things, they happen for a reason. Everything will turn out for the best, I promise you.'

'What possible reason can there be for something like this? This is my fault, I'm a hateful, awful person, and I'm responsible. I'll never forgive myself.'

'You're going to get through this, I promise. I'm leaving right away.'

'Thank you, Cam. Please hurry.'

'I'll do anything for you, Hannah. You know that.'

20

I've been up for an hour when Sean finally comes downstairs. Amber's breakfast things have been cleared away and we're sitting together; she's chattering away happily. This quiet time we share of a morning, before Sean comes down and Siobhan arrives, when it's just me and her, is precious to me.

But this morning, I can't help but think about Cameron. With all the other things happening in my life, it was nice to see him, and to my relief he was attentive and sympathetic when I explained the situation with Diane. Most importantly, he didn't dismiss what I said, or make me feel like I'm overreacting, or turn it all into a joke like Sean would.

I'm sorry that this has happened to you.

I wonder what would have happened if I hadn't banished him from my life. Would we have stayed together? Would we still be together now?

Probably not, because if I'm honest with myself, I liked Cameron – who was quiet and attentive and loyal, and just the kind of person I needed at the time – but he was also a little bit dull. The bald truth is, he was always more smitten with me than I ever was with him.

He seems happy, his eyes lit up when his wife called him,

but there was also concern in his voice when he spoke to her – he mentioned she was taking medication – so I hope everything's okay at home.

At least now I've finally got someone on my side where Diane is concerned, and in whom I can confide.

'Where's my tie?' Sean dashes into the kitchen on the hunt for various bits and pieces he needs for work. 'Have you seen a blue folder?'

Finally, he stops long enough to pour a coffee and eat a slice of wholemeal toast, which he chews as he checks his phone.

'That thing kept lighting up in the middle of the night,' I tell him.

'Sorry.' He dabs at the screen. 'There's been an emergency with one of our clients in Asia.' He finally glances up at me. 'You look shattered.'

'I didn't sleep.'

'It's the heat,' he says.

It's also the insinuations Diane made about my husband and Izzy, and the coke and condoms I found in the shed, that made me unable to sleep, because I couldn't stop wondering what Sean was doing while I was out last night.

When I got home, the patio light was switched on and a couple of empty beer bottles were left on the garden table. Did he sit outside in the warm evening, texting my best friend? Or sexting her? Were they playing out fantasies on the phone; laughing at me behind my back?

The end of the garden was shrouded in darkness when I walked to the shed. The door was ajar, the lock still placed on the sill, but when I lifted the empty pot, the white powder and condoms were gone.

'Worried about the television thing?' he asks. 'Don't be, you're going to smash it.'

Those are the exact words Izzy used the other night. When Sean absently pats the breast pocket of his jacket, I can't help but wonder what's in there. Maybe it's the coke and condoms.

'Forgotten something?' I ask.

He drops his hand quickly. 'No, got everything now.'

My pulse quickens, it's on the tip of my tongue to have it out with him. But then he makes a big fuss of Amber, kissing and cuddling her, and I don't want to start a fight in front of her.

'So how was last night, anyway?' he asks. For a moment, the lie I told about where I was slips my mind. 'With the producer?'

The *Morning Brew* producer, right. 'It was good, she just wanted to run through the format of the slot with me one more time.'

'Exciting stuff,' he says, but he looks preoccupied. 'So you're going to do the dirty deed this morning? To Shiv, I mean.'

'As soon as she comes in.'

'Well, it's your choice,' he says. 'But it's not like we can't afford to keep her on, if that's what you're worried about.'

'I've made up my mind,' I tell him firmly.

'Good luck with it, then.' He cups his hands around my cheeks, intending to kiss me hard, but I jerk my head away so that he only manages a glancing peck on the side of my mouth.

'I'll see you lovely ladies later.' At the door, Sean slaps his head as if something's just occurred to him. 'I just remembered, Han, I'm out tonight. It's the birthday of one of the lads from football, and I said I'd pop in for a quick one.' He grimaces in apology, because he knows we've had this conversation many times. 'I'll try not to be too late.'

His fingers once again flutter to his breast pocket, and I open my mouth to ask him what he's got in there, but he's already out of the door.

When I unstack the dishwasher, I find the dish Diane brought the lasagne in, which sparkles now it's clean. Taking Amber upstairs, I shower and dress, and at nine the front door opens downstairs.

'Who is it?' I call tensely from the bedroom.

'Just me, Mrs Godley,' Siobhan calls.

Lifting Amber from the bed, I whisper to her as if she's a co-conspirator, 'Let's get this over with, my darling.'

Sacking Siobhan is one of the most difficult things I've ever had to do, and despite what Sean believes, it's not a prospect I relish. My thoughts are on spin cycle about it. *You're being mean, she's not done anything wrong*, I tell myself. But also, *she's cold, there's a lack of communication and trust.*

If it doesn't work out, if I find it too hard to juggle my workload and my responsibilities as a mother, we can always get another nanny in further down the line.

Siobhan will land on her feet. She's a bit reserved, and may not be the best at keeping her employer informed about her whereabouts – I know some parents don't mind that – but she's dedicated and flexible, and good with kids. If she was just a bit warmer where adults are concerned, she'd be the full package.

Downstairs, she's filling the baby bag with nappies and

wipes and creams, and all the other accessories she needs when she goes out with Amber.

'Siobhan, can I have a word?'

'Of course,' she says, giving me that slightly robotic smile as she fills Amber's sippy cup with juice.

'Just... stop doing that, will you?' If I'm going to do this, I should get it over with now. 'Sit down for a moment.'

Sensing my unease, Siobhan gives me a searching look, then places the beaker on the draining board and goes to sit at one of the tall stools at the kitchen island. Amber reaches out her arms, she wants a morning cuddle from Siobhan, and I hand her over. The last thing I want to do is give her the impression that I don't trust her with my daughter, which is not true.

'Look, Siobhan.' I'm happy to negotiate the terms of her severance, and of course she'll have up to a month to find other employment, but it's my hope she'll find somewhere long before that. 'There's no easy way to say this but—'

And then there's a muffled noise from her pocket, the sound of a phone, and Siobhan makes a face. 'Sorry about this,' she says. 'At least it's switched on.'

It's the worst possible time for someone to ring, and I hope she ignores the call. But she frowns at the screen. 'I don't recognize the number.' She looks worried.

'You'd better answer it.'

'Hello?' Her face becomes a terse mask as she listens into the phone, and it's obvious there's something wrong.

'When did this happen?' she says, beginning to pace. I take Amber from her, so she can concentrate. 'Please may I come there now? Is now a good... Okay, I'm on my way.'

She kills the call and tells me, 'My grandad's been rushed to hospital.'

'Oh no, is he all right?'

'He's had some kind of seizure.' Agitated, Siobhan walks back and forth. 'They've got him in intensive care, and said I should... I really should go to him.' She points vaguely at the front door. 'Do you mind?'

'Of course you should go,' I say. 'Where did they take him?'

'He's at a hospital in Enfield.'

It's a trek to get there by public transport, and it'll cost a fortune by cab. I feel intensely sorry for Siobhan, and immediately want to help her. 'I'll drive you.'

'That's very kind,' she says, edging towards the door. 'But you don't have to.'

'You could be waiting all morning for a cab, it'll be much quicker if I take you.'

Siobhan looks pale and preoccupied as I pick up Amber, the bag and the folded stroller, and grab my keys.

A few minutes later, with Amber strapped in the back of the Fiat, we're driving across London. I'm going as fast as I can, but it's the rush hour, and parts of the journey are snarled or diverted.

'Do you know what kind of seizure he's had? Is it a heart attack or a stroke?' I try to make conversation and bring her out of her shell, but Siobhan sits tensely beside me. 'I promise you everything is going to be okay. If he's in hospital, he'll be getting state-of-the-art care. What's his name?'

She looks at me blankly. 'His name?'

'Your grandfather.'

'Peter,' she says tersely. 'Pete Linden.'

'Presumably someone found him, was it your gran?'

Siobhan just stares straight ahead. 'She's dead, he lives on his own.'

'A neighbour, then?'

It's obvious Siobhan isn't in the mood to talk, so I concentrate on driving. It strikes me that it's the first time I've learned anything at all about her, or her family, and I can't help but ask, 'Are you close?'

'I went to his flat just last night.' She turns to me now, her mouth a thin, straight line, as if she's trying to hold in her emotions. 'He was talking about football.'

'Oh, really?' I say, as if we're standing in the kitchen enjoying a cup of tea, rather than dashing across the city to see her hospitalized grandfather. 'You know, this seizure, or whatever it is, could be nothing. Ninety-nine times out of a hundred these things are a warning, and not as bad as they look.'

She attempts a smile. 'I hope so.'

'Is he very old?'

Siobhan blows out her cheeks, thinking. 'He's seventy-seven, but he keeps himself fit. He walks everywhere, and still plays bowls, so...'

'Keeping active is the best thing you can do at that age,' I say encouragingly. It occurs to me that she's not called anyone else to tell them. 'Do your parents know what's happened? Should you speak to them?'

When she looks away again, I can see how hard she's finding it to speak to me right now. 'Dad's in Norfolk. I'll... I'll phone him later, once I know how Grandad is.'

Considering I was about to sack Siobhan a few minutes ago,

it seems hypocritical to bombard her with more questions, so I concentrate on steering through the thick morning traffic.

When we get to the hospital, there's a slow-moving queue for the car park. It's going to take me time to find a space, so I tell her to jump out, and I'll meet her in reception.

She opens the passenger door but turns to me. 'I don't know how long I'll be.'

'Take all the time you need, I'll be here.'

She nods, *thank you*, and climbs out, slamming the door behind her. Stuck in the queue, I watch her half walk, half run to the entrance of the hospital.

By the time Amber and I arrive in reception, Siobhan is nowhere to be seen. Most likely, she's upstairs in intensive care, or wherever her grandad is now. Finding a seat, I pull Amber's stroller beside it, and we sit and wait.

21

Waiting in reception for nearly two hours, I call Izzy. I'm trying not to get paranoid, but she doesn't answer her phone, which isn't like her at all. Amber's getting hungry now, and I could really do with a coffee, so I wheel her buggy over to the hospital café and order a cheese roll and a drink. Sitting at one of the tables, we watch people coming in and out of the reception.

Finally, after another quarter of an hour, I spot Siobhan in the middle of the floor, trying to find me.

'Siobhan, over here!' I wave from the café. When she walks over, looking tense and miserable, I try to ignore once again her eerie resemblance to Natalie. 'How is he?'

'He's unconscious but stable, and the doctors said he may be like that for some time.' She sits in the chair on the other side of Amber's buggy. 'They think he's had a stroke.'

'Oh, Siobhan, I'm so sorry.'

'Hey, baby.' Siobhan's face lights up when Amber giggles at her, and she leans over to give her a kiss. They both look happy to see each other. Maybe my daughter is just the comfort she needs right now, and once again it makes me feel guilty for wanting to let her go.

'Do you mind if I spend another hour or two here,

Mrs Godley? I don't really want to leave, just in case his condition changes.'

'Oh God, of course you should stay.' Siobhan must think I'm a monster if she believes I'm going to insist she comes back home immediately. 'Take the next few days off, as long as you need.'

She nods, and the corners of her mouth almost turn up in a smile. 'Thank you.'

'Is there anybody you need to call? Family?'

'I'll call them in a minute,' she says. 'You probably had better things to do with your day.'

There are things I should be doing, yes. Articles to write, and a podcast to prep, but they'll have to wait. 'There's nothing more important than something like this, Siobhan. I'm just glad I've been able to help.'

Exhausted, Amber finally falls asleep in the buggy, her fingers clinging to Siobhan's hand. The coffee in front of me has turned cold. My anxiety about Sean and Izzy still swirling around my head, there's something I feel I need to ask her. It's not fair to put her in such a position, not while she's consumed with worry about her grandfather, but I figure I might not get another chance in the near future.

'I've got a question, and I'd be grateful if you answered me as honestly as possible.'

Siobhan places Amber's hand in the buggy and turns to me, perhaps grateful for the distraction. 'Of course.'

'Has Sean ever had anyone at the house when I've not been there?'

Siobhan immediately looks uncomfortable. 'At the house?'

'A woman, maybe…' I try to smile. 'I may not have known was there.'

She glances away. 'I haven't seen anyone.'

I should be relieved by her answer, but my anxiety spikes; I'm sure there's something she's not telling me. 'Are you sure? It's… important that I know, Siobhan.'

'No.' She shakes her head at the floor.

'What is it?' I lean across the table towards her. 'Has someone been there? Have you seen something?'

She won't look at me. 'It's not that.'

'Then what is it?'

Siobhan's voice falters. 'I can't…'

'Has something happened?'

It's a punch in the gut when she says, 'Mr Godley… he tried to kiss me.'

My fingers clutch the plastic rim of the seat tightly, because otherwise I may fall sideways; the ground beneath my feet feels like it's whiplashing, and I'm about to be hurled off my chair. Her words make me dizzy, faint.

Aren't we all living a lie?

When I finally feel strong enough to speak, it's with barely a whisper. 'He did what?'

'It was one afternoon,' she says. 'You were working upstairs, and he came in… and kind of lunged at me.'

'What did…' My voice flaps wetly in my throat. 'What did you do?'

'I pushed him away,' she says quickly, because she can see how upset I am. 'And then Mr Godley went upstairs, and I took Amber out.'

My heart thumps. 'Is that all he wanted?'

She won't look at me. 'He said a few things, *suggested* things. 'He was drunk.'

'What things? What did he say?'

'I don't know.' Siobhan shakes her head, flustered. 'I was too shocked to catch – I can't remember, honestly, I can't.'

'When did this happen?'

She flashes me a frightened look. 'It was a few weeks ago.'

The air conditioning chills the air in the café. But it's not enough to prevent a molten river of shame and shock and disgust surge inside of me.

Sean came on to our nanny. In my own house. In *our* house. While I was upstairs working.

It hardly seems possible, but she has no reason to lie, and after what Diane said about him, and what I found in the shed, I believe her instantly.

I need to take action; I need to do *something*.

'Oh, Siobhan,' I say. 'Why didn't you say anything?'

But of course she couldn't tell me, because that would open a can of worms that would make it extremely difficult for the three of us going forward. Whatever else happened between me and Sean, it would almost certainly have led to Siobhan not working for us any more, and very possibly the police getting involved.

I remember now that afternoon Sean came home pissed, it was maybe a month ago. He'd had a boozy business lunch, and was steaming drunk when he thumped heavily upstairs while I was trying to work in the office. Stumbling everywhere as he tried to step out of his trousers, at one point he crashed into the dresser and I had to help him into bed. I was so angry with him.

'Later, babes,' he mumbled pathetically, pressing his face into the pillow and closing his eyes. 'We'll talk about it later, I promise.'

According to Siobhan, only a couple of minutes earlier he'd made a pass at her.

Tried to kiss her, made lewd suggestions.

'I didn't do anything to lead him on, I swear,' she says now, looking beseechingly at me.

'I know you didn't,' I tell her quietly, trying to get my thoughts into some kind of order, to work out where we go from here. 'And I'm very sorry that it happened to you. I apologize unreservedly for his behaviour.'

And then I remember what Sean said last night, when I told him I was going to let Siobhan go. *What if she spreads rumours about us?* Maybe he wasn't so drunk that he can't remember what he did, and was frightened I'd find out. 'I just… I wish you had told me.'

'How could I?' She looks stricken. 'I really need the job, and I thought you would blame me, Mrs Godley, because I know you don't…' Her mouth snaps shut.

'Go on,' I urge her. 'Say whatever it is you want to say.'

'I didn't… I don't really think you like me very much, and I'd be sacked.'

Her statement makes me ashamed, because I realize I've projected a lot of my own anxieties onto Siobhan and made her a scapegoat for certain things, when, let's face it, she's been a rock during a difficult time. The fact she knows I've blamed her for silly mistakes makes it worse.

It's obvious it's not Siobhan who's the viper in the nest.

'I'm sorry if you think that I've not been a good employer.' I place a hand to my heart. 'And once again I apologize if I've made you at all uncomfortable. It's unforgivable.'

She shakes her head and is about to speak, but I hold up a trembling hand, because there's more I want to say.

'For the record, Siobhan, I'm grateful for what you've done for me, and Amber. I do like you, but maybe I've let some of my own insecurities show, and I'm sorry if I've made you feel... unappreciated. Thank you for being so honest, and rest assured that I take what you've just told me very seriously. Will you leave it with me?'

She looks upset. 'I don't want to cause any trouble.'

'You haven't done anything wrong.' It's important I assure her. 'It isn't your fault.'

22

The stroller collapsing slowly at my knees, I stand in the car park and call Izzy again. But she doesn't answer, which is completely unlike her – she always calls me back – and of course that makes me even more anxious.

Sean isn't answering his phone either. It can sometimes take hours for him to return my call if he's in a meeting or tied up on urgent business. But what Siobhan said about his pathetic, drunken pass has shaken me and I need to speak to him urgently.

Amber's already strapped into her baby seat in the car. She's still sleepy; her head lolls against the headrest of the chair.

'It's been a strange morning, hasn't it, baby?' I say as I finish folding the buggy and shove it in the back. It's not ideal she's had to spend half the morning at the hospital, but she's been very patient. 'Don't worry, we're going home.'

There are things I should be doing – I've never missed a deadline, *ever* – but when I get in the car, cranking the air conditioning to full blast because it's like a furnace inside, all I can think about is how Sean tried to kiss Siobhan and propositioned her while I was upstairs. It seems incredible, a bolt from the blue, but I instinctively know it's true. The cocaine and condoms hidden in the shed, where I was never likely to look, are proof of that.

Then there's Diane and her sly comments implying that something's going on between Izzy and Sean.

We all live a lie, don't we?

Shoving the key in the ignition, Sean's betrayal feels like the last straw; things have gone too far now. I can't work, I can't just go home and carry on as usual, as if everything's normal. I need to speak to him, and if he's not answering his mobile, I'll phone his work number instead.

'Hang on,' says the woman who answers, when I tell her his wife is calling. 'I'll put you through.'

But when his extension doesn't connect, she tells me she'll to try to find him. After a minute of muzak, she comes back on. 'Apparently Mr Godley has taken the afternoon off.'

'He has?' I ask, surprised.

'Oh,' she says uncertainly. 'He didn't tell you?'

'Of course he did!' I say, as if I've just remembered. 'I've had a bit of a brain freeze.'

When Sean left the house this morning he never said anything about taking the afternoon off, just that he'd be home late.

'We're going to find Daddy,' I tell Amber over my shoulder in an anxious sing-song. 'And make everything right.'

Before I even realize it, I'm opening the 'Find-Your-Car' app on my phone. It'll tell me where he is. Part of me desperately hopes to find his car is parked outside our house, he's driven home while we've been at the hospital and is wondering where the hell I am. But it's not there at all…

According to the app, his car is parked on Izzy's street.

Closing my eyes, I take a deep breath. Despite the cold air blasting from the dash vents, the small of my back is sopping wet against the car seat.

Oh God.

My eyes drop to the keys dangling from the ignition, because Izzy's front-door keys are hanging from the small bunch. She and Ollie used to have a cat, which they asked us to keep an eye on when they went on holiday, and then she asked me to keep the keys in case of an emergency.

'We just have to pop somewhere quickly,' I tell Amber, who's asleep again. 'And then we'll go home.'

And so I drive back across London to Izzy's house in Crouch End. My movements feel numb, robotic. My hands thread carefully along the steering wheel; my foot trembles above the pedals. The journey to Izzy's house is second nature to me, I've been there countless times – screaming with laughter with her over a bottle of wine, helping clear out her attic, curled up on her sofa watching terrible romcoms – but I've never driven there with such a feeling of dread. Because if Diane is right, if her insinuations are correct, not only will my marriage be finished, but I'll lose my best friend too.

Part of me yearns to prove Diane wrong, and to take back control of my life. Thanks to her, I've begun to think the worst of the people closest to me. Sean's drunken attempt to snog Siobhan, as abhorrent and treacherous as it is, isn't in the same league as him having an affair with my dearest friend, and I simply won't believe it. With her comments and stupid messages, Diane is doing her best to poison my trust in two of the most important people in my life, and I'm going to prove her wrong.

On the way there, I try to call them again. There's not a hands-free system in the car, so I surreptitiously thumb the screen of my phone in my lap.

When I call Izzy: the phone rings and rings.

When I call Sean: the phone rings and rings.

I just want one of them to answer and immediately allay my fears, assure me they're not with each other, and what on earth makes me think they would be?

In the end, I throw the phone angrily into the footwell. I really hate Sean at this moment for what he did to Siobhan, and for keeping secrets from me.

If he's the kind of man who could do that to our own nanny, then what else is he capable of, and with whom? Has he been taking me for a fool all this time, and committing adultery with my best friend? When he's out of an evening with his mates, if that's even where he is, is he flinging himself at women in bars and clubs?

When I pull into Izzy's street, I feel sick because Sean's car is parked right outside her home. The ground-floor windows are shuttered, the curtains pulled in the bedroom.

Parking further up the street, I sit and look at the house, my heart pounding with fear and anticipation.

Am I really going inside?

The engine idles. All I have to do is release the clutch, put my foot down and drive home. The sensible thing would be to calm down, take the heat out of my raging emotions, before I speak to them both. That's exactly the advice I'd dish out to other people in the same situation.

But instead, I kill the engine and pull the keys from the ignition. Because it's obvious what I'm going to do. I've tried to contact them both, I've given them plenty of opportunity to answer the phone and explain, and neither of them has.

'Come on, baby.' Pulling Amber out of the car, I hold her close. She's a warm weight against my chest, and her head rolls against my shoulder as she sleeps.

We walk up the pathway towards the house where I've enjoyed parties and meals and barbecues, some of the most fun nights of my life, and I find the right keys. There's a deadlock, and I slip the key quietly into that and turn it. It's not locked, which means someone's definitely inside. I use the Yale key to open the door very gently.

The long white hallway is empty, and so is the living room, with its on-trend furniture, immaculately placed cushions and tall, bright ornaments. Izzy likes to keep everything just so, but the remains of two lines of coke are a powdery smudge across the glass surface of the coffee table. Sean is here.

Muffled voices come from the main bedroom above my head, and the bed creaks. Placing Amber on the sofa and making her comfortable, I walk softly up the stairs. I can make out Sean's voice now, urgent and excited, as the creaking quickens. At the top of the stairs, the bedroom door is ajar.

Standing outside, I know this is my last chance to leave. I can turn around, pick up Amber, and slip out of the house. Neither of them will ever know I was here.

I don't have to go inside. I don't have to confront this.

I don't have to face the reality of Sean's betrayal with my best friend.

But it's too late now, I've got to know, I've got to see, and my heart feels like it's about to leap out of my chest.

Sean's moans become louder and hurried over the rapid creaking of the bed. I hear the hard, rhythmic smack of skin against skin.

I open the door.

And see Sean and Ollie.

23

I've been sitting in the car for... I don't know how long. It's probably only a matter of minutes, but it feels like hours.

My hands on the wheel feel cold and numb, despite the incredible afternoon heat. Finally, Sean comes out of the house and walks slowly towards me, shoulders slumped, head bowed.

One of the curtains in the bedroom twitches, but it's impossible to see Ollie inside. The only thing I can think about is how I'm going to tell Izzy I found our husbands fucking; the conversation is going to be awful. Frankly, I'm struggling to work out my own confused feelings.

When Sean opens the passenger door and climbs in, I can't bear to look at him. And he doesn't – or can't – look at me, so we both stare ahead. With my hands on the wheel, it's like we're driving somewhere with Amber sleeping in the back, a happy family on holiday.

Out of the corner of my eye, I see him lift a hand to his chin, and it's shaking. It's obvious he's not going to break the hideous silence, so I guess that's going to be up to me.

'So.' My voice is full of bitter irony. 'That was unexpected.'

Sean bursts into tears.

'I've fucked up,' he says, dropping his head into his hands. 'I know that, and I'll be better, I promise.'

'We're not going to talk about it now,' I tell him quietly.

In the white heat of the moment, my head is full of questions, and I need time to process what I've discovered this afternoon – about his activities, his proclivities. It wasn't just another man I found him in bed with, but the husband of my best friend. There are so many betrayals stacked up here, one of top of the other, that my head swims. It feels like my whole life has been cracked open and its rotten core exposed.

I've been gripping the car key so tightly in my hand that it's left a deep impression in my palm.

Sean wipes the tears from his cheeks with the back of his hand and sniffs. 'Do you want me to drive?'

I probably shouldn't drive. My arms and legs feel like jelly, but he's offering because he wants to make things better, and to give him a chance to try and explain his actions on the way home.

'No,' I say. 'You have to drive your own car.'

The ironic thing is, this is the kind of situation I'm always telling other people how to cope with.

My husband is having an affair, Hannah. He came on to our nanny, and then I caught him having sex with a man, a mutual friend, and I don't know what to do. I don't know how I can ever trust him again.

What do I do, Hannah? Please tell me…

In such a situation, I'd probably tell them to… what?

Sit down and talk with him about what he wants from your relationship, about what you both want. Get him to open up about a lot of things: his emotional needs, his dependency on drink and drugs, his sexuality. There's a whole lot of issues to unpack. I don't even know where to start, and I'm pretty sure that Sean doesn't either.

Has my whole marriage, our whole relationship, been one gigantic lie? Does he love me, does he even desire me? Am I what he wants, or a convenient facade for a whole other life he's living that I know nothing about? And this thing with Ollie, this whatever it is he's been having – an affair, a relationship, a fling? – what does that mean?

It's impossibly hot and stifling in the car, my fringe sticks damply to my forehead, and I lower the driver's side window.

'Look, Han,' he says in a wavering voice. 'It's really not what you thi—'

'No!' I shout, making him jump, and I have to force myself not to let my anger and frustration boil over, because Amber is in the back and I don't want her to wake up and get upset. When I continue, my voice is low and harsh. 'I'm *not* going to talk to you about it here, not sitting in a car outside the house of your... boyfriend, or whatever Ollie is to you.'

'Don't be ridiculous.' He grimaces. 'He's not—'

'Your fuck buddy, then.'

He looks like he's about to protest, but sucks down a breath instead. 'When we get back home we can—'

'I need a few days,' I say. 'To get my head on straight and work out what I feel about... all this. Because right now, Sean, I'm trying to understand what's going on, and what's been happening behind my back, and none of it makes sense.'

'I understand.' He nods, and his oh-so-reasonable response makes me seethe. 'I messed up.'

Oh God, poor Izzy doesn't realize a thing. She's madly in

love with Ollie, she worships the ground he walks on, and this is going to destroy her.

'Where's Izzy while you've been shagging her husband all coked-up?'

'She's up north at a conference,' he says. 'She's back tomorrow.'

'I see. And this…' I said I wouldn't talk about it now, but I can't help gesturing at the house. 'Whatever is going on between you and Ollie…'

He shakes his head violently. 'It's nothing.'

'How long has this *nothing* been going on?'

He shrugs. 'Not long.'

'How long, Sean?'

'A few months, on and off… I can't even remember how it started.'

The question is, do I leave a message for her now, or wait till she gets back before I talk to her? It doesn't feel like the kind of thing that can wait, and I don't know how she's going to cope with this catastrophic news.

Sean pulls his hands wearily down his face. 'I'm exhausted.'

'Must be all that shagging,' I say sarcastically. 'Are there other men… or women?'

'No,' he says after a hesitation, and turns away. Amber has been asleep the entire time, thank God, and he hasn't turned to look at her once.

'I want you to go,' I tell him.

'What?' He looks at me in shock.

'For a couple of weeks, at least. We need a circuit break. I need some space, and so do you.'

'Can't I just stay in the spare room?' he asks. 'I know how it looks, but it was just a stupid mistake.'

'And if I didn't catch you here, Sean?' I say. 'Would you be so contrite and distraught about it? Or would you have just come home tonight and got on with being mister happy-go-lucky family man, as if nothing had happened?' My voice sounds cold and hard, even to myself. The Queen of Hearts has left the building. 'And just carried on shagging our friend.'

'We can get over this,' he pleads. 'Han, I'll do anything to make this better.'

'Siobhan told me today that you came home drunk one afternoon and made a pass at her.'

He looks shocked. 'Something happened with her, but it's not… Look, I will do anything, *anything*, to make it up to you. You and Amber are my life.'

'Do I even know you at all?' I hiss, making him flinch. 'Do I?'

He thinks all he has to do is fall to his knees and I'll forgive him. Maybe I will, maybe I won't, I don't know yet; I'll have to cycle through a lot of emotions before I can come to a decision. But I'm not going to just let him worm his way back into my life in the space of five minutes.

'I'm sure someone will give you their sofa,' I tell him, reining in the anger and disgust I feel. 'We'll talk in a couple of weeks.'

'What about Amber?' His voice rises in frustration. 'When will I see her?'

Sean's bottom lip quivers and he bursts into tears again, his shoulders heaving as he sobs. He's distraught, we both are, but I'm determined not to cry. When I don't react to his emotional outburst, he flings open the door and walks to his car.

I'll text him to say I'll stay out of the house for the afternoon, I'll take Amber to a café, or to the movies, to give him enough time to pack a bag and move out.

24

But when Sean finally drives off and I'm alone, I begin to physically shudder from the shock and upset, and it's my turn to weep.

I have to make a decision about what to do. The obvious thing would be to call Izzy, but I really can't face having that conversation so soon. Besides, it was her I suspected of sleeping with Sean, and that makes me burn with shame.

Damn Diane and her insinuations. A woman who walked into my life a week ago seems to know more about what's going on behind the flimsy facade of my marriage than I do. I can't help but hold her responsible for this. Somehow – because she's a crazy stalker, a lurker, a plotter, because she wants to *hurt* me – she's made it her business to find out about what Sean has been getting up to, and must have been watching him very closely; although she seemed to believe he was having an affair with Izzy. Unless she encouraged me in that mistaken belief, in order that I receive one final, devastating shock.

Diane said she wants to be my friend, but she threatened revenge on the radio – and now she's got it. To look at her, you'd think she wasn't capable of such manipulation. Will this satisfy her, or is she going to keep sticking the knife in? What more does she have up her sleeve? At this point, I wouldn't put anything past her.

What is clear is that trying to stay on her right side, encouraging her to believe she's a friend, hasn't worked.

If I can't call Izzy, I have to speak to someone who'll understand what I'm going through. It feels intrusive to contact Cameron already, I only saw him last night, but I don't have any choice.

He gave me his mobile number before we left the pub, so I don't have to phone the switchboard at his surgery, and when I've blown my nose and got my breathing back under control, I call him.

'Hey, Hannah.' To my relief, he sounds pleased to hear from me. 'You've caught me at the right time, I'm on a break.'

'I hope you don't mind, you did say I could call.'

'I've just talked for an hour with a patient about his ingrown toenails,' he says, 'so whatever you have to say is going to be an improvement. What's up?'

Shock and bewilderment still press hard against my chest, and I have to fight hard not to burst into tears again. When I'm sure I'm able to talk, my voice sounds small and strangled. 'It's nothing, I shouldn't have phoned.'

'It doesn't sound like nothing,' he says quietly. 'It sounds like a whole lot of something.'

'It's just been a... bad day.'

'Let me guess, is it our friend Diane?'

'Yes, no – kind of.' I want to tell him what's happened, but I barely know him. Yet I feel as if I can trust him. 'She's... done something and I'm... I want to tell you, but...'

'I understand,' he says when it's obvious I'm not going to be able to. 'You don't have to. I'm glad you called. I've been thinking about what you said, and think we should meet Diane together, the both of us, and put a line under this whole episode once and for all. We'll put on a united front. From what you tell me, I believe Diane's the kind of leech who attaches herself to one person, and me turning up out of the blue will likely give her a big shock. I'm confident it'll make her back off.'

'And what if it doesn't?'

'If it doesn't, then we go to the police. We can look at getting a restraining order.'

'But what we did to Martin…'

'It's our word against hers,' Cam says. 'It was all such a long time ago, and Diane is clearly confused about a lot of things. Look, half the time a lot of my patients don't even have anything wrong with them. They're lonely and isolated and miserable, and all they want is a bit of human contact. I think that's what Diane needs, to the point where she's desperate to embed herself into someone else's life. You're a connection to her dead brother, maybe the only one she's got, and by doing this stuff, she's trying to insinuate herself into your world. If we challenge her about it, she'll run a mile.'

'I don't want to upset her,' I tell him. 'I don't want to make things worse.'

'Hey.' He pretends to be offended. 'Us doctors are famous for our soothing bedside manner. I'll be firm but fair.' He waits for my response. 'How does that sound?'

The thought of seeing Diane again doesn't fill me with enthusiasm, but this time I won't be alone, Cam will be beside me.

'It'll be the old team back together again,' he says.

'It was the old team who got us into this mess.'

'Oh, yeah.' He snorts. 'Forget I said that.'

'What do you want me to do?'

'Call her, or text if you can't face speaking to her, and say you want to meet. Let's get this thing done.'

'Thank you, Cameron,' I tell him.

'Hey,' he says sternly. 'What did we agree about you calling me that?'

'Cam.' I give a short, bleak laugh. 'Thank you.'

'We never saw Martin again after that night, and we can make his sister go away too,' he tells me. 'I promise you, H.'

25

The house is filled as usual with Amber's laughter, her joyous stream of lively chatter, but it feels quiet and lonely without Sean.

My first appearance on *Morning Brew* is only a week away, and it really can't come at a worse time. His betrayal has made me feel numb, hollowed out, but I'll be expected to be bright and bubbly in front of presenters Simon and Maria. I'll do my best, but I'm terrified that the press will go absolutely crazy if they find out that the new agony aunt on the show has just thrown out her husband after discovering him in bed with another man. I hope their make-up person is good, because, unable to sleep, I look terrible: pale, with dark, puffy circles under my eyes. The bed, *our* bed, feels big and empty.

It's Monday afternoon, three days since Sean left, and I haven't heard from him. I was expecting to be bombarded by frantic messages and appeals to be allowed home, but it looks like he's following my advice and taking time to think about what he wants; I hope that's the case.

But of course I'm not able to hide his absence from Siobhan, who has come back to work today. She tells me her grandad's condition has improved, he's still unconscious but the doctors say he's out of danger. It's a huge relief that she's even here. If I'd gone ahead with my plan to fire her, maybe she'd have left immediately, and there'd be nobody to help with Amber.

Siobhan can see how tense and preoccupied I am, and just as she's leaving she asks if I'll be okay till Sean gets home.

'There's something I need to tell you.' I've thought long and hard about how I should bring up the fact, but there's no good way. 'Sean isn't... he's not going to be here. He's moved out, temporarily.'

'It's not...' Siobhan turns a deathly white. 'It's not because of what I told you?'

'It's not your fault. It's the culmination of a lot of things that have been happening. We decided it was maybe best to spend a bit of time apart.'

In all honesty, his adultery was a thunderbolt from the blue. But I don't want her to think that she's to blame, not when I'm going to need her even more.

When Amber drops one of her toys on her foot and begins to cry, I pick her up and try to soothe her.

'There's something else you should know.' It's obvious that Diane is disturbed, and the chances are, her meddling isn't going to stop. 'There's a woman who has a kind of... grudge against me.'

Siobhan looks up. 'The woman who had your phone?'

'That's her.' Amber won't stop crying and I bounce her frantically, but Siobhan lifts her from my arms and whirls the tips of her fingers in a gentle motion across the back of her neck. Amber's screeches immediately begin to soften.

'I don't believe Diane would ever approach you, or try

to do anything to Amber, but if a stranger comes up to you, or attempts to strike up a conversation, you should be aware.'

Diane seems awkward around people, I don't think she would willingly approach Siobhan, but she's so full of contradictions it's better to be safe than sorry.

'Okay,' Siobhan says, jogging Amber, who is calm now; she even looks like she's forgotten her trauma. I've seen Siobhan do that motion with her fingers before.

'Where did you learn that trick?' I ask her, in wonder.

Siobhan smiles awkwardly. 'My mum used to do it to me when I was a baby.'

Once again, I thank my lucky stars that I didn't sack Siobhan.

The conversation with Izzy when she finally returns my call is as difficult as you can imagine, particularly because Ollie clearly hasn't told her what's happened. It's not something I want to talk about on the phone, and keep suggesting that we meet, but she suspects immediately that something is wrong and demands to know what's going on.

Telling someone by phone that her husband has been having sexual relations with mine isn't ideal, and at first Izzy doesn't believe me, she thinks it's some kind of weird joke. Then she accuses me of lying and finally – I don't know how long we've been talking, but it feels like hours – she becomes angry and accusatory, as if what's happened is my fault. By the end of the call, when she hangs up on me, we're both in floods of tears.

I leave numerous messages asking her to call back, but Izzy ignores them, and I have to tell myself she'll get in touch when she's ready. I don't know what will become of her and

Ollie, but I'll be there for her if she'll let me. It's bad enough losing Sean, I don't want to lose her too.

And there's something else I need to do, which is to contact Diane, as Cam suggested. She's continued to send me inspirational messages, bland Hallmark-card-type stuff about how the universe loves me, and every new day is the first day of the rest of my life, and every one of them makes me tense and angry. When Siobhan and Amber are out of the house, it's time.

Diane answers within seconds of the call connecting, and says brightly, 'Hannah, I was just thinking about you!'

'Diane.' I try to keep my voice neutral, because I don't want her to think this is a social call, but nor do I want to alarm her. 'I think it's time we met up again.'

'Oh yes,' she says eagerly. 'I would really love that.'

'Let's go back to the café where we met the first time. Can you make tomorrow afternoon? Say, three o'clock?'

'What a good idea,' she says. 'Did you enjoy the food I made you, I hope you did?'

It takes me a moment to remember the lasagne she left on the doorstep. Telling her I didn't eat it may upset her, so I say, 'It was delicious, thank you.'

'And Sean?' Diane asks. 'Did he enjoy it too?'

Is she playing games with me, does she know what's happened? I haven't seen her, but it wouldn't surprise me if Diane's been watching the house. She may even have seen Sean leave with a packed bag, or noted his absence.

'He wanted me to tell you how much he enjoyed it.'

'I don't have much of a kitchen, you should see it, but I love to cook,' Diane says brightly after a long moment. 'So there's plenty where that came from.'

'That's kind of you, Diane, but don't go to the trouble, we don't eat a lot of meat.'

'Oh.' She sounds disappointed. 'You can tell me the kind of things you like when we meet. I'm sure there's something I can make. Martin used to love my meals, he always told me how delicious they were.'

She talks eagerly, and in such an unselfconscious way, that she hardly resembles the quiet, nervy woman I first met. It's like she's a vampire feeding off my own unhappiness. The more she takes from me – my peace of mind; my nights of sleep; the husband from my bed – the more self-assured and confident she becomes.

But Cameron and I are going to remove her from my life.

We're finally going to make it happen.

26

This time I make sure to arrive at the café twenty minutes early, so I can grab a table that is out of the sun, but where I've also got a good view of the street. Diane's casserole dish is in a plastic bag at my feet. I'm going to give it back to her so that she has no excuse to keep pestering me for it.

As I order coffee, Siobhan texts to say that she's taking Amber to the swimming baths; bless her, she's really trying hard to let me know at all times where they are.

But when the clock strikes three and Diane's still not turned up, I get nervous. I was sure she'd be here on time, or even arrive earlier; it's certainly not like her to keep me waiting. People walk past on the street, and I know Cam is hiding in a doorway nearby. Our worry was that if Diane saw him sitting with me, she wouldn't come in.

Fifteen minutes pass and I'm convinced she's not coming. But when I text Cam, he replies, *don't worry*, and a moment later I see her rushing down the road in her leggings and sandals. Seeing me, she gives a little wave.

Coming inside, her top lip curls in a grotesque smile that makes me shudder. It takes all my energy to return her grin. If she sees how uncomfortable I am, she doesn't show it. Diane doesn't seem like someone who's able to read people's moods very well, and she's probably oblivious to my tension.

'I'm so sorry,' she says, fanning her red face with a hand. 'It took forever to get here. There are delays on the Tube. I thought you would be gone, I was so sure of it. But you're here!' Collapsing into the chair opposite, she dabs at her sweating forehead with a scrunched-up tissue she takes from her clamshell bag. 'I'm amazed you even came.'

'Why would you think I wouldn't come?' There's so much I want to ask her, but Cameron warned me not to confront her by myself.

'I know how busy you are, and you're on the television soon, I know that because Simon and Maria have already started mentioning you. I couldn't believe it when they said your name, I wanted to rush outside and tell everyone, that's my friend! The Queen of Hearts! My friend's going to be on TV! I thought, what with everything going on, you wouldn't have time to see little old me.' She grins. 'But here you are!'

'This is yours.' I pick up the plastic bag at my feet and hand it over. The dish gleams, and Diane runs a thumb over the smooth surface in wonder. 'I've never seen it so clean. How do you manage to get it like this? I just… I wouldn't even know where to start.'

'Sean sends his regards,' I tell her, because I want to see her reaction.

'Oh.' Diane's smile falters for a second. 'That's nice.'

'Would you like something to drink. Tea or coffee?'

'I'm happy with this, thank you.' She reaches for the decanter of water on a tray in the centre of the table and picks up one of the small tumblers beside it. 'I need to cool down after all that running!'

And as she's doing that, and telling me again about the delay on the Tube, the café door opens and Cameron walks in, and I feel a massive sense of relief.

'Diane,' I say, as he drags a chair from another table and brings it over, positioning it beside mine. 'I'd like you to meet Cameron.'

'Hello, Diane.' Cam holds out his hand. 'It's nice to meet you.'

Diane stares up at him in shock.

'I wish the circumstances were a little different,' he tells her, withdrawing the hand when she doesn't take it, and adjusting his jacket as he sits. 'Okay, so the reason I'm here is, I know you contacted Hannah because you blame her for what happened to your brother, and she's told me she's already apologized to you for what happened. But I think it's important you get an apology from us both.'

All her previous energy drained from her, Diane lowers her gaze to her empty glass.

'Because I was there with her that night, Diane, as you probably know.' Cam nods, and I take out the photo Diane gave me the last time we were here and place it in front of her, the way she did to me.

'Alas, I've put on a bit of weight since then,' Cam tells her gently. 'But you can tell it's me, yes?'

When I glance at him, his smile is friendly, encouraging, but his eyes have a steely intensity; he's not going to let her off the hook. Diane refuses to meet his gaze. She looks as uncomfortable and awkward as when she met Sean, and it occurs to me that I know nothing about her relationship with men. Has she ever had a romantic relationship, does she even have any male friends? Or was her brother Martin the only male she's ever trusted in her life?

'I've spoken to Cameron about you, Diane,' I start to say. 'And he—'

But Cam lifts a finger, *let me take it from here*, so I bite my lip.

'Diane,' he says, more forcefully. 'You can see that's me in the photo, can't you?'

Finally, Diane's eyes lift to his, and she gives a nod that is almost imperceptible.

'Why...' She clears her throat. 'Why are you here?'

'I told you, Diane,' Cam says sternly. 'I'm making an unreserved apology for what happened. But that doesn't mean, of course, that either of us accept any responsibility for your brother's death.' He hunches forward. 'When did he kill himself, Diane?'

She shakes her head, as if she's forgotten. 'I don't remem—'

'But you must know, surely?'

Diane shakes her head. 'Five... or... four years ago.'

'Four or five? Which is it?'

'Four years,' she says, breathing quickly. 'It was four.'

'So a considerable time after his encounter with Hannah and me. More than fifteen years later, in fact.'

Folding his arms, Cam sits back in his seat and considers her calmly. There's a long, tense silence at the table.

'We've both apologized now, Diane,' he continues. 'We've made amends. And now you must promise us something in return, which is to not contact Hannah again.'

Diane's gaze lifts quickly to his, and her eyes blaze. Once again I glimpse the buried fury bubbling behind the meek and simpering facade. But if Cam sees it too, it doesn't seem to faze him at all.

'Do you understand, Diane? The harassment has got to stop.' Diane's shoulders slump, her eyes drop again to the table. 'Do you *agree*, Diane?'

She says something, but too quietly for us to hear.

'I'm sorry,' Cam says sharply. 'I didn't hear that.'

'Yes, I understand,' she mumbles. 'Thank you for the apology.'

Cam's shoulders relax; his smile returns. 'You're welcome.'

I've never seen Diane look more pathetic, and I know it's hypocritical but I want to hug her right at this moment. Confused and unpredictable as she is, she's still a vulnerable woman. She needs help from someone before it's too late. But I can't be that person. Despite what she says about wanting to be my friend, Diane clearly harbours a toxic resentment against me, and it would be unhealthy – and I think counterproductive – for us both.

And even if I wanted to, Cameron was very firm on the phone about giving her encouragement. If I give her the slightest hint that we can remain 'friends,' she won't get the message, he said. And he's right.

But it doesn't make me feel any better when her eyes lift to mine. She looks desolate, and I wonder about all the body blows she must have taken in life to make her like this: meek, lacking in confidence, isolated – and treacherous. I can't help but give her a helpless smile, as if to say, *I'm sorry it's come to this*.

And then Cameron does something that makes the charged atmosphere even more electric. He takes one of my hands in his. Diane's eyes widen, but her reaction is nothing compared to the shock and excitement I feel, and my fingers instinctively return his pressure. Then he removes his hand, pats the edge of the table as if to symbolize that our business is concluded, and says, 'Thanks for coming, Diane.'

He stands, nudging my elbow discreetly on the way up, and I jump to my feet beside him. Our apology, curt and formal, doesn't feel adequate. But maybe it will be enough to satisfy the demons that plague Diane. I'm afraid to look at her, but I know she's staring at me, her eyes full of hurt.

'Goodbye, Diane.' Cam is pleasant but firm; that's her cue to leave. 'Thanks for the opportunity to set the record straight.'

'Bye, Diane,' I murmur, darting a look. Stunned, and clearly intimidated by Cameron's presence, she turns to go.

'Diane.' Cam lifts the bag containing the dish. 'Don't forget this.'

She takes it in silence and then leaves the café.

As she walks past the window, Cam tells me in a low voice. 'Give her a few minutes, and then we'll go.'

My legs feel a bit wobbly, and I sit down and exhale. I must look a bit green around the gills because he touches the small of my back and says, 'You did brilliantly.'

'I feel awful,' I tell him.

'Of course you do,' he tells me gently. 'Because you're a nice person. She totally retreated into her shell when I came in, which is what I thought she'd do. If you ask me, we let her off lightly. We should have challenged her a lot more about the things she did.'

It's not like I did anything at all, really; I just sat there maintaining radio silence. But I'm grateful that he was here with me, and so firmly took charge of the situation.

'The main thing is, she's gone,' he whispers. 'I'm confident she's going to leave you alone now.'

'If you're so confident,' I tell him just as quietly, 'then why are we both whispering?'

He laughs at that, and I do too.

'Sorry about taking your hand. It was a wild improvisation. I thought it might demonstrate shared resolve.'

'She looked completely shocked.'

Cam checks his watch, says, 'She should be long gone by now, so let's get out of here.'

We hurry down the road, trying to put distance between us and the café, as if half expecting Diane to come charging around the corner brandishing a knife. But a couple of streets later, Cam touches my arm. *Let's slow, we're being ridiculous.*

'She's not what I expected at all,' he says finally as we stroll into the tangle of streets around Fitzrovia. 'I suppose I was expecting someone more, I don't know, aggressive or manic. But she seemed kind of... sad.'

'That's what she's like,' I tell him. 'But she's unhinged, I think.'

He stops, thrusts his hands in his pockets. 'As I say, if she doesn't leave you alone now, we should consider going to the police. At the end of the day, it's your word against hers, and she seems like a fantasist. If Diane wants to air her grievances, then let her, and let's see who the public believes.' The idea that she may not go away makes me sigh, and he adds quickly, 'Having said that, I really think she's going to leave you alone now.'

Diane certainly seemed far more intimidated with Cam there; I think she was surprised – and mortified – that I brought him along. Maybe she'll finally get the message that her friendship with me, or whatever it is she thinks we share, is well and truly over.

'I'd really like a drink,' I say. 'Do you want to grab a quick one?'

Cam frowns. 'I'm not much of a drinker, as you know.'

'Sure.' I shrug, but I'm a little disappointed, thinking he's going straight home.

Then he smiles. 'But I am starving.'

27

'What if she goes home and ends it all?' I ask him over a cobb salad at a posh burger restaurant north of Oxford Street. 'Like Martin did.'

'She won't do anything like that.' Cam chews his club sandwich. 'She'll lick her wounds, and then attach herself to someone else. People like Diane are parasites.'

'That seems a bit harsh.'

'Parasite is a bit strong, I suppose,' he admits. 'A survivor, then.' He drops the uneaten crust of his sandwich on the plate. 'As I've said before, I meet a lot of people like her, and I'm afraid to say, it's what they do.'

I can't help but worry that I'm letting Diane down, or making her someone else's problem. 'She needs help.'

'Yes she does, but your getting involved isn't going to be the solution to her problems.' Cam pushes away his empty plate and wipes his hands on a serviette. 'That really hit the spot.'

He pulls his coffee mug closer to him and sits with his fingers clasped around it. The fact that he's not drinking makes me self-conscious about my bottle of beer. Cam saw me fall over many times when we were together. I was drinking heavily back then. It was just as well that he was always sober, because he probably had his hands full putting out the fires that I started. Remembering his attentiveness, his quiet solicitude, only makes me feel worse about how I treated him.

'I'm sorry,' I tell him now.

He frowns. 'For what?'

'For everything I put you through.'

'You didn't put me through anything.' He sips his coffee and grimaces; from the bitter taste of coffee or what I've just said, I can't tell. 'You were the most exciting person I'd ever met.'

'I was a mess.'

'But what a beautiful mess. Chaotic and utterly unpredictable. You made me feel alive. I loved every moment of being with you, so stop apologizing for everything.'

Cam's smile is unguarded and honest, and so different from Sean's. Sean smiles all the time, but he uses it very cynically. To charm people, to present to the world the facade he wants them to see; it's a blunt instrument to get what he wants. But there's nothing false about Cameron's smile, which is sympathetic and warm and spontaneous.

'The way I ended it, the way I did it…'

'My goodness, we're all about the apologies today.' He shrugs. 'Come on then. Let's get your big apology to me out of the way.'

When I try to explain, it's hard to find the right words. 'I…'

'What you want to say is that you're sorry you dumped me,' he says. 'You had your reasons, and even if you didn't, you weren't in your right mind. Even though I was utterly irresistible, after everything that happened you needed to wipe the slate clean. You're sorry that you never gave me a proper explanation, or even a chance to change your mind, and you've regretted it ever since. You are very, very sorry and embarrassed for all the hurt you caused me.'

'That about covers it.'

He lifts his mug in a salute. 'Apology accepted.'

'But also...' He laughs when I won't leave it alone, but I have to say something else. 'I'm sorry if I made you do anything that made you uncomfortable, like that time at the restaurant.'

'You didn't make me do anything, H. I had a choice about doing those things.'

'But I was hard work back then, and I encouraged you in... bad behaviour.'

'I did those things because I loved you,' he says quietly, and his intense gaze gives me goosebumps. 'I would have walked to the ends of the earth for you, or jumped off a cliff. You really don't know how much I loved you back then or what...' He shakes his head.

'What?' I ask. 'What were you going to say?'

'Look...' He shakes his head in frustration. 'It's all water under the bridge now.'

I can never tell Cam that I never loved him in the same way as he obviously did me. All I really needed back then was a sidekick, a good friend. Cam was a safety net, someone to catch me when I fell, and I think he knows that. The truth is, I was too busy battling my own demons, I was too trapped in my own headspace, to be able to love him. And I don't think we ever had a future, not in that way. That fact makes me feel sad, and awful, but it's true.

'Anyway,' I say, trying to draw a line under the conversation. 'Thank you for being so understanding.'

'Yeah, it's old news now.' It's obvious he's thinking about something else. 'It's possibly a personal question, but how do you feel about Natalie all these years later?'

His question about my sister takes me by surprise. 'I feel sad that I didn't make more of an effort to get to know her and understand the pain she was in. Maybe if she'd lived, we'd have become closer as time went by. I like to think we'd have become more like sisters, and maybe even friends.' I move the beer bottle around, smearing condensation onto the table. 'It's funny, I've been thinking about her a lot recently. The nanny who looks after my daughter is the spitting image of her.'

Cam pulls his mouth down in a rictus, as if to say, *awkward*. 'How do you feel about that?'

'It bothers me, I'm not going to pretend otherwise. It's uncanny, actually. Sometimes I see her and I just want to scream. It's not her fault, of course, she has no idea. I was even determined to get rid of her because I couldn't stand it any more. But then...'

My gaze drops to the table, because I can't finish the sentence.

Cam lowers his eyes to mine. 'But then, what?'

Just saying it out loud makes me upset, and I have to pick up a serviette. 'I've split up with my husband.'

'Oh hell.' Cameron grimaces. 'I'm sorry, I didn't mean to upset you.'

'It's okay.' My chest feels packed with emotion. 'He's moved out, at least. I don't know what's going to happen next.'

'You have a little girl,' he says gently. 'So it can't be easy for either of you. Is it something that's been on the cards for a while?'

'No.' I gulp from the bottle, but the beer is tepid now. 'It came out of nowhere. I'm still... processing it.'

Cam holds up his hands. 'I'm not going to pry, but it sounds as if you're still in a painful place, and us doctors have a reputation for being good listeners. If you ever want to talk about it, or anything else for that matter, I'm always available.'

'He cheated on me,' I say suddenly. 'With another man, actually.'

He blinks. 'Okay then, that's—'

'An eye-opener,' I tell him, trying to make light of it, but my throat feels like it's full of glass, and I discreetly brush tears from my lashes. 'The weird thing is, Diane knew more about what he was getting up to than I did.'

And then I can't stop myself telling him all about Diane's insinuations about Izzy and Sean, and my suspicion that she must have been following Sean to her house.

'He was having an affair with your best friend's husband?' He touches my hand briefly. 'Oh, H, you've been through the wars. And Diane...' He shakes his head. 'What a piece of work.'

'She planted those suspicions about Sean in my head, but she's not responsible for him sleeping with Ollie.' I sigh. 'You know what, I'm sick of hearing about my problems, and talking about myself constantly. I know hardly anything about you.'

Cam is nodding slowly, obviously thinking about how to reply, when my phone rings. The screen flashes on the table between us and we both look at it, because we instinctively suspect who it is.

I turn the screen so he can see who's calling. 'It's Diane.'

'Well, that didn't take long.' He looks disappointed. 'Block her number.'

'You think?'

'From now on, don't engage with her. Don't give her the time of day.'

'Maybe I should tell the police.'

'Let her sleep on what we said first, I still think she'll back off, and if she doesn't...'

So I kill the call and immediately block the number, then drop the phone in my bag as if it's contagious. 'I don't think she's going to go away.'

'Don't be so sure. She's just got to get used to the idea. And you're good at ghosting people, remember, so you've got this.' He winks, but his comment makes me blush. 'Do you trust me?'

'Yes.' Because if I have to go to the police, I'm confident it will be with Cameron at my side. He's right, it's our word against hers, and I will fight tooth and nail for my career and reputation if I have to. 'I trust you, because you're a doctor.'

He nods gravely. 'Is the correct answer.'

I'd like to stay out with Cameron for a bit longer and get to know him better – Siobhan said she's happy to look after Amber till I get home – but he looks at his watch and I know he's going to leave.

'Penny?' I ask him.

'Because my wife is ill,' he tells me sadly, 'I don't like to leave her on her own for too long.'

'I'm sorry to hear that, is it... bad?'

But he won't meet my eye as he decides how to reply.

'She's not very... she's housebound.'

I don't want to put him on the spot, so I change the subject. 'I'd better be getting back anyway.'

'Yeah.' He nods, and perhaps I'm imagining it, but he looks reluctant. 'We should go.'

It looks like we're calling it a night, but I can't help but say, 'It's mad.'

'What is?' he asks, but I'm sure he knows what I'm going to say.

'What we did to Martin that night long ago was the end for us. But all these years later, because of his sister, we're back in touch again.'

'Good old Diane, I always liked her.' He grins, and holds up his coffee, encouraging me to lift my beer in a toast. 'To Diane. May she live long and prosper... but preferably far away from us.'

We clink our respective drinks, and I say, 'And to a friendship renewed.'

'Yeah.' He looks gratified. 'And that, too.'

28

Twenty Years Ago

'The funeral would have finished by now.'

Neither of us had spoken about it all afternoon, but the fact that hundreds of miles away my sister was being laid to rest and I wasn't there was the cause of a fierce unspoken tension. It was inevitable Cam would bring it up sooner or later.

And he was right, the ceremony would be over, and the mourners at my family home drinking tea and eating sandwiches; and they would all be wondering why Natalie's sister was missing. And what would Mum and Dad say if a guest inevitably asked where I was? They would have agreed on some unlikely excuse: *Hannah is ill. The trains let her down.* They wouldn't admit the truth, *She's too selfish and self-involved to pay her last respects to her sister.*

My parents were incredulous when I told them I wouldn't go to the funeral. Dad got seriously mad about it, and I don't know if he'll ever forgive me. I tried to explain my feelings about Natalie, and how after all the conflict and bad feeling it would have felt hypocritical to stand beside her grave. Also, my non-attendance was cowardice on my part, it was self-sabotage, and I knew I would feel awful about it for the rest of my life; maybe that was even the plan. If I had gone, I told myself, the day would surely have ended in a terrible row, and my parents didn't deserve that.

Instead, I phoned Cameron and told him to meet me in a bar in Kennington, South London; a basement dive with gloomy lighting, wood interiors and curling posters on the walls publicizing long-forgotten gigs by long-forgotten bands.

'I hope it went well,' I told him, and smirked. 'But what if she faked her own death? What if she's still alive somewhere?'

Knowing Natalie, she would be absolutely lapping up all the attention. All those people standing at her funeral, all of them thinking about her, talking about her.

'Come on, Cam,' I goaded him. 'Stranger things have happened.'

Even Cam looked annoyed then. 'She's dead, H.'

'But how do you know, yeah?' I snapped.

He looked at me carefully and sighed. 'There'll be a body, a coroner's report, all that. Look, drinking all day isn't going to help.'

I turned my bottle of beer in my hand; as usual, he was sipping a Coke.

'Don't worry,' I told him. 'That's not why we're here.'

He looked around the room, trying to work out what I was talking about, because it wasn't our usual kind of place. Where we were sitting, we could see a group of lads playing pool; balls clicked noisily off each other as they ricocheted across the table. There must have been something in my tense expression that excited him, because he leaned closer. 'Go on.'

'Do you trust me, Cam?'

'Always,' he said.

It was wrong to keep expecting reassurance from him, because I'd almost run out of patience with Cam's clinginess, but there was something I'd come here to do, and I needed him as partner in crime. 'And will you do anything for me?'

'You know the answer to that.'

I nodded at the pool table. 'Over there.'

He followed my gaze. 'What am I looking at?'

'Him,' I said. 'The big one.'

The man I pointed to was a young guy, not much older than us; in his early twenties, maybe. He was tall, six foot or so, but his big build had softened to fat. He wore a slack hoodie with the Harley-Davidson logo on the front, grey sweatpants, a pair of old white trainers. Greasy hair fell over his eyes, so that he had to keep sweeping it away. Leaning over the table to take a shot, his stomach sagged to the baize. Moist bottom lip protruding beneath his large mouth, his hooded eyes blinked fiercely along the cue at the balls that he invariably missed.

The guy had placed money on the table to challenge the winner of the previous game, but he was losing badly, and the way he shuffled around, shoulders hunched, nostrils flaring in disgust whenever he fluffed a shot, made him look like a petulant baby.

'That's the one I was telling you about,' I told Cam, speaking quietly. 'The one who attacked Lisa.'

'Him?' Cam looked at me in surprise, because he couldn't believe it.

But I knew it was him, because I'd been doing my homework. A couple of months ago, a girl on my course had come to this bar, she was already a bit drunk when she walked in, and somehow she ended up talking to him. His name, he told her, was Martin. It's not like she was even remotely attracted to him, but he bought her a couple more drinks and then lured her back to his flat around the corner with the promise of smoking weed. She was so wasted that she fell asleep on his sofa, and woke up to find him trying to get her clothes off. She shoved him away and tried to leave, but he got aggressive and locked the front door, angrily accusing her of leading him on. When she tried to get past him, he pushed her to the floor, and kept her locked in for a couple of hours.

The experience was terrifying, she told me, and she feared for her life. It was only when he fell asleep and she swiped his keys from a pocket that she managed to escape.

I tried to persuade Lisa to go to the police, but she refused. She was embarrassed about the whole episode, and scared of her parents finding out about it; said she just wanted to forget it. But her experience made me furious, and I couldn't get it out of my mind.

It made me angry that this guy Martin had got away with it, and I'd come to this basement bar in Kennington several times to find out more about him. He'd told Lisa he was often here at the weekend, so it was easy to discover who he was and when he came in.

The whole episode became a kind of focus for the anger and guilt I felt at my sister's sudden death, and I became consumed with the idea of teaching the toad a lesson he'd never forget. I demanded it, and it felt to me like the universe demanded it.

I took a plastic bottle from my pocket and placed it on the table between me and Cam.

'What's this?' he asked, picking it up.

'Martin has to learn that he can't go around terrifying women, or hold them against their will, and not face the consequences.'

He tipped the bottle and watched the dark red liquid slope up the glass inside. Unsettled, he looked at me. 'Are we going to hurt him? Physically, I mean?'

That's not something I could ever do. 'We're not going to touch him, we're not going to stoop to his level, but if you don't want to be involved, tell me now.'

'Whatever it is, you can't do it on your own. I won't let you. Tell me what you're thinking.'

As I explained to Cam what we were going to do, Martin stood grimly watching his opponent grandstanding at the pool table, finishing the game with an audacious shot on the black, which rebounded off three cushions and into the centre pocket. Martin threw down his cue and shuffled to the bar, where he ordered a pint of cheap lager and stood furtively watching a couple of girls who had just walked in.

'Last chance to back out,' I told Cam.

'We'll do it together,' he said.

I reached over and touched his hand, but quickly withdrew, mostly because I didn't want Martin to get the wrong idea if he saw us.

'When do you want to do it?' Cam asked, with the same fevered look in his eyes that he had after we'd robbed that restaurant a few months back.

'No time like the present,' I said, and took a deep breath. Then we both walked over to Martin.

'You remind me of someone,' I said, arriving at his side.

Martin fixed me warily with his dark, droopy eyes,

expecting a humiliating punchline. But I wasn't interested in antagonizing him, or making him feel small; I wanted him to like me, and to want me.

'Yeah?' he asked.

'A film star,' I said. 'Tom Cruise or somebody like that.'

'He's a lot taller than Cruise,' said Cam.

Martin drew himself up to his full height. 'Your mate talks a lot of sense.'

'So I've never been to this bar before.' I maintained eye contact, to give him the idea that if he played his cards right tonight, he might get lucky. 'This your local, is it?'

'Yeah,' said Martin. 'I'm in here sometimes.'

I knew how often he came here and when, because I'd made it my business to find out. I'd even followed him to his grotty flat above a betting shop, so I knew where he lived.

'What's your name, anyway?' I asked.

'Martin,' he said, rolling his shoulders.

'I'm Hannah.' My name and Cam's were probably the last truthful things we told him that day. Martin was so overwhelmed that anyone would take any interest in him, let alone fancy him, that he swallowed our lies easily. Afterwards, he probably wouldn't remember much of our conversation anyway.

'We should go.' Cam gestured to the door, as if impatient to leave. 'Find someplace else.'

'Let's stay here. It's cosy, and it'd be rude to leave Martin on his own.' I touched his wrist with a finger. 'And he seems like a fun guy to talk to.'

'I am.' Martin scratched a soft patch of hair below his ear he'd missed shaving. 'I'm a lot of laughs, me.'

When Cam went back to the table to get his corduroy

jacket from the back of the chair, Martin eyed him resentfuly. 'He your boyfriend, then?'

'Nah.' Holding his gaze, I worked hard to convince him he was the only man in the bar I fancied. Unnerved, Martin gulped his pint. 'He'd like to be, but he's just a mate. He's all right, really, but... Tell you what, film star, why don't you buy us a drink?'

Martin's tongue slid along his protruding bottom lip as he decided whether he was in with a chance with me, if I was worth the investment. 'Why not?'

'Better put your card behind the bar because I've a feeling that it's going to be a long, fun night.'

'Yeah?' When Martin looked away, trying to hide the excitement he felt, I winked at Cam, because we already had the guy wriggling on the hook.

He gave me a look, as if to say, *are we really going to do this?*

I felt the small plastic bottle in my pocket. *Oh yeah, we were really going to do it.*

The idea was to get Martin drunk, really drunk – he was halfway there already – and then give him the biggest shock of his life.

29

It feels like Diane is finally getting the message and staying away, because for a few days she doesn't try to contact me. She's blocked on my phone and doesn't come to the house. Thankfully, she doesn't seem to be on social media either – of course I've looked – because I haven't received a friend or message request.

But it's difficult not to feel tense whenever I leave the house, particularly if I'm with Amber; I keep expecting Diane to come running around the corner towards me. It wouldn't be the first time she's appeared out of the blue, she turned up at the bar where I met Izzy, and has already admitted she was creeping around the restaurant when I met my parents – and look how that turned out.

But I keep Cameron up to date on everything, and we send each other messages several times a day. He'll write:

Any sign of our 'friend'? x

And I'll reply:

Nope xx

Phew! Looks like we're in the clear! xx

It's sweet the way Cam implies that we're both the target of Diane's unwanted attention, that we're in this together, when of course she still has no way of knowing how to contact him, even if she wants to; she doesn't have his surname or address. She's been tenacious in the way she's stalked me, but I can't imagine how she'd go about locating him.

Cam also makes a point of phoning every night when he's on the way home from work, and we'll talk for up to an hour.

He'll ask me how I'm getting on with Siobhan, or about my appearance on *Morning Brew* next week; we had a good laugh when I told him about dressing up and posing for the show's publicity shots.

'Get you, you glamorous thing,' he says.

He's told me a lot about his work as a GP but I know hardly anything about his home life, except that he's married to a woman called Penny who is sick, and to whom he is obviously devoted.

The awkward fact that I'm texting and calling a married man after I discovered my own husband has had an affair isn't lost on me, but Cam assures me Penny understands that we're old friends.

'I'd love you to meet her,' he tells me. 'She tells me that I have to bring you round.'

'I'd like that too.'

The reason Cam calls every night is that he knows how worried I am about Diane; but I've also come to look forward to our evening chats, and I'm always disappointed when I hear him park his car and turn off the engine.

'I'm home now, so I'd better leave you alone,' he'll say, and I imagine him lifting his satchel from the passenger seat; the car door slams and he walks along the pavement to his house, where Penny waits inside. 'I'll call again tomorrow... if you want me to?'

'Yeah,' I tell him, as if he's being kind and thoughtful, when really I'd like nothing more than for him to phone. 'But only if you have time.'

He laughs on the other end. 'I'll make time for you, H, because we're mates.'

'Yeah,' I agree. 'We're mates.'

But of course it's inevitable that Diane will turn up sooner or later, and that Friday lunchtime when Amber's taking a nap and I'm just coming downstairs from my office to make a cup of tea, the doorbell rings. Behind the glass, I see her familiar shape.

Sitting at the kitchen island reading a magazine, Siobhan sees me stop in my tracks on the stairs, and follows my tense gaze towards the door.

'Is that her?' she asks. 'The woman?'

I can't remember what I've told Siobhan about Diane; probably just that she's someone who has an imagined grievance against me. But she can see how freaked out I am, and she stands.

'What do you want me to do?' she asks.

'Get rid of her, please,' I say in a tight voice, and I move out of sight to the side. From there, I can see through the gap a needle-thin sliver of Diane when Siobhan opens the door.

'Can I help you?' Siobhan asks her.

'Is Hannah there?'

'She's not in.'

'Can I come in and wait?' asks Diane, and I close my eyes wearily, because it feels like I'm never going to be free of her.

'No, you can't,' Siobhan tells her and her tone is terse. For someone so young, she's calm and controlled. If I'd had a small amount of her self-possession at that age, I wouldn't be in this mess in the first place. 'She doesn't want to see you.'

Diane's face is hidden from me, but I imagine her eyes widening a little bit, the way they do when she's told something she doesn't want to hear, and then she says, 'It's very important that I talk to her.'

'I'm not going to tell you again,' says Siobhan. 'She doesn't want to see you, so please leave.'

'I don't think her phone is working, because I can't contact her.'

'It's Diane, isn't it?' insists Siobhan. 'Hannah doesn't want you to contact her.'

'Her phone isn't working,' says Diane crossly. 'Because I can't get through.'

While Siobhan's talking to her, I tap a message to Cam on my phone.

Diane's turned up!

It's a long shot that he'll actually see the message, let alone have the time to respond while he's at work, but the three little dots immediately throb on the screen.

Don't let her in! Do you want me there?

I reply,

Don't worry, Siobhan is getting rid of her! xx

He writes,

I'll pop round later. If you want me to…?!

'I've made her this,' says Diane, and I look up from my phone to see her hand come into view across the threshhold, holding out a plastic bag to Siobhan.

'I'm not taking that,' says Siobhan, lifting her hands up and away from it. 'I don't want it, and I know she doesn't want it, she wants nothing to do with you.'

A little muscle ticks in Siobhan's jaw as she blocks the doorway. I'm only a couple of feet away, but she doesn't glance at me once, or give any indication I'm there.

I type to Cam,

Yes please, I'd like that.

The reply comes:

Sure thing. What's your address?

My heart pounds, and not just because Diane is standing so close to me, as my message rushes away.

'Seriously,' continues Siobhan. 'She doesn't want it, and I want you to leave right now.'

'She needs to check her phone is working,' says Diane.

'She doesn't want to see you, Diane,' Siobhan says. 'I'm not going to tell you again.'

'I have something to tell her, it's very important.'

'You can't, and if you come here again, or I see you hanging around, I'll call the police.'

Cam sends me a final smiley face emoji, just as Siobhan closes the door in Diane's face. We both peek through the stained glass as Diane walks away, the plastic bag hanging from one hand.

When we're both sure she's gone, I lean against the door. I feel exhausted, and I didn't even speak to her.

'Thank you,' I tell Siobhan. 'You did brilliantly.'

My only worry is that Diane will come back again, and Siobhan won't be around.

But when she's due to leave, Siobhan has misplaced her travel card so she hasn't gone when Cam arrives. He stands on the doorstep looking a bit bashful in that threadbare grey jacket, his navy knitted tie pulled down from his shirt collar. The battered leather satchel hangs from his shoulder.

'Hey,' he says.

Just seeing him makes me happy, and the shy smile on his face suggests he feels the same.

'Everything okay?' He kisses me on the cheek and I smell his aftershave. 'She hasn't come back?'

'Siobhan did a great job of telling her to never darken this doorstep again, and she sloped off with her tail between her legs.'

'And you?' He squeezes my shoulders. 'You're okay?'

Cam's concern is lovely to see, but slightly embarrassing in front of Siobhan. 'I'm absolutely fine.'

He nods gravely, but studies me to make sure I'm not putting on a brave face for his benefit. Satisfied I'm not, he goes over to Siobhan, hand stretched out.

'Hi,' he says. 'I'm Cameron.'

We've talked about her at length, but I realize I should formally introduce them. 'Cameron, this is my nanny, Siobhan. Siobhan, Cameron.' And I add quickly, 'Cam's a friend.'

It's somehow important to me that these two people, both of whom I've come to depend upon in different ways, like each other.

'I've heard a lot about you,' Cam tells her, and that makes me tense, because I think I told him that I almost fired Siobhan. 'Good to finally meet you!'

As self-effacing as usual, Siobhan barely meets his eye when she shakes his hand. Cam turns in a circle, looking at all the windows in the room.

'Have you changed the locks?' He slides the patio doors open and shut, checking the lever on the lock. 'You said she got into your house.'

'The front door was left open that night, and she walked in, is what I think happened. I don't think Diane is the breaking-in type.'

'To look at her, you wouldn't think she was violent, but she attacked your father. Better to be safe than sorry.'

My eyes slide quickly to Siobhan, who looks shocked. She hasn't heard any of this before.

'She attacked your father?' she asks, and Cam grimaces because he knows he's put his foot in it.

'Attacked is maybe putting it a bit strong,' I say quickly. 'She gave him a bit of a shove. Why don't I make us some tea?'

As I pour the tea, I tell Siobhan about the night of the party, when I'm certain Diane came in the house, and what happened at the restaurant. While I'm doing that, Cameron introduces himself to Amber.

'May I?' He asks to pick her up. Maybe it's because he's a GP, but it's obvious he has a natural way with kids; Amber takes to him immediately.

Siobhan watches carefully as he plays with my daughter, and I'm grateful that she's so protective. 'But if she did those things, why would she make you food?'

'It's probably nothing, but I'm glad you never ate it,' says Cam with a shrug.

It takes me a moment to realize what he's getting at. 'You think she poisoned it?'

'I think it's something you should consider.'

The idea never once crossed my mind. Diane is clearly confused and damaged, but trying to poison me and my family is a whole different level of crazy, and the possibility makes me shudder.

'I still think she's just going to fade away,' Cam insists, because maybe he realizes he's scared me. 'But the next time she turns up here, call the police.'

'When I told her that's what I was going to do, she looked shocked,' Siobhan says.

'You did really well, Siobhan.' To me, Cam says, 'It's not ideal that you're here on your own of an evening.'

It's not ideal when you throw your husband out, no, but there's little I can do about that.

But then Siobhan suggests, 'I can move in.' Cam and I look at each other in surprise. 'It doesn't have to be forever, just for as long as you want me here.'

'It's kind of you to offer,' I tell her. 'But it's really not necessary.'

'I mean it, because I can see how upset you are about everything,' Siobhan insists. 'When Diane turned up earlier, you nearly jumped out of your skin. To be honest, I've been staying at a friend's flat in Wanstead and have been looking to move out for a while. Staying here would give me time to find somewhere else.'

Cameron raises his eyebrows, as if to say, *that's really not a bad idea.*

She's right, Diane has really spooked me and there are two spare bedrooms, so there's plenty of space. But it was only days ago that I was going to sack the poor girl and I don't want her to feel suffocated by working *and* living here. 'You'll soon get tired of being with me and Amber.'

'It doesn't have to be forever, and if it gives you peace of mind...'

It's undeniable that I would feel safer if there was someone here with Amber and me.

Picking up Amber's floppy rabbit and giving it to her, Cam asks, 'What do you think?'

I'm not sure I want Siobhan here, particularly if Sean and I are going to try to patch up our differences, but she showed a cool head when Diane came to the door earlier, and would be a reassuring presence.

'Well, if you don't mind, Siobhan. We can try it for a month or so, until you manage to find someplace else.'

'I can move in tomorrow, if you want. My friend will understand, she's got a boyfriend, so she'll be happy to see me go.'

To my surprise, I'm actually relieved. The idea of having someone here makes me feel immediately more safe.

'This is… what's the big word, Amber… synchronicity.' Cam glances at his watch and places my daughter on the floor. 'I'd better get off.'

'Is everything all right?'

'Yeah, sure.' But there's a tension behind his smile, he looks like he wants to tell me something but Siobhan being here is possibly holding him back. 'I should get home.'

'Of course,' I tell him.

'Good to meet you, Siobhan. Take care of Hannah.' He turns to me. 'And good luck with your television appearance. I'd love to watch, but we don't have a TV at the surgery. I'll be thinking of you.'

When he's gone, I pick up Amber – it's nearly time for her bath, and then I'll put her to bed – and Siobhan finishes her tea.

'I'd better be going as well.'

'Did you find your travel card?'

She holds it up. 'In my pocket the whole time.' Then she looks at me uncertainly. 'I don't have to move in, if you don't want me to.'

'No, it sounds like a good plan.'

Having her here will give me an opportunity to get to know her better. I feel that I've misjudged Siobhan in the past; behind that sometimes icy exterior is a warm and caring person. And it will undoubtedly be good for Amber too.

Only a few days ago, I was dead set on getting rid of her, and now here she is on the verge of moving in. It's funny, the hairpin turns life takes.

'Let's do it.'

Then Siobhan says, 'I like him.'

'Who, Cam?' I must be blushing, because she gives me a rare smile. 'I know what it looks like, but he's just an old friend who's helping out while Sean is…'

'Of course.' Siobhan picks up her phone and plops it in her bag. 'He seems very nice, Mrs Godley, and he obviously thinks the world of you. It's good that he makes you happy.'

'He's married and I'm married,' I tell her quickly, trying to close down the conversation.

Pulling her bag over her shoulder, Siobhan says, 'My parents were married for years, but they were never right for each other. Dad was in love with someone else the whole time.'

'That's sad,' I say.

'Yeah.' Her gaze drifts as she thinks about it. 'And their marriage just…'

'What?' I ask, when she doesn't finish the thought.

Her focus comes back to me. 'Ended.'

I've never heard her say anything about her family background, and now I know why. 'I'm sorry to hear that.'

'So if you like each other, Mrs Godley, then I say, go for it.'

'Mrs Godley makes me sound ancient. Please call me Hannah.'

'And call me Shiv,' she says. 'Only Dad calls me Siobhan.'

'Shiv.' I nod. In the past, getting her to talk about herself has been like getting blood from a stone, but I feel like we've made a breakthrough. 'How's your grandfather doing now, by the way?'

'He's on the mend, thank you for asking. I'll get here early on Monday, so you can get ready for your TV show.'

'Thanks, Shiv.' It feels strange calling her that, but I guess now that she's going to be my employee *and* my lodger, I should get used to it.

30

The building that houses the *Morning Brew* studio and production offices is a warren of corridors. I've been there several times for meetings, and to record other shows, but if I had to find my way around it on my own I'd get lost within minutes. So when the cab drops me outside reception, a young woman with a clipboard runs over to meet me.

'Hi, Hannah.' Her big smile suggests I'm the only person in the world she wants to see at that moment. 'I'm Christi, one of the production assistants!'

She presses her ID to a keypad on a security gate and leads me into the depths of the building. I've been on TV many times, but this regular slot is a massive opportunity, a chance to become familiar to a huge and loyal TV audience, so I'm very nervous.

'Everyone's thrilled to have you on the show,' Christi says as she leads me quickly down one corridor and along another. There's always a buzzy energy behind the scenes of live television, with people rushing back and forth making sure the show runs smoothly. It's just gone on-air, and on a monitor I can see the presenters laughing about something on the famous *Morning Brew* sofa.

'Simon and Maria asked me to tell you that they're looking

forward to your appearance – the first of many, we hope! – and said to make a big fuss of you.'

I met them briefly when I came in for a meeting, and they were both very friendly and enthusiastic, and we hit it off straight away.

Christi leads me into one of the green rooms, where guests who are appearing on the show wait before they go on-air.

'Would you like a coffee while you're waiting?' she asks, and I politely decline. I don't want to be sitting on-air with my legs crossed tightly because I'm busting to go to the loo. 'I'm going to leave you here for a couple of minutes before we get you to make-up.' She takes sheets of paper from her clipboard. 'These are the calls we'll be taking this morning.'

It's the fact sheets about the callers who'll be on the show. With a quickening pulse, I shuffle through them. One woman is pregnant by her on-off boyfriend and doesn't want him to have anything to do with the child. Another caller wants help with his addiction to online gambling, and there's a man who can't stop self-harming. I read all the names more than once.

'Just to confirm,' I ask her. 'All of these people have been checked out?'

'We may not identify them on-screen,' Christi tells me, even though I already know this. 'But we insist they give us their real names.'

'And you won't be putting anyone else on-air?' I ask, because at the back of my mind is the fear that somehow Diane will slip through the vetting procedure in an attempt to humiliate me all over again.

'Only the people on those sheets.'

'And when these people called into the show, none of them asked about me, or made any reference to me in any way?'

Christi frowns. She must think that my new job has already gone to my head. 'No, should they?'

'No, there's no reason.' I smile. 'When am I going on?'

'You'll be on-air in twenty minutes. I'd say good luck, but you don't need it, I just know you're going to be a big part of the *Morning Brew* family for a long time to come.'

When Christi leaves, I reread the information about each caller to make sure I've got everything covered. The one thing I've learned about live broadcasting is that the discussion can often shoot off in unexpected directions.

But I keep getting distracted because my phone buzzes with texts and emails. One comes in just as I'm looking at the screen. It's from Cam and says,

Knock 'em dead xx

Just looking at his message makes me feel calmer. But I don't want to be constantly interrupted, so I turn off the phone and drop it in my bag.

On a screen on the wall, Simon and Maria are larking about in the studio kitchen with the show's resident chef, who's waving an aubergine. Then the reality hits me that I'm going to be on the show in just a few minutes. It feels like a dream come true, but I've got to impress. By the time Christi pops her head back into the room and invites me to make-up, I've read the sheets several times, and made notes. There's nothing more I can do.

She leads me down a rabbit run of more corridors, turning left and then right, and right again, and slams through a pair of fire doors.

'I don't know how you don't get lost,' I tell her.

Christi laughs. 'You'll be running along these corridors blindfolded after you've been doing the show a few weeks.'

We come into a dressing room, where there's a row of chairs in front of mirrors. A woman in a clear visor waits with a brush in her hand and a pot of face powder.

'Don't worry,' she says brightly when she sees how nervous I am. 'I'm not going to be doing any dental work. We just don't want you looking hot and bothered under the studio lights.'

Inviting me to sit in the nearest chair, she places a gown over me, and dabs at my face with the brush.

A moment later, Christi comes back into the room. 'Hannah, there's a telephone call for you.'

'For me?' I haven't given anyone the production office number at the studio.

'They say it's urgent.' The call is inconvenient, I'm due on-air in less than five minutes.

'Tell whoever it is I'll call them back after the—'

'It's your nanny.' There's something in Christi's tense smile that makes me alarmed. 'I think you should take it.'

A moment later, I'm following her to a room with a phone in it, and cursing myself for turning off my mobile. When I pick up the handset, Christi stands behind me looking grave.

'Hello?'

'Oh, Mrs Godley.' Siobhan sounds tearful and afraid. She's talking so quickly and her words are so garbled that for a moment I don't understand what she's saying. 'I'm so sorry!'

'Slow down, Siobhan.' I have to speak over her because she's talking too fast. 'You're not making any sense.'

'She's gone.' Siobhan sucks down a deep breath. 'Amber is *gone*.'

They were at the shops, she says. In a supermarket. She looked away just for a second, a split second, and Amber was in the buggy behind her, but when she turned back...

What she's saying makes me feel sick. 'When did this happen?'

'Half an hour, forty minutes ago, maybe. We've been looking. I thought she just wandered off.'

Amber can't have just wandered off, she's barely able to toddle more than a couple of yards. 'Where are you now?'

'I'm still here. We've been looking for her everywhere, but she's not... I can't find her. She's not here!'

My blood runs cold, my heart hammers in my chest. 'The police...'

'They're here,' she says in a strangled voice. I've never heard her sound so emotional, so distraught. 'They're going to keep looking, but I've got to go home because they say someone needs to be there.'

I don't understand why she didn't tell me earlier; she should have called as soon as it happened, I should be there.

'I'm coming now,' I tell her quietly.

When I put the phone down, I turn to Christi, who must see how stunned I am. I'm meant to be on-air in a few minutes, we're only feet away from the studio where it's being broadcast.

'My baby.' A tight band of steel tightens around my chest. 'I need to go.'

'Of course,' Christi tells me gently. 'I'll order you a car.'

My first instinct is to apologize. 'I'm so sorry.'

Morning Brew was meant to be my big break, but there's no way I can stay.

Amber is gone, somebody's taken her, and I can't be here.

31

'Please hurry,' I tell the driver as I fumble with my phone in the back of the cab.

I yearn for Siobhan to call me back to tell me Amber's been found, she's safe, or that there's been some foul-up in communication; Sean's taken her without letting me or Siobhan know. In my heart I know it's not true, he's not just going to grab her in a supermarket when Siobhan's back is turned, but I'm clutching at straws.

When I try to call him to find out, he doesn't answer.

'Sean,' I say urgently when the call goes to voicemail. 'It's Hannah. Do you have Amber? If you do, please let me know. Call me straight back. Let me know she's okay, yes?'

As soon as I end the call, I know it was a mistake to ring him, because now he'll be worried too, and because I know he hasn't got Amber.

I know all too well who's taken her.

The windows are open in the cab, there's a breeze blowing inside, but the air is scorching and the chemical smell of the pine freshener that swings crazily from the rear-view mirror makes me feel nauseous. All I can think about is the things Diane could be doing to Amber. This is my fault for encouraging her to think of me as a friend and then believing I could just dismiss her from my life.

One thing is clear, she's dangerous – she proved that when she pushed Dad down the stairs at the restaurant – and my chest almost bursts at the thought that she's got my daughter. It's been over an hour since Amber was taken, and anything could have happened in that time.

The phone rings, it's Siobhan, and I blurt out, 'I'm nearly home, just a couple of streets away. Is she there? Tell me she's back.'

The driver watches me closely in the rear-view mirror. He must see the tears of terror and frustration on my cheeks, hear the panic in my shrill voice.

'I'm at home with a pair of police officers,' Siobhan says.

'There's no point in you being at home, she's not going to be there,' I snap. 'You need to be looking for her. I know where she may be.'

'They want to talk to you,' Siobhan says quietly, and I hear voices in the background.

'Tell them I know who's got her.'

'Who?' she asks in surprise.

'Diane, of course.' We're so close to my house now, driving quickly along the tangle of streets near mine. 'I know where she lives, I can't remember her address exactly, but I've been there. As soon as I get back I'll take them.'

My fear is that Diane has no intention of taking Amber to her house, because she'll know it's the first place the police will go. Her intention may be to run away with her, smuggle her abroad, or even – I place a hand to my mouth to swallow the acid bile that surges into my throat – maybe even kill her. Has that ultimate act of revenge always been her endgame? Her brother is dead, and now Amber must suffer the same fate.

'The police say we can discuss it when you're back,' she tells me.

'Discuss it? Amber is missing, Siobhan,' I shout into the phone. 'My little girl is gone!'

I don't want to blame Siobhan, she must be feeling awful about what happened, but it's hard not to feel angry. Amber was in her care; her first priority must always be to keep her safe, and I simply don't understand how such a thing can have happened. She shouldn't have taken her eyes off my daughter, not for a single second.

'Hang on a moment, Mrs Godley,' she says. I don't want her to go, I want her to stay on the phone until I get home – we're so close, just round the corner – but I can hear her talking to someone on the other end.

'Siobhan, are you there? Please speak to me,' I say, but then I hear raised voices, and the phone goes dead. 'Hello, Siobhan, are you there?'

'This is the street, yeah?' says the driver, as I keep repeating her name into the dead phone. We're just turning onto it now, and I fight the impulse to jump out and run the last few hundred yards. But as we come round the corner there's some kind of commotion going on outside my house. Leaning forward between the front seats, I see Siobhan struggling with Diane, Amber between them; a pair of police officers are rushing out of the house.

'Pull over!' I scream at the driver and within a moment I'm out of the car and running. Just ahead of me, Siobhan manages to pull a crying Amber from Diane's grip, as the police grab and restrain her.

'Siobhan!' I shout, in a flood of tears. She's heading to the house, but as soon as she sees me, she rushes over, so that I can grab Amber and hold her tight. The both of us are sobbing as we hurry towards the house.

'Hannah!' Diane has seen me too, and she tries to get my attention. 'I haven't been able to speak to you!'

'Go away!' I scream at her over my shoulder. 'Just stay away!'

'Your phone isn't working,' Diane shouts, as one of the officers pulls her away. 'I need to speak to you, Hannah. Please, it's very important.'

Her eyes swivel wildly in her head as she's led to a patrol car. The other officer stands between us, shielding me and Amber. I don't want to hear her voice, I don't want to see her, the sight of her makes my blood run cold.

'Hannah, please!' is the last thing I hear her say as the car door slams, and I hurry inside with Amber in my arms.

32

The first thing I do when we get inside is check Amber for injury: bruises, cuts, any signs of assault. She's crying because she's upset, tired and hungry and bewildered, but physically she seems fine, thank God.

'We should get her to a Safe Centre, where she can be properly examined,' says a police officer as I walk up and down, holding her tight, talking to her, trying to calm my little girl.

Right at this moment, I've no intention of letting her go. 'She seems okay.'

'A doctor should look her over,' says the second officer. 'For your peace of mind, and to gather evidence.'

Walking to the window, I look out and see the patrol car still parked at the kerb. Another pair of officers stand beside it talking into their radios. In the back of the car, I can see the dark outline of Diane's profile.

'What happened?' I ask Siobhan, who's standing very still in the hallway with her arms clutched tightly around her. She looks pale and shaken.

'While I was on the phone to you, I looked out of the window and saw her stood with Amber at the top of the street, watching the house.'

'She was coming here?' one of the officers asks.

'She was just standing there, as if she was waiting for a bus,' says Siobhan. 'I didn't want to take the chance that she would go, so I rushed outside. It all happened so fast.'

'Thank you.' I'm grateful for her quick thinking, because Diane may well have slipped away without anyone seeing her. 'But what I really want to know is how she managed to take her in the first place.'

Siobhan takes a quivering breath. 'I'm so sorry, I was in the Tesco on the high street, and Amber was in the buggy beside me, and I turned my back to get a sandwich from one of the chiller cabinets, and then my phone rang… I thought I was only turned away for a couple of seconds.'

She's trembling, I can see how upset she is about what's happened, so I bite my lip. The main thing is, Amber is safe in my arms. It's a mystery why Diane came back here with her, but who can fathom what goes on in the mind of that damaged and dangerous woman? At the window, I once again look at the silhouette in the back of the police car, and get the feeling that she's looking back at me.

'Did she say anything?' one of the officers says. Her name badge says she's PC Todd.

'*Get off me, you bitch*, stuff like that,' Siobhan says. It's odd to think of Diane swearing, I've never heard her do it, but she seems to have completely lost her mind. 'She wouldn't let go, she had Amber by the arms, and for one moment I thought she was going to wrench her away. But I wasn't going to let go, I couldn't, because we were beside the road and she could have just thrown her into it. I honestly think she would have done it, too.'

Amber could have gone under a car – it only takes an

instant. The thought of it makes me feel sick, and I have to place a hand over my mouth in case I throw up.

'But it was only seconds, really, because the police came outside and then you arrived.'

PC Todd offers a hand to steady me. 'Do you want to sit down?'

'I'm so sorry for losing her,' says Shiv. 'I don't know what I would have done if...'

She looks stricken, and I tell her, 'Come here.'

Placing Amber in her chair, I hold out my arms to Siobhan. It takes a moment for her to respond, but then she shuffles forward and lets me hug her. She feels stiff against me at first, maybe she's holding back because of my earlier anger, but after a few seconds her head rests heavily on my shoulder, and her arms tighten around my waist.

'Thank you,' I whisper into her ear. 'For saving Amber.'

When we've finished, the male officer, PC Carlton, says, 'Your nanny says you know the woman who took your daughter?'

Outside, the police car pulls from the kerb and drives away.

'Her name is Diane. Diane Clemence.'

'And do you have any idea why this person would want to take your daughter?'

'Because she's not well, clearly,' I tell him. But I know that's not a good enough answer. In trying to protect my reputation, I allowed Diane to get too close to my family, and it's time to admit the truth, or as much of it as I dare. 'She blames me... for something she says I did to her brother a long time ago, and about which she's completely wrong.'

Cameron is right, that photo of us and Martin doesn't prove anything. All it does is put us in the same bar. I should have gone to the police much earlier.

'She phoned a radio show I was on and made a threat against me.' Amber squirms in the chair and Siobhan goes over and picks her up. 'I stupidly thought that if I showed her a bit of kindness and empathy, she'd go away. She keeps saying we're friends, but she's been harassing me.'

Then I tell them about the mirror, and how she turned up at the bar. 'She pushed my father down some stairs at a restaurant. He's old and frail, and she could have seriously hurt him.'

PC Carlton looks up sharply. 'Did you press charges?'

'Nobody saw her do it,' I tell them in frustration. 'But she admitted she was at the restaurant. It's like she just... blanks out all the bad things she does.'

'What did she accuse you of doing to her brother?' asks PC Todd. I'm standing with my hands on my hips, building up the courage to tell them Diane's accusation, when my phone rings. It's Sean, calling me back.

'It's my... husband,' I tell the police officers.

Carlton gestures, go ahead.

'Where is my daughter?' Sean asks as soon as I connect the call.

'Don't worry,' I tell him. 'It was just a misunderstanding.'

'What the hell is going on, Hannah?' he says. 'You left a message accusing me of taking her and pleading with me to bring her back, so something's happened.'

'Everything's fine,' I tell him, and can't help adding, 'it's nice of you to call me back, finally.'

'I'm out of town,' he says.

Turning away from the officers, who are talking quietly with each other, I say, 'Having a lovely time, I presume.'

'It's business,' he says indignantly. 'Don't change the subject, you gave me a fright.'

'It's nothing you have to worry about. It was a false alarm. Look, the police are here, I'll call you back and explain properly later.'

'That was your husband?' asks PC Todd when I've finished the call.

'He's out of London on work,' I say, feeling self-conscious.

'In the light of what you told us, we should talk to your father,' she says, writing in her notebook.

'Do you have to?' Dad won't thank me for dragging him into this. 'He didn't see whoever pushed him.'

Carlton frowns. 'You're now saying it may not have been her?'

'I'm sure it was her. She stole my little girl.' I feel my chest tighten with frustration. 'What more do you need?'

'If Diane Clemence is responsible for trying to injure your elderly father, it's important we speak to him.'

'He lives up north,' I tell him quietly. 'But I can give you his number. What will happen to Diane?'

'She'll be interviewed, and we'll search her home. We'll also need a statement about your relationship with her.'

'You'll keep her in custody, surely?'

'Not necessarily,' says Todd gently. 'Only if we believe she'll continue to be a threat to you and your family, or anybody else.'

'What happens when she gets out?' I say in alarm. 'I don't want her to come near me or my daughter again.'

'If she's stalking you, and in the circumstances I think that's pretty clear, it won't be difficult to get a restraining order. You and your husband don't have to worry about that.'

'He doesn't live here,' I tell them. 'We're... estranged. But Siobhan is here, she's moved in.'

'We should get Amber checked over, and then we'll need you to make a statement about your relationship with this woman.'

'I don't *have* a relationship with her,' I tell him. 'It's not like she's a friend.'

'But earlier you said you paid her some attention, and that she considers you a friend,' says PC Carlton.

'And what a mistake that was,' I tell him bitterly.

33

It doesn't take long for the press to find out what happened. Someone at *Morning Brew* or connected to the police must have tipped them off, because my mobile starts ringing as I'm coming back from Amber's health check – she's totally fine, thank God – and after giving a statement at the local station.

The reporters speak in soft, sympathetic tones and call me Hannah as if we're good friends, as they try to find out more about the morning's events. It's not like I'm a big celebrity or anything, but I've been on TV and radio numerous times, and that makes me fair game for the tabloids. All I can do is tell them that the matter is in the hands of the police, so I'm unable to make any statement.

But one of the journalists asks me if it's true that I've separated from my husband, and that shocks me, because I've no idea how they got hold of that information. If they think the story has legs, it's only going to be a matter of time before they discover the circumstances of the split. I long to phone Izzy to warn her not to talk to reporters. Usually, I'd call her like a shot, but that's not possible now.

The producers at *Morning Brew* are sympathetic about what happened, but they may not be so understanding if all the salacious details of my marriage split are splashed across the front pages. I'm meant to be an agony aunt, after all, and they may decide I'm not the right person to give other people advice on how to surmount their problems if my own personal life is a train wreck.

At least Shiv is living here now. The following day, she comes back with a bag and a rucksack and moves into the spare room next to mine.

'You're sure about this?' I ask her once again, because she probably feels she sees more than enough of me already.

Shiv places her bag on the bed with the same care that she does everything. 'I don't want you and Amber to be here on your own, Hannah. Thanks for the opportunity to stay.' She presses her hands into the mattress. 'It's so much more comfortable than my old room.'

I've got to admit, it's good to have someone to chat to and watch a bit of television with in the evenings. But maybe Shiv feels self-conscious, or she just wants a bit of privacy, because at eight-thirty she goes to her room.

One thing's for sure: it's a relief to know there's someone in the house, even though I've had the locks changed on the doors and windows. Looking down at the empty street one last time from the bedroom window, and even though I know Diane is still in police custody, I feel more at ease knowing that Shiv is just next door. I've brought Amber into my bed tonight, she's going to sleep next to me. When I'm finally under the covers, I pick up my phone and text Cameron.

> Hi. Do you mind me texting this late?

A couple of minutes later, I get the reply…

No, go away! (Only joking!!) I've been
thinking of you. Everything OK?

Shiv is here now, so that's good. Can I ring u?

There's a pause before he replies,

Better not... Sorry.

Maybe it's because I'm exhausted after a traumatic day,
but his reply is a bitter disappointment. I've gotten used to
our evening chats on the phone, and it's frustrating that I
can't just chat to Cam any time I want.

But I understand it's not fair on him, or his wife.

So I reply,

No probs. Just wanted to check in.

How're things with Siobhan?

Good, it's a relief not to be in the house alone!

I'm pleased. I'll try to come and see you
tomorrow... there's something I need to tell you...

Ok, now you've got me worried!!

No need to worry!!!!

It looks like he's writing something, because the ellipsis at
the bottom of the screen pulses. Maybe whatever it is he wants

to tell me can't wait, and he's writing a mammoth message to explain. But when it finally drops into my phone, it just says,

Honestly, don't be. Xx

I'm so sorry for contacting you so late. XX

The reply comes,

Please stop with the sorries (sorrys?!). You have nothing to be sorry about. Take care. Xx

And I say,

Night. Xx

And then I place the phone on the bedside table, switch off the lamp and turn to face Amber. It seems crazy that I'm texting a married man late at night, the world feels like it's been turned on its head, and it makes me think once again of Sean. He's not been in touch since after Amber's abduction. I don't even know where he's staying. What with everything that's happened, I haven't had the headspace to consider where my marriage – if I still have one – goes from here. We're going to have to talk about it soon, Sean and I.

A couple of days later, Amber's eating wholegrain toast and banana slices – both foodstuffs squelched into a pasty goo between her fingers and all over her high chair – and Shiv has gone to see her grandfather at the hospital, when the police come back.

'Thank God for you, my beautiful, precious girl,' I tell

Amber gently, as I do my best to wipe her hands and face. She's my world and I can't even contemplate what it would have been like if Diane hadn't brought her back, if she had never come back... Just the thought of it hits me again like an aftershock.

When the front doorbell rings, it's the same two officers who were present on the day of Amber's abduction, PC Carlton and PC Todd. They've come to tell me that Diane was held for twenty-four hours and then let out on bail, but is forbidden to come anywhere near me. She'll likely be charged with abduction.

It's a shock to know that Diane's been released. I understand that they can't keep her locked up indefinitely, but even with a restraining order in place, I'm not going to feel comfortable with the idea that she could be out there somewhere, waiting for me and Amber to leave the house. And this time she could have a knife hidden in that clamshell bag of hers. We've all read the terrible stories about how cases of stalking escalate into violence and murder.

'What did she say in the interview?' I ask, as Shiv comes in the front door. 'Did she say why she did it?'

The two officers have this infuriating way of glancing at each other before answering, as if neither of them wants to be responsible for giving me bad news.

'All she said was that she was frustrated at being unable to get in contact with you,' PC Todd says. 'You didn't answer the door, and she couldn't get through on the phone.'

'Of course not, because I blocked her.'

'She said that she was forced to take Amber to get your attention,' says PC Carlton. 'Because she wants to tell you something.'

'She's mad,' I tell them. What kind of person would use such an excuse to justify snatching a child?

'She point-blank refused to tell us anything else,' says PC Todd. 'I imagine the enormity of what she did probably hit home and she panicked, then tried to make things better by bringing her back to you.'

'She insists she'll only talk to you about it,' says PC Carlton. Shiv looks alarmed. 'You mustn't.'

'I don't want to speak to her,' I agree.

Carlton takes a computer tablet from a pouch. 'I can assure you that will never happen.'

'What about her house, did you search it?' I ask. 'She may have a journal or a diary or a laptop. She might have written something down about what she was planning to do with Amber. A travel itinerary or something?'

'It was searched... in a fashion.' The two officers glance at each other again.

'What does that mean, *in a fashion*?'

'Our colleagues went to her house, and it was a bit of a mess. I think the council is getting involved in that side of things.'

Carlton dabs at the screen of the tablet and comes to stand by me. 'We thought you'd want to see this, it's the footage taken from security cameras in the supermarket when your little girl was taken.'

Shiv comes over as the officer opens a video file. The footage comes from a camera positioned high up. At the top of the screen is a timestamp, its numbers changing at a furious speed. Below it, Shiv pushes Amber's stroller down the middle of a long aisle, looking in the chiller cabinets.

'I went in to get a sandwich,' she explains.

On the footage, she pauses at one of the cabinets, her hands still resting on the handles of the stroller, and then bends over to look more closely at the contents of a shelf.

'Look up there.' Todd points at the screen, and I see a figure lurking at the top of the aisle. My heart leaps, because it's Diane watching Shiv and Amber from behind a display. Shiv lets go of the stroller and walks to the chiller cabinet. Her back is turned from Amber now, and I feel sick. I know what's going to happen, but my stomach cramps in anticipation. Beside me, Shiv tenses too. On the screen, she reaches into a pocket, and takes out her phone and looks at it. With a final cursory glance over her shoulder at Amber, she puts it to her ear to speak.

'It was a friend,' Shiv says. 'I wasn't even going to answer it, but...'

While Shiv's distracted on the phone, Diane walks quickly down the aisle, and as she passes the stroller, she scoops Amber into her arms and hurries off. A moment later, Shiv puts the phone away and turns to the buggy – to see Amber is gone.

'You see,' says PC Todd sympathetically. 'That's what we always try to tell people. It only takes a single second.'

It's history now, Amber is safe and sound, but watching this footage still makes me uneasy. Shiv looks urgently up and down the aisle. She turns one way and then the other, you can practically see the panic on her face, because my daughter is gone. Shiv runs towards the bottom of the image and disappears into another aisle.

'If you'd headed the other way, you'd probably have seen her,' says PC Carlton. He opens another video file to show footage from a camera that shows Diane hurrying out through the sliding doors to the street, Amber in her arms.

'By the time Miss Linden approached a member of staff—'

'It was only a minute later,' Shiv interrupts.

'—Miss Clemence was already outside.'

There's more footage they can show me, they say, captured on different cameras. Shiv doesn't give much away, but I can tell she's upset; her breathing is heavy and her mouth twitches. I don't want to see any more anyway.

'That's enough,' I tell the officers.

The crazy thing is, I could have lost Amber forever if Diane hadn't inexplicably decided to bring her home. Was it to goad us, or did she intend some kind of showdown? She wanted to get my attention, she says; to talk to me. I guess we'll never know what about.

There's a knock on the door. I don't want to answer it in case it's a journalist, but a muffled voice calls, 'It's me.'

When I let Cam in, he gives me a big hug.

'Everything okay?' he asks and eyes the police. 'I hope I'm not interrupting.'

'We're just going,' says PC Carlton, turning to me. 'We'll keep you informed of any other developments. But rest assured, Miss Clemence is under strict instructions not to contact you in any way. If she does, she'll be rearrested.'

'Diane says she wants to speak to Hannah,' Shiv tells Cam tensely.

'You mustn't go anywhere near that woman,' Cameron tells me.

'Don't worry, I've no intention of doing that.'

I'd be mad to even consider it.

34

With Shiv and Cam here, I feel more relaxed than I have for days, even after finding out that Diane has been released on bail. Telling Cam about the video footage from the supermarket, we discuss how desperate Diane must have been to do such a thing.

'I'm sick of talking about her,' I tell them both finally.

'She's history,' says Cam. 'Put her behind you.'

'I'm starving.' Looking at the time, it's almost six. 'Let's get a takeaway.'

'Sounds great.' He reaches into his satchel. 'I forgot, I brought this, I thought it might take the edge off your hideous week.'

It's a bottle of wine, which he places on the kitchen island. There's an Indian takeaway around the corner, the food is always decent, and we each select a main dish to share, lamb, chicken and prawn, and a couple of sides, and I order a delivery on my phone.

Cam reaches into a pocket. 'Let me give you some money.'

But I shake my head. 'Too late, I've paid already. It's my treat, and anyway you brought a bottle.'

Shiv cracks the screw cap. Cam doesn't want any, of course, and she pours a single glass of wine.

'Aren't you having any?' I ask her.

'I've got a bit of a headache.' She frowns. 'I may have a small glass later.'

'Anyway.' Cam lifts a glass of lemonade in a toast. 'Here's to our merry little band.'

It doesn't take long for the takeaway to arrive, I hear the buzz of the moped as it pulls up outside, and Shiv takes plates and cutlery from the kitchen cupboards. We stand around the counter chatting as we serve ourselves from the plastic containers of curries and sleeves of naan and poppadoms, and it all smells fragrant and tasty. The white wine is crisp and cold.

'What's your story, Siobhan?' Cam asks as we sit eating. 'Where are you from?'

She glances up at him. 'My dad lives in London.'

'Oh,' I say in surprise. 'I thought you said he lived somewhere else?'

She swallows the korma she's eating and says, 'He lives here most of the time, but he's actually got a place on the Norfolk coast, it's practically on the beach.'

'Oh man, that sounds good,' says Cam. 'I wish I could get out of town more.'

'And how's your grandad?' I ask her. 'Is he... still in hospital?'

She nods, in that embarrassed way.

'Oh no, nothing too serious, I hope.' Cam tears off a piece of naan to dip it in his biryani. 'Is he okay?'

'I think he'll be all right.'

'He had a stroke,' I explain to Cam, because it's obvious that Shiv isn't going to elaborate. 'But he's on the mend, isn't that right, Shiv?'

She smiles at her plate. 'I hope so.'

'And how are you two getting on with each other?' Cam asks. 'It must be a little strange for you both, this new normal.'

The phrase irks me a bit. I don't want to give either of them the impression that it's going to be a long-term arrangement.

'It's early days.' I smile at Shiv. 'But it's working out fine, I think.'

'It's nice,' Shiv agrees, and goes back to her food. She eats quietly, using small, precise movements. When Cam finishes eating, he wipes his mouth with a napkin.

'I like being here. Thank you for having me.' He points at the empty plate. 'And the food was delicious.'

It doesn't take long for Shiv to pick up the plate – Cam lifts his arms from the table in surprise – and take it to the dishwasher.

'Siobhan… Shiv, you don't have to clear up everything as soon as we've finished.' I noticed earlier that she didn't start eating her own food until she had binned all the empty boxes and bags.

'I'm sorry,' she says over her shoulder. 'It's just the way I am.'

'You've got her well trained already,' Cam tells me.

When I've finished my food, she does the same thing. Puts the plate in the dishwasher, and then rinses out a cloth to wipe down the surface of the island. There's no point in telling her not to, because I know she'll just wait till I've left the room and do it anyway.

Cam watches her, amused and fascinated. 'Feel free to come and clean my house next,' he says, laughing.

'I'd better get Amber up for her bath,' I tell them, and lift her from her chair.

'I'll come up and help you in a minute,' Cam says, picking up my empty glass. 'But go ahead, I can't let Siobhan clear up by herself. She's making me feel bad.'

Cam and Shiv start a conversation as I climb the stairs, but they're speaking quietly and Shiv is running the tap, so I can't hear what they're talking about. Cam doesn't come upstairs for a quarter of an hour, and in the meantime I get Amber into the bath.

She splashes about happily, almost hidden by a towering mountain of bubbles. Her favourite bath toy is a tubular piece of rubber that fell off a bigger toy; she uses it to scoop water into multicoloured plastic cups, which we both pretend to drink from like we're enjoying afternoon tea.

'Cheers,' I tell her, touching my cup against hers.

'Gears,' she replies.

Afterwards, I wrap her tightly in a towel, and we go into my bedroom to get her into a sleepsuit. I've just snapped the last popper in place when there's a light knock on the door.

'Can I come in?' Cam asks, gesturing at the room.

'Of course.'

'I brought this up for you.' He steps inside, handing me a glass of wine. 'Thought you might need it.'

'It's very full,' I say.

'You only live once.'

When I take the glass from him, our fingers touch. I feel an odd sense of excitement that Cam is in my bedroom.

'It's spotless down there already. Shiv's like a cleaning machine, you've landed on your feet having her here.'

'I keep telling her she doesn't have to do it.' I gulp from the glass. 'She makes me feel slovenly.'

'She was telling me about her grandad,' he says, explaining

why it's taken him so long to come upstairs. 'And how you raced her to the hospital.'

'Sounds like you both had a good chat. You have to tell me your secret about how to get her to open up.'

'GP bedside manner and all that. Sometimes a chat is the best medicine, etcetera. I can be a silver-tongued devil when I want to be.'

'It must be that.' The truth is, I'm glad we're alone now because I'm anxious for him to reveal what he wanted to tell me. 'You mentioned in your text that there was something on your mind.'

Cam nods, but his smile is uncomfortable. 'It's nothing,' he says. 'Forget about it.'

'That's not fair, Cam.' I place Amber on the floor, where she starts playing with some toys she's left there. 'You know absolutely everything there is to know about me, but I know hardly anything about you.'

He grimaces. 'That's kind of true.'

Maybe it's the way his whole body seems to twist away from me, or the guarded expression on his face, but it makes me say, 'I take it back, I don't want to know.'

'No.' He takes a deep breath. 'You deserve to know… I want you to. I'm married, as you know, to a lovely lady called Penny.'

He sits heavily on the edge of the bed, on the side I usually sleep. The top I wear at night is beneath the pillow that he absently brushes with his fingers. Legs apart, elbows rested on his knees, he stares at the floor, and for a moment I think he's going to cry.

'We've been together five happy years. But Penny's not well, she's sick.' Tears sting his eyes when he looks up at me.

'It's cancer. And she's only going to get worse. I'm going to lose her, Hannah, she's going to die.'

He rubs his face with his open palms. Feeling self-conscious standing with a glass of wine, I put it down on a cabinet and sit beside him. I've been so wrapped up in my own problems, our conversation is always about how terrible things are for me, and all this time he's had to deal with this. It's no wonder he races off so quickly, and no wonder he doesn't want me to call of an evening.

'Cam, I'm so sorry.'

'Yeah, sorry.' He tries to smile, but his lips are clamped together in a thin line. 'That news always takes all the oxygen out of the room. I've had a lot of time to get used to the fact, but the crazy thing is, H, I'm a doctor. I spend every day helping other people get well, but I can't save my own wife. She's our age. It's obscene, it doesn't seem fair.' His face twists in pain. 'I'm going to lose her.'

His sudden forward movement as he drops his head into his hands makes the mattress springs move, so that we incline towards each other. Our shoulders touch, our arms and hips and thighs dip together. Heat comes off his body, I smell the lotion on his skin. We're so close that all he has to do is turn his head and I'll feel the warmth of his lips on mine. And if he does, if he wants to kiss me, I know I'll respond.

It won't be right, it'll be totally inappropriate, but I'll let it happen. Because I know how much I want him right now, and how I need him; how much I sense we need each other. But I can see how lost he is, how unmoored and troubled, and I know I'm being selfish again.

He's married; his wife is dying, for God's sake.

'I'm sorry.' His face lifts close to mine, his soft breath brushes my face. 'I just ruined the afternoon.'

'No, thank you for telling me. It… puts a lot of things in perspective.'

Maybe Cam's uncomfortable that we're sitting so close together on my bed, but he stands quickly. He's preoccupied and anxious as he looks down at the crumpled duvet and pillow. 'I should get going.'

'I'll come down with you,' I say, and stand.

'You get on with putting Amber to bed,' he suggests. 'I can manage.'

'We'll come and see you out,' I tell him, and he gives me a small smile.

But then the front door slams downstairs.

'Where is she?' I hear Sean's voice. 'Where's Hannah?'

35

When I come down, Sean is standing at the bottom of the stairs, with Siobhan – who answered the door – beside him.

'You've changed the locks, I couldn't get in.' The smile drops from his face as soon as he sees Cam. 'And who the hell is that?'

'Cameron is a friend,' I tell him, perhaps too defensively.

'I don't know him.' Sean makes a face. 'I've never seen him in my life.'

'He's an old university friend. We haven't seen each other for years.' I hand Amber to Shiv, who watches from the kitchen doorway. 'Do you mind taking her to bed?'

'Good to meet you, Sean.' Cam offers a hand, but Sean just stares at it.

'Didn't take you long to replace me, did it?' He smiles bitterly. Angry confrontation isn't Sean's style, but he gets sarcastic and sulky when things don't go his way. 'What were you doing upstairs together?'

'Just giving him a tour of the house,' I say, blushing. 'What are you doing here, Sean?'

'I live here,' he tells me, but he's still staring at Cam.

'Not any more you don't,' I say, raising my voice to bring

his gaze back to me. Maybe it's his sudden appearance, the wine, or the stress of everything, but I feel a headache thicken behind my eyes. 'You can't just turn up out of the blue without telling me.'

'My name's still on the mortgage last time I looked.'

'I can understand how upset you must be, Sean,' says Cam. 'But the main thing surely is that Amber is safe and unharmed.'

'Hey, *old university friend*,' Sean says, making quotation marks with his forefingers, 'this is between me and my wife.' He turns to me. 'Why have I never heard of this guy, and why is he suddenly here in *our* house?'

Cameron smiles amiably. 'I'm just looking out for Hannah.'

Ignoring him, Sean says to me, 'Shoulder to cry on, is he? Someone to moan to about your nasty husband?' When Shiv comes back downstairs, he says, 'Look at you all, one big happy family.'

I appreciate Cam's trying to help, but Sean's upset, and his being here is only going to make things worse, so I say, 'Thanks for coming round, Cam.'

He hesitates. 'You're sure you're going to be okay?'

'Yeah, she's going to be okay, fella,' snaps Sean. 'Because she's with her *husband*.'

Cam kisses me on the cheek and nods at Shiv. 'Nice to see you again, Siobhan. Take care.'

Standing behind Sean at the door, he gives me a surreptitious signal that he'll call.

'*Nice to see you again, Siobhan*,' Sean repeats when Cam's gone. 'Sounds like he's got his feet well and truly under the table.'

'Why are you here?' I ask him, changing the subject.

'I'm worried about my daughter.'

'Yes, someone took her. But she brought her back to the house within an hour. Amber never came to any harm, she's fine.'

'Who brought her back?' he asks. 'Who took her?'

'You remember Diane,' I say. 'The woman who came round the day after the party?'

'That odd woman who showed up here?'

'Yes, Sean,' I say acidly. 'The one you invited in.'

He sucks down a breath. 'I think you had better tell me what's going on, don't you?'

Shiv kneels in front of the washing machine, taking out a load she put in this morning. I think about asking her to leave us alone, but she knows almost everything already, so I tell Sean that Diane took Amber after getting it into her head that we were friends. What I don't tell him is that it was Diane who made me suspicious about his adultery in the first place.

He shakes his head, bewildered. 'But why is she doing this?'

'People get obsessions about people in the public eye, it sometimes happens.'

'Then why did you meet her at that café?'

'It was a mistake,' is all I say. 'And not one I'm going to repeat in a hurry.'

I sense Shiv listening as she quietly folds clothes on the floor.

'These odd people think you're going to fix them, to sort out their problems, and get angry when you can't.'

'Yes,' I tell him, because it's easier to do that than to tell the truth about Diane's grudge against me. 'You're probably right.'

'She can't get away with it,' he says. 'She can't just take our little girl.'

'It's in the hands of the police now.'

'She needs to be taught a lesson, given a fright,' Sean insists, 'or she'll come back and do something worse.'

'That's not going to help,' I tell him.

But his anger is building. 'Amber's not safe here.'

'That's not true, Sean.'

'It'll happen again.' Sean likes to think of himself as being laid-back, but his temper can go from nought to sixty when he doesn't get his own way. 'She'll come back, or another nutter will attach themselves to you, and the same thing will happen.'

'Shiv is here now, and together we'll provide Amber with a safe environment.'

'She's moved in?' Sean looks at Shiv in astonishment. 'Not so long ago, you couldn't wait to get rid of her.'

His statement makes me blush with shame, because of course it's true. But if his accusation makes Shiv uncomfortable, she doesn't show it, and she carries Amber's folded clothes across the hallway. 'I'll put these upstairs.'

'No, Shiv, wait.' I want her to hear what I'm about to tell Sean. The headache is really crashing against my skull. 'That may have been the case, yes, but it's certainly not true now. Shiv's been a rock since you've gone, she's been here for Amber and me, despite what you did... despite your advances.'

Sean cocks his head at her. 'You want to tell Hannah what really happened, Shiv?'

Shiv listens with her head bowed.

'What are you talking about?' I say.

'Yeah, I came in drunk, I was totally out of order, I admit it. But I wouldn't have tried it on if *she*—' Sean jerks a thumb at Shiv. 'Hadn't given me the come-on. Admit it, Shiv, you led me on, you were bang up for it.'

Shiv looks helplessly at me – he's gone too far now. Upset that I've discovered he'll throw himself at literally anyone, he's lashing out, trying to sow discord and distrust between us.

'I'd like you to leave,' I tell him in a low voice.

'Han, please.' He realizes he's gone too far and holds up his hands. 'We can work things out.'

'Not when you're being like this.'

'This is my house too,' he says petulantly.

'Sean.' All the stress of the last few days feels like a perfect storm. My head throbs, my thoughts are sluggish, and I can't handle his aggression. 'Please, just *go*.'

Sean glares at Shiv, and when he speaks again, it's more quietly. 'I keep getting journalists calling, they're all over me like flies. They want to know why we split up and say they'll pay good money. Maybe I should just come clean, tell them the truth, and earn myself a few quid.'

'If you do that, you wouldn't just be hurting me, but Izzy and Ollie, and Amber, too.' When he doesn't reply, I say, 'Let's talk later, when we've both calmed down.'

'Sure,' he says shortly and walks out.

When I've shut the door behind him, I look longingly at the white wine on the kitchen island. Despite my tiredness and headache, I'm going to go upstairs to get my glass and finish the bottle.

Shiv looks upset, her lashes flutter. 'It's not true,' she tells me.

'Of course it isn't. I'm very sorry for the things he said to you, he was out of order.'

'I think I'm going to go to my room,' she says. 'If that's okay.'

But I can't just let her leave without trying to reassure her. 'Shiv, for the record, I want to thank you for everything you've done for me, and if I've not done the right thing by you in the past, I apologize for that too. I'm glad you're here with me and Amber. *We're* grateful you're here for us.'

She smiles uncertainly and then goes upstairs.

36

When Shiv goes to bed in the evening, I unwisely sit in front of the TV and finish the bottle of wine. There's a film on, but my head is fuzzy and I barely register anything happening on the screen. My mind keeps looping back to the memory of Shiv's struggle with Diane in the street, Amber being pulled one way and then the other. Diane didn't look hysterical or angry, her lips were pressed together in a determined line, even as police officers rushed out of the house to detain her.

She took my daughter to get my attention, the police said, because she's desperate to talk to me; she wants to tell me something. Knowing Diane, she'll say anything to get to me, but I can't help wondering what could be so important to her that she would take my child.

The movie is finished, the credits are rolling, but already I can't remember a thing about it. All the stress and anxiety of the last few days must be catching up with me. I feel totally exhausted, my muscles ache with tiredness, my head feels heavy on my shoulders. Finally, I pick myself up off the sofa and stumble upstairs to bed.

As soon as my head hits the pillow I sleep, but it's fitful and filled with disturbing dreams. Sean shouts at me again, he paces so quickly back and forth in front of me that he's a vibrating blur when he moves; one moment he's so close to my face that I flinch, and then he's behind me, making me turn in a frantic circle. And then Cam appears and pulls off my duvet, flicking it up into the air so violently that it billows above me, spreading darkness. I try to snatch at it to cover myself, but my movements are slow, clumsy, and a cold breeze wafts over my exposed legs and stomach as it drifts down.

Despite the heat of the night, I'm freezing and shiver when he looms over me, his body dropping horizontally towards mine. His face shrouded in gloom, his hot breath brushes my cheeks and lips as his stubble grazes the slope of my neck. The weight of his body finally comes to rest on top of me, I feel his bare skin as he presses down. I try to speak, and he jerks up; his eyes peer into the darkness of the room. Because there's someone standing there.

And then Cam fades away, and all I can see is a figure at the end of the bed. Diane has Amber in her arms. She looks at me sadly, with pity, and I scream at her to *put her down, let her alone*. But Diane turns slowly away from me, so slowly that she barely seems to move at all, and I try to scrabble up, arms and legs windmilling against the loose bed sheet, which laps and splashes and sucks against my shaking body, refusing to let me rise. I'm hot now, burning in a fever, and my panicked heart pounds in my chest. *I can't get her back, I can't get my baby*.

And when I rear up in the dark, silent room, and my eyes snap open, there's still a figure at the end of the bed. It's a density, barely more solid than the darkness that surrounds it, because the shutters are closed, despite the fact I don't remember pulling them shut when I came to bed last night, exhausted. There's movement, but I can't tell if it's in the room or it's the ghostly shapes drifting across the surface of my eyes. Maybe I hear a faint scuffing sound, a soft tread on the carpet, the slightest sense of someone moving their weight from one leg to the other.

My breath rasps in my throat and blood rushes in my ears, as I try to clear my head and force my unseeing eyes to adjust to the pitch-black room.

Somebody's in the room; somebody's here. I *know* it's her, but I can't move. My arms and legs are heavy and stiff, my bare legs and stomach chilled to the bone.

And then the shape begins to expand above me and all around, pulsing out on every side like surf riding a wave, racing up the wall and the surface of the bed. I scrabble away from it in terror, kicking out my heels, because the dark wants to swallow me whole. Huddled against the headboard, I hug my knees against me as it races towards me, and—

My own scream pulls me suddenly out of the deep well of sleep, and I pivot forward as the final strangled sounds of my voice die away. Panting, blinking, squinting into the blackness. My eyes finally find focus, and light bleeds into the room at the edges of the shutters. The tall, straight lines of the dresser and wardrobe begin to reveal themselves in the gloom.

I'm awake. Finally, I'm awake. But I'm sure I wasn't dreaming. There was someone here. *She* was here.

There's movement on the landing, a creak, and I freeze in fear. But then light clicks on behind the half-open door. Usually, I keep the door closed, but I was almost insensible with tiredness last night. Did I close it, or just stumble into

the room and go straight to bed? And close the shutters too?
I don't remember doing either, but I must have before I fell
into bed. My brain is so fogged with sluggish sleep, and an
aching weariness.

Then there's a knock on the door and a shadow falls against
the wall beside it. 'Mrs Godley, are you okay? Hannah?'

It takes a moment for me to realize who it is: Shiv lives
here now. She's in the spare room. The door opens, throwing
more light into the room, and I look around wildly. The
room is empty.

When I swing my legs off the bed, my head throbs; my
mouth feels parched, it's been a long time since I've had such
a terrible hangover. I'm sweating, feverish, and wearing a tee–
shirt and knickers – I must have undressed, at least – and my
arms and legs are cold. The duvet hangs off the end of the bed.
It's been so hot this summer that every night I kick it away.

And then the panic returns. 'Amber!'

Stumbling past Shiv, I run to Amber's room. Every
movement makes my stomach lurch. 'She's here!'

'Who is?' Shiv stares at me.

To my relief, Amber is asleep. On her back, her arms and
legs flung out easily, eyes moving under the lids; she's asleep
and oblivious to my panic and distress. When I turn, Shiv
stands in the doorway.

'Check all the doors, I think she's here!'

'But she can't be,' she says.

'Please, just check the doors and windows.'

She looks at me doubtfully, but then leaves the room.

I spend a few moments trying to clear my head – it's been
a while since I've had a whole bottle of wine, and it's really
knocked me for six – and then close the door to Amber's

room. Downstairs, the patio door to the garden slides open, and then there's silence.

'Shiv?' I call at the top of the stairs. From the landing I can only see a tiny part of the kitchen, the light is on, but it's impossible to see the garden. 'Are you there?'

Walking down, I see her come in from the garden and slide the door shut. 'Why didn't you reply?'

'I'm sorry, I didn't hear you, I was checking outside,' she says. 'There's no one here.'

I'm still trembling. It's so hot still that the tee-shirt clings to my damp body, and my hair is plastered to my head. 'The security light… why didn't it come on?'

She looks at our black reflections in the sliding door. The sky, just about visible outside, is the colour of a fresh bruise. She shakes her head, as if I'm overreacting. 'I've no idea, but there's no one here. You don't… you don't look well. Would you like some Nurofen?'

Shiv locks the patio door and then goes to the cabinet where they're kept. The flip clock on the wall says it's four in the morning.

'She's driving me crazy,' I tell her. 'I'm dreaming of her.'

'It's no wonder you feel like this,' says Shiv as she fills a glass at the tap. 'You've had an upsetting few days.'

She hands me the glass and pills, and I gulp them down. My head pounds, I feel weary. There's no sign that anyone tried to break in, or that Diane was ever here, and yet the dream was so vivid.

'You must think I'm losing it.'

'You've been under a lot of strain. Go back to bed and get some sleep, and please don't worry about getting up tomorrow morning. I'll take care of Amber.'

'I don't expect you to look after her twenty-four-seven.'

'And I'm not going to,' she insists. 'But you need rest, and in the circumstances I'm more than happy to do it.'

The terror has passed, but I feel a hot surge of bile in my stomach and race to the bathroom.

37

It's gone Friday lunchtime when I finally manage to pull myself out of bed, trying not to think of the shape I saw in my bedroom last night. Diane has even poisoned my dreams now. When I stand, I feel dizzy, light-headed, exhausted, as if I haven't slept at all.

When I went back to bed at four, I fell straight back to sleep and slept all the way through the morning without having any more nightmares. A couple of times, as I drifted uneasily in and out of consciousness, I'm sure I woke up and heard Shiv speaking softly downstairs; to Amber, probably, or on the phone.

Standing at the kitchen island packing Amber's baby bag, Shiv looks up when I finally come downstairs. 'How do you feel?'

'I've felt better,' I say, catching a glimpse of myself in the mirror: I look pale and ill.

Kissing Amber on the top of her head, I lift her into my arms. She chats and laughs happily; at least my daughter doesn't have a care in the world.

'Sorry about last night.' It can't have been nice for Shiv to be woken in the dead of night by my shrieks.

'You don't have to apologize. I checked all the doors and

windows again,' she says. 'Honestly, Hannah, I don't think she was here.'

It's another hot, fine day. The sliding doors are open and light floods into the house, along with the sweet smells of the summer plants and flowers. Amber's stroller is ready at the door, and Shiv loads a bag full of food, wipes and nappies into the webbing beneath it. It's obvious she's been waiting to take Amber out, but wanted to make sure I was okay first.

'Where are you going today?' I say, clicking the kettle on.

There's work to do, emails to reply to, but it's obvious that I'm not going to be good for anything, and I'm about to tell her that she can take the day off, so I can spend the afternoon with Amber, when she looks at me in surprise.

'Oh, I'm taking her to my friends' house,' she says. 'The ones I told you about.'

'What friends?'

'I did mention it yesterday, and you said it was okay. They live in Clapham, but they're moving out of the city soon and they're having a get-together. There'll be lots of other children there for Amber to play with, so I thought it would be nice to take her.'

If she told me about it yesterday, I have no recollection of it, but I'm not firing on all cylinders today. 'What time does it start?'

'It's been going on all day, but I thought I'd wait till you were up.'

It seems crazy to let Shiv take Amber across the city when I'm so worried about Diane, but if I've already said yes, I can't change my mind now.

'That sounds like a great idea, it'll be good for her to meet other kids.'

When the kettle boils, Shiv takes a mug from the cupboard and I ask her, 'What are you doing?'

'Making you a cup of tea,' she says.

'You don't have to do that,' I tell her, because she's always making me tea, and I slide the mug away from her.

'We'll be at the party all afternoon.' She gives me an uncertain smile. 'I hope you don't mind.'

The truth is, I'm glad she's going out, because I want time on my own to pull myself together, relax, and shift this headache.

There's no point in telling Shiv to be careful, because after what happened at the supermarket I'm sure she won't take her eyes off Amber for a second, but I do anyway.

And when she's gone, lifting Amber's stroller over the doorstep and down the path, I finish making the tea, and then take a long shower, standing with my face tilted to the powerful jet of spray, letting the water pound against my head and shoulders as I try to wash away the weariness I feel. There are bruises on my upper arms I haven't seen before; I read somewhere that bruising can be caused by a vitamin deficiency. Towelling off, I can't help but examine the sunken brown hollows beneath my eyes.

I spend the next couple of hours listlessly sprawled on the sofa, doom-scrolling on my phone, with the television burbling in the background. But I can't shake the feeling that there's something I need to do if I'm going to put this sorry episode in my life to bed once and for all.

After another nap, and when I've drunk a couple of coffees and taken more Nurofen, I feel much better. Rested, more alert – and determined. Pulling on a pair of trainers, I snatch up my car keys and my mobile, and leave the house.

The police, Shiv and Cameron all told me to stay away from Diane, and they're right, I shouldn't go anywhere near her. But I feel there's unfinished business between us. When she took my daughter, she could have taken her anywhere, done anything with her, but instead brought her home within an hour of snatching her. The police suggested she did it out of remorse, or a lack of nerve, but Diane also told them she wanted to get my attention. She tried to talk to me when I got out of the cab, she wanted to tell me something, but in the panic of the moment I didn't give her the chance.

It was a mistake to let Cam do all the talking when we met Diane at the café, I should have spoken to her, and allowed her to say more. So I'm going to give her the opportunity to speak now. I'll find out what she wants to say to me – it'll be nonsense, it always is with Diane – and then we're done; then she's gone.

I'm probably breaking all kinds of rules. The police told me that Diane is forbidden to approach me by the terms of her bail, but technically I'm approaching her.

It was late at night when the cab dropped Diane at her house, but I think I remember where she lived, in the tangle of streets behind Bounds Green Tube, and I've already driven halfway there when my phone rings.

Cam's name appears on the screen. He's the last person I want to speak to, so I drop the phone on the passenger seat, and after several rings it goes to voicemail. Moments later it rings again, and I feel compelled to answer it.

'Hi,' I say, picking it up.

'Hey,' Cam says. 'Just thought I'd call to see how you were.'

'Yeah, good… I've just been sitting about the house, really.'

'You don't sound like you're in the house,' he says brightly.

'I can't really talk right now, I'm driving.'

'Yeah?' he asks. 'Going anywhere nice?'

It's exactly the question I don't want to answer. 'Please don't get mad, but I'm driving to Diane's.'

'No,' he tells me firmly. 'Turn around.'

'I'll just talk to her, find out what it is she wants, and that will be the end of it, I promise.'

'The police told you to stay away, H,' he says sternly. 'Turn around and go home.'

'I'm not going inside her house,' I insist, 'or to put myself into a dangerous situation. I just want to know why she brought Amber back to me. Once I know that, I'll go straight home. It's crazy, but even after everything she's done, I still don't get the sense that she means me harm.'

'I've met plenty of people like Diane,' he says impatiently. 'To look at them, you'd think they were meek and harmless, but they're not, they're confused and damaged, and some of them are plain malicious. Look at what Diane's done: harassed and stalked you. She snatched your daughter, for God's sake.'

Pressing an elbow into the steering wheel to keep it steady, I rub my tired eyes. 'I think she may have been in my bedroom last night.'

There's silence on the other end for a moment and then Cam asks, 'Did you see her?'

'Yes, no – I don't know. It felt like a terrible dream.'

'Please, H, don't go.' When I don't reply, he sighs. 'You're making a mistake.'

'I'm sorry,' I tell him. 'I'll call you as soon as I leave, so you know I'm safe.'

'No, please don't—'

But I cut the call and throw the phone on the passenger seat. Approaching Bounds Green, I concentrate on getting my bearings, trying to retrace the route of the cab that took Diane home the other week. It doesn't take me long to find her street, and her shabby house near the end of the row. Parking outside, I walk up the pathway, past the dumped furniture and boxes and mattress, and knock on the door.

38

Twenty Years Ago

My only wish as I lay there was that I could have seen his face, watched his every reaction as the reality of what he had done dawned on him. But I couldn't, so all I could do is imagine what was happening based on what I heard.

'Oh God, Martin... You've killed her!'

I imagined Martin's eyes open as he was roughly shaken awake. Tangled in the duvet, he lifted slowly onto his elbows, hair hanging lankly over his brow, his puffy red lids slowly parting. He was so hungover that despite the panicked voice in his ear and the hand on his shoulder, all he wanted to do was bury his face in the pillow and go back to sleep.

'Wake up!' Cameron's voice was shrill with fear. 'What have you done? Look what you've done!'

The insistent tone finally forced Martin to drag himself into full consciousness. Early-morning light knifed into his eyes – the curtains were open, he probably kept them closed all day – and he lifted his arm to block out the painful glare.

His head spun, his stomach churned, his mouth was sandpaper dry. He wouldn't have understood why there was a man in his bedroom, or who he was, and why he looked so scared. It would have taken Martin a long moment to remember that he spent last night drinking with this guy, and a woman he really fancied. But the man looked upset, terrified in fact, as he stood with his hands clenched in his hair, staring in horror at the end of the bed.

It was then, I'm sure, that Martin felt the first stab of fear and confusion settle in his gut.

'What have you gone and done?' I heard Cameron screech at him.

Martin rubbed his face, trying to get his head together, and when he pulled his hands away he saw they were smeared red; blood was splashed up his arms, the duvet was a sodden red. And it was when he saw at the end of the bed the body of a woman lying on the floor in a pool of blood that he was overcome with fright – revulsion – panic.

Martin clambered quickly off the bed and pressed against the wall as far as he could from the bloody scene.

'You did this,' Cam told him angrily. 'You killed her.'

'No.' Martin stared dumbfounded at the body on the floor, and tried desperately to recall the events of the previous day. He would have remembered the bar, a night of drinking beer and downing shots, one after the other; but after that it was a blur. And as I lay there pretending to be dead, my eyes half closed, it took all of my strength not to laugh out loud.

A name – my name: Hannah – would have sprung dismally into his mind. With blood streaked all over his duvet and pillow, his hands and chest, and with Cameron's angry accusations ringing in his ears, he knew he must be responsible for my violent death.

'You killed her,' hissed Cameron again and again. Unable

to concentrate, disorientated by the harsh voice in his ear, Martin wished he would shut up; he couldn't bear it. 'Look what you've done to Hannah!'

You killed her, you killed her, you killed her.

But when Martin tried to talk, all that came out was an odd keening sound.

'What happened?' he finally managed to say.

'What does it look like?' Cameron spat. 'You both came in here last night, and I slept on the couch, and when I knocked on the door this morning and nobody answered, I found her, she was my friend. I found my Hannah...' Cameron's face crumpled in misery. 'Why, Martin? Why did you do it?'

'I don't... I can't...'

Martin wouldn't have been able to get his thoughts together, or untangle his memories of last night. Terror overwhelmed him.

The girl had fancied him, *I* had fancied him, I'd made that plain enough, because I was all over him like a rash. Touching his hand or his shoulder or his leg, making suggestive remarks in his ear; coming on to him, but then slapping him away when he responded. It drove him fucking crazy, I remember that much. He couldn't wait to get me back here, and told me he wished my friend would go away, but I refused to come back to smoke spliff without Cameron. Martin probably had a vague memory that I suggested I sleep in his bed, and he had eagerly agreed. But then I'd refused to let him touch me, and he was too drunk and exhausted to do anything about it, and fell asleep.

As he stood frozen, I could feel his mind whirring. Did something happen after that, something he blanked from his mind? Did he come on to me, and I resisted? Did he lose his temper? He's done that before with girls, I know that about him, he's got angry. But he'd never do anything like this, he wouldn't kill, he *couldn't* do it – could he?

But the blood everywhere, the body on his bedroom floor...

'I can't... I don't...' I could sense that the reality of what would happen was starting to hit him. His life was ruined, he would go to prison; for years, probably. He was a murderer, the lowest of the low, and they would lock him up and throw away the key. Martin dropped to the floor and began to cry. Big, wracking sobs.

Playing his part beautifully, Cameron said with venom, 'People like you die in prison, and you deserve it!'

Martin tried to scuttle away from him, but glimpsed the body again and pulled his legs to his chest to hunch into a tight ball.

Sickened, petrified, Martin couldn't look at me as I lay perfectly still, covered in fake blood. His head dropped into his hands as he wept bitterly.

Which was when I opened my eyes.

'I'm calling the police.' Cameron crouched in front of him, whispering that he was a murderer, and going to prison, where men who killed women were treated like vermin; he didn't give him a moment's respite. 'And I'm going to tell them what you've done.'

Martin's head was tucked behind his knees, his tears and snot mixing with the fake blood we'd smeared onto his chest and arms and duvet while he was asleep. He cried because he was convinced of his own guilt: in a moment of madness he couldn't even remember, he'd killed me.

Pleased with Martin's terrified reaction, Cam smiled at me

as I walked over, the fake blood sticky on my face and neck, and in my hair.

I'd gotten the idea because I'd almost convinced myself that somehow Natalie had faked her own death. Because the way she died, walking out of the house one afternoon and into the path of a train, was so inexplicable, and so obscene, that it couldn't possibly be true. I had so desperately wanted to believe that she was alive, she *must* be alive, because if that was the case then it wasn't too late to tell her how sorry I was that things had been so difficult between us.

But that was ridiculous, because deep down I knew that she was gone. Natalie was dead, and I'd never be able to tell her how much I loved her; that despite what she thought, and what I had told myself, I loved her, and wished I had been kinder to her and more understanding. She was gone and I would never be able to say how sorry I was.

And now that we'd played this awful prank on this pathetic man, my eyes were open. All the anger I had felt this morning, last night, all these weeks and months and years, left me immediately when I saw how broken he was.

I didn't feel any kind of triumph, or sense of justice. I just felt shame for what we had done. I knew I had hit rock bottom, and jagged tracks of tears ran down my bloody face.

I wondered about Martin's family, and what his mum and dad – maybe he had a brother, or a sister who doted on him – would think if they could see him reduced to such a cowering, sobbing wreck.

Martin didn't deserve what we'd done to him, and he wouldn't learn any lessons about how to treat women; all it would do is fuel his resentment, and make him more suspicious and withdrawn. What we did wasn't *kind*, and it wasn't justice, and no good would ever come of it.

The triumphant smile on Cam's face sickened me. I'd encouraged him to participate in this joke, goaded him into it. He was a nice guy, and I'd made him do bad things, he'd ended up stealing from that restaurant because of my taunts. He deserved better than me.

I think it was in that moment that I knew I had to finish with Cameron once and for all; set him free. It was wrong to lie to him, and allow him to dream of a future together. We had done a bad thing, one I would never forget, and I knew I must never see him again; for his sake, as well as mine.

Cam backed away so that I could kneel in his place. 'Martin,' I said softly.

His wracking, helpless sobs were so loud that he didn't hear me. So I took his wrists and lowered his hands from his knees. He stared incredulously at me, his face a mess of snot and tears and fake blood; I had come back to life.

'We're going now, Martin.'

When he realized that I wasn't a vengeful ghost or apparition, his whole body began to shake. The juddering sobs became faster, because now he was crying with merciful relief. He hadn't killed me; his life wasn't ruined; he was free of the stain of murder.

A moment ago I was his victim, and now I was his saviour.

Martin stared pathetically into my eyes as if I was an angel, and I knew I had to change the trajectory of my life, and do something good with it before it was too late.

'Don't ever lay your hands on another woman again,' I told him quietly. 'Do you hear me?'

'Please.' His head dropped back to his chest. 'Just leave me alone.'

He was still sobbing, rocking back and forth, when Cam and I left the flat.

39

'Come on, Diane, open up. I want to talk to you.'
        The bay windows are covered by heavy curtains that conceal the inside. The sun has disappeared over the top of the roofs, and shadow cools the front of the house. Diane doesn't come to the door when I bang on it, and I'm afraid she's not at home. Cupping my hands against the dirty rain glass, I see a faint blur of light coming from the end of the hallway.

Stepping back to look up at the windows above, I'm momentarily distracted by movement in the window of a neighbour's house, and when I turn back, the dim light at the back flickers, as if someone has walked in front of it.

I slam my palm against the glass. 'I know you're in there, Diane!'

I'm about to bang on the door again when a light goes on in the hallway, and a figure approaches. Then the door opens, just a crack, and one wild eye peeks around the side.

'What do you want?' There's none of the usual ingratiating shyness in Diane's voice. 'You shouldn't be here!'

'I just want to talk,' I tell her.

She considers me warily, as if I'm the dangerous one, and then retreats, leaving the door ajar.

I don't want to go inside – I promised Cam I wouldn't –
but she's gone from the hallway. When I try to push the door
wider, it bumps against something blocking it on the inside,
and I have to squeeze through the gap.

Looking inside, I'm stunned. The reason the door won't
open is that the hallway is filled from floor to ceiling with
piles of junk and towers of boxes. The stacks block out most
of the sallow light from the low-watt bulb hanging from the
ceiling, and run the length of the hallway.

'Diane?' I'm reluctant to venture further inside. The
tottering wall of junk looks incredibly unsafe, and makes
it impossible to do more than shuffle sideways down the
narrow space against the wall on the right.

The boxes are old and dry and many of them are partially
crushed by the pressure of the junk in the compressed boxes
stacked above and below them; they lean haphazardly
against the stacks on either side. Packed into the spaces
between are bulging plastic and paper bags, and flimsy
cardboard containers crushed out of shape, containing God
knows what.

There's a door to the right just ahead, and further along
the narrow path to the back of the house, stairs lead up
to the gloom of the first-floor landing. On each stair are piled
more boxes, bags, and fat black sacks.

'Diane, are you there?' I call, but she doesn't answer, and
against my better judgement I move further down the hall
beneath the unstable towers. Just ahead, one pile of boxes
has even toppled near the ceiling; it's propped up against the
opposite wall, forming an arch, and I have to duck beneath
it, as if it's a narrow fissure in a wall of rock. 'Where are
you?'

I'm not usually claustrophobic, but pressed against the wall my anxiety builds, and I dare not look up. *This is a bad idea, just leave.* There's an overpowering smell of damp and mould, the stink of blocked drains. When my fingers brush against the wall, it feels cold and clammy, despite the heat of the afternoon. The frayed carpet beneath my feet feels tacky.

Some of the boxes are full of piles of yellowing newspapers; the rest contain old appliances, clothes, knick-knacks, tools, plastic containers full of screws and nails, mysterious pieces of wood and metal, broken china from items long fallen apart, discarded packaging and rolls of bubble wrap.

'Diane?' It's only a couple of feet behind me, but over my shoulder I can barely see the front door any more. 'Are you there?'

The hallway continues past the stairs. The smudge of lamplight comes from behind a doorway ahead, and I go towards it.

The kitchen is also filled with piles of rubbish and clutter, a wall of mess everywhere. Smelly black bin bags are ripped open by the density of all the contents stuffed inside, clothes and jagged wooden frames and bits of metal, but also food wrappers and containers. A mousetrap sits against the dirty skirting. It's unbelievable to me how anyone can live like this. It occurs to me that this chaotic and disordered house is the physical manifestation of the inside of Diane's head.

My shin scrapes against a metal strut jutting from a pile of junk, and when I rear back into a stacked tower of stuff behind me, it ominously shifts.

'Diane, we need to talk.'

It's impossible to see too far into the room because there are tables, chairs, a sofa, even an old bedstead, piled on top of each other. It's as if someone has tipped the entire contents of a house into this single room. All the other rooms in this house, I know, will be exactly the same. Diane is a hoarder. She's filled her house from top to bottom with junk. This place is a deathtrap; it's no wonder the police got the local council's environmental health people involved.

When I get past the heap of furniture, I finally see a sink straight ahead, but it's piled with bowls and dishes; the draining board is filled with cups and mugs and opened food packaging. One cupboard door is left ajar, and it's empty inside. There's a cooker, but the hob is covered with stacks of dirty plates and pans. There are flies everywhere. My stomach flips when I remember she told me she made that lasagne here.

Stained blinds are drawn over the windows, and where they've come off the rail, a black sack has been taped over the remaining pane, so it's gloomy, despite the fierce brightness outside, and the windows are sealed with screw locks, which is why it's so hot in here. The worst thing is the smell of rotten food. When I accidentally touch the top of a table, my fingers come away smeared in grease.

'Welcome to my home,' says a voice, making me jump. When I turn, I see Diane sitting on a chair in a tiny space by the back door, which has chipboard nailed to it where the glass should be. Beside her is a cabinet, and on the Formica surface is a kettle plugged into the wall, a mug, a dish containing sugar.

'How long have you been living like this?' I ask her.

She looks around the room, or what can be seen of it from

this small space by the door, as if she's only just noticed it's a mess.

'You get used to it,' she says. 'I've always had a lot of belongings, and I don't like to throw things out because you never know when they're going to be useful.'

I gesture at the heaps of furniture. 'This is all yours?'

'I'm a bit of a collector.'

'You can't live here, Diane,' I tell her. The environment is so cluttered and oppressive, it's inconceivable that anyone could live like this.

'It's my home,' she tells me forcefully. 'My home, and it's nobody's business how I keep it. The police came here and they said—'

There's a noise from the front of the house, a rustle, the sound of something shifting in the hallway, and we both look up.

'Mice, probably.' Diane's lips quiver. 'Anyway, I don't want people here, I don't want them judging me. You shouldn't have come here.'

The light I saw from the front door comes from the bare bulb of a lamp on an upturned chair. In the gloom, it casts spidery shadows on the walls behind the jagged clutter.

'The police say I mustn't talk to you, you're going to get me into trouble.' Diane looks up at me. 'So you have to go.'

'I'm sorry you live like this, Diane.'

'They're going to make me leave now, because they came here and said it's unsafe, and it's thanks to you. It's just like the last time. I lived in Chattersea Close in Ealing, I loved that house, but the neighbours complained and then the council came round.'

'I'm sorry,' I tell her, because she looks upset.

'I don't want your pity,' she says.

'I came to ask you why you brought Amber back to my house.'

But Diane isn't listening. 'You set the police on me,' she says angrily. 'They put me in a cell.'

'Can you blame me, Diane?' I ask, incredulous. It's important that I make her understand that actions have consequences. 'After what you did?'

She shakes her head. 'After what I did…?'

I'm sick of this constant state of denial that Diane lives in, the way she buries her head in the sand, and I feel my temper rise.

'So you didn't take my daughter. Like you didn't steal my phone, like you didn't attack my dad, or set out to ruin my marriage. Like I suppose you weren't in my house last night!'

She leaps out of the chair in front of me and this confined space at the back of her house suddenly feels a long way from the world outside. I feel a tinge of fear and wish I hadn't been so stupid as to follow her.

'You sent the police here,' she tells me, and there are tears in her eyes. 'They'll evict me again, they'll throw me out on the street.'

'Why did you bring her back?'

'Because you won't *listen* to me.' She stomps a foot. 'I thought you were my *friend*.'

She tries to say more, but I've had enough. 'You brought this on yourself, Diane. You've had your fun and games now, you've had your… what did you call it on the radio… your *revenge*, and now it's got to stop.'

'You have to listen to me—'

'Because if it *doesn't*,' I tell her, raising my voice to speak over her, 'I'll make sure you won't be able to come a hundred miles near me or my family or my home.' My face and neck flush red with anger. 'Do you *hear* me, Diane?'

'Yes, I took Amber,' she says, her mouth trembling. 'But you told lies to the police. You're not a good friend, you're not a good person, you're not *kind*.'

I need light and space and fresh air; I need to get out of this dark, claustrophobic, stinking space. My breathing is quick and ragged, and the hairs stand up on my arms; my whole body is screaming at me to take flight. But I've got to have my say.

'I *am* a good person,' I tell her in a rage. 'I'm a much better person than Martin ever was, and he deserved what we did to him. He *deserved* it. He attacked a friend of mine, Diane, he locked her in his flat. And I bet he did it to other women too. *That* was the kind of man he was.'

Diane blinks in bewilderment. 'Who are you talking about?'

I stare at her in disbelief. 'Martin, Diane. Martin did that. Your brother.'

'I don't...' Her eyes lift to the ceiling. 'I don't care about any of that. About... Martin or whoever... I don't...' She whispers. 'I just want to be your friend.'

'So why?' I ask her finally. 'Why did you take her?'

'You were ignoring me, so I had to – it was the only way.' She lunges to grab my arm, but I rear back. 'You need to *know*.'

'Know? Know what?' But Diane's eyes have lifted to the ceiling again, she's staring.

And at that moment, I smell something, and taste it at the back of my throat: acrid, cloying, harsh. When I follow

Diane's gaze to the ceiling, I see tendrils of smoke drift above our heads. There's a fire somewhere, and this house is packed full of dry paper, fabrics, plastics, foam and wood.

'The door,' I tell her, because now a flicker of light comes from the hallway, and there's the soft whoosh of something igniting. Fire is spreading fast in the cramped space. We have to get out immediately. But when I turn the handle of the back door, it doesn't open.

Thick black smoke is pouring into the room now from the hallway; orange light pulses in the door. The fire is spreading fast in the cramped space among the boxes of paper and cardboard and plastic.

My eyes sting from the cloud of burning toxins, but when I try again to open the back door, it doesn't move.

'It's not opening,' I say, sucking down smoke, which makes me cough and retch.

'There's a key,' she says, looking around frantically. 'But I don't know where it is.'

'We have to get out,' I scream, as I claw at the wood nailed over the broken glass. Giving up, I go to the window, but the black smoke is already too thick for me to find the locks.

'This way.' Diane shoves past me, heading back towards the hallway.

'We can't!' I tell her, but already she's moving into the smoke. Squinting, using the hem of my top to cover my mouth, I have no choice but to follow her. Coughing and spluttering, hunching beneath the sheet of smoke swirling above us. It hurts to breathe, and my eyes sting. We have to get out of this room before the flames reach the furniture in here, with their cheap foam and wooden frames, or we'll be trapped.

'Wait,' I call to Diane. She's already disappearing ahead, and in a hurry to keep up with her, I blindly stumble into a wall of junk, stabbing my rib into a protruding chair leg.

Diane has stopped in front of me. The contents of the hallway ahead of us are being consumed by raging fire, the narrow pathway to the front door obliterated by licking flame. There's no way through.

'I'm going to get you out.' Her eyes blinking furiously against the smoke, she places her hands on my shoulders for a moment, then pushes me away. 'Stand back!'

Diane claws at a big pile of boxes at the side of the kitchen where I've just been standing. Heavy boxes crash at my feet, spilling plates and bowls, which smash across the lino.

I want to ask her if she has a phone, so we can call someone, because I left mine in the car. But I know it's lost somewhere in the swirling smoke.

'Over here,' she tells me, pulling a chair from the stack and throwing it into the hallway. Another door is revealed behind the remaining boxes, which come to waist height. She pushes it open as far as it will go, and then climbs over the boxes and squeezes through the gap into the room beyond. Her legs scrabble in the junk, and I have to push her over the landslide of rubbish. The heat is intense at my back as I climb up behind her, the boxes and their contents sliding and shifting under me. Diane reaches back through the gap to grab my arm and pull me through.

We're in another room, but I'm disorientated and scared, because I've no idea where we are, or what direction we should be going in. We're parallel to the kitchen and hallway, in a dining or living room, I think, but we're surrounded on every side by more towers of junk. Smoke pulses above our heads, racing down the narrow canyons between the stacks.

Diane grabs my wrist and leads me into the thick blackness. I can barely stand, I keep dropping to my knees to splutter out a choked gasp. My lungs feel scraped out, my throat full of glass. We stumble along another narrow pathway. For all I know, Diane could be leading me into the fiery heart of the blaze. There's a banging coming from somewhere, and I'm sure I hear someone shouting my name, but my head spins.

Terrified, I just want to sink to the floor and wait for it all to end. Choking, gasping for breath, blindly falling against the junk on either side of me, I'm convinced I'm going to die. I can't get air into my lungs at all. Finally, I crawl on my hands and knees as the smoke swirls above me. I'm sick, nauseous. And when I look up, Diane's gone.

'Dia…' I try to say, heaving for breath, terrified that she's left me.

But then a hand reaches down and drags me to my feet. 'This way.'

Diane pulls me around a corner and into another narrow alley. The room feels like a never-ending maze with no way out. We could be near the front of the house, or the back.

'Hannah!' That distant voice again, coming from somewhere. 'Hannah!'

As Diane drags me along, the shoulder of my top snags on a coat hanger protruding from a box. I pull blindly at it, the fabric tears, and the tall stack sways above me – and begins to topple. Diane lunges at me in the dark. Her eyes wide and frenzied, she lets out a strangled, 'No!' and smacks me backwards.

She barely has time to lift an arm before the junk crashes

on top of her. Falling to the floor, I scream, but it comes out as a jagged, throaty howl.

When I blindly crawl over to her, she's lying on her front, the upper half of her covered by a school desk. Climbing to my knees, I try to lift it off.

'Diane,' I croak, frantically try to breathe. 'We… have to… go!'

I pull at her, try to drag her to her feet, but she doesn't move. She's a heavy weight, and I'm too weak. I'm sucking ever more smoke into my lungs, and my head feels increasingly sluggish, my chest as if it's about to burst. When I look up, one entire wall is being consumed by flame, and I realize it's the curtains at the front of the house. We're close to the front door, so close, but we'll never make it through the hallway.

I'm only moving out of instinct now as I weakly tug at her, spluttering her name, trying everything to get her moving. The smoke thickens, and then I can't see anything but an orange smudge ahead of me.

I can't think, I can't pull, I can't live any more. The easiest thing to do is rest on the floor.

And let everything go black.

40

My eyes feel sore and gritty when I open them, as if they're full of sand, and the world comes gradually back into cloudy focus. My head throbs, and my breath flaps wetly in my raw throat; it hurts when I swallow. It takes me a few moments to realize where I am.

I'm lying in a hospital room, which is sterile, almost empty. There's an oxygen canister beside the bed, and a bulky machine in the corner, which isn't hooked up to anything, its blank monitor screen turned to the wall.

There's an empty chair near the door, where two people are talking. Cameron is one of them, and he's nodding at something a nurse is telling him, arms folded across his chest in concentration. Someone walks past in the corridor outside, shoes squeaking on the floor. When Cam looks over and sees I'm awake, he comes over quickly.

'Hey.' He wears a big, relieved smile. 'Welcome back.'

'Am I dead?' I ask. It hurts when I speak, my throat feels like it's been lacerated by glass, and my voice sounds different; guttural, muffled. When I lift fingers to my face, they tap against the bulbous plastic of an oxygen mask.

He pulls the chair over from the door and places it close

to the bed, squeezes my hand on the sheets. 'No, you're not, you're alive, thank God.'

'My chest hurts.' It feels like there's a heavy weight pressing down on it. 'Everything hurts.'

'You sucked down a lot of smoke.' Cam's voice cracks with emotion. 'I thought we were going to lose you, H. I really thought…' But he doesn't finish the thought. His head drops to his chest, and he exhales slowly, composing himself. When he looks up, the smile is back in place. 'But you're back.'

When I close my stinging eyes, I see Diane stumbling ahead of me; then on the floor at my feet, her face barely visible in the thick, cloying smoke. I can't move her, she won't get up.

'Diane,' I croak.

'I'm sorry, H.' Gently stroking my palm with a thumb, he shakes his head. 'She's gone.'

In my distress and shock, I feel claustrophobic: in this mask, trapped beneath the sheets of this bed, in this small, bare room; the walls feel like they're closing in. When I pull it off, the mask detaches from my face with a soft hiss. Cam gently stops me from getting out of bed.

'You can't do that,' he says, but I won't let him replace the mask, weakly batting away his hand when he tries to put it back in place.

'You don't have to wear it if you can breathe unaided,' says a young nurse, coming into the room. Cam steps back to give her space to check me over. The first thing she does is to lift my wrist to check my pulse.

'You'll be fine,' she says, when she's finished. 'But your lungs have been through a trauma, so it's going to take a little time for you to recover. Don't think about running a marathon anytime soon. You're lucky you're here at all, and you have this man to thank.'

She gestures at Cam.

'What... what happened?' I ask.

'The way I heard it,' says the nurse, 'this gentleman rushed into a burning house and carried you out.'

Because my previous exertions have exhausted me, I'm barely able to lift my head off the pillow to look at him. 'You saved my life.'

'We'll talk about it later,' he says, embarrassed.

'Tell me now.'

'There's not much to tell. When I arrived at the house it was on fire. When I kicked the front door in, I could hear you inside hoarsely screaming at Diane, so I knew you were close, somewhere in the living room. The heat and smoke made it almost impossible to get inside, but I knew I had to try. I would never forgive myself if...' He has to compose himself before continuing. 'Then one of the neighbours came over with a blanket soaked in water, and I threw it over my shoulders and rushed inside. The heat was intense, H, and the smoke... I couldn't see a thing, but thank God you were lying just inside the living-room door, and I was able to pick you up and get you out. If you had been any further inside the house, we would have lost you.' He takes a steadying breath. '*I* would have lost you.'

'And Diane...'

Cam shakes his head. 'I managed to get you out and I was going to take my chances again, Diane was so close to the door, but by that time the hallway was an inferno. I just couldn't find a way back inside, and then firefighters turned up, and ordered me away. I think… I think they went inside eventually, but it was too late for her. I'm so sorry.'

Closing my eyes, I try to make sense of what he's said. Diane is dead, killed in the disordered chaos of her own home, burned alive or suffocated by smoke.

'I want to go home,' I tell the nurse.

'We need to keep you in overnight, to do some more tests, and then we can decide about that.'

Cam waits for the nurse to leave, then drags the chair closer to my side, says quietly, 'My God, Hannah, what happened in there?'

It's all coming back to me. We were in the kitchen, we talked, tempers got… frayed. And then tendrils of smoke drifted across the ceiling. Diane did her best to get me out, but the house was a deathtrap. The back door was locked, there was no key, and if there had been a clear route to the front door, we could have got out in seconds, we'd both be alive now.

'It wasn't me.' My throat feels scraped raw, but I'm terrified he believes I'm responsible for the blaze, and that I killed Diane. 'I didn't start that fire!'

He nods gravely, *yes*, but I yearn for him to say it out loud: I believe you.

'We were in the kitchen. It was difficult to move because the room, all the rooms, were packed with furniture and junk. We talked, we… argued.'

'Argued?' he asks quickly. 'What about?'

'Everything that's happened. Cam, I didn't kill her!'

'Go on.'

'And then smoke began to pour into the room.' Something occurs to me. 'There was someone else in the house.'

He leans forward. 'Did you see who?'

'No, I heard a noise in the hallway, Diane dismissed it as mice, but I think someone was there. Someone who started that fire.'

He listens carefully, his face a tense mask, and I can't tell whether he believes me.

'Amber,' I say in a sudden panic, trying to lift myself up, Cam places a hand gently on my shoulder to ease me back down.

'She's fine, she's good, Siobhan's with her at home. They both send their love and are looking forward to seeing you.'

All I want is to go home and try to put this nightmare behind me. But how can I, knowing that Diane is dead? My relationship with her was short and complicated; she exploded into my life like a bolt of lightning, turning everything on its head in a matter of weeks. All the terrible things she did, threatening revenge, attacking my father, snatching my daughter, were like a feverish nightmare; and her bittersweet attempts to be my friend desperate and contradictory, just like Diane herself. But neither of us could ever imagine that our story would come to an end in such an awful, tragic way.

Diane was an unhappy and lonely woman, but she didn't deserve to die in such appalling circumstances. I don't think I'll ever understand her, in life or in death, but I owe it to her to try.

Maybe it's all the burning detritus of Diane's house I inhaled, the carbon monoxide and particulates and toxins, but it hurts when I begin to cry; my tears are literally painful. Cam sits quietly holding my hand until I finally stop and compose myself.

'What were you doing there, anyway?' I ask.

He nods, as if he's been waiting to explain.

'I didn't want you to go there, you know that.' I remember now the frantic conversation we had on the phone as I drove to Diane's house. 'And I didn't like the idea of you being alone at her house. I don't know…' His free hand clutches at the air as if he's trying to find the right words. 'Maybe it was instinct, but it just felt wrong. As soon as you hung up, I left work, and drove there as fast as I could.'

I can't make sense of it. 'But how did you know where to come?'

'You'd told me she lived in Bounds Green, I didn't know any more than that, but my heart leapt when I saw smoke lifting into the sky, I just *knew*, so I drove towards that. When I got there, I saw your car and… I couldn't lose you, H.'

'Thank you,' I croak, and we sit quietly holding hands.

'There's another thing you should know,' he tells me finally. 'The police want to talk to you.'

I expected as much, but the way he looks at me steadily, as if I've got something to hide, makes me anxious. It feels even more difficult to breathe.

'All you have to do…' Cam glances at the door to make sure we're alone. '…is tell them what you told me, that you went there to talk to her. I wouldn't mention an argument.'

'I'm not going to lie to them, Cam.'

He tries to smile. 'Of course not.'

'Why would I lie?' I ask.

'That's good, then.' His gaze searches my face, and then he places both hands around mine. 'But you're not going to be alone, H. I'm going to be here for you every step of the way.'

41

'Sit yourself down and I'll make you something to eat,' Cam tells me as he unlocks the front door the following morning.

Dropping the keys into his pocket, he helps me inside. I may be a bit short of breath but I can walk okay, and the way he's fussing around me, you'd think I was an invalid.

'I'm not hungry.' It hurts when I swallow, so I don't feel like I want to eat or drink anything ever again. All I want to do is go to sleep and hide from the world. Details of the fire and Diane's death have been on the news, but I haven't yet been identified; it's only a matter of time.

'Not eating isn't going to solve anything. You need to get your strength back up.'

'My throat and chest still feel like they're on fire.'

'Because you sucked down a lot of nasty toxins, and you need to flush them out. Come and sit.' He leads me to the sofa in the living room and plumps up the cushions. 'There you go, fit for a queen. A Queen of Hearts, even.'

'You don't have to stay here.'

He pivots me forward to prop a cushion at the small of my back. 'I want to, until I'm sure you're shipshape.'

'Cam, you should be with your sick wife,' I tell him as he's walking out of the room.

That stops him in his stride. He looks at me sheepishly. 'Penny says she's happy for me to stay for a little bit. She says she doesn't like it when I mollycoddle her.'

'I need a shower, I feel filthy.'

'I think that's a really good idea,' he calls from the kitchen. 'As soon as you've had something to eat.'

'Where's Amber?' I ask. 'Why isn't she here?'

'Siobhan's taken her out.' I can hear him banging all the cupboards open and closed. 'She'll be back in an hour or so.'

'You two have really got this all organized,' I call.

He pops his head back in the door and grins. 'Oh yeah, we're working as a proper team now. We've got walkie-talkies and everything. Honestly, though, H. Siobhan's a good kid, you're lucky to have her here.'

It feels wrong to just sit on the sofa. 'I should tell Sean what's happened.'

'Rest first and then worry about that,' he calls back. I hear the metallic shiver of the bread-bin lid slapping shut.

'We've run out of bread,' I call, if that's what he's looking for.

'There's bread, of course there is.' He comes to the door, holding up sliced sourdough. 'Because Siobhan lives here now.'

A few minutes later he comes in with a sandwich, with quartered tomatoes and cucumber sticks placed on the side of the plate, and a mug of herbal tea. He's got a tea towel flicked over his shoulder, as if he works in a restaurant.

'Smells great,' I say, enjoying the sweet fragrance of the drink. 'I didn't even know I had camomile.'

'Found it in the back of the cupboard. Your sense of smell is coming back, at least.'

He places the plate and mug on a coffee table, moves a footstool closer to me and lifts my legs onto them.

'I could get used to being treated like this.'

'You deserve it,' he agrees, and heads back into the kitchen, tugging the tea towel into his hand as he goes.

When I bite into the ham sandwich, it feels like a soggy, tasteless mass in my mouth, and I replace it on the plate. But the mug warms my hands, and I listen to him moving around in the kitchen.

'Where do you keep your washing-up liquid?' he calls, and then, 'Oh, here it is!'

His phone rings, and I hear him pick it up.

'Sure,' he says after a short silence. 'I'll let her know. Tomorrow at nine is fine. We'll be here. Thanks... yes.'

Then he comes into the living room and perches on the edge of the coffee table, eyeing my uneaten sandwich.

As much as I wanted to, I just couldn't enjoy it. 'I'm sorry,' I tell him.

'Bah.' Cam smiles. 'Don't worry, I'm used to it. Penny's not got much of an appetite either.'

'Thank you for looking after me.'

He takes the plate. 'Eat when you want to, but drink the tea. Doctor's orders.'

I give him a weary salute. 'I will, but it tastes funny. Bitter.'

'Everything's going to taste funny for a while.'

The tea makes me think of the empty mug on the tabletop littered with brown tea rings in Diane's kitchen. She runs ahead of me, her broad back disappearing into the swirling smoke.

Emotion surges inside me again, my heart flutters, and I sit up quickly, spilling tea down my front. Cam quickly takes the mug.

'I keep seeing her,' I tell him. 'Diane.'

'You're in shock. It's going to take a few days, weeks or longer, but it's all perfectly normal, and won't last forever.'

'I killed her,' I tell him.

Cam stares at me.

'What I mean is,' I say quickly, 'if I hadn't been there, maybe she would have been able to get out. She knew how to get out, but I slowed her down.'

'So, look, that was the police on the phone.' He squeezes my hands. 'They're coming to ask you tomorrow morning about what happened, and the last thing you should do is use loaded phrases like *I killed her* or *it's all my fault.*'

'Yes.' I meet his concerned look. 'I understand.'

'What happened was terrible, inexplicable, and I understand how upset you are, but don't let Diane's final legacy be to send you to prison.'

His saying it out loud like that makes me clench with anxiety, because it's never occurred to me that could happen.

'You were the last person to see her alive,' he says. 'Diane's neighbours saw you banging on her front door shouting to be let in, they saw you go inside.'

'I *didn't* kill her,' I say again, because I'm scared now, and I couldn't bear it if he doesn't believe me.

'We're going to get through this, me and you, I promise,' he assures me. 'It's a tragedy, what happened to Diane, but... well, at least you won't have to always be looking over your shoulder any more.'

But he must see how shattered I am, how exhausted; I feel overwhelmed, my head throbs as if it's still clogged with smoke. 'Come on. Go up and take that shower. It'll help make you feel better.'

42

Despite lifting my face to the almost scalding heat of the shower, I shiver with cold. Whenever I close my eyes, all I can see is Diane disappearing like a ghost into the smoke. I'd do anything to turn back the clock, to make her live again, but the water can't wash away the helplessness I feel; all I can do is let the spray pound against my aching muscles.

But when I turn off the shower and reach for the towel, it's not on the rail. There's no hand towel either. I'm cold and wet and I've no choice but to move naked across the bathroom to open the door.

'Cam.' A chill comes into the bathroom through the crack. Shaking, I call his name again, but he doesn't answer. 'Cam, are you there?'

I'm ready to rush across the landing to my bedroom when he appears at the bottom of the stairs.

'Hi,' he calls up. 'Everything okay?'

'There's no towel,' I tell him, poking my head out of the door. Shiv must have washed the one in the bathroom and forgotten to replace it. 'Do you mind going into my bedroom and getting another one? It's in the top drawer of the dresser.'

'Sure,' he says, and as he climbs the stairs, I close the door. A minute later, he knocks.

'It's here,' he says.

'Just leave it out—'

But the door's already opening, and I stand back quickly as his arm reaches inside the narrow gap to hand me the towel. When I look up, I see him reflected in the fading steam of the bathroom mirror, which means he can also see me standing naked behind the door. Our eyes meet for a moment, and then I hurriedly take the towel and shut the door.

A few minutes later, just as I'm finishing getting dressed in the bedroom, the front door opens downstairs, and I hear Shiv come in with Amber. The idea of holding my daughter in my arms sends me rushing to the stairs. As I come down, Cam is talking pleasantly to Shiv while she lifts Amber out of the stroller.

But when I get to the bottom, I freeze.

Cam claps his hands and says, 'How about I make us all a nice cup of tea?'

'What are you doing?' I ask her under my breath. With Amber in one arm, she's crouching to take the travel bag from the webbing beneath the stroller, and I say again, 'What do you think you're doing?'

Shiv looks up uncertainly as I lurch forward.

'How dare you,' I hiss, my throat exploding in hoarse pain. 'How dare you look like that!'

Because Shiv doesn't just resemble my sister Natalie any more. The way she's dressed, in a red striped summer frock – an exact copy of my sister's favourite dress, the one my parents told me she was wearing on the last day of her life

– the way she's styled her hair, the colour of her eyeshadow, even the sandals she wears: she's identical to Natalie.

Picking up on the charged atmosphere, Amber begins to babble. Shiv stares, wide-eyed. 'I'm sorry, I don't—'

'That dress, where did you get it?' She looks bewildered that I've taken against her again, but I don't care, and step forward to pull Amber from her arms.

Shiv appeals to Cam. 'I don't remember, I've had it a few years now, it was from a charity shop, I think.'

'You've never worn it before,' I say. 'Not once, or had your hair like that, or worn make-up like that.'

'Okay.' Cam lifts his hands. 'Let's just calm—'

But Shiv says, 'But I have worn it before.'

'No,' I say. 'That's not true, you've never worn it. Not once!'

Cam walks between us. 'There's been some kind of misunderstanding, I'm sure.'

'She's dressed like my sister. Her hair, her make-up, everything! It's her. It's what she wore when...' It feels like I'm gargling glass when I spit out the words; my chest feels as if it's packed with concrete. 'That was the dress in which she *killed* herself.'

Shiv turns deathly pale. Her face trembles.

'Hey, Siobhan,' Cam tells her quietly. 'Why don't you go upstairs and change into something else?'

Her voice cracks. 'I'm sorry, I didn't—'

'Get out of my sight!' I scream. She rushes up the stairs. Breathing hard, I hold Amber close. She squirms in my arms, and I press my lips to her hair, shushing her, trying to make her feel better, as if it isn't me who just made her upset.

'I'm sorry,' I tell Cam, immediately embarrassed.

He looks at me with concern, but also disapproval; his look *hurts*. 'It's not me you need to apologize to.'

'She looks just like her,' I insist. 'Just like Natalie.'

'I'll have to take your word on that.' He folds his arms, thinking. 'But I'm going to be honest with you, H, she doesn't look much different to how she usually does. She's done her hair in a different way, maybe.'

'No.' I shake my head. 'That's not the way it is.' Cam glances at Amber, as if worried that her mother is a deranged woman. 'Don't look at me like that, don't you dare!'

'Fine,' he says quietly. 'You probably want to be on your own, so I'll just go.'

But that means I'll be left here with Shiv, and I can't face that, not now. Right at this moment, I can't face any of it. The fire, Diane's death, speaking to the police tomorrow. Shattered, exhausted, I press the heel of my hand hard into my temple. 'Please stay. I'm confused, tired. I must have made a mistake.'

'What did I tell you?' Cam sighs. 'You're in shock, you have nervous exhaustion. It's all completely understandable right now. You should go to bed.'

'It's the middle of the afternoon.'

'Listen to your body.'

'But Amber...'

'I'll ask Siobhan to look after her.'

'You can't, not after—'

'Siobhan is a grown-up. She's concerned for you, and she understands that you're not... in the right headspace. She'll be fine about it, I promise. Go and lie down and I'll speak to her.'

He takes me by the hand and leads me upstairs.

'You've a big day tomorrow,' he says outside my room. 'The police are coming, so you need a clear head. Get yourself into bed, and I'll bring you a drink.' He takes Amber from me, kissing me on the forehead; I can't help but lean into the soft press of his lips.

'I should speak to her,' I tell him. 'Apologize.'

'Let me do that for now,' he says in a whisper, because we're close to Shiv's room. 'There's plenty of time tomorrow.'

Inside my room, I stand against the wall listening, as Cam knocks softly on Shiv's door.

'Hey, Siobhan,' I hear him say when it opens. 'May I come in?'

The door closes and I can hear them talking quietly in the next room, but can't make out what they're saying.

Pulling on a tee-shirt, I get under the duvet, and my body sinks gratefully into the mattress. The voices murmur next door. Then Cam leaves and goes downstairs. A few minutes later, he comes into my room.

He hesitates at the door, frowning. 'Sorry, I should have knocked.'

I give him a weary smile. 'I'll let you off.'

He's got another mug of herbal tea in one hand and a glass of water in the other, and places them both on the bedside cabinet. Then he goes to the shutters and closes them, blocking out the daylight.

He comes over and helps me prop myself up against the headboard, then picks up the water.

'Take these.' In his palm are a couple of pills.

'What are they?'

'Painkillers.'

'I'm not in pain.'

'They'll help you relax. Doctor's orders.'

I gulp down the pills with water, and then ask, 'What did Shiv say?'

'Of course she's happy to help,' he assures me. 'She understands the trauma you've been through, and that you're not yourself. I think I can predict that you won't see that dress again.'

'I'm so tired,' I tell him, resting my head on his upper arm, which feels warm and solid beneath my brow.

'It's only been a day. Your body is still in recovery mode.'

'Is that your professional opinion?' I ask.

'I'll go and get my stethoscope and tell you again, and then maybe I'll look like a real doctor. I'll try and get here early tomorrow before the police arrive.'

There's something I need to tell him again. 'I didn't start that fire. I didn't kill Diane.'

He nods, which isn't the overpowering reassurance that I need. He stands. 'I'd better let you sleep.'

I don't want him to go. I can't face being alone. Not now, not tonight. And Cam has been a rock. He's been there when I've needed him; he saved my life.

Conscious that Shiv is next door, I keep my voice low. 'Do you have to go? Please stay tonight.'

'Sure,' he says after hesitating. 'I'll make up the couch.'

'No.'

I need more. I need him to stay with me, someone to hold me, and I pull him down onto the bed. He presses me close. Our faces almost touch, I feel his soft breath on my lips, and we both know what's going to happen next. It's wrong – he's married, his wife is sick. I'm being selfish, but I don't care, because I want him, and I can't bear it if he were to leave.

Moving my mouth onto his, I give him every opportunity to resist, but he responds. His kisses are gentle at first, and then harder. He takes my head in his splayed fingers to hold my face steady and I grind my body hard against his. My tears wet his cheeks.

'I want you here,' I whisper. 'Please, stay.'

A long time ago I dismissed Cam from my life in the most callous way, but he's with me now, keeping me safe.

43

Twenty Years Ago

When I dumped Cam, I gave him no explanation or warning, I just stopped seeing him, removed him from my life as if he never existed. He turned up at my bedsit and rang the bell, banged on the door, waited outside for hours on end. He called and called, until at last he left one final message on the answering machine:

'Hannah? Are you there? Please answer... please, Hannah. Just talk to me. Tell me why you won't talk to me... I love you... There's something you need to know, but I can't tell you like this. You have to let me in. Please, H. I did something for you, and it shows just how much I love you, Hannah. I did something and it'll change everything between us, it'll make you love me. I can't... I can't tell you it like this, so please let me in. Or call me, tell me what you're thinking. I'm so afraid of losing you... I'll leave you alone now, I won't pester you, I promise, but please call... I love you so much.'

Eventually he got the message, and stayed away.
And then I was able to begin again.

44

'Why did you go to the home of Miss Clemence?' asks the detective.

I had hoped that I'd feel better after a long night's sleep, but I don't. My head is still thick with anxiety and fear, my body aches. Cam says it's because of all the trauma, but I know I look jittery and nervous.

The police detective, DS Sheehy, watches me carefully every time I rub my hands or rake my nails along my arms.

'I'm sorry,' I say, distracted. 'Can you repeat the question?'

'Why did you go to the house of Miss Clemence?'

Glancing at Cam, who sits on the sofa beside me, I take a deep breath.

'I needed to... talk to her.'

Sheehy nods. 'About what?'

'It didn't make sense to me why she snatched Amber and then brought her back here. One of your officers...' I glance at the two PCs who stand in the room behind Detective Sergeant Sheehy, but don't recognize either of them, '...told me that when Diane... Miss Clemence... was interviewed, she said she wanted to tell me something, but she refused to say what it was. I thought that by going to her house, I could find out, and put my own mind at rest.'

Sheehy smiles pleasantly. He's a tall, slim man. His neck doesn't seem to make any contact with the buttoned collar of his white shirt, and his long legs are folded awkwardly in the small space between the armchair and the low coffee table.

'You went to her house alone?'

'It was a spur of the moment thing. Cam phoned when I was in the car and tried to persuade me not to go. God, how I wish I'd listened to him now.'

'We spoke for a minute or so,' Cam tells him. 'And when it was obvious that Hannah was intent on speaking to Diane, I left work immediately to try to—'

'I'll get to you in a minute, Mr West,' Sheehy tells him pleasantly – Cam holds his hands palms out in apology – and turns back to me. 'And what did Diane want to tell you?'

My chest clenches just thinking about it. Diane is gone, she died in that blazing inferno, and if Cam hadn't turned up and dragged me out, I'd be dead too.

'I don't know, I got there and we… argued, and everything seemed to happen so fast after that.'

'You argued,' repeats Sheehy. But before I can elaborate, he says, 'Oh, by the way, do you mind if we look around the house while we're here?'

'Why would you want to do that?' The request fills me with a paranoid dread, and I instinctively reach for Cam's hand. 'Do you suspect me of something?'

'You don't have to agree,' Sheehy says, avoiding the question. 'But it could save time going forward.'

'That won't be a problem, will it?' Cam squeezes my hand. 'It's not like you've got anything to hide.'

Sheehy unfolds a piece of paper. 'There's just a form you need to sign. Or we can come back later... with a search warrant.'

'My baby is outside.' The door of the living room is open and I've got a clear view into the kitchen and garden, where Shiv sits playing with Amber on the lawn.

'You'll hardly know we're here,' says Sheehy.

'I don't see how it can hurt,' says Cam. 'Of course Hannah is very happy to cooperate.'

The idea of the police poking around my house fills me with a nameless dread; I don't feel in control of anything that's happening, but reluctantly agree. Sheehy goes over to the two officers and speaks quietly to them, and they leave the room.

'So.' Sitting down again, the detective adjusts his long legs behind the table. 'Take me back to what happened when you went inside Diane's house?'

'I didn't want to go inside, because there was so much junk,' I tell him. 'It was piled everywhere. I wanted to talk to Diane at the door, but she disappeared off down the hallway, so I had to follow her in.'

'Did you go straight to the kitchen, or did you look around elsewhere?'

The question makes me pause. I don't know what he's trying to imply; that I went around the house lighting fires?

'I followed her. I mean, it took a while to get to the kitchen because of the piles of junk in the hallway.'

'So you didn't go into the living room at all.' He's writing in his notepad. 'Or upstairs?'

'No.' When I glance at Cam, he gives me a surreptitious nod, *you're doing well*. 'Why would I?'

'And when you followed her, did you shut the front door or leave it open?'

'I think I closed it. I know it sounds crazy in the circumstances, what with the state of the house and everything, but I was trying to act like everything was normal. And also...'

'What?' Sheehy looks up when I don't finish the thought.

'I guess I wanted privacy.' Cam's still smiling as I speak, but his expression is strained. Sheehy must easily be able to pick up the tension in a room. 'I tried to talk to her, and that's when we began to argue.'

'What did you argue about?' says Sheehy quietly.

'About her brother.'

The detective pinches the bridge of his nose. It's not the answer he was expecting. 'Go on.'

'The reason Diane had a grudge against me, why she got in contact out of the blue, is that she blamed me for something that happened nearly twenty years ago. She claims I was responsible for traumatizing her brother.'

'Both of us.' Cam squeezes my hand again. 'She blames both of us.'

'I...' It's hard to concentrate because I can hear the uniformed officers walking about in my bedroom above our heads. The thought of them opening drawers and cabinets, touching all my personal things, makes me lose my train of thought. 'We made him believe that he'd killed me.'

Sheehy blinks. 'And why would you do that?'

'It was kind of a prank,' says Cam. 'A childish prank.'

'But it was also a revenge,' I tell the detective, because I feel compelled to be as honest as possible. 'I'd discovered that this man had attacked a friend of mine, he'd seriously assaulted her at his flat, and we… *I* wanted to teach him a lesson. Whatever Cam says, it was my idea. We got him drunk and went back to his flat and then pretended that he'd killed me; we used fake blood and everything. It was a stupid thing to do, very infantile and mean, and he was shaken, but there was no harm done, and we never saw him again after that night.'

Sheehy looks at us both. 'And what's his name, her brother?'

'Martin,' says Cam.

'He's dead now,' I blurt out, and Sheehy looks at me. 'According to Diane, he killed himself.'

'She said he died four years ago,' says Cam. 'Which is many, *many* years after that incident.'

The detective runs a finger along the gap between his neck and collar. I've no idea if he knows who I am, if he knows I'm the Queen of Hearts, but if he does, he's probably deeply unimpressed with my often repeated mantra of *always be kind*.

'Diane was a troubled woman,' says Cam. 'It wouldn't surprise me if she started that fire herself.'

'I'll be coming to you in a minute, sir,' Sheehy reminds him firmly.

The detective probably already knows the sequence of events that led to my final, tragic encounter with Diane, but I tell him anyway. About how she phoned the radio show, and came into my house that same night to vandalize my mirror; how she pushed Dad down the stairs at the restaurant, and snatched Amber.

'So you argued in the kitchen,' says Sheehy. 'And then what happened?'

'Smoke started pouring in from the hallway. It all happened so fast. The back door was locked, Diane couldn't find a key – I mean, it would be impossible to find anything in there – and then she tried to lead me to the front of the house. The hallway was full of flame and smoke so we had to climb over a pile of rubbish into another room – the living room, I think. The smoke made it impossible to see anything, I had no idea where we were going, I just followed her. We got almost to the door apparently, we could probably have got out, but then... Diane fell.'

'The post-mortem suggests Miss Clemence sustained a head injury when she was struck by a heavy object.'

Sheehy speaks in such a matter-of-fact way, but he watches my clammy fingers rub against the seat of the sofa. The ground beneath my feet feels like it's sliding away. The officers are coming downstairs; their heavy shoes clatter on the steps.

'We were running between two massive piles of junk,' I tell him quickly. I need him to know the truth, and to understand that I would never, *could never*, be responsible for her death. 'It was impossible to see anything because of all the smoke, and I could hardly breathe. My top got snagged on one of the piles and I pulled at it. The next thing I know, something – a desk, I think – toppled down and fell on her.'

'You pulled it down?' asks DS Sheehy lightly.

'No!' He's trying to imply that I did it on purpose, made it crash onto her, or even swung it into her head. 'She pushed me out of harm's way as it came down, and it fell on her instead. I tried, I really tried, to get her off the floor, but she wouldn't move. I couldn't... she wouldn't wake up... and then I couldn't breathe... I just felt so tired.'

'Smoke inhalation,' Cam tells him.

Sheehy peers at his notes. 'You say she pushed you.'

'I think Hannah has been very clear about what happened,' says Cam in irritation.

'She saved my life. If I could have picked her up and carried her the rest of the way, I would have. But I didn't have the strength.' I'm in tears. 'And I will have to live with that knowledge for the rest of my life.'

Sheehy looks at me for a long moment.

'You were very lucky, because Dr West turned up.'

As he makes a note in his pad, I watch the uniformed officers move around the kitchen, opening cupboards and drawers. One of them walks into the garden.

'But Diane wasn't lucky,' I say, wiping away my tears with the back of my hand. 'I'd do anything to turn back time.'

'And it's lucky that you got there when you did,' DS Sheehy tells Cam. 'If emergency services had been at the scene, there's no way you would have been allowed to go in.'

'Do you know yet how the fire started?' asks Cam.

The detective considers his reply carefully. One of the officers is walking up the garden. He nods amiably at Shiv, who gets Amber to wave at him, and carries on to the shed.

'We believe it was started deliberately, probably by firelighters. Fire investigators found evidence of several points of ignition in the hallway, in the living room and on the stairs.'

Standing at the shed, the officer pulls at the lock, then cups his hands at the window to look inside.

My heart leaps, because the opened pack of firelighters is sitting on the lid of the barbecue in the corner. It's the first thing you'd see looking in, and he can't miss it.

'Because there was so much combustible material in that house, and it was started in multiple places, it took just seconds for the fire to spread,' Sheehy is saying.

The second officer joins the first to look through the window of the shed; they talk for a moment, then walk back towards the house.

'Diane had a grudge against Hannah, and as soon as Hannah stepped inside, she saw her chance.' Cam turns to me. 'You said yourself, she hurried off after she opened the door, she could have thrown matches as she walked to the kitchen.'

I know he's trying to take the heat off me, and maybe it's too little, too late, but my instinct is to protect poor Diane.

'That doesn't make sense,' I say. 'She tried to save me.'

'What's more likely is that she realized she was trapped in that house too,' Cam says. 'Which is typical Diane. Or she was willing to kill you both.'

Sheehy looks slightly irritated by Cam's constant interruptions. 'If the fire was set on purpose, then there's only two ways it could have happened. The perpetrator entered the house at some earlier point to place those firelighters – they would have been easily missed, because the house was full of boxes – and then returned to the house when you were there. Or they were already hiding in the house when you arrived.'

'We heard a noise,' I tell him. 'Diane said she thought it was mice, but I'm sure there was somebody there.'

'Can you tell me more?'

'It came from the hallway, it was a rustling, as if someone was brushing past the refuse bags. I'd only been there a couple of minutes.'

The officers are walking back into the room.

'When you arrived at the house,' Sheehy asks Cam, 'was the door shut?'

'Yeah, I had to break it down. The lock was flimsy, it was just a Yale lock. The neighbours watched me do it.'

The officers nod at Sheehy, and I'm certain they're going to tell him about the firelighters in the shed, or take Sheehy outside to show him. I can't help but squeeze Cam's hand even more tightly. I'm sweating so much that his fingers are slippery in mine.

'All done,' one of the officers says, and then they leave.

'Well, I think that's all we need from you now, Mrs Godley,' Sheehy tells me, running the tip of his pen down the notepad to double-check everything.

Cam is about to stand but Sheehy smiles at him. 'But I'd like to take a statement from you, Dr West, if you don't mind.'

'Of course.' Cam sits back down, but I sense his unease at having to leave me.

'It won't take long,' the detective tells me.

Shutting the door to the living room behind me, I rush to the garden.

45

Cam will be telling Sheehy how he called me while I was driving to Diane's house on Friday – about our brief, frantic conversation, and how he left work to try to find me – and it gives me the chance to go to the shed. I still haven't apologized to Shiv properly since yesterday's outburst, and it's a reflection of my panic that it doesn't even occur to me to say anything to her or Amber as I walk past them on the lawn.

If the police looked inside the shed – and I definitely saw them cup their hands to the glass – they surely can't have missed the crumbling bricks of firelighters on the lid of the barbecue.

The officers are waiting outside the house for the DS to finish taking Cam's statement. Are they waiting for Sheehy to leave before telling him what they saw? Will they return with a proper warrant to search the house more thoroughly, or will I be arrested straight away?

Unlocking the shed with the key kept in the kitchen, I step into the suffocating heat inside – but the box of firelighters is gone. The barbecue hasn't been used for weeks and it's sitting in the corner, as usual. And yet those firelighters – the kind in a waxy slab that can be snapped into square chunks that ignite easily, and then dropped into cardboard boxes and plastic bags full of paper – are gone.

The only person who knew they were in here, because he placed them on the lid, is Sean. And that makes me remember his fury at Diane the other day. Sean must have taken those firelighters. But the idea that he could have used them to torch Diane's house while we were both inside shocks me to the core.

It's stuffy in the confined space of the shed; the sun beats down through the scuffed glass of the window. Inside the house, Cam and the detective come out of the living room. They stand talking for a moment, and then Cam shows Sheehy out. A moment later, he comes into the garden, crouching in front of Shiv to ask her if she knows where I am. She points towards the shed, and he says something quietly as he strokes Amber's hair. A moment later, Shiv picks up Amber and her toys, and the pair of them go into the house.

Then Cam comes into the shed. 'Doing a bit of gardening?'

'Are they still here, the police?'

'Gone,' he says. 'Do you want to come inside?'

'There were firelighters.' I point at the lid of the barbecue. 'A packet of them right there. But they're not here any more, they're gone!'

He frowns. 'Hold on a minute—'

'Sean did it. He took them and he started the fire. I can't believe it, but he killed Diane.' Something occurs to me suddenly. 'Maybe the plan was always to kill both of us, because he couldn't bear that I threw him out.'

'Look,' says Cam. 'I'm no fan of the guy, but do you really believe he could do such a thing?'

'Yes, because he hates me.' My voice is becoming shrill. 'They were *here*!'

Cam raises his voice over mine. '*I* took the firelighters.'

'You did?' I look at him, stunned. 'Why would you do that?'

'Because when you were in the hospital, I knew the police would come here, and I knew it wouldn't look good if they found them. I found the key to the shed, you keep it in that little dish on the shelf, and took them away.'

'That's tampering with evidence, that's a crime.'

'Is it, I don't know?' He looks flustered. 'If it is, I don't care, because all I care about is you.'

What he did should make me feel better, because he's trying to protect me, but it doesn't. 'You think I did it. Despite what you said, you think I killed Diane.'

'That's not what I meant.'

'Be honest with me, please.'

Cam takes me in his arms, holds me tightly. 'I don't care what you did, I'm going to protect you.'

He thinks I took the firelighters from here, scattered them around Diane's house and set them alight. He believes I confronted Diane, smashed her over the head with a piece of furniture, and left her for dead in the fire, despite the fact that I was almost killed too.

With my face crushed against his shoulder, tears soak into the cotton of his shirt. His mouth presses into my hair, and he tells me again and again, 'I'm going to protect you, I'm going to protect you…'

'Why are you here if you think I could do such a thing?'

'Because I love you,' he says quietly.

His statement hits me like a hammer and I pull away so that I can look into his face. 'You don't mean that.'

'I'm afraid I do,' he tells me sadly.

'You're married,' I tell him, trying to make sense of it. 'Your wife is—'

'I know all that,' he tells me and sighs. 'I can't help what I feel.'

He looks at me expectantly, I can see he wants me to say the same to him, but my mouth opens and nothing comes out. It's too much. On top of everything else, it's just *too much*. I need time to think about what's happening. And maybe he understands that I'm overwhelmed, because he smiles.

'Nothing's going to happen to you. You've been under stress, you've not been thinking straight, you were scared for your daughter's safety, and terror makes us … irrational. One bad thing doesn't make you a bad person, it doesn't define who you are. But you *will* come out the other side of this, you have my word, and I'll be beside you every step of the way.'

'I didn't do it,' I whisper dismally.

He seems so convinced I did it that I try to remember the sequence of events again. I was here alone on the afternoon of Diane's death, I remember that much; my head a fog of angry, conflicting emotions. Had Diane told me about the state of her house? Did I get straight into the car that afternoon to drive to her home? Or did I come first into this small, hot shed, to break off a slab of the firelighters, then take matches from the drawer in the kitchen?

I don't even know any more.

'You still have them?' I ask him. 'The firelighters?'

'They're hidden. In case there are… residues at Diane's

house.' Cam squeezes my shoulders. 'You don't have to worry about anything. I'm here and Siobhan is here for you too.' He frowns. 'Talking of which, I want you to do something for me... apologize to Siobhan about yesterday.'

Nervous about the impending visit of the police this morning, I've not had a chance to talk to her since my outburst.

'You've got a lot on your plate at the moment, things are... uncertain, and she's been looking after Amber without complaint. It would be a shame if she walked out now.'

As I let Cam lead me up the garden path and back inside, my head swims with the knowledge that he thinks I killed Diane.

And my own dread suspicion is that in an unwell and confused state, I may well have done it.

46

Amber patiently waits in the stroller as Shiv loads her bag beneath the seat. She looks completely transformed from yesterday, more like her old self. Her hair has been straightened, she's not wearing any make-up, and she's dressed in jeans and trainers.

After chatting to Amber, I turn to Shiv. Desperate to make things better between us, my question comes out too loud and ingratiating. 'Where are you going, anywhere nice?'

'I thought we'd go to the park,' she says, avoiding my eye. 'And get an ice cream on the way, if that's okay?'

I don't want her to think that I don't trust her judgement. 'That sounds like a great idea.'

Satisfied that we're communicating, Cam walks away.

'Shiv.' I take a calming breath. 'I want to apologize about what happened yesterday.'

'You don't have to apologize. Cameron explained why you reacted the way you did. I honestly had no idea about… your sister, and I'm sorry if I caused you any distress. It was never my intention.'

'I know that,' I tell her. 'I overreacted, I was seeing phantoms. Everything that's happened recently, it's all getting to me. I'm so grateful you're here in difficult circumstances, and… please don't leave us.'

Shiv smiles tensely. 'I'm not going anywhere, Hannah. You and Amber are like family to me now. Please know that you will be happy again, I promise.'

'Thank you,' I say in a grateful whisper.

'Hey, look.' Shiv swipes open her phone screen. 'I took photos of Amber at the party we went to, do you want to see them?'

I'd almost forgotten that Shiv had taken her to a friend's house on the afternoon I made the fatal decision to drive to Diane's. It's good to see Amber with other kids of her own age. She's smiling and happy as she plays, full of life and love. But it's bittersweet to look at these photos. They were most likely taken at the same time as I was fighting for my life in a smoke-filled room. And I could yet be convicted of Diane's murder and go to prison; I may not see my daughter for years, maybe ever again.

A knot of fear tightens in my stomach. 'She looks like she had a lovely time.'

'She really did.' Shiv looks pleased at my reaction to the photos. 'Hannah, it's not my place, but—'

She wants to say something, but shakes her head.

'What is it?'

'It's just, well, you've got a lot on your mind, and Amber's been grouchy for the last few days. I think it's… the atmosphere.'

'What are you saying?' I ask her.

'I'm happy to take her away for a few days.'

'Sounds like a plan,' says Cam, listening on the other side of the kitchen. 'Till everything blows over.'

'I don't know,' I say doubtfully.

Right now, Amber is the only thing keeping me going, and I don't like the idea of not having her near. It's not like my parents will want to take in Shiv, either, and I don't want to impose on friends who live out of town.

But at the same time, the future is uncertain. I could be interviewed by the police at any time, even arrested and kept in a cell overnight. Only yesterday, I lost my temper in front of her, and it would destroy me to think I was projecting my own fears and anxieties onto my baby.

'It would really cheer her up,' says Shiv. 'I think I mentioned Dad has a lovely cottage on the Norfolk coast, right on the beach, and it's empty most of the year. It would be a wonderful holiday for Amber. We could all go.'

'That part of the coastline is beautiful,' says Cam, wiping his hands on a tea towel and coming over. 'I know it well.'

'It really is,' Shiv agrees.

'Let me think about it,' I say, because as much as I'm grateful for what Shiv's done for me, I really want to keep Amber near.

Returning the phone to Shiv reminds me that there are things I need to do. I should contact the *Morning Brew* office to explain what's happened, and I need to call Sean too. Only earlier, I was convinced he was a murderer. My emotions are all over the place.

'Where's my phone?' I ask Cam, when Shiv and Amber have left.

'Destroyed in the fire,' he says, as he clicks on the kettle.

'No, I left it in the car when I went inside.'

Cam gives me a long, appraising look. 'The detective who

came here told me it was found in the doorway of the house, don't you remember taking it in?'

'No.' I pull my hands down my face, because nothing makes sense any more. 'I didn't, I'm sure of it.'

'When the mind has been through a trauma, H, it can block out certain memories to protect itself.'

Cam winces a little at his poor choice of words, because we both know I may have blocked out the most traumatic memory of all: that I killed Diane. It makes me sick to think I could be capable of such a thing. But Cam has seen me at my absolute worst in the past, humiliating Martin, and maybe a part of him believes I am capable of going that far.

'Anyway.' He turns away to pick up the boiling kettle, so he doesn't have to meet my gaze. 'It's all perfectly normal, and those memories will come back.'

'Where's the landline?' I ask, because the home phone isn't in its usual cradle on the counter.

'No idea,' he says brightly, grateful perhaps that I've changed the subject. 'I didn't even know you had one.'

'I need to make some calls, can I use your phone?' It's on the kitchen island and I pick it up, but he comes over quickly and snatches it from me.

'I don't want you going outside or making calls, not until this situation has died down,' he says.

'I can't just hide away, Cam.' I'm surprised at his tone. 'I've got to get on with my life. And there are people who'll be worried about what's happened.'

'All that can wait.' He takes a couple of pills out of his pocket.

'I'm not Penny,' I tell him. 'I'm not an invalid.'

'No, you're not.' He sighs, and I have to remind myself

307

that he's got a lot on his plate at home, and doesn't have to be here. 'I'm sorry I snapped. I just want... I want you back on your feet, but you can't rush it, it's going to take time.'

He comes over and we hold each other, and then he picks up the herbal tea he's made for me. 'Come on, you need a nap. Let's get you to bed.'

47

Thin blades of light blur the edge of the shutters in my bedroom. My head is groggy, thick with tiredness. After what feels like another long, dreamless sleep, my arms and legs feel heavy. I can't believe how much time I'm spending in bed.

My first instinct is to reach for my mobile, but the only thing on the bedside cabinet is the empty mug that contained the tea Cam gave me. Then I remember that my phone was apparently destroyed in the blaze.

The house is eerily quiet. Usually, I'd hear Shiv and Amber downstairs, or the burble of the radio, but there's no sound at all. My watch says that it's nearly five, which means I've slept most of the morning and all afternoon, so I get up and climb into a pair of leggings.

But when I try to open the bedroom door, it's locked. One of the quirks of the house is that the bedrooms all have keys in the doors, which are part of the original features. Sean and I never used them, there was never any reason, but the key that usually sits in the lock on the inside of the door is gone. When I look through the keyhole, I can see a small portion of the banister on the landing, which means it isn't even in the lock on the other side.

'Hello?' I call. 'Shiv? Cam?'

There's no point in panicking, I tell myself, because Shiv is probably in the garden with Amber. And if Cam is still here, he'll probably be with her.

But my heart begins to thump, because I don't understand why it's been locked in the first place.

'Cam!' I call again, trying to stifle my panic. 'Shiv! Up here!'

Banging my fists on the door, I shout and shout, but nobody comes. The door is old and slightly warped, and rattles when I pull the handle, but it won't open.

Bright light floods into the room when I open the shutters. It's still hot and sunny outside. Pulling up the sash, I look down. It would be impossible for me to climb down from the first floor, I have no idea how I'd even dare attempt it. But there are people walking past, and I'm just about to call to one of them when I see Shiv coming along the pavement, pushing Amber in the stroller.

'Shiv!' I shout as she arrives at the gate and stares up at me in surprise. 'I'm locked in. Can you let me out?'

Pushing the buggy quickly up the path, I hear Shiv let herself into the house directly below. Less than a minute later, she's standing on the other side of the door. The handle turns when she tries it, but the door doesn't open.

She says, 'There's no key.'

'Is it out there?' I call to her. 'Is it on the floor?'

'No,' she says. 'Hold on, I'll look downstairs.'

As her footsteps retreat, I rest my forehead against the soft fabric of Sean's dressing gown, which still hangs on the door. But I dare not close my eyes, because Diane's nailed-shut garden door keeps flashing into my mind. For one chilling moment, I think I smell burning, and the rippling shadows of the leaves on a tree outside shimmer like smoke on the wall. Trying to control my breathing, I tell myself it's not happening again, that I'm going to be free in a few seconds, but Shiv doesn't come back.

I bang on the door again. 'Shiv, please, let me out!'

It must be minutes now, it feels much longer, and she still doesn't return, so I shove my shoulder as hard as I dare against the door. I have to get out, I can't stay in here, I need air and space. I feel like I'm suffocating, I can't breathe.

'Shiv!' I scream, slapping the palms of my hands against the door, making them sting. She must have gone out again. 'Shiv! Let me out!'

And then there's a click on the other side of the door and the handle turns. The door opens. Shiv stands there, but I stumble past her, across the landing, down the stairs and into the open space of the garden.

'Where did you go?' I ask when she comes outside. 'You took forever!'

'I'm sorry,' she says, and holds up the key. 'I couldn't find it anywhere.'

'Where was it?'

She nods at the counter. 'It was here, but it had been left behind the fruit bowl.'

'Who locked me in?' I ask, as I walk inside to lift Amber from the stroller. 'Was it you?'

'We've been out most of the day,' she reminds me, looking surprised.

'I don't understand why anybody would do that, why would Cam lock me in?'

'I wasn't here.' Shiv shakes her head. 'I don't know.'

'It's okay,' I tell her, conscious that I've already had to apologize to her once today.

'What's that noise?' she asks, and I realize there's a phone ringing. Cam's jacket hangs over the back of a stool in the kitchen, and it's coming from there. His mobile is in the breast pocket and when I take it out, I see Penny's name on the screen.

'Maybe you shouldn't,' says Shiv when she sees I'm thinking about answering it. She's probably right, but I'm annoyed with Cam, and press the screen to connect the call.

Walking over to Shiv, I give her Amber and walk back outside.

'Hello,' I say.

There's a long pause on the other end and then a faint voice says, 'Is Cameron there, please?'

'I'm afraid he's not. Is... this Penny?'

'Yes,' she says uncertainly. 'Please tell him I called.'

'Penny, it's Hannah. Cameron's friend.'

Turning on the lawn, I look back inside. Shiv holds Amber while she cleans up, but every now and then she glances over at me.

'Yes,' says Penny. Her voice is weak, the fragility of it shocks me, and I wish I'd never answered the phone. 'I know all about you. I hope you will make him happy, in the way that Charlotte and I weren't able to.'

'He's not... I'm sorry if you think...'

'I understand what's happening,' she says sadly. 'Cameron has told me all about it, of course he has, and you have my blessing. I just hope... I want to know what's going to happen to me.'

'I'm just a friend,' I lie, and the treacherous reality of my growing relationship with Cam makes me feel awful. 'You're married, and I know how much he cares for you, and that you will always be his first and only priority.'

'I'm not a fool. I know what's going on between you. It was inevitable, really.'

'That's not true. He's told me how much he lo—'

'*Please.*' A sudden sharpness in her voice stops me in my tracks. 'I wish you all the best. Tell him I called, will you?'

And then she hangs up.

Walking back inside, I place the phone on the kitchen island and take Amber to the living room – it's not something I feel comfortable talking about to Shiv – and we spend time together for what feels like the first time in ages, looking at picture books and playing with her toys.

Forty minutes later, Cam lets himself back into the house. I don't remember giving him keys.

'Hey,' he says, when he sees me. 'You're up.'

'Where have you been?'

'I just popped to the high street to get you some stuff.' He opens a plastic bag to show me food he's bought, including a loaf, a carton of milk, fruit and vegetables. He also pulls a phone from the bag and holds it up. 'And I got you this. It's charged and I've put the number on the back so you know what it is.'

'You locked me in the bedroom.' I climb to my feet and show him the key.

'Ah.' He looks mortified. 'I'm sorry.'

'Why would you do that?'

'I just wanted to make sure you were safe while I was out,' he says, embarrassed. 'I thought you'd still be asleep.'

'I was trapped in the bedroom, Cam, and I imagined smoke. I honestly thought I was going to die.'

'I didn't want you to wake up and panic if there was nobody in the house. It seemed like a good idea at the time.' He winces. 'I made a mistake, and I apologize completely.'

'Shiv, do you mind?'

She comes over, and I hand Amber to her and then fetch a pair of trainers by the door.

Cam watches as I force my feet into them, one after the other, without undoing the laces. 'What are you doing?'

'I'm going out.' Stomping the second trainer onto my right foot, I snatch my keys off the kitchen counter. 'I need some fresh air.'

'I'll come with you,' he suggests.

'No, I need to be alone for a while.'

Shiv gives a little nod from the living-room doorway, as if to reassure me that Amber will be fine. Part of me wants to take my daughter with me, it feels like too long since I've gone anywhere with her, but there's somewhere I need to go alone.

'Look,' I tell Cam, because he's frowning. 'I've got things to do, and I can't stay *locked up* here all day.'

Cam blushes. There's a tinge of frustration in his voice when he says, 'I apologized for locking you in. At least take this, in case you need it. It's got the internet and everything.'

He comes over and gives me the phone he's bought. It's a cheap Android model, more basic than the all-singing, all-dancing smartphone I lost. I'll replace my own phone as soon as possible, but this one will do for now; and I have to admit that it was generous of him to get it.

'That reminds me,' I tell him. 'Penny called.'

Cam looks astonished and reaches for his pocket, but I nod at his phone on the kitchen island. When he goes to get it, I slip out of the house and walk quickly down the path.

I don't have any pressing chores, and it's true I need to be on my own for a while, but there's also something else I want to do, and I didn't want to tell him what, because he'll try to convince me not to be so foolish – and he's dead right.

48

It's odd being back on Diane's street. Her house near the end of the row still stands, it has walls and most of its roof still, but the structure is a blackened shell. The windows and front door are gone and the gaping holes left behind are scorched, and covered in yellow police tape.

It would be dangerous to go inside, even if I wanted to. There's nothing for me to discover, no evidence left, even if I knew what it was I was looking for; nothing that will make me understand Diane any more than I do now, or provide any clue as to why she came into my life and did all those things.

Standing on the pavement in front of the house, my anxiety spikes. I don't even have to close my eyes to visualize Diane disappearing into the smoke in front of me, or the avalanche of rubbish falling at my feet as she clambered into the living room. If someone sees me, they may recognize me as the woman who was carried out of the burning building. My coming here could even convince the police that I'm guilty of Diane's murder.

'Excuse me,' says someone. 'Can I help you?'

When I turn, a middle-aged woman is coming out of a house on the opposite side of the street and walking towards me. She has curly brown hair turning grey at the roots, and her spindly arms are folded across her chest, as if she's trying not to look too nosy.

'Did you know Diane?' she asks.

'A little bit,' I tell her, edging away. 'I was just... looking.'

'So you heard, then, about what happened?'

'Yes.' My voice is still a bit hoarse, and I'm worried that at any moment she'll realize I was the woman pulled from the blaze. 'I suppose I did.'

'Was she a friend of yours? Or are you a social worker?' I shake my head, unsure of what to tell her. 'You look a bit upset, if you don't mind me saying. Would you like to come inside for a cup of tea? I knew Diane.' Her eyes roll to the sky. 'As much as anyone could be said to know her.'

There are so many different reasons why I shouldn't be here, but maybe I can learn more about Diane, even if it is too late to help her.

'Thank you,' I say. 'That's very kind of you.'

It's cool and dark inside the woman's house – she tells me her name is Linda – because the sun has already dropped behind the stretching limbs of a tree in the garden. Walking inside, I realize that the layout in this house is the same as the one in Diane's. It's cluttered, there are shoes kicked everywhere and schoolbooks dumped on the floor as you come in, and I have to walk around two mountain bikes leaning against the wall in the hallway, but the disorder in this comfortable family home is nothing on the scale of the chaos of Diane's house.

As she stands making tea, Linda talks about the fire. 'I was at work at the time, but I heard all about it from the neighbours. There were three fire engines, and one poor woman was taken away in an ambulance. A man broke the door down and managed to save her, but not poor Diane. It was a brave thing to do, but foolhardy, if you ask me. I wouldn't let my husband go inside, no way. Still, the chap saved a life, so fair play.' Placing the tea in front of me, Linda sits opposite at the table. It's still too hot, but she sips at her own cup thoughtfully. 'I'm just amazed Diane even had a visitor.'

The door to the garden is open and there's a slight breeze coming in. We'd be able to get outside in a heartbeat if a fire broke out now.

'How well did you know Diane?' I ask, and she thinks about it for a moment.

'I knew her better than most people around here.' Linda frowns, choosing her words carefully. 'Which had its challenges, let me tell you.'

'Why do you say that?' I ask, when she doesn't elaborate.

'Well, you know what she was like, I imagine.' She sets her cup on the table. 'I feel awful saying that, actually, because at heart she was a kindly soul. I got to know her quite well at one point. When she moved in, this was about four years ago now, and before the house became a...' She crinkles her nose. 'Disaster zone, I introduced myself, as you do when someone new arrives in the street. A lot of the people around here soon complained about all the stuff she was already dumping in the front garden. I don't know where she got it all, I think she spent most of her days going from one junkyard to the next, bringing it all back, like a little magpie.'

She waves a hand. 'Anyway, that's irrelevant. I told Diane she could pop over any time she liked. It was meant as a polite gesture, you understand, I was just being neighbourly.

I never expected her to take me so literally.' Linda blows out her cheeks. 'My goodness, did she take me at my word. I couldn't get rid of her, she was coming over four, five, six times a day. Bringing food and gifts. She must have been watching the house, because when I had guests she'd turn up too. It got so bad that I had to keep the curtains shut and not answer the door. And when she wasn't doing that, she was texting silly inspirational messages to me. I discovered that letting Diane into your life can be a bit... overwhelming.'

'Did anything happen to you during that period?' I ask.

Linda frowns. 'How do you mean?'

'Were there unexplained incidents, or... accidents involving you or your family?'

'Oh no.' Linda looks slightly shocked. 'It's not like she meant any harm, that's not her at all. She was like a little puppy, really, she just didn't have any boundaries.'

Sipping her tea, she says, 'It became very difficult, I'm afraid. Finally, my husband had to tell her to sling her hook. He was quite rude to her, and I was mortified, but I suppose it had to be done. Even then, Diane didn't get the message, and kept coming over as if we were best friends.'

'But she did leave you alone?'

'Yes, eventually, but it took a few months. It's not nice when you have to ignore one of your neighbours in the street, particularly when all they want is to be friends.' Linda gives me a strained smile, as if she's afraid I might judge her. 'But she really left me with no choice.'

'Did she have... other friends?'

'Not that I knew of.'

'So she didn't have visitors?'

'Nobody visited her during the day, that's for sure, although the door was often slamming late at night. Brian, that's my husband, joked that it was because she was bringing in a piece of junk from the front garden to take to bed with her.'

'I know she had a brother, but he died a number of years back.'

'Did she?' Linda is surprised. 'I didn't know that. I can't recall her ever revealing much about herself.'

'Did she speak about her parents?'

'Never mentioned them. They're dead, I presume. I know Diane lived in Ealing for a while, before she moved here. Chattersea Close, I think. I always remember the street because I had an aunt who lived there many years ago.'

Linda starts to tell me about her aunt, but I lose track of what she's saying, because something about the name of that street rings a faint bell in my mind.

'It's such a shame about her, don't you think?' Linda says. 'She wasn't a bad lady, just lonely. She's gone now, and what will she leave behind? Nothing much.' She shakes her head. 'What a terrible way to go.'

She gazes at me thoughtfully. 'Diane would do anything for you, you know? I remember one time, she saw me running down the road when I was very upset. It was my daughter's birthday party and I'd only gone and dropped the cake all over the floor. I rushed to the supermarket to buy a replacement, but all they had was a cheap sponge cake, and I felt awful. Just as the party was about to get going, Diane turns up on my doorstep with the most beautiful cake, it really was special. It must have cost an arm and a leg, that cake, and I'm sure she didn't have the money, but she wouldn't let me pay a single penny for it. She was a lovely lady in that way.

'I don't feel good about how things turned out between us, but at least I tried to be a good neighbour, which is more than some people around here.' She looks at me tensely. 'Do you know what I mean?'

'I know exactly what you mean.'

'That's the thing about people like Diane, isn't it? Lonely people, those poor souls who yearn to make a connection with anyone at all... It's just that sometimes they can be so needy and desperate and overwhelming. I wish there were more happy endings for people like that.'

Linda's got to get to the shops, she tells me, so I thank her for the tea and head towards the Tube, giving Diane's ruined home one last look.

At the very least, it was useful to know Diane had behaved obsessively with someone else. Cam has hypothesized that she ingratiated herself into the lives of other people more than once, and that her clumsy and toxic efforts inevitably got her rejected. Was her vow of revenge against me a weird and desperate way to insinuate herself into my life? It seems bizarre if, as Linda suggested, she was at her core a kindly person.

On the way to the station, I take out the phone Cam gave me. Concerned that the police are at my home right at this moment, intending to arrest and charge me with Diane's murder, I call DS Sheehy.

'This is a temporary number,' I tell him. 'Just in case you needed to contact me. I'll get my old number back in a day or so.'

'Thanks.' I hear him tapping a keyboard, making a note of the new number. 'Actually, while you're on, I wanted to clarify something with you. You told me Diane Clemence contacted you because you played a prank on her brother twenty years ago.'

'Yes, that's right.'

'And this Martin. Did he mention a sister?'

'It happened so long ago, I wouldn't remember.'

'Uh huh,' he says, after a moment.

'Why, what did you manage to find out about him?'

There's silence on the other end. I hear ringing phones in his office, a door opening and closing.

'Nothing,' he says finally. 'Because Diane Clemence didn't have a brother.'

49

What Sheehy told me doesn't make sense, it's surely not possible Diane didn't have a brother, but he insisted his team had checked her background thoroughly and found no record of any siblings.

The news is a shock – even in death, Diane is a woman of surprises and contradictions – but it also makes me uneasy. I've got the photo of me and Cam and Martin she gave to me; she told me, *that's my brother.*

My first instinct is to go home and tell Cam what Sheehy told me, but part of me doesn't want to find him still there. It feels ungrateful, Cam has been like a rock – he saved my life, for God's sake – but I have to let this bewildering new information sink in. And also, his declaration of love reminds me too much of the student Cam who followed me around like a devoted puppy, and I really need some space.

My new phone doesn't have Cam's mobile number on it, and I don't remember what it is, so I call my landline. To my surprise and disappointment, he answers it immediately.

'Hey,' I tell him. 'It's me.'

'Are you coming back?' he asks brightly. 'Tell me where you are, and I'll pick you up.'

'I've some errands to run and then I'll head back.'

There's a tense silence, and then Cam says, 'Penny told me you spoke to her.'

It's difficult to tell if he's annoyed, but his statement makes me defensive. 'You left your phone in your jacket pocket. I didn't know where the ringing was coming from.'

There's a pause, and I wonder whether he wants to say something else, but then he sighs. 'You really shouldn't be out. I'm worried about you.'

It crosses my mind to remind him again how he locked me in the bedroom, but at this point I just want him to go. Lifting my face to the sun, I say, 'Penny needs you, Cam. You should be at home looking after her, not with me.'

'You're right,' he says. 'I should go home and see Penny, make sure everything's okay.'

It's for the best. Everything between us has happened so fast, and it's not fair on Cam either. After everything that's happened with Diane and Sean, I've probably been using him as an emotional crutch, the same way as I did all those years ago. With Penny the way she is, he thinks he's found solace in me, and perhaps I've fooled myself into thinking he's the one to help me out the other side of my own problems. But the whole situation is becoming suffocating, I need to take a step back, and so does he.

'I understand if you feel awkward or embarrassed,' he says. 'The situation isn't ideal for any of us. But Penny knows about my feelings for you. And, well, she understands that she's not going to be around forever, and she's given us her blessing.'

'Cam,' I sigh. 'She needs you right now.'

'Wait a minute, let me just take this next door,' he says, and I hear Shiv talking to Amber in the background. He closes a door, says, 'I'll do everything in my power to make sure you're not charged.'

'I know that,' I tell him, but I'm positive I'm not guilty of murdering Diane, whatever he may suspect, and I don't want him hiding evidence. He's only going to land us both in more trouble.

There's another thing that's on the tip of my tongue to ask him.

I couldn't make him happy, Penny told me, *and nor could Charlotte*.

Who's Charlotte?

'Go home, spend time with Penny, and then we can talk.'

'I'll come back tomorrow after work,' he says, 'if you think you're going to be okay tonight.'

I didn't say come back to my house, I said we'd talk, which is a different thing, but I let it go for now.

'I'm going to be fine, Cam. Honestly.'

Finally ending the call, I walk to the Tube station. There's an internet café on the opposite side of the street. I can use my laptop at home, it'll be easy to do that, but I want to give Cam time to leave, so I run across the zebra crossing and go inside.

I'm curious about Charlotte, whoever she is; she can't be his sister because he's an only child. The first thing I do when I get online is open a search engine and type in her name. And, of course, there are lots of hits. It's a common name, and there are all kinds of entries about all kinds of Charlotte Wests, who work in every industry under the sun.

I'm not even certain if Cam was married to this woman, it may not even be her surname, so it feels like I'm searching for the proverbial needle in a haystack. But then one news article headline catches my attention, only because Cam once told me he liked skiing.

BRITISH WOMAN DIES IN SKIING TRAGEDY

An Ealing woman has died in a skiing accident in the French Alps after falling from a cliff.

Local medics tried in vain to save the life of Charlotte West (24), who was on holiday with her husband and three-year-old daughter in the popular sports resort of Courchevel, after she took a wrong turn on a slope.
Her husband Cameron West (23) remained in France until the local coroner completed an inquiry but has now returned to his London home.
'Charlotte was an experienced and enthusiastic skier,' Mr West said after the hearing. 'I can only imagine that she became disorientated in the poor weather conditions. We will miss her deeply.'

There's a photo beside the article of a young, flame-haired woman, holding a child in her arms. She looks a lot like me, but more beautiful, with piercing green eyes, a pale complexion and an enigmatic smile. Younger and thinner, looking only a few years older than when I first knew him, Cameron stands beside her. The article is fifteen years old, which feels like a lifetime ago now.

Out of curiosity, I've searched for Cam online more than once in the past, but I've never seen this local news report before, probably because his name is buried in the body of the article.

So Cam was married a long time before Penny, not so many years after I first knew him, and his first wife died in a skiing accident. On top of the revelation that Diane didn't have a brother, this new piece of information is unsettling. I understand that he may still be upset by the tragedy all these years later, but he's had plenty of time to mention the fact that he's been married twice, and that he has a child of his own, who would be grown up now.

Consumed by my own problems, I realize now how little I know about Cam and his home life, and the idea makes me deeply uneasy.

I may not be able to remember Cam's number, but Sean's is etched on my memory, and I call it.

'Sean?' I ask, when he answers. 'It's me.'

'Thank God.' He sounds eager and friendly, in sharp contrast to his mood when I saw him last. 'I've been trying to call you, I even came round, but that fucking guy wouldn't let me in. He said you didn't want to see me.'

'When?' I ask in surprise. I don't remember him coming around.

'I've been round at least three times, Han,' he says indignantly. 'But you changed the locks so I couldn't get in, and nobody's answered the phone. Then I hear that you've been injured in a fire – what the hell?'

'I'm sorry, I've been... sleeping a lot.'

'And Amber?' he asks, and I can hear the emotion in his voice start to spiral. 'I'm serious, Han, if I can't access her I'll get lawyered up.'

'That's why I'm phoning.'

'What were you thinking, going to that deranged woman's house? The police asked me about you and her.' His voice drops to a stricken whisper. 'Bloody hell, Han, what's going on?'

I'm not going to tell him on the phone that Diane's death is being investigated as a murder, and that I'm the number one suspect. 'I need to ask a favour, Sean.'

'What's with the new number?'

'Uh, I lost my phone.' I pick up my bag and head to the counter to pay. 'Look, do you mind coming round later?'

'What about that guy?'

'Cam won't be there,' I tell him.

'Cam.' Sean sarcastically repeats his name, but then exhales deeply to calm himself, maybe realizing that resentment isn't going to get us anywhere. 'Of course I will. You know I'd do anything for us to get back together, Hannah.'

With everything that's happened, Sean and I making another go of our relationship is the last thing on my mind. But it's true that I need him right now; and Amber needs him.

'Can you have Amber for a few days?'

'I'll drop everything.'

'Good,' I tell him. 'I want you to take her out of London. Somewhere far away.'

50

When I get home, it's a relief to find that Cam has been as good as his word and gone. But he's left behind the satchel he carries with him everywhere, which sets off alarm bells, because it's a convenient excuse to come back and get it. The door keys he was using are on the kitchen island, but the new locks came with multiple sets of keys, so there's nothing to stop him having sneaked off with a spare set.

Shiv is upstairs in Amber's bedroom; I can hear them on the baby monitor. Amber is a bit grouchy, though, and Shiv is softly talking to her.

'Things will be back to normal soon, Amber, I promise. *Sssshhhh*. Your mum is just under a bit of pressure, that's all, and it's making her so tired. But soon we're all going to get back to normal. *Sssshhhh*. Then we'll all go on a nice trip, how does that sound, my lovely girl?'

Shiv sounds tired, too, and no wonder, she's been looking after Amber for days, but her loving patience for my daughter is inexhaustible. Whatever my previous misgivings about her, it's incredible she's stayed here, considering the difficult position Sean put her in, and then all the drama with Diane.

Because it's hanging by the strap over the back of a

kitchen stool, I can't help but pick up the satchel and look in it. It's snooping, really, but I'm curious to see what's inside. All I find are some files from work, admin stuff about minor procedures, a medical textbook, a catalogue of various drugs, a toothbrush, an opened roll of mints; a tie is stuffed in the front pocket, along with a bill addressed to his house in Clapham. But as I'm looking, I get the fright of my life when he texts me on my new phone.

What are you doing? xx

It may be a combination of my jumpy nerves and guilt, but I get a horrible sense that he knows exactly what I'm doing, and quickly close the flap and step back. Picking up my phone, I reply,

Just having a quiet sit down.

You're living your best life! xx

Another text comes in almost straight after that one.

I've left my bag at yours but I can
come and get it tomorrow. Xx

I don't want him to come back here, I feel strongly that he's beginning to make himself too much at home. And if he's hiding evidence he thinks could incriminate me, he's going to make matters worse and get himself into big trouble too. Whatever the police think, and whatever Cam believes, I didn't kill Diane.

There's no doubt he's been kind and attentive, and done his best to help me, and I will be forever grateful that he saved my life, but the fact that he hasn't told me about his ex-wife and his child is weird; and anyway, everything's happening too fast. I'm going to have to be honest with him. We'll meet tomorrow somewhere in town, he deserves for us to talk face to face, at least. We can grab a coffee, and I'll tell him firmly that I'm not looking for a romantic relationship, and that he must give me back the firelighters, because I've got nothing to hide; I'll hand them straight over to the police.

So I reply to his message, saying,

> Let's meet somewhere nice outside. I'll bring your bag. (Do you have any more keys?)

A few moments later, he replies,

Are you mad at me!?

The mention of the keys was probably a bit much. I reply,

> Let's chat tomorrow.

You're definitely mad at me!
I'll come tomorrow morning.

'For God's sake,' I say out loud, because he's not getting the message, and try one last time.

> Let's meet in town. It'll make a nice change!

I watch tensely as the three dots at the bottom of the screen pulse. He's writing something. But when his reply finally appears on the screen, it just says,

You're definitely mad at me! ☹ I'll call in the morning. Xx

And then he adds,

And bring my bag. That way you'll have to meet me!!! xx

It's a relief when he finally stops replying, and I lean against the kitchen counter to rub my face. The fact that I discovered Penny wasn't his first wife, and Charlotte died, and that somewhere he has a child, has rattled me more than I want to admit.

The doorbell rings; there's a familiar figure behind the stained glass of the front door. I don't want Sean to go into a strop, so I place the satchel in a cupboard, and open the door.

'Hi,' he says.

It's weird and sad that he waits to be asked to step inside his own house, but I stand aside and gesture for him to come in. It seems absurd that only yesterday I was convinced he killed Diane, but that's the rollercoaster of emotions I've been on.

'Shiv, can you come down here?' I call from the bottom of the stairs, and when she arrives with Amber, Sean looks sheepish.

'Sean's going to take Amber away for a few days,' I tell her, taking my daughter in my arms. 'So that he can spend some time with her.'

She looks at us both in surprise.

'Sure,' she says uncertainly.

'I'm not sure how this situation with the police is going to play out, and the fact is, I could...' Emotion builds in my chest; it feels scary to say it out loud. 'I could be arrested, even charged. If that's the case, I don't want her here.'

Sean is shocked when I tell him about how the fire was probably started on purpose, and that I was in the house at the time.

'Holy shit, Han,' he says, upset.

'Where are you going to take her?' I ask, because he's probably still staying in a friend's spare room or even sleeping on a couch.

He grimaces, and I know that he hasn't given any consideration to it. 'We can book into a hotel for a few days, I thought, make a little holiday of it.'

'There's my family cottage on the Norfolk coast you can use,' Shiv reminds me. 'It's empty, so there's plenty of room. You can stay there as long as you like.'

'I'd feel uncomfortable at a stranger's house,' says Sean.

'I'll come with you,' Shiv suggests. 'We can both look after her.'

Sean looks embarrassed, because of how his drunken pass at her soured everything between us.

'You'll probably have to work at least some of the time,' Shiv tells him. 'Someone needs to keep an eye on Amber.'

'What about your grandad, don't you want to be near him?' I ask.

Shiv thinks about it. 'I can give him a call at the hospital to say I'll be away for a few days, but he's a tough old guy so he won't mind. He's doing much better now, anyway, the doctors are really pleased with his progress.'

'It's your call, if you're happy to go,' I tell her doubtfully, jogging Amber in my arms. It's unfair to expect her to go anywhere with Sean, but I know she'll provide emotional continuity for Amber. 'I'll try to get out of London as soon as I can, once the situation here becomes clearer. You can go now with Sean, or you can wait for me, and we can travel together.'

She smiles. 'I'm happy to go now.'

'Sure.' Sean smiles awkwardly. 'If you're comfortable with that. Where is this cottage, anyway?'

She tells him the address, which is near a fishing village called Weybourne, and I write it down.

'If it's that far away, we should get going, or we won't get there till late.'

'I'll pack a bag for me and Amber,' says Shiv. 'It won't take long.'

'I'm trusting you,' I tell him when she's gone.

He places a hand on his chest. 'Nothing like that will ever happen again, I swear. I've knocked the drinking on the head, Han. We don't even have to go away, if you like. I can stay here with you and we can look after Amber together, just like we always have.'

I know what he wants me to say, that I'd like him to move in again, but our relationship – whether we have any future at all – is the last thing on my mind right now. 'I'll follow you to the coast as soon as I can.'

'I would do anything if we can try again, Han,' he says. 'I want to come home.'

The look he gives me is so pathetic and full of yearning that it's hard not to feel something for him. We shared a good life, it's true, but then I remember what he was getting up to behind my back, and I strongly suspect there's plenty more shenanigans I've yet to find out about.

'I'll join you up there when I can,' I tell him again. 'And then we can talk.'

'Did you sleep with the guy?' he asks.

'I'm not going to talk about it right now,' I say, and he turns away, his eyes filling with tears.

Shiv comes down a few minutes later, with a hastily packed rucksack, and I promise her I'll bring more of her clothes when I come. Giving Amber one last hug, I hand her to Shiv with a solemn promise that we'll be reunited very soon. We all go outside while Sean puts the rucksack and stroller in the car, and once the baby seat has been fitted, I watch the three of them drive off.

Back inside, I find another message from Cam, asking if he can call. But I don't want to hear from him, not tonight, and I power down the phone and put it in a drawer.

Then I take a long shower. It's peaceful having the house to myself and I take my time in the bathroom, then climb into a hoodie and sweatpants; use the landline to order a takeaway from a nearby Malaysian restaurant. Finishing the meal, washing out the containers, placing them in the recycling, and putting the plate and cutlery in the dishwasher, I head up to my office and open my laptop.

The first thing I do when I get online is to open up Google Maps and look at Chattersea Close in Ealing, south-west London, where Diane used to live, because something about that address has nagged at me since Linda told me about it. The area means very little to me. I used to have friends who lived there, and there's a radio studio nearby where I did an interview once, but I haven't been there for a long time.

Frustrated, I'm just about to click out of the map when I notice something, and the connection I've been trying to make in my mind slides uneasily into place.

Because Cam's former GP surgery is at the end of that street. He hasn't worked there for years, I don't think, but I distinctly remember looking online once and seeing that was where it was. Diane's former home is literally a few hundred yards away. She was well within the catchment area of the surgery. There's every chance he would have known her; maybe he was even her GP. But if that's the case, why wouldn't he have told me about it? Linda said Diane moved to her street in Bounds Green four years ago, and I'm sure Cam moved to his most recent GP surgery around the same time.

It's too much of a coincidence. Something is happening – just out of the corner of my eye where I can't see it properly.

And I have to know what it is before it's too late.

51

This morning, I messaged Cam and we agreed to meet in Soho within the hour, but that's not going to happen; rather, I'm not going to get there on time.

Instead, I'm standing in a doorway at the bottom of his street, watching his front door. I've been here for half an hour already, and if he's going to meet me on time, then he's going to have to leave soon.

I've got his satchel over my shoulder, so that if he finds out I came here, I'll say I brought his bag to his house before we went out so he didn't have to carry it around, and unfortunately just missed him.

All I want to do is speak to Penny, to get a better idea of how she feels about the situation with me and Cam, and to find out whether she's as comfortable with it as he says she is, then I'll leave. But that odd coincidence that Diane lived near the surgery where Cam once worked is playing on my mind too, and she may be able to shed some light on that.

My temporary phone unexpectedly rings. It's Shiv, calling from Norfolk.

'Just thought you'd like to know we're all settled in.'

'Oh,' I say, just as the door of Cam's house opens and

he steps outside. My heart leaping, I press back into the doorway, so he can't see me.

'Hello? Hannah, are you there?'

I peek round the corner to watch Cam walk off with a spring in his step, heading towards the Tube. He doesn't look back once.

'Sure, I'll be up soon. Everything okay with Sean?'

'He's gone to the village to get supplies,' she tells me. 'I took Amber to the beach this morning. She played in the sand, and loved all the space and sea and seagulls. But she misses her mum.'

'Bless her, tell her I'm coming soon,' I say, as Cam disappears around the corner. 'Shiv, I'm sorry, but I've got to go. I'll give you a call a bit later.'

'Of course,' she says.

As soon as the call is finished, I cross the road and ring the doorbell of Cam's house. It takes several moments before a small, frail-looking woman opens the door.

'Penny?' I ask, and when she nods warily, 'I'm Hannah Godley.'

'I know who you are.'

'I hope you don't mind me coming here. The thing is, I haven't told Cam… Cameron I was coming, but I wanted to talk, just the two of us.'

'I know you haven't told him,' she says.

'Can I come in?'

Looking up and down the street, her breathing begins to rasp, as if the decision is making her anxious. Finally, she shuffles back and motions me inside. Then she shuts the door and locks it, pops the key in her pocket.

I tense because it makes me think of the locked back door at Diane's house. 'Do you have to do that?'

'Cameron doesn't like it if I keep it unlocked.'

He's told me about her illness, cancer he said, but her frailty is shocking. Penny's only in her late thirties, but she looks old before her time. There are photos on the wall in the hallway of her and Cam. He looks younger but not much changed – slightly thinner perhaps, and with more colour in his hair – but Penny is completely different to the hunched and broken woman in drab cardigan and elasticated trousers in front of me. In these images, she's a healthy and vivacious woman, with a sparkle in her eye and a devastating smile. She's gorgeous.

'What's wrong with you?' I ask her.

'I'm not very well,' she says.

'But what is wrong with you? What kind of cancer is it?'

'Cancer?' She's flustered, and I see terror in her eyes; she's scared. 'It could be, I suppose. Does it matter?'

A dreadful, dizzy feeling comes over me; it's as if a curtain is lifting in front of my eyes, revealing a terrible reality. Cameron's first wife died, and his second is a shadow of the young, beautiful woman in the photo on the wall.

'Is he keeping you like this? Is he making you ill?' I expect her to deny it, to tell me not to be so ridiculous, but she doesn't. 'He's using drugs to keep you like this, isn't he?'

'You should go.' Penny speaks in quick panting breaths. 'He won't like you coming here, he won't like it at all.'

'He doesn't know that I'm here.'

'He'll know,' she says, and her tired red eyes flick to the front door.

'He's got a camera out there?' I ask.

'He'll know where you are. He always knows.'

Staring at her, I take the phone he gave me from my pocket,

and she nods. He must have set it up so that he can track the GPS signal, in the same way I was able to track Sean's car.

He knows I went to Diane's street yesterday. He may well know I'm here now.

'You must go,' Penny tells me in a strained voice. 'Before he comes back.'

My mind whirls with all kinds of terrible possibilities. 'What happened to his first wife?'

'Charlotte,' she says.

'He killed her, didn't he?'

'He didn't love her either,' she tells me, as if it explains everything. 'He's only ever loved one person.'

'Who?'

'Isn't it obvious?' she says sharply. 'He's only ever loved *you*. All he ever talks about is Hannah *this* and Hannah *that*, day and night.'

'He's a psychopath,' I say, incredulous. 'He killed Charlotte, and somehow he killed Diane, and… he's done this to you, Penny, he's made you ill.'

He'll kill her, too, I'm sure of it. She'll die of whatever terrible condition it is he's given her, using the medication she's forced to take. As a GP, he'll know which drugs will make her body slowly fail, and make her docile, compliant, and wracked night and day with pain and fatigue.

'You're blessed to have his love,' she tells me sadly.

'I don't want his love, I never asked for it, and I don't give my love to him.'

'He'll take it anyway,' she tells me. 'He can't live without you. He's tried, but he can't. Charlotte and I have always lived in your shadow, Hannah.' She shakes her head. 'Cameron tried his best to find his love for you in us, but he never managed it, and he'll only be happy when you're back together.'

'I'm going to get you out of here,' I tell her. 'The police need to know what he's done to you, Penny, and what he did to Charlotte. He killed Diane, too, didn't he?'

'She'd do anything for him. We all would, really.'

'He groomed her,' I say, stunned. 'Used her as a Trojan horse to get back into my life.'

'He did what he had to do. I'm not going to begrudge him his happiness. He can't love me if I'm like this.'

'He *made* you like this.' I think of the pills he gave me, and the food he made, the wine he brought. It all made me feel terrible, and made me begin to lose my sense of time and reality.

It's obvious to me now that there was somebody in my bedroom when I had the nightmare; but it wasn't Diane, it was Cameron. The realization that he was there – creeping around, watching me, climbing *onto* me – makes me feel sick.

I'm going to get Penny out of here, to a hospital, and together we'll talk to the police.

'Get your shoes on, we're going out.'

'I don't have shoes,' she says, looking down at the cheap slippers on her feet. 'Cameron tells me I can't go out.'

'Then you'll have to go like that.'

'He'll be furious,' she says.

'He's not going to tell you what to do any more,' I assure her. 'We're getting out of here. But first, does he have his own personal space somewhere? A room he doesn't let you go inside?'

'His office is upstairs at—' Before she's even stopped talking, I'm racing up, taking the steps two at a time. Because if I'm going to go to Sheehy, I'll need evidence. People like Cameron are slippery as hell. As soon as he knows he's been rumbled, he'll destroy any evidence that could convict him.

At the top of the stairs, there's a security gate of the kind that stops toddlers from getting downstairs. With Penny's lack of mobility, it would be easy to use it to keep her trapped upstairs.

Looking along the landing, there's only one room where the door is shut, it's at the back of the house, and I rush inside. There's a single bed, but a desk too, and a bookcase full of medical textbooks beneath the window, overlooking the tidy garden at the back. On the desk is a laptop and a tray full of papers, and I rifle through them. There are bills and medical reports, receipts for drugs with very long names – I have no idea what they are, but I pull the satchel off my shoulder and stuff them inside – and at the bottom of the tray is a photograph.

Of me and Cameron in a bar. It's the same photo that Diane gave me, with one important difference. There's no Martin in the middle. In this photo, Cameron and I are sitting beside each other, so close that our hands almost touch. The photo wasn't taken at the Banshee Bar on the night with Martin; it was from a completely different evening, a completely different bar. I don't know who the man is in the photo that Diane gave me, but it's not her brother, because I know now that he doesn't even exist. Cameron photoshopped that person, a complete stranger most likely, into the middle of this photo.

Pocketing the image, I want to get out of the house quickly, but force myself to open the laptop. A password box comes up. My fingers hover over the keyboard as I try to think of what it may be, but it could be absolutely anything. Running onto the landing, I call down to Penny, who's still standing at the bottom of the stairs.

'Do you know what the password for his laptop is?'

She shakes her head, trying to think. It'll take too long to think of the password, and I decide to take the laptop with me; maybe we can figure it out at the hospital. But then she says, 'I think I can probably guess, and so can you.'

Rushing back into the bedroom, I type in:

HannahGodley

The laptop screen winks on. Cam's got a lot of windows open on the screen and it takes me a moment to realize what I'm looking at...

Live feeds from the inside of my house.

There's a view of my empty kitchen, my bedroom, my office, and another of my living room, all from high up on the wall. One even shows my bathroom and shower cubicle. There's an odd low-level throbbing sound coming from the computer, and I can't work out what it is, until I take out the mobile and ring my home number. When the call connects, I hear my landline phone ring on the laptop speaker.

It doesn't seem possible, but it's true. Cameron has got spy cameras set up all over my house. Microphones, too. He's got a tracker on my phone. It's no wonder he called when I was driving to Diane's house that fateful afternoon, because he probably has one fitted to my car too.

It takes me a moment to realize I've been holding my breath and I let out a long, trembling exhale. I slam the laptop shut, and fumble it into the satchel. I've got everything I need. I can't bear to be here a moment longer.

'Penny,' I shout, turning. 'We've got to—'

But then an arm goes around my middle, forcing my arms to my sides, and something pungent is pressed against my mouth.

My scream is muffled; I can't move.

And within a moment, I lose consciousness.

52

'Hey,' says Cam gently when I open my eyes. 'Don't try to get up, take your time, you're going to feel a bit groggy.'

My head feels heavy, my thoughts sluggish. Bile surges into my throat, making me gag. I'm disorientated. I don't know where I am, I don't recognize the bedroom, or why I'm lying down.

'It's not as nice as yours, admittedly.' Cam follows my gaze around the strange room. 'But regrettably we're a single income household.'

And then everything begins to come back to me. The last thing I remember, I was snapping shut the laptop in the room at the back of the house, frantically pocketing evidence, and about to leave. I was going to get Penny to safety – away from Cameron.

And now I'm in another bedroom, his own, I think, on a double bed facing a large bay window. My eyes jerk to his. He's sitting on the edge of the bed, smiling, happy to see me. He turns away, and lifts a mug of tea from a bedside cabinet. 'Take a sip of this.'

'No!'

My instinctive reaction is to swipe it away, and it flies out of his hand and across the room, the liquid arcing through the air. The mug smashes against a wall.

'Oh dear,' he says, looking at the tea dribbling down the wall and soaking into the carpet; at the smashed china on the floor.

The door is only a couple of feet from me, but Cameron is in the way, and I don't even know if I can move.

'Your fingers and toes are probably a bit numb, so wiggle them a little and the feeling will come back. If you feel nauseous, don't worry, that will soon pass.'

'Where's Penny?' I say, clenching and unclenching my fingers.

But Cameron doesn't appear to have heard me, because he gives me a loving look.

'You're the one that got away. You don't realize how utterly spellbound, how besotted, I was with you, H, and still am. I would have done anything for you – hell, I *did* do anything for you – and then you just…' He clicks his fingers. 'Made me go away. It was so brutal the way you did it, and I was so lost without you. For weeks and months, I couldn't get over it, I didn't understand, because we shared something special, me and you. But then I thought, *Cameron, you've got to get on with your life, plenty of fish in the sea, and all that.*' He sighs. 'And, yes, there were plenty of other women out there. But the trouble is, none of them were you. Not a single one of them could possibly measure up to you.' He clenches his hands over his heart. 'All the years without you have been wasted and empty.'

'Where's Penny?' I ask again.

'There have been a few women, I guess. But none of them have had a fraction of your charisma or character, H.'

He sits up straight, stretching his spine. 'I mean, I thought Charlotte was exciting, I really thought I saw something in her... for a little while, at least. But I soon discovered she was a fake, a fraud. Boring, mundane, she couldn't hold a candle to you. Well, that marriage didn't end well. After that, there were one or two other women, but it was clear that they weren't fit for purpose, so I just—' He mimics putting a phone to his ear. 'Got rid. And then finally I met Penny, and I thought she was exciting, I really believed I could be happy with her; that she could help me forget you. Sure, it was fun for a short time, but it soon became painfully obvious she would never fill your shoes. That nobody ever could.'

'Where's Penny?'

'I was a nervous little boy until I met you, H, I was a child, but you changed everything for me. The fun we had!' He rolls his eyes to the ceiling. 'Remember the time we robbed that restaurant? I felt like an outlaw, we were like Bonnie and Clyde. I felt like the most exciting guy ever when I was around you. How could I settle for second best after that?'

He claps his hands on his thighs and stands. 'But listen to me go on! There's plenty of time to chat. How are you feeling?'

'Cam,' I ask again, 'where's Penny?'

He tilts his head from side to side, as if trying to decide how to answer. 'You know what, let's not talk about her. Penny is ancient history now. From now on, H, it's all about us. The future is ours, my darling.'

He reaches out to touch my cheek, but I bat away his hand. Cam frowns, but holds up his hands. 'I understand, it's a lot for you to take in all at once, and you're not firing on all cylinders at the moment, but...' He grins. 'We're together again, at last. Finally! And the best thing is, H, we've already got a family.'

His words are like an electric shock. 'Amber.'

Because Cameron had my house fitted with hidden cameras and listening devices – I only managed a quick look at his laptop, and there could be even more I don't know about – he'll know Amber's gone away. Shiv told me the address of the cottage in Norfolk in the kitchen and he may have heard that. Or if he's gone to such extraordinary lengths to pry into my life, there could even be a tracker on Sean's car.

'Amber's waiting for us, isn't that right?' he says, as if reading my mind. 'My car has a full tank of petrol, if we leave now we'll get to Norfolk before nightfall.' He claps his hands. 'Let's get going.'

'I can't just leave now,' I say, playing for time. 'I've got to go home, get some clothes.'

'Surprise!' He goes to the end of the bed to pick up a bulging holdall, and the grin he gives me is sickening. 'I took the liberty of taking a few of your clothes from your bedroom when I left yesterday, because I knew sooner or later we'd be going away, you and me. I mean, I don't want to start our new life in this horrible city, do you?'

He dumps the bag on the bed and comes to me, drops his hand to my forehead so quickly that I rear back against the headboard in terror. Cameron pulls up my right eyelid with his thumb, examining the eye as if I'm one of his patients. 'You look fine to travel, let's go.'

When he turns away to pick up the bag, I scramble off the bed and fling open the door to rush onto the landing.

'Penny!' I scream. 'Penny!'

I don't know where she is, she could be anywhere in the

house, and the only way I'm going to be able to help her – to save us both – is to get away and return with the police. But when I get to the top of the stairs, the child's security gate is locked. In normal circumstances, I'd be able to climb over it, but in my panic, and with Cameron rushing out of the bedroom, I can't get my leg over. Forced to make a split-second decision, I rush into the bathroom and slam the door behind me. There's no lock, of course there wouldn't be, and I press myself against the door, hoping to keep him out.

'Hey, H,' he says softly on the other side, and I feel the pressure against my back as he yanks down the handle and begins to push the door open. 'We don't have time for this.'

'Keep away,' I scream, but my feet slip on the tile as he slowly and steadily pushes the door open behind me. I can't stop him; I don't have the strength to keep him out.

And when I see Penny's body underwater in the bath, her mouth gaping, her lifeless eyes staring up at the ceiling from beneath the water, her hair limply splayed across its cold surface, I shriek, because all is lost.

53

Grasping me tightly with one hand, Cameron checks his watch as he pushes me downstairs.

'It's going to take us a few hours to get there, so let's go.' At the front door, he stops. 'It was unfortunate you saw Penny in her condition... I appreciate you probably have a lot of questions, which I'll gladly answer, but please don't scream when you step outside.'

'In her condition?' I'm physically shaking in his grip.

'I'd like to explain, but if you make a scene it will be better for the both of us to put you to sleep again. That may be better, actually, because you'll wake when we get there, and then we can chat.'

I can't let him put me under again, because anything could happen to Sean and Shiv – or, oh God, Amber – while I'm unconscious in the back of the car.

They don't know what he's like. He could turn up there with a cheery hello, and take them by surprise. He'll have a weapon in the bag, or drugs he'll use to knock them out, then drown them in the sea. He said he wants us to be a family, so I pray that he'll spare Amber, but Sean and Shiv are in his way, and he'll do anything to keep me to himself.

'Sean is going to be there,' I say, trying to frighten him.

He shrugs, and I know by that single dismissive gesture that Cameron intends to kill him. 'Let's cross that bridge when we come to it.'

'No.' I force myself to stay calm, trying not to tremble at his touch, despite the terrifying sight of Penny's lifeless body in the bath. 'I won't scream, I promise.'

'Thank you.' He looks pleased, as if my response has confirmed something in his mind. That we're really going to be a couple, and have a future together; most of all, that he's in control. Cameron picks up the bag and opens the door.

The street is empty as he throws the holdall in the boot of the car, slams it shut. For the first time in what seems like forever, it feels cooler, the sky overcast. Storms are forecast to roll across the south-east in the next couple of days.

Cameron pulls me discreetly to the passenger side, but then changes his mind.

'You can drive,' he says, pulling me back to the other side and opening the door. 'I'll give directions.'

He forces me down into the seat, but with a big smile on his face, as if he's a loving, attentive husband helping his wife inside.

'Morning,' I hear him say brightly to a neighbour, but before I can even think about jumping out, he's beside me in the passenger seat, clamping a warning hand around my wrist until they've gone.

'Seat belt.' I pull the belt across my chest, click it in the central arm between us, and he does the same. 'Right,' he says. 'Let's go.'

'Keys,' I tell him.

He laughs and reaches into his pocket. 'Silly me.'

When I've pushed the key into the ignition, I say, 'I don't think I can drive. I feel groggy.'

'You're fine. It's easier this way, H, because we don't want you jumping out the car while I'm driving. You could seriously hurt yourself.' He grins. 'Trust me, I'm a doctor.'

'That joke is getting old,' I tell him sourly.

So I start the car and drive along the street, trying to work out what to do. Maybe when we get to the cottage I'll have enough time to warn Sean and Shiv. But Cameron's hand keeps patting his pocket, and I have no idea what he has in there. More chloroform, or a syringe filled with some kind of stupefying drug he'll plunge into my neck as soon as we arrive.

Cameron is a murderer. He killed Penny, and his first wife, too; he's capable of doing anything to get what he wants.

And what he wants is me.

54

The gears grind angrily as I push the stick back and forth with a shaking hand, trying to change up to fourth as we head out of the city.

I don't want to head to that place. Every minute we spend in this car, every mile I drive, takes us – takes *him* – closer to Amber, and I can't let that happen. It's me he wants, and if I can escape from the car, he'll have to come after me. But he's right beside me, the knuckles of his right hand rest against my hip, and I know that before I could even get my seat belt undone he'd put me to sleep once again. If I can somehow make eye contact with other drivers or passers-by, maybe they'll realize something is wrong. But nobody looks at me, nobody cares; we're just one car among a million.

'Tell me about Diane,' I say finally, because I need to keep him distracted while I frantically try to work out whether we'll be passing a police station.

'Ah, our poor friend Diane,' he nods sadly. 'She was a patient of mine in Ealing. She was a lonely soul, who craved emotional connections the way a man lost in the desert craves water, and she came into the surgery every single day, attaching herself to me in the same way she did to you. She was banned from the surgery eventually, there was even talk of a restraining order, but I was soon going to be leaving that surgery, she didn't know where, and besides, she was getting chucked out of her own home down there. You've seen how she lived, so that would probably have been the end of it.

'But even back then I had a glimmer of an idea that one day Diane may prove useful to me, because she was highly vulnerable to suggestion. I met her in secret, spent time with her and gave her gifts, so that by the time I left that practice, Diane had grown heavily dependent on my attention. She even gave me a key to her new house.

'You were in what seemed like a loving marriage, but the closer I looked into your so-called happy relationship, the clearer it became that your husband was a promiscuous slut, and it gave me an idea.' He points at a junction. 'Turn right here, and follow the signs to the south circular.'

'You've been watching me for years?'

He leans over to pat the satchel with the laptop in it at his feet. 'I wasn't able to see inside your house or listen to your conversations back then, but yes, the twists and turns of your life have long been a hobby of mine.'

He lifts his chin to scratch his neck. 'I'd follow Sean of an evening, and see what he'd get up to, and when I discovered things were more precarious between you than you could ever know, I had an idea. There was no point in engineering a chance meeting, or trying to make contact – after all, you had ditched me once and could still point-blank refuse to let me back into your life – so I had to find a way to get you to invite me back.'

My hands thread tightly along the steering wheel. 'Diane.'

He lifts a finger in exclamation, *got it in one*. He tells me how he set about grooming her, and painstakingly placing into her mind all kinds of false statements, even going so far as to convince her that she had a beloved brother who had died.

When Diane didn't do as he told her to, or faltered in believing what he insisted again and again was true – that she had a brother who I had humiliated – he refused her love and attention. He didn't visit or take her calls, he cast her into a lonely wilderness. Threats to withdraw his love soon brought her into line.

Once he had planted the seed of what he and I had done to Martin, Cameron told Diane that he would help her get revenge against me because I was a cruel and heartless person. He gave her the photo he'd photoshopped, seemingly of him and me and Martin; her lost brother at last made physical in her mind.

'I told her that I deeply regretted the whole sorry episode, and that you had orchestrated the whole thing.' He shrugs. 'Diane wasn't a vengeful person, really, but she was excellent at following commands.'

There are speed cameras above the road. If I drive too fast, maybe we'll get pulled over by the police, so I press my foot softly on the accelerator, hoping he won't notice that we're steadily picking up speed. But no sooner have I done it than the traffic thickens ahead, and I have to slam on the brakes.

'Easy does it,' he says, placing his fingers on top of mine on the wheel. 'You're doing just great, H.'

It takes all my willpower not to snatch my hand away, and I ask quickly, 'So then it was easy to insert Diane into my life.'

He can't keep the pride out of his voice as he tells me

how Diane became his puppet; how he made her contact the radio show and told her what to say; then sent her to the bar where I met Izzy, and to the restaurant where I met my parents. When she warned me about Sean's behaviour, all she was ever doing was repeating what he'd told her to say.

But Diane didn't sneak into my home to smear the mirror, and she didn't push my father down the stairs, she was completely oblivious to any of that, because there's only so much you can make a person do against their better instincts.

All she had to do was provide the appearance of a threat, he says, and to feed my suspicion that my husband was having an affair. The triumphant way he speaks disgusts me, and I have to swallow down my anger.

I've got to concentrate, to think of some way to escape. But as soon as we slow to a stop in traffic and I lift my hands off the wheel, he takes hold of my wrist and leans close.

'Sean doesn't deserve your love,' Cameron says with distaste. 'He's a vile creep and you're well shot of him.'

Diane's seemingly vengeful behaviour – her apparent acts of violence and vandalism, but also her stupid inspirational messages and clumsy attempts to curry favour by making me food – was erratic and alarming, and she proved the perfect threat to make me contact Cameron in desperation, begging him to solve the problem of Diane. He reeled me in like a fish wriggling on a hook.

'The trick was not to seem too keen at first, even though I cherished every second I spent with you.'

'But she liked me too much,' I tell him bitterly as the traffic begins to move.

'Yeah.' Cameron shakes his head ruefully. 'That was the problem with Diane. Give her the tiniest bit of attention and she was yours forever. She kept asking me why I didn't like you because you seemed so nice. Holding your hand at the café was a mistake, because I suppose it dawned on her that I had been using her, or had an ulterior motive. But I was still convinced that if I told her to go away and stay away, she'd do as I said.'

Cameron tells me how he warned Diane off. He threatened and charmed and manipulated. He made promises he had no intention of keeping, but this time she ignored him because she had transferred her affections to me, and in her desperation to get my attention, she even went so far as to steal Amber.

He knew then that Diane would never give up trying to warn me about him, and he had no choice but to arrange for her to be killed. Cameron knew her cluttered house would be easy to burn down, but he panicked when he discovered that I was on my way to confront her at the very same time as it was due to be torched. Stuck at work, he couldn't believe it. He was likely to lose the person most precious to him in the world, the woman he was so close to winning back, and raced there.

'It would have been a devastating blow,' he says with emotion, 'a sickening joke, if you had died too.'

His self-pitying tone makes me want to laugh, despite everything. Another innocent woman died. 'You killed Diane.'

'I placed the firelighters – the ones from your shed – in the house the final time I visited her there, yes, and arranged for someone else to start the fire. But if you died, everything I'd done would have been for nothing. I was desperate to get you out of there, and when I arrived at the house, nothing on earth would have stopped me going in to get you out, nothing.' He looks close to tears. 'And I saved you, H. I rescued you, because it's our destiny to be together.'

'And what about Martin?'

He looks confused. 'What about him?'

'Whatever became of the man in the bar?'

'That guy?' He makes a face. 'He could be alive, he could be dead; he could be a family man with a wife and daughters, or a sad loner still propping up bars. Who cares? All that matters is the *idea* of Martin, and what we did to him: all these years later, he was the key that enabled me to walk back into your life.'

'Then who's the man in the photo with us?'

'That's just some random I found in an old photo who looks a bit like he did. I think so, anyway. I don't remember much about him, do you?'

My shoulders slump as I speed onto the motorway. We're out of the city and there's nowhere to run now, just miles of road ahead. If I had a chance to get away, it's gone. 'So what happens now?'

Cameron rubs his hands, as if everything is settled. 'What happens now is that we live happily ever after, me and you. After twenty wasted years, the future is ours.'

'We have no future, Cameron, because there never was an *us*,' I say tearfully. 'You were just a guy who was hanging around me at a bad time in my life.'

His face twists in denial. 'That's not true.'

I don't care any more about trying not to get him angry, and tell him viciously, 'You were a wingman, a sidekick, one of those creepy guys who prey on the emotions of vulnerable women.'

Cameron smiles tightly. 'I was a bit more to you than that, and you know it. We were in love.'

'I didn't love you.' Tears roll down my face. 'I *never* loved you, and I never will.'

'We'll see.' Cameron holds up his hands. 'Look, I know it's probably all too much to take in right now, but after a while you'll see how perfect it all is.'

That makes me snort with derision. This so-called love he thinks he has for me is just a twisted, disgusting excuse to kill and control.

'I don't think you have the slightest idea of what love is. If you loved me, you'd know what you're doing is wrong.'

'*You*,' he says tersely, 'can't tell me how to love.'

'And what happens when I disappoint you, Cameron?'

'Call me Cam,' he says in irritation.

'When I don't live up to your expectations.' My foot pressed on the accelerator, the car surges in the middle lane as I turn to him and snarl, 'Like Penny didn't, or Charlotte. My God, I don't even know what happened to your own daughter.'

Cameron smirks. 'You won't disappoint me, you never could. I've thought about you every single day for twenty years, and about the life we should have had together, the magnificent memories we'd have shared. We've wasted twenty empty, meaningless years.' He gazes glumly out of the window. 'But it's not too late to start again. We're together now, and in love.'

'Do you seriously believe I'm going to live the rest of my life with you?'

'We'll have a happy life together, I promise.' Cameron squeezes my hand on the steering wheel, but when I snatch my hand away, his face trembles with anger. 'I'd do anything for you, Hannah. You'll see.'

'Will you let me go? Will you leave me alone? Or go to prison to serve time for all your crimes – for the murder of Penny and Charlotte and Diane?' Something uneasily occurs to me. 'Or are there more?'

He smiles, as if there's something I don't know, and I feel a cold dread tumble down my spine.

'What?'

'I've told you before, I'd do anything for you, H. I *did* do something for you.'

'You haven't done *anything* for me, Cameron.' I wipe the tears from my face with the heel of my hand, trying to stay calm. 'Except come into my life and destroy it.'

He turns to me again, grinning. 'I never got the chance to tell you.'

'Tell me what?'

'There's something I once did for you that proves just how much I love you.'

My hands grip the wheel tightly, but the road ahead and all the cars around us seem to shimmer and blur, because I *know* what he's going to say.

'I killed your sister for you. I killed Natalie.'

55

For a moment, I lose control of the car, which veers across a lane, causing the van behind to slam on its brakes and blast its horn.

Cameron grabs the wheel to pull us gently back into the middle.

'Steady,' he says tensely, and keeps his hand on the wheel until he's sure I'm in control once again.

'It's not true,' I whisper hoarsely.

'That's how much I loved you, H, even back then. Natalie made you so unhappy, and I just couldn't bear to see you like that. The way you spoke about her made me hate her so much, you were in so much pain. So that half-term you stayed in London, I got on a train to Lancashire.'

'No.' I shake my head in disbelief, because it can't be true. 'You told me you went home.'

'I told you that, yeah, but I actually went to your childhood home and stood in that little copse of trees opposite.'

Cameron smiles at my shocked recognition. How else would he have known about those trees unless he'd been there?

'I didn't know what I was going to do when I went there, I think I just wanted to see her and work out for myself why she made you so unhappy. I hadn't even met her and I felt a deep and burning hatred towards your sister. When Natalie came out of the house – she was going to the shops, I think – we got talking. I made up some story about moving in around the corner. It was hard but I managed to hide the massive disgust I felt for her. How I did, I'll never know.

'It was dark and drizzling with rain, so there was no one about. She was obviously lonely, and I persuaded her to walk with me. Your sister was naïve, unsure of herself, and I don't think she was used to the attention of strangers, so she was easy to persuade. We walked along the canal, and then came to some railway tracks, and just at that moment, a train was approaching.

'And I thought, this was the only chance I may ever have to show you how much I love you, H. So I pushed her down the bank. It wasn't a good push, and my heart was in my mouth because I thought she was going to scramble off the track. But then she touched the electrified track, and the train did the rest.'

He doesn't say anything for a long moment, just stares out of the window. 'I longed to tell you what I did, but you were upset at her death and I thought it may take some time before you could appreciate it, and then... we split up. But I'm able to tell you now: that's how much I've always loved you, H. I did it for you. I killed her for *you*.'

Every part of me is shaking. Cameron killed Natalie. My shoulders heave as the silent tears come again.

She didn't commit suicide, it wasn't an accident – Cameron killed her; and his first wife, too, and Diane. God knows what became of his own daughter. In my mind's eye, Penny's eyes stare at me from beneath the bathwater.

He's going to kill Sean and Shiv, I know that. He'll have to, if he wants to keep me to himself. And sooner or later he'll kill me too. Because this so-called love he has for me is a poisonous sickness, a deranged fever; a toxic obsession that destroys everyone it touches.

Even if I try to go along with his madness, how long will I manage to survive? He'll only be able to deny the truth – that I will *never* love him – for so long. How many weeks, months or years will it be before he becomes tired of keeping me captive, of trying to force me into being his soulmate?

Maybe he'll do to me the same as he did to Penny, which is to ruin my health with drugs in order to impose control over me.

But I will never love him. *Never*.

How long will it be before he finally admits defeat?

And then what happens to me?

What happens to Amber?

I can't let this monster near her.

'You're a lucky person, H,' he says gently. 'You're getting a second chance at the kind of love that most people only get once in a lifetime. I promise I won't be like that snake of a husband, I'll be devoted to you, we'll be devoted to each other. I can't wait till we get to the cottage, because you're going to get such a surprise.'

A long time ago I did one bad thing. All these years later, it's finally been my undoing, because it's let a monster back into my life.

But to protect myself, to protect my family, I'm going to have to do something worse.

We're already speeding when I press my foot hard on the

accelerator and swerve into the fast lane of the motorway, accelerating behind the cars ahead so fast that I have to pull back to the middle to overtake them on the inside.

'Slow down,' says Cameron, pressing his feet tensely against the footwell. 'We'll get there soon enough.'

Keeping my foot pressed down, I jerk the wheel so that the car swerves hard into the slow lane.

'This is ridiculous, H,' Cameron tells me, his hands bracing the sides of the passenger seat.

When I just miss a car, jerking hard into the middle lane, he braces his hands against the dash.

'That's enough,' he commands.

And then I see it: parked on the hard shoulder ahead is a lorry. It must have broken down, because the driver is out of the cab, making a call on the verge – and I know what I have to do.

Swerving, cars braking to the left and right of us, horns blaring, I press my foot down hard on the accelerator, and it dawns on Cameron what I'm doing, because his face fills with panic.

'Slow down,' he shouts. 'Slow down now!'

I did a bad thing once, but this man beside me, he's done worse. He's killed several times, and he'll kill again, I'm absolutely certain of that. He says he'll love me forever, but I'll never reach whatever pedestal it is he's put me on, and I'll resist him, I'll spite him, and then he'll kill me, and move on to some other poor woman. It's what he does.

The back of the lorry looms up ahead of us. As Cameron leans across to snatch at the wheel, I reach for his seat-belt button and punch it hard with the joint of my finger, releasing it, so that the belt whips back across his chest.

He scrabbles at it wildly. 'What are you doing, you stupid fucking bi—'

Yanking the wheel hard to the left, the car lifts up the steep verge, throwing us about; the back wheels slide crazily on the dry grass, and Cameron falls across me. He snarls, claws at my face, but scrabbles to get the seat belt back in.

It's too late. Pulling the wheel hard to the right, we skid back onto the hard shoulder behind the lorry and smash into it.

My body snaps back and the seat belt locks across my chest when I'm hurled forward—

56

Cameron was killed instantly. Without the protection of a seat belt, he was thrown through the windscreen and across the twisting, screeching metal of the bonnet.

I escaped with whiplash injuries, cuts and bruises, a torn muscle in my shoulder and mild concussion, but the doctors assure me I've no internal injuries, and there'll be no lasting damage.

Hours after being rushed to hospital, I'm already sitting up in bed telling DS Sheehy about the events leading up to the crash. How, terrified that Cameron was going to kill me and Amber, and still groggy from the chloroform, I lost control of the car, which veered across the road. In the ensuing struggle, Cameron's seat belt came loose in a million-to-one accident, just before we smashed into the back of the lorry.

'You had a lucky escape,' Sheehy says. 'In more ways than one.'

The detective says that traces of chloroform were found in my bloodstream, a smashed bottle of the liquid in his satchel; there was also a broken syringe, filled with an as yet unidentified drug, in his pocket. Whatever it is, I'm certain Cameron was going to use it to subdue Sean and Shiv when we arrived at the cottage.

I'm able to tell him about Cameron's intentions, and where the police will be able to find Penny's body. There's the smashed laptop, too, with the camera and microphone feeds of my house. Sheehy says that forensic technicians will rebuild the hard drive to collect the evidence of his stalking. Cameron more than likely used the laptop to photoshop that image of us with the man he told Diane and me was Martin. The firelighters will be somewhere in his house, too, and the drugs he somehow managed to procure from work to keep Penny weak and compliant, and always teetering on the edge of death.

'He killed his first wife, and my sister too, and I don't know how but he killed Diane. I want to tell you everything.' I try to sit up in bed. 'About Diane and Cameron – everything.'

'We want you to take us through it thoroughly,' Sheehy says with a patient smile. 'But you've just been in a major car crash, Hannah, and the most important thing is your recovery, so there's no need to tell me everything now. There's plenty for us to be doing in the meantime.'

Poor Penny's body will be examined, and Cameron's house searched thoroughly for further evidence.

'Nobody knows where I am,' I tell him suddenly.

'We can let someone know that you're here,' says Sheehy, 'if you give us a number.'

Sean and Shiv have been at the coast less than a day, and I don't want to worry them, not until I'm sure I'm no longer a suspect in Diane's murder, so I ask him to call Izzy instead, she can tell my parents, and I give him her number.

I so dearly want to see Amber again, Shiv too, and even Sean. I can't wait to hold my little girl in my arms and spend time together. We'll go for walks on the beach and let the fierce North Sea air blow away all my previous cares. I'll put the past behind me once and for all. From now on, she'll be my focus, my sole priority.

That afternoon Izzy comes in, bringing a big bunch of flowers. She bursts into tears as soon as she sees me and rushes over to give me a hug, trying to embrace me without hurting me in the process.

'Are you okay?' she keeps asking. 'Is there going to be any lasting damage?'

'I'm fine, a bit bruised, but I'm going to be fine.'

'I'm so sorry about how I reacted on the phone.' She presses a mushy tissue to her nose as she sobs. 'I treated you so badly, and I'm so, so sorry I haven't been in touch. I didn't know what to do or say, Han, I was devastated, and took it out on you, and that's unforgivable. Will you forgive me?'

'Of course,' I tell her. 'It's so good to see you, Iz.'

'You could have *died*, Han,' she says, and bursts into tears again. 'I could have fucking lost you.'

When she's pulled herself together a bit, I tell her everything that's happened with Diane and the blaze, and all about Cameron, and for once she's speechless.

'I should have been there for you,' she keeps saying, 'and I let you down.'

'You had stuff to process and it takes time,' I assure her gently, and can't help but ask, 'You and Ollie?'

'We're going to make another go of it.' She looks embarrassed and I get the feeling she's choosing her words carefully. 'I think he was sucked into a situation that he regrets deeply.' Her eyes brim with tears again. 'It's just...

I love him so much, Han. Even now, I do, and I can't lose him.'

'I'm glad,' I tell her. What she and Ollie decide is none of my business. I just want Izzy to be happy.

'What about you and Sean?' she asks, looking at me carefully.

'We haven't managed to talk yet, so we'll see,' I tell her. But the truth is, I don't think I can trust Sean any more, and after everything else that's happened, it's best we both go our own way. I've had more than my fill of duplicitous men. I think he'll understand; maybe, deep down, he'll be relieved too.

'Friends, then?' Izzy asks, squeezing my hand.

'Oh yeah.' I roll my eyes. 'You ain't getting rid of me so easily.'

When Izzy leaves, I try to sleep, but it's hard.

Cameron's gone, he's dead – he'll never hurt another woman again. But every time I close my eyes and try to sleep, I see Diane disappearing into the smoke ahead of me; or Penny's blank, staring eyes beneath the water; the back of that lorry surging towards us, the obliterating impact.

Cameron never stood a chance.

'When can I go home?' I ask a nurse who comes into the room, trying once again to climb onto my elbows, making my bruised ribs shriek. 'I feel fine.'

'You may feel fine, but it's best to keep you in overnight for observation. You don't have any broken bones or internal injuries, so with luck you should be able to leave tomorrow.'

'Thank you,' I tell her.

When she's gone, and I'm alone, I begin to cry, desperately relieved that I'll be able to see Amber soon.

But also thinking of Diane and Penny, and Charlotte, and poor, poor Natalie, who died because of the unkind words of a sister who was too young, and too selfish, to know better.

57

A taxi drops me home the following day. The police have already removed the cameras and microphones and taken them away as evidence. Sheehy tells me there were five cameras, so small that you would never know they were there: in the kitchen and living room, one hidden above the picture rail in my office, in the bathroom, and my bedroom. There were four microphones: in the kitchen and living room – both of which were able to pick up conversation in the hallway – and in my office and bedroom.

It's impossible to know how long they've been here, and for how long Cameron watched and listened to everything that happened in my house. It makes my flesh crawl that when I came home from the hospital after the fire, Cameron was probably on his phone downstairs watching me shower. He would have watched Sean too, and heard his furtive phone calls to Ollie. Did he even watch us in bed together?

And even though there was no camera in the spare bedroom, I'll have to explain to Shiv how he would have been able to see both of us as we unwittingly went about our daily business.

I don't know how Cameron got the spyware into the house in the first place, but he was planning his return to my life for a long time, and I understand now that he was a man capable of going to any length.

As much as I've loved living here, and that I know Cameron's gaze will no longer follow me everywhere, my home feels spoiled now. It gives me the creeps. My body aches from the crash, I'm hardly in any condition to drive, but I don't want to stay here a moment longer than I have to. I need to get away, and to see Amber again.

Shiv said we could stay at her Dad's holiday cottage for as long as we want, and I'm going to take her up on that offer. We'll enjoy long walks along the coast, breathe in the fresh sea air; and I'm going to tell Sean that I want to sell up and move on. I'll stay at the cottage for as long as I'm able before I'm required to come back to assist the police.

Dragging a suitcase from the top of the wardrobe, trying to ignore the shooting pains that crackle up my side as I pull it down, I fill it with my clothes and Amber's. Remembering I promised Shiv I'd bring more of her clothes with me, I go into her bedroom. The room is so tidy and clean, you'd hardly know anyone was sleeping here.

The duvet on the bed is as flat and square as a postage stamp, and the hem of a nightdress pokes from under the pillow. There are just two personal objects on top of the chest of drawers: a hairbrush, with barely a hair trapped in it, and a photo of herself as a young girl in a plain silver frame.

She's walking along a beach, maybe the one she's at now, and there's something inexpressively sad about her smile. It's a curiously lonely photo. At Shiv's age, you'd think she'd be surrounded by photos of her with friends and family.

When I pull out the top drawer, there's one or two other things. A notebook covered in fabric, with a pen snapped in place beneath the elastic on the cover, a luxury purchase from a posh stationer. Treacherously, I'm unable to resist opening it, but there's nothing written inside.

Opening the second drawer, I take out tops and leggings and numerous pairs of knickers for her. And when I open the third drawer, I get a shock.

Folded neatly at the top is the summer dress she wore that made her look the spitting image of Natalie. Just the sight of it makes my sore head throb. I don't want to touch it, I don't want to see it, and I'm about to close the drawer when I spot her make-up bag. In the rush to leave, she didn't take it, so I lift it out, intending to pack it. It feels thin to the touch, Shiv's not one for make-up, but my thumb and fingers feel a bulge inside, and I unzip the bag to find out what it is.

It's an empty lipstick. When I touch a finger to the hollow rim, it comes away smeared a dark, faintly glittery red colour. But the lipstick is gone, as if it's been completely worn down – or broken off.

I'm sitting on the bed looking at it, trying to understand the implications of it, when the landline rings.

'My darling,' says Mum immediately. 'We've been so worried about you.'

'I'm fine,' I tell her. 'I'm safe.'

I can't face telling her about the man who died in the crash, and I don't really want to talk right now, because my mind is reeling from my discovery.

'I've got to go back to the hospital, Mum,' I lie. 'They want to do more tests, so I've got to go. I'll call you back later if you—'

'Your father has been worried sick,' she interrupts. 'He wants to speak to you.'

I can't bear the thought of another difficult conversation with Dad. But before I can say anything, Mum has handed over the phone. To my surprise, he sounds upset.

'We saw it on the news,' he says. 'Is it true a man has died?'

'I'm afraid so,' I tell him warily, expecting him to question me about who the man was, and why I was with him, and where I was going.

Instead, I hear a shudder in his voice. 'I don't know what I would have done if...' Mum murmurs consolingly in the background. 'Come home, Hannah, come and see us, and bring your lovely child and husband. We... we want to see you.'

Maybe it's taken something like this, the idea that he could have lost me, to make him realize life's too short to carry grudges to the grave.

Mum and Dad are going to find out soon enough about what happened to Natalie, that she was murdered rather than committed suicide or was killed in a tragic accident. After all these years, there'll be no proof Cameron killed her – unless he wrote his confession in a diary – but I can't face telling them about what he said, not while Dad is already upset. There'll be an investigation, and they'll be interviewed once again about Natalie's last day. Maybe it will be another stick that Dad can beat me with, but I don't think so; not now.

'Dad, there's something I need to ask you,' I say. 'It's very important.'

'Of course,' he tells me.

'Remember in the restaurant when you fell down the stairs?'

'When I was pushed, you mean?'

'Yes, when you were pushed. You said at the time you

thought it was a woman but didn't see them properly. Why did you say it was a woman?'

'Why does it matter?' he asks, getting flustered.

'Please. It just does.'

He sighs. 'Because of the buggy.'

'The buggy?'

'There was a child's buggy in the corridor, with a small child sleeping in it... Hannah, are you there?'

The broken lipstick tube trembles in my shaking fingers. I manage to say, 'Dad, I've got to go.'

'We would really love to see you,' Dad says. 'Please come up soon.'

'I will, *we* will, I promise. I must go, I'm sorry.'

The police have taken my laptop, looking for spyware that Cameron may have planted on it, but I still have my temporary phone, so I find the number of the hospital in Enfield the old-fashioned way, by calling Directory Enquiries. When I've got the number of the hospital, I tap it in with a shaking hand.

'I'd like to speak to someone about Peter Linden,' I tell the person who answers. 'He was admitted a couple of weeks ago after suffering a stroke.'

'Who are you, please?'

'It's his granddaughter, Siobhan.'

'Hold on, please, I'll pass you to the stroke ward.'

When I'm through, I tell them the date of the morning he was admitted and that I rushed to see him. But nobody on the ward knows who I'm talking about.

There was never a Peter Linden admitted to the hospital on that date, or any other time. Shiv made it up. Struggling not to panic, I try to understand the sequence of events.

Siobhan met Sean in the park and convinced him she was a nanny looking for employment. Being manipulable and a sucker for a pretty face, he persuaded me to employ her, and the whole process was completed so quickly that we didn't even go through a proper vetting procedure. We looked at a couple of CVs, and I emailed one of her former employers – who was probably Cameron – to check her references, but looking back, our efforts should have been more rigorous.

Because she was often alone, Shiv had plenty of time over the weeks and months to place cameras and microphones around the house.

She sneaked back in during the party to vandalize the mirror using the lipstick I found in her make-up bag.

It was Shiv who pushed my father down the stairs. Good God, Amber was with her when she did it.

Cameron knew I was going to sack Shiv, because he was watching and listening in real time on his laptop as I discussed it with Sean. In order to stop me doing it, he and Shiv made up a story about a sick relative, knowing that in those circumstances there's no way I would throw her out. I'd at least delay my decision, and might even change my mind, which is exactly what happened. They even persuaded me that it would be safer if she moved in with me.

Shiv let Cameron into the house while I was sleeping. Despite my sluggish and bewildered state, caused by the drugged food and drink they gave me, I was convinced someone was in my room. I'd thought it was Diane, but it was Cameron; and Shiv helped him escape through the patio doors when she said she was checking the garden.

She kept my nerves on a knife-edge by dressing as my

sister, in the same dress that Cameron saw Natalie wearing on the day he threw her in front of a train.

It was Cameron who ordered Diane to encourage my distrust of Sean, but it was Shiv who confirmed my worst fears by saying he'd made a drunken pass at her. Sean denied it, he said she'd come on to him, and maybe that's the truth – because she was setting him up for a fall.

Cameron told me in the car that he'd arranged for someone else to light the fire that killed Diane. He was nowhere near Diane's house when the blaze started – his phone records confirm that – and I know instinctively in my gut that Shiv started it. She showed me photos of Amber at her friends' party, which means she must have left her there with strangers, then gone to Diane's house and slipped inside – using a key Cameron had given her – to light the firelighters he had earlier scattered in bags and boxes, not knowing that I was there.

It makes my flesh crawl to think what would have happened if Cameron had grown tired of me in the future. I would never, I could never, live up to his expectations, and he would kill me. And then Amber would be left in the care of them both.

She'd grow up under Cameron's malign influence, dominated and controlled by him; forced – maybe even brainwashed – like Siobhan has been to become involved in his sociopathic schemes. That sad photo of Shiv looking lonely and isolated on the beach may one day be my daughter.

The thought jarringly brings me back to the moment, and the sickening knowledge that Amber's with Shiv right now.

If I tell the police about her, and they turn up at the cottage, my daughter will be put in danger. The only thing I can do is phone Sean's mobile and tell him to leave: don't tell Shiv, get in the car immediately and drive away. As soon as I know they're both safe, I'll call Sheehy and tell him about her.

When I call Sean's phone, it rings and rings. Finally, after six, seven, eight rings, it connects.

'Sean?' I whisper fiercely, trying not to betray my panic. 'You have to take Amber and get out now!'

But when nobody replies, I know it's not Sean on the other end.

'Hi, Shiv,' I say brightly, trying not to betray my terror. 'Are you there?'

'He died,' she says finally in a flat voice. 'We saw it on the news. You killed my father.'

'No,' I tell her. 'It was an accident. Please, Siobhan... Shiv, put Sean on the phone.'

'I'm waiting for you,' she says, and hangs up.

58

The last thing I want to do is get in the car, in my condition it's probably too dangerous for me to drive, but I don't have any choice. All I can do is take a couple of painkillers and then make my way carefully from London to Norfolk. I follow the GPS's instructions to the cottage, which is on the coast near a village called Weybourne. I try to stay calm and focus on the road, but all I can think about is what I'll find when I get there, and all kinds of terrible visions flash through my mind.

I'm waiting for you, is what Shiv said.

Her father, a man who has controlled and manipulated her all her life, a man who coldly involved her in an evil conspiracy to ensnare his former love, is dead, and I can't even imagine what she must be feeling. All I know is that she blames me for his death.

With a father like that – a psychopath, a twisted, obsessed killer – Shiv never stood a chance in life. It's obvious how remote and unconfident she is around adults, and I can see now that it's because she's always been forced to view the world through his eyes. He's made her do things that nobody should ever make their child do. She's inveigled herself into my life and family, sown discord and chaos, lied again and again; worked tirelessly to ensnare me in her father's trap.

She's killed.

She'll want revenge for his death; she'll demand vengeance.

But she must also know that sooner or later the police will discover her relationship to Cameron, for all she knows I could have told them already, and I cling to the hope that when I arrive at the cottage, she'll have fled, and I'll find Amber and Sean safe and sound.

My worst fear, the thought that I can't get out of my head, is that she'll have taken Amber, or even... I cling to the wheel in the darkness because I don't even want to contemplate it... maybe she's even already taken her revenge.

Finally, this far out of London, and with night long fallen, there's a flash on the horizon. A jagged fork of lightning cracks, followed moments later by booming thunder. Rain sheets down suddenly, gusts sending it across the windscreen and bonnet of the car. The hot, swollen sky finally unleashes on the earth after weeks of drought, so that it becomes almost impossible to see anything as I drive towards the village, the ghostly, dancing map of the GPS readout leading me to the coast.

The phone rings on the passenger seat. I know who it is before I pick it up.

'Hannah,' says Sheehy urgently.

'I can't talk to you, I'm sorry.'

'Hannah, wait, your nanny is not who you think she is. We got into Cameron West's hard drive and went through the footage. We saw her let him into your house late at night, he... came into your room.'

'Shiv's his daughter. I know everything.'

'You said she took your baby to a cottage, Hannah, so tell us where—'

'It's Cameron's cottage,' I tell him. 'You'll find the details on his laptop, I'm sure. I'm nearly there.'

I'm driving through Weybourne now. A picturesque fishing resort surrounded by fields, woods and heathland. This late at night, and with the lashing rain causing flash floods that make the water sheet down the winding roads, it's completely empty.

'Hannah,' Sheehy says, 'don't—'

But I cut the call.

The wipers move frantically back and forth as I drive carefully out of the village, water spraying high on either side of the car. Because of the driving rain and lack of street lamps, the headlights don't illuminate much of the twisting road ahead. Gripping the wheel tightly, my aching limbs shudder; it takes all my focus and concentration to negotiate the tight bends in near-zero visibility.

And then the GPS leads me off the road and down a narrow, bumpy dirt drive towards the shore – the dark mass of the sea is a black band ahead – and announces that I've arrived at my destination.

Sitting on a grassy rise with a view of the beach below, Cameron's Norfolk cottage has traditional walls, a gable roof and mullioned windows. To my alarm, all the lights are off.

Jumping out of the car, I run towards it and get drenched immediately, my feet splashing in the many puddles on the gravel path. Above the sound of the rain pummelling the ground, and the wind shaking the trees, I can just about hear the angry surf crashing rhythmically on the beach, hidden beyond the grassy dunes below.

'Shiv! Sean!' I pound at the door. 'Let me in.'

But nobody opens it. Soaked to the skin, I rush around the cottage to the side facing the beach, which is all clean modern lines and glass. Rain punches the roof of the veranda. In the pitch-black of the night, the glass blankly reflects swaying grass and racing cloud.

Cupping my hands to peer inside, I see the soft light of a single lamp on a coffee table illuminating one big room; half the space is an open-plan kitchen and the other half a comfortable living area with sofas and chairs. When I pull a handle, the glass slides open smoothly and I step inside. The cottage is dark and quiet.

'Shiv,' I call. 'Where are you?'

It's warm and comfortable in the room, as I trail water behind me on the stone floor. The driving rain is a rythmic thrum in my head. The central heating hums. Amber's stroller is folded against a wall, her toys and clothes scattered across a sofa. A boiler begins to roar softly as the blue blur of a pilot light fires on a wall-mounted unit in the kitchen. I'm afraid to go too far into the gloom of the cottage in case Shiv leaps out at me. A pair of doors at the back of the room, one on either side, lead to the other parts of the house.

'Shiv!' I call again. 'Please talk to me!'

And then I hear a faint banging from somewhere in the house, and without even thinking, I rush to the door directly ahead and open it. The corridor beyond is long and narrow, the ceiling low.

'Down here!'

'Sean?' I shout.

His voice calls weakly, 'Hannah? Let me out!'

Light comes from under a door to my right, and when I

open it, narrow stone steps lead to a basement door. I head down quickly.

'Sean?'

Sliding back the bolt, I open the door.

Sean's in the small basement room inside, slumped against a wall, and bleeding badly. He's pressing his tee-shirt against the gash in his forehead to stop blood pouring into his eyes. When I come inside, he tries to get up.

'Where is she?' I ask him. 'Where's Amber?'

'I don't know,' he says, wincing. 'Shiv attacked me. Swung a bloody pot plant into my head.' He touches his temple and grimaces. 'The next thing I know I woke up down here.'

'Take this.' I place my phone in his hand. 'Call the local police, get them here now.'

'Wait, where are you going?' he calls. 'She's dange—'

But I'm already rushing up the stairs and into the main room and out of the sliding door. Rain still crashes against the ground as the summer storm swells. I can just about make out the churning mass of the sea ahead and the inland landscape seems to sway and undulate. The dark mass of trees crack and creak; leaves spin crazily on the wind in front of me. A coastal path passes in front of the cottage, and a bolt of lightning illuminates a figure in the distance. I stumble towards it, the sopping grass slapping my shins. Another flash of lightning on the horizon turns the turbulent world yellow for an instant, to reveal waves crashing furiously against the rocks below the rising cliff edge, spray exploding skyward. Norfolk is renowned for its flatness, but this part of the coast is jagged and dangerous.

'Shiv!' I call. She must see me, because a moment later the

figure begins to move. Running frantically towards her, I try to keep my balance on the slippery, uneven ground.

'Shiv!' I scream. 'Please, stop.'

I can hear Amber crying now, and I see them both. Shiv has my baby in her arms, and they're close to the edge of the cliff. But then they disappear, and for one awful moment I think they've both gone over. Amber would be killed instantly.

'Shiv!' I scream, falling to my knees, before getting up and plunging forward.

They're visible again now, had momentarily gone out of sight down an incline, and when I shout for Shiv to stop, she finally turns towards me, Amber pressed to her chest. They're both sopping, I don't know how long they've been out here in the storm.

'He told me we would finally have a family!'

Her hair plastered to her skull, Shiv's face twists in despair. I know she's crying, even in the rain. 'I didn't want to do those things, but he made me. How am I meant to live with myself?'

She steps backwards, towards the edge.

'Please come closer,' I say pleadingly, because she almost stumbles. But she's not listening, she's too distraught. Amber's crying, holding out her hands to me, desperate for me to take her, and I would do anything to hold her safely in my arms right now.

'He promised me we would be a family, and that we would all be happy! But you killed him!'

'It was an accident.' It's a lie I will have to repeat for the rest of my life. 'But I'm not sorry, Shiv. He hurt you, he made you do things, and he's never going to hurt you or anyone else ever again.'

'I didn't want to do any of it, but he made me,' she cries, her angry tears lost in the wind and rain. 'He said it was the only way for us all to be together. And now I have nothing – no one!'

'Cameron... your father is gone, but I promise you will never be alone again, because I'm here for you, and so is Amber, and we won't leave you.' Amber wails in her arms. 'But you're scaring her, Shiv, you're scaring both of us, is that what you want?'

'I've done terrible things.' She steps back again and I gasp, because one more step and they'll both plunge to certain death. 'And now he's gone, and I have to live with myself.'

'We've all done terrible things, Shiv, but we've both got to move on. I let Diane down. Like everybody else in her life, I rejected her friendship. All she wanted was to make human contact with another person, but I pushed her away like so many people in her life have done. And I will not do the same to you.' My hand trembles as I hold it out to her. 'Please, Shiv, Amber is scared, I'm scared, let's go inside.'

'I didn't want to do any of it, I swear!'

'I believe you,' I tell her, and I see a glimmer of something in her eyes: hope.

Shiv has been cut off from the world, bullied and controlled by her father, and taught to hate and manipulate; forced to do things nobody should ever have to do. I saw how haunted and isolated she looked in that photo in her room.

Her eyes are blurred with tears. 'After everything I did?'

'He made you do those things, because he's all you've ever known since he... since your mother died. You're as much a victim of him as anyone else. I can only imagine what your life has been like. The police will want to talk to you about everything, and I can't tell you what's going to happen, but I promise you that we'll be here for you, me and Amber. We'll be your family.'

And I mean every word of it. Shiv has never known a healthy, loving family. I can only imagine the psychological abuse and manipulation she has suffered over the years and decades by Cameron, and the things she's had to do to survive his malign influence. She'll have to live with the guilt of the things he's made her do. But never again will she have to fear the sound of his voice.

Yesterday, I did a bad thing, I killed a man. Tonight, and for the rest of my life, I will make amends by helping this vulnerable young woman.

'Please, Shiv,' I say. 'Let's go inside.'

She looks back over her shoulder, sees how close she is to the edge, and seems mesmerized by the angry, leaping sea and jagged rocks.

For a moment I think I've lost her; that she's going to jump with my baby in her arms. But then she gasps, as if freed from a terrible spell, and staggers forward, bundling Amber into my arms.

I hold Amber and Shiv close, ignoring the wind and rain and flashes of lightning. Shiv's shoulders heave as she cries in my arms.

'Thank you,' I tell her. And then I take her hand and we walk back towards the cottage, where the darkness is fractured by the flickering blue light of police cars and an ambulance. Uniformed figures stride quickly towards us.

And later that night, when we're both dry and in clean clothes, and when Shiv is arrested and placed in a police car, I get in beside her and we go to the station together.

The future is unclear; I don't know what's going to become of her, but I'll be there, I'll stay at her side as much as I can, because I owe it to Natalie, who needed my love and support, and to Diane, who had no one to protect her when Cameron came into her life; and to Charlotte and Penny too.

One day, it could be soon or at some unknown date in the future, Shiv will have a chance to start all over again, and she'll need a family.

I'll be there for her, if she'll let me.

Acknowledgements

Many thanks for reading *One Bad Thing*. If you enjoyed it, please consider leaving a rating or review, it really does help people find the book.

And bear with me for just one more page and a bit so that I can thank a few people who helped in the writing.

I've been asking questions about police procedure of Michael Gradwell and Inspector Kevin Horn for five books now and they have continued to respond with patience and kindness. And the same goes for Senior Paramedic Jason Eddings, who helps me with medical detail.

Many thanks to the talented crew at publisher Head of Zeus: editor Laura Palmer, editorial assistant Anna Nightingale; Rachel Hart and Christian Duck in production, Jessie Price and Matt Bray in the art department, Jade Gwilliam in marketing; copy editor Jenni Davis, proofreader Sophie Scott and Sophie Ransom for the PR. Emma Rogers designed a cover to die for.

Thanks to my agent Jamie Cowen at The Ampersand Agency for all his amazing work in a rollercoaster year, and to Rosie and Jessica Buckman at The Buckman Agency.

My four-legged work colleagues Jason and Gracie kept

me company during the days and weeks and months, and thanks to Archie for kicking me out of my office in the evenings.

And always, always, *always*, there's Fiona, without whom there would never have been any books; not a single one.

About the author

M. K. HILL was a journalist and an award-winning music radio producer before becoming a full-time writer. He lives in London. Visit him at MKHILL.UK